A Demon's Dark Embrace

The Elite Guards

AMELIA HUTCHINS

A Demon's Dark Embrace
Copyright © November 10, 2015 by Amelia Hutchins

ISBN-10:0997005513   ISBN-13: 978-0-9970055-1-6

Cover Art Design: Vera DC Digital Art & Photography
Cover Art Illustrations: Vera DC Digital Art & Photography
Copyright ©November 10,2015Amelia Hutchins
Edited by: E & F Indie Services
Copy Editor: Gina Tobin

Published by: Amelia Hutchins
Published in (United States of America)
10 9 8 7 6 5 4 3 2 1

ALSO BY AMELIA HUTCHINS

The Fae Chronicles
Fighting Destiny
Taunting Destiny
Escaping Destiny
Seducing Destiny

The Elite Guards
A Demon's Dark Embrace

A Guardian's Diary
Darkest Before Dawn

WARNING!

This book is intended for mature and adult audiences.
A Demon's Dark Embrace is the first book in The Elite Guards
Series. This is a companion series to The Fae Chronicles
Series; Reading The Fae Chronicles is not absolutely required
to enjoy The Elite Guards Series, however you will have a
much greater enjoyment of it if you do. The first book of The
Fae Chronicles Series is Fighting Destiny and it can be found
with reputable book sellers for your convenience.

A Demon's Dark Embrace tells the behind the scenes story
that the reader did not see in Seducing Destiny and then
some! Just like The Fae Chronicles Series: If you prefer
adorable and sparkly Fairies, Demons and Vampires...look
elsewhere.

This story is told in narrative format rather than the first person.
The story is dark, gritty, tear jerking, panty soaking, edge
of seat grabbing, and does have some questionable scenes
that more sensitive readers may not enjoy. It does contain hot
asshole alphas that seduce and wreck sensibilities. Explicit
language is used liberally as is the use of magic in acts of
naughtiness. The author strongly advises buying batteries
or securing a willing victim to your bed while reading this
book. (Handcuffs are optional.) Side effects include, but are
not limited to: lip biting and/ or chewing, screaming at the
author, wet panties, unexplained leaking from the eyes, or
other parts of the body. Some people may experience strange
attachment to characters, and may scream for the next book
in the series immediately after reading. If you experience
one or more of these symptoms, do not seek a health care
professional. Thank the author and wait for the next book
in the series. (Stalking the author is normal behavior. Rest
assured she has already started the next in the series.)

DEDICATION

This book is for my mother.
You've shown me that in every storm, there's sure to be a rainbow afterwards. That learning to dance in the rain is a glorious feeling that will free your soul from many burdens. And for teaching me that there is nothing so bad that a good song and dancing cannot fix.

For my husband, for standing beside me no matter how stressful things can get, or how crazy I may be.

For the fans of these stories, for understanding that I am human and that my family's needs always have to come first.

To Gina, thanks for sticking through this journey with me, even when we don't agree, we always make it through it together. There's not another I would prefer to be with me through this. Your undying love for these characters is amazing.

Tomorrow is not promised to us. Start dancing in the rain and look for your rainbow through the storm clouds. Once you find it, don't ever let it go.

A Demon's Dark Embrace

The Elite Guards

CHAPTER ONE

Ristan watched the Guild, his eyes scanning the area around it and those damned doors. Doors that were meant to keep creatures like him out, but failed to. The Guild never worried about Demons, though they would be terrified if they really knew what creatures like him could do. Not these fuckers; they were more worried about the Fae, which he also was.

Half-Fae, as if that mattered lately; his Demon half tended to be more prominent, but when combined with who his father was, it was fifty-fifty as to which half was more powerful or barbaric.

He tipped up his second bottle of Pepto-Bismol and downed its contents. With an air of nonchalance, he watched as Witches and Warlocks came and left the Guild, all oblivious to what was really going on around them. Or maybe they just pretended to be unaware of everything.

Not even five yards away sat a dark-haired Fae, his green-gold eyes inhuman as he watched one of the

1

librarians move towards the steps, her lithe frame barely discernible through the outfit she wore. A block away from the Guild was a Bás Mall, a creature that could skin a Human while leaving them alive. The pain of their skinning would feed the nasty beastie for months.

It amazed him how the Guilds were oblivious to the real monsters in this world, sitting right under their noses, and yet they sought to police those who fed mostly from sex. As if both parties in that situation weren't reaping a benefit? He turned his eyes back to the Guild, waiting for the old man to exit those doors and escort him in.

He'd been doing this for a few weeks and it hadn't made entering the Guild any easier. The Guild was heavily warded against the Fae castes, such as the High Fae, Vampires, and Shifters. Long ago, he had discovered that it hadn't been spelled against his breed of Demon, and he had been trawling under their noses ever since, using an invisibility glamour. Now that he was going into the Guild daily with Alden's knowledge, he could get away with a simple glamour to disguise his features. Using this disguise had quite a few advantages, and no one had questioned him or his right to be within the walls of the Guild. Of course, they saw him as 'Justin,' a tall, muscular, blonde, Guild Enforcer with blue-gray eyes. One who was doing research for the New Orleans Guild as a form of punishment, and was reporting directly to Alden.

Having a Guild Elder backing your story helped immensely.

Alden exited the building, his eyes scanning the area and stopping briefly on both of the Fae that Ristan had just noted. He was surprised that the Elder had seen the Bás Mall, as those creatures usually took on the glamour of an attractive Human to disguise themselves from the Guild, as well as to attract victims. It was just one of many reasons that this was a man that Ristan had come to respect over the past couple of months. His eyes followed Alden as he slowly made his way to the bench Ristan was sitting on.

"Justin," he said cordially, his blue eyes sharp as he took in the discarded bottles of the pink stuff. "Bad morning?"

"Not any worse than any other morning that I have to pass through those doors," Ristan belched softly as he brought his fist up to softly tap his chest where another pain from indigestion was trapped. "Maintaining glamour all day and putting up with the Guild's sanctimonious bullshit gives me a sour stomach. Sometimes I miss just being able to wander around the Guild, invisible to those idiots who think they're smarter than us."

"Takes a toll on you, I suspect," Alden said as he sat on the bench and let his eyes wander to the Bás Mall, or Skinners, as he and his brothers called them. "Fucking monsters are out today," he acknowledged with an almost imperceptible tip of his head.

"Glad you noticed," Ristan replied with a cross look and a snarky grin on his lips.

"You're not a monster, trust me. I've seen them things up close and personal; those are real monsters."

"And yet the Guild focuses on the ones paying attention to pussy," Ristan remarked crudely.

"If we were all dead-set on bedding your women,

would you not take offense?" Alden asked with no malice buried in the question, only genuine curiosity.

"Point taken, old man," Ristan said with a nod of his head. "I just think there are bigger fish that need to be put down, or fried. You know, those Skinners taste amazing when you're in a pinch and need a substitute for meat. Add some sauce and they're not half bad. I personally enjoy them with Tabasco Sauce," Ristan said with a small grin.

"Good to know," Alden said, but the look on his face said otherwise as it twisted with a smile and a soft shake of his head at Ristan's culinary options. Alden looked over his disguise, as he did every time they were about to enter the Guild. Ristan was dressed in a black long-sleeve Henley shirt with black cargo pants; typical for an Enforcer to wear during the winter months. The Guild Elder's eyes narrowed at the black Doc Martens he wore.

"Feeling a bit rebellious today?" Alden chided.

Ristan shrugged it off.

"They're shit-kickers."

"That may be, but you know how the Guild feels about…"

"Personality, individualism, thinking…got it." Ristan interrupted impatiently. He flicked a finger as if he were removing lint, and the boots changed to steel toe boots that were more in line with what the rest of the Enforcers would be wearing. "So, what's the plan for today?" Ristan asked quietly.

"Olivia pulled more of the boxes containing items recently obtained in raids on Fae houses and brothels."

"Fae don't run brothels; Humans do. They just know

good business. Selling your cock for an endless supply of money and food is just smart. No harm done in those places, not if we know about them. We take care of our own, even the sick dogs that need to be put down," Ristan replied as he set his eyes back to the Skinner. "They know Faery is in trouble; like sheep jumping the fence because a wolf is slaughtering the herd."

"I'm not sure many would consider that thing a sheep," Alden said, his eye on the same monster Ristan was tracking.

"I'll be right back," Ristan said, his inner Demon growling with the upcoming kill. Normally he'd leave it alone, but this one was using compulsion to lure a child into a nearby alley. Visiting Tèrra and having a snack or a little fun was fine as long as death wasn't involved in the equation. Killing Humans, much less children, was against the Horde King's laws. Seeing that the Horde King was Ristan's half-brother, he had a pretty good understanding of how Ryder would feel about what the Bás Mall was doing right now.

Ristan entered the dark alley, his eyes scanning the area before he finally let the glamour fade, revealing his true form. His hair fell just past his shoulder blades, and his blackish-blue hair was muted from lack of regular feeding. His silver and black patterned eyes saw more than most Fae, which, unfortunately, was a blessing and a curse.

He heard the kid scream and glamoured his Guild-issued sword into one with a serrated edge to make a lasting impression. He slowly moved in further, the garbage piled up on each side of the alley making his nose itch with the need to plug it. Another scream, but this one was closer than the last.

The kid came rushing at Ristan, almost plowing him over in the poor thing's haste to get away from the monster which had probably exposed the oozing pustules that would cover its skin when his true self was exposed.

"Run kid, now," Ristan growled as his skin reddened and his fangs descended, making his Demon parentage more obvious. "I said, *fucking run*!" he shouted harshly when the kid fell to the ground and scurried backwards. He smiled coldly at the kid.

"M-m-monster!" the kid screamed, turning a pasty color and stammering over his words as he scooted back using his hands to crab-walk.

"I am; now run, before I take you back to the one you just ran from," he growled, knowing it would get the kid moving. He hated scaring kids. They were innocents in a war they had no business being in. He waited until he was sure the kid was running before he moved on to the monster.

"You shouldn't have left Faery," he said as he approached the Skinner. It was a mess of a thing, with nasty boils that openly oozed pus. Its teeth were jagged and razor sharp, perfect for skinning their prey. "You know the rules of the Horde."

The Skinner was shorter than Ristan; whereas he was just less than seven feet tall, it barely came up to his nose. Where he was slim and graceful, it wouldn't be. He held the sword at his side in a non-menacing pose, knowing this thing wouldn't be leaving the alley alive.

"I hold no ties to the newly-crowned king, no allegiance to the whelp," the Skinner sneered.

"No?" Ristan asked, knowing this creature had no idea who the hell he was.

"No; why would a Demon care who the hell I answer to?" it hissed, splattering spittle with each word it spoke.

This creature was no threat to him; it was a threat to the Humans if he was hunting in the open. It was definitely breaking the laws of the Horde King, and that in itself was an invitation for trouble. If one could get away with doing so, more would follow its lead.

"I don't," Ristan said as he swiftly brought the blade up and severed the creature's head from its body before it could react. Ristan heard a commotion and swore as he quickly glamoured on the face that wasn't his, and formed his body to do the same.

He turned in time to find Olivia, one of the librarian's from the Guild, standing with the boy at the entrance of the alley, her arm protectively around the kid's slim shoulders.

A crowd was growing and he swore again, his eyes searching for Alden, only to sense the man's presence behind him, his own weapon drawn and covered in some kind of ooze. The ooze had more than likely come from the same monster. He watched as the monster toppled from his feet, unaware that he'd lost his head. The headless body hit the ground with a sick thud that brought a smile to Ristan's mouth.

"Good job, Justin," Alden announced loudly, his hand slapping Ristan a little harder than he should have on the shoulder. "Great teamwork taking down that thing, but the other one sifted. It's all right, we'll get him eventually. Those kinds are always coming back for more."

"Right," Ristan said roughly, his eyes on the little redhead that was looking at him like he'd just saved the fucking world.

"We should get back, Justin," Alden offered, and Ristan agreed.

He smiled and nodded to the kid, who watched the two men as they emerged from the alley. His young eyes moved from Alden to Ristan and back again. He couldn't see the Demon who'd just saved his ass, just the Guild Enforcer who returned victorious from killing one monster and chasing the other one off.

"Let's do this," Ristan said, confirming his glamour was fully in place. His eyes skimmed the crowd, finding the male Fae with the green-gold eyes. In Ristan's eyes was a silent warning, which made the Fae turn and run.

This day already fucking sucked, and it was about to get even worse. He followed Alden as he made his way through the gawking bystanders and trailed him up the steps of the Spokane Guild.

CHAPTER TWO

Ristan paced in the library, his eyes taking in the simple things around him. Librarians moved around the library and the maze of catacombs further below this level. Most split their duties and also taught Math, English and History lessons to the younger groups of soon-to-be Guild Enforcers, or wherever they ended up being placed in the Guild's organizational chart.

The students housed at the Spokane Guild had been sent by their parents from various Guilds around North America to learn all they could about being good little Witches and Warlocks. There was also a pretty impressive setup here for those children with magic that had ended up orphaned or abandoned by their parents. Kids with powers, such as those as Synthia had been brought here, and the Guild had accepted them with no questions asked. The true Dark Fae Heir had been found on the steps to this Guild as a child with no knowledge of who he was, and had also been accepted because of people like Alden, who actually gave a shit about these kids. Of course, Synthia hadn't been left there; she'd been hidden with Alden's own sister to protect her from her destiny.

He tried to shake off the battle high left over from the monster in the alley. He missed fighting and was itching to go another few rounds. He could kill easily, and hadn't really been challenged since Synthia had thought him dead. The only reason those assholes got to him was because he had been more worried about her. He knew she had an important part to play in saving his world, and he was stuck here—babysitting.

"Justin?" Olivia's sweet tone made him turn, and he narrowed his eyes on her.

She was beautiful, but not his type. She was a little too innocent. Too easy to kill. She was tiny, and by tiny he meant that she didn't even reach five feet tall, and she was a wisp of a woman. She was thin, but she did have plump breasts that rose perkily beneath her light green sweater, both nipples erect and inviting his eyes to feast on them. Her hair was loose today and flowed enticingly down her back to her hips. It was red, a bright coppery color that drew and held the eye, until you caught sight of her beautiful, vivid dark blue eyes.

He loved that her eyes were an open portal, which seemed to lead him right to her pure, innocent soul. She'd be an easy catch, but it would be just that. Catch and release; it was how he liked to play his cards. It was like a two-step program. He caught them, and when he was finished rocking their world, he simply released them. No harm done.

"Can I help you?" Ristan asked after a moment

of openly staring at her since she was doing the same to him. It was only fair. He had adopted a light Cajun drawl in order to keep his Guild disguise in character, and based on the pretty blush currently spreading over her porcelain skin, it was a good choice to go with.

"I can help you," she said softly, shyly. That shit made his cock twitch—bad news. He stepped back, his eyes never leaving hers.

Olivia watched him, and when he took a giant step away from her, she had to struggle with the urge to sniff herself. She'd showered this morning and had only been outside for a few moments before the child had come barreling up the steps of the Guild for help.

She'd been flabbergasted to find Justin standing with a blade, the creature's dead body at his feet. She'd never before seen what the Enforcers did on the job. She just read about it in the mission logs and archived the stories. The summaries and reports the Enforcers detailed had never seemed real. They were more like an adventure or an escape from her everyday world, kind of like one of her romance novels. She loved books, and here, in the catacombs and libraries of the Guild, she was surrounded by them.

"I just wanted to thank you, you know, for saving the kid from the Demon and that monster today," she said as she shot him a small smile and continued. "Also, I pulled some of the books you needed in addition to the confiscated items, and even took notes for you on some of the things the NOLA Guild requested via email this morning."

"That was nice of you," Ristan said with a roguish smile. Zahruk was coordinating remotely from a false

IP address and running interference when shit got close to Ristan's cover being blown. Alden had helped set it up, and it was an easy matter for Zahruk to use the portal to the Spokane mansion, log into the computer and send 'instructions' to the Spokane Guild from the 'New Orleans Guild.'

It was all part of the cover, and the Spokane Guild bought the story pretty easily. All of the archives from the Guilds around the country were in the process of being sent to Spokane for safety. The New Orleans Guild had a lot of hairy shit going on down there, so that Guild had been chosen as the most plausible one to send an Enforcer for research on how to solve some of their issues. Ristan feared that Guilds' troubles had more to do with the Mages—and the knowledge that Faery was in trouble—than any of the Guilds were currently willing to admit. There were Fae that were already jumping ship due to the uncertainty in Faery—as if Ryder would ever allow Faery to go down to something as insidious and evil as the Mages.

They would meet their end, and it would be as brutal as they'd been to the Fae. The evil fucks had loved torturing, and it would only be right for the Fae to return the favor.

"Did anything else come up the line from down South?" he asked as he accepted the box of assorted books and scrolls.

"Just a message that said your punishment has been extended indefinitely," she replied softly, her voice hesitant to relay what she thought was bad news. "Or at least until you finish what they sent you here to do. I'm sorry they're making an Enforcer like you suffer in this dusty old library," she finished.

"It's not so bad," Ristan replied as he absently reached up and tucked a stray curl behind her ear. "The scenery is outstanding and breathtakingly beautiful," he muttered as his fingers grazed her ear. He tried to connect and read her mind, and once again, he couldn't get a single image or thought.

She blushed and he smiled inwardly. Yeah, his mind went there. And by there...he was imagining her in a schoolgirl outfit. She would have that thick, gorgeous hair in a tight ponytail that he could use to direct her lips with... She'd be decked out in stockings, with nothing blocking his direct route to her sweet flesh... He groaned and shook his head to dispel the image, and crossed his arms over his chest.

He had a fucking hard-on for a librarian... One that reeked of sweetness. She was nothing like the willing, skilled bed partners he normally chased. He went after ones that he knew Danu wouldn't harm; her strange obsession with him bothered him. Daily.

Danu was one of the most powerful Goddesses and creator of his race; she'd used him since he'd Transitioned, and she'd been there in the room with him, watching as he killed most of his bed partners. Later, he discovered the Fae thought that the strength of his Fae sire would make him immune to his curse, his need to consume souls... It hadn't been the case. Instead, Danu had been witness to it, and she'd laughed at his horror, saying afterwards that what he'd done was natural.

As if his life hadn't been fucked up enough? He'd barely come out of the killing haze of his Transition; when his own father had sliced his wings from his back, and took his tail and horns. He'd taken his identity. He'd wanted to kill him, to take from his father as he had done to Ristan, ever since he was a child. He'd been haunted by vacant eyes, and it was what he'd seen as his father took his Demon markings and scarred him for life. What was supposed to be a time of joy that he'd survived was tainted with the knowledge that he hadn't thought he deserved to live at the cost his survival came with.

Ryder had saved him and, away from their father's ever-watchful eye, had been kind, everything Ristan had needed. That's what created the bond of loyalty between them. Even though it took him months before the flesh of his wounds completely healed, the emotional shit had never gone away, and yet he managed it daily, hiding it behind snarky comments and a whole lot of women.

Fuck, he loved women. Loved to take them to their dark side, and show them just how much fun it was there. Show them things they'd never known they were capable of doing with their minds and bodies. They were made for sin, and he knew just how to get them there. Easily.

A hand on his chest made his eyes lower and brought him back to the task at hand.

"Are you okay?" Olivia's voice penetrated his mind, dissolving his thoughts to focus on her.

"I was just thinking how lucky that kid was, and how easily that could have taken a turn for the worst. He's lucky we were out there, otherwise his parents would be picking out a casket." Unlikely, since the Bás Mall would have hidden the body, and kept the kid alive for a very long time, savoring his pain until nothing but a husk remained.

"He's very lucky, and I for one am glad you and Alden caught it, but what worries me is the Demon that kid spoke of. He said there were two monsters in that alley, and that the Demon helped him. A genuine Demon; since when do those monsters come here?"

"A lot more than you'd think," Ristan said as he gave himself a mental shake. A lot more than any of them knew. What with Lucian and his group in close proximity to this place, he was surprised that the Guild hadn't taken note of it yet. Then again, the Guild spotted and documented a few Soul-Seeking Demons long ago and mistakenly thought that his race was what all Demons looked like. Lucian and his men blended in with the Human population far better than most of Ristan's people could do, which was probably why the Soul-Seekers rarely left Faery anymore.

"I guess it makes sense why Kendra keeps coming back, asking for more information on Demons, and the early history of the Witches."

"Kendra?" he asked, his curiosity piqued.

"I think she's doing some family history searches. She's not Guild like us, though, she's from one of the separatist Covens. Alden said she's not anything to worry about. We get a lot of them coming in lately, people searching for family lines, or things to put in the news. We are getting busier now that the archives from all the Guilds are being housed here. It's good business for the Guild; shows we're here for them. They need to see us as their allies, and not in league with the Fae, right?"

Ristan shook his head; the girl could talk the ear off a

fairy. That much he was sure of. Funny, considering she hadn't talked to him very much before today. He smiled and nodded slowly in understanding. He didn't agree nor disagree with what she'd just spit out. He wouldn't know what the hell she'd just said next because his eyes had strayed to her cleavage, and his mind had gone back to his earlier fantasy.

Talking was overrated when he needed to feed.

CHAPTER THREE

"*You need to be careful with her; she's* a lot smarter than you think she is," Alden said quietly once Ristan had entered the study carrel they'd been using for research so curious eyes wouldn't grow too interested in what they were doing. It was a nice workspace with a large conference table in the middle for group studies. A desk sat off to the side, and there was even a little sofa with a small table for smaller group discussions. There was even a small galley kitchen in the back of the carrel so the researchers wouldn't have to leave if they didn't want to.

"She's safe from me, don't worry, old man. I'm going home to feed and check on other things."

"I'm not worried about her safety with you. I am concerned that she's shown very little interest in the men here, unlike the others, who seem more than willing to engage and procreate. Most seem oblivious to her differences, but those who have noticed her lack of interest tend to stay away from her or view her as a little sister. As you know, we encourage them to interact, but Olivia is different than most of the girls here; more shy and intellectual than anything. It's nice to see that she has taken notice of you," Alden said as he watched Olivia through the window that looked out to the library.

"You know how I feel about the feeding from Humans, so of course I'd prefer, if you do end up having a dalliance with her, that you not feed from her. Maybe you can help her build a bit of confidence in the process. One thing I am concerned about, though, is that she's taking notes of everything you're asking her to pull. That list is being handed off to Cyrus, and he's been cagey lately. He also asked for one of the lots she pulled for you and took it out of the Guild today. Anything in there we should worry about?"

Ristan considered it and dismissed it easily. "It was most likely the one with the location of one of the relics, but it was the one Synthia and I found in the maze. If he is also looking for relics, we should be worried in that aspect, but not that he would find it."

Ristan watched Alden as he watched Olivia. "You think she might be in league with them?" he asked, his eyes sliding over her lithe frame as she worked behind the librarian's main desk.

"I wouldn't encourage you to fool around with her if I did. She's a sweet girl, timid little thing. But it's getting harder to tell what people are like anymore. People I trusted have fled, and with the Seattle Guild demanding that we send most of our Enforcers to them, it leaves me unsettled. If the Fae or Mages attacked this place, we'd be hard-pressed to defend it. I don't buy the bullshit about it being budget cuts; I've seen the accounts firsthand and know for a fact that we've got enough gold in the vault here to get hundreds of thousands of dollars for it," he said as he turned away from the window, dismissing Olivia. "New Orleans is silent. Has Zahruk reported to you on the condition of the Guild there?"

"Just that it's operational, at least from what our people can see from the outside," Ristan replied, his eyes still on the redhead, but now with *what ifs* playing in his head. "They run training exercises on time and patrol the bayou for any Fae who have decided to use the myths surrounding the history of New Orleans for feeding frenzies. I'm not sure what you expect him to report back with since you know we mostly played around here. Vlad's bar filled most of our needs, and Sidhe Darklands did the rest. The Light Fae are a lot more prominent down there, as they enjoy the heat. But then those twisted fucks also like playing royalty in front of the Humans, more so than they do in Faery. Do you think there is a possibility that the Mages could be manipulating her?" Ristan asked as his eyes finally lost the little redhead as she fluttered out of sight of the main desk, probably into the catacombs.

"I may have helped raise her, but she reports to Cyrus. I'm pretty sure he's looking into you, as you look into us. I also think he's the one who has been spreading rumors that I'm on the take. It's a mess," Alden admitted, his light blue eyes tired, and his shoulders slumped.

"I can pull us out at any moment. All you got to do, old man, is say, *go*."

"I can't leave those kids, not now. Most have parents who can take them, and protect them, but the rest? The rest of them are just innocent kids who have no one who could give a shit if they die tomorrow, except me. Some are like Adam; just showed up and had no one. Those kids, they make me feel needed, and when you get to my age, it's good to have at least someone who needs you."

Ristan grunted his agreement, his eyes taking in the old man with new respect.

"How's our girl?" Alden asked.

"The tamest dame in the universe," Ristan replied with a grin on his lips.

"As if; I didn't raise any tame creatures. I raised a woman who would take no shit, and I know she is giving you guy's hell."

"Miserable, but dealing with it. She thinks she's the size of a house, but she's beautiful. Seeing her pregnant with the future of Faery is something I never tire of. She's handling it, and Ryder is dealing with the repercussions of taking the throne. He's allowing her to do more than any other queen of the Horde has before—even though she hasn't been officially crowned.

"I suspect that is because he's testing her. She has a lust for knowledge, and she has one hell of a head on her shoulders. I was given a vision just before they dried up, of her leading beside him, and fixing some of the shit our father had done."

"Always knew she was special, but never this. I wish my sister could see her; I think she'd be proud of the woman she's become. Do you believe in fate?" he asked offhandedly.

"Do I believe fate played a part in the death of your sister? No; I think that was the action of a true monster.

Do I believe in Synthia's destiny? One hundred percent," he said with a knowing smile. "It's not so much her destiny that scares me, but the unknowns of how we get there. I see what needs to happen, and what could happen. I've never been shown the entire way, or what all of the sacrifices are."

"Do you think Synthia will kill Faolán, and avenge her mother?" he countered.

"Absolutely," Ristan said without hesitation. "I knew she would from the first time I watched it happen, courtesy of Zahruk's gift. Even as a child she fought to become strong enough to get the job done and you knew it. It's why you pushed her harder; because you knew it couldn't be you, but she could. You pushed her, trained her, and created the perfect killing machine. I have a feeling that Marie must have worried about what would happen when Synthia's secret came out; that perhaps even you would turn on her. You already suspected it, though, and you used it. So the question isn't, Do *I think she will*? It's, *when do I think it will happen*? I don't have that answer, old man. No one does."

"I'm glad you can't lie," he said with a wide smile.

"I can lie, and do. I'm only half-Fae, which is what allows me to be inside this shit hole protecting you. I'm more Demon than Fae in some aspects. I just choose to tell you the truth," he said as he watched the window and noted Olivia was indeed with Cyrus.

The Guild Elder towered over the little librarian and her posture was one of professionalism as she seemed to be reporting to Cyrus. He wished he was close enough to hear what they were discussing. The Elder had aged well, just as Alden had; he was still fit and had only a bit of salt and pepper in his brown hair and his brown eyes were sharp and always assessing. Something about the man made Ristan uncomfortable though and there wasn't any reasonable way for him to get close enough to Cyrus to have a chance of touching his skin to get a 'read' on him.

"She was a chatterbox today, which isn't normal. She's usually really shy," Ristan noted out loud.

"Olivia was chatty?" Alden asked in surprise. "That's weird," he admitted, his bushy eyebrows lifting as he reached up to scratch his head.

"It's interesting mixed with the knowledge of what Cyrus is doing, to say the least. I'd like to get you out of here soon. I'd also like to be around for Synthia when her time comes."

"I'll think on it."

"If Olivia is in on it, I'd be surprised. I don't know how you handle staying here, surrounded by so many people that are guilty of treachery. I'd kill 'em all and let your Goddess, Hecate, sort them out. I need to go feed, though, so I'm out of here. I'll have Zahruk send Olivia more shit for tomorrow. She's pulled most of what I'd planned to do today. I'll also have Zahruk work with Dristan on pulling some of our history around New Orleans. Send them on a merry chase so we can get back to it. There were a few references I found today that look like they could lead to at least one of the relics we are looking for. If that's the case, I'll need to send my brothers in to find it."

"See you in the morning," Alden said as he poured himself a glass of bourbon.

Ristan left him in the study area, his mind heavy

on the little redhead and Alden's problems. Who knew that agreeing to protect Synthia's uncle could lead to so much shit that he was practically wading in it?

He walked down the Guild steps and watched the dark-haired male Fae with the green-gold eyes who had returned to the spot he'd occupied earlier in the day, his eyes still fixed on the doors of the Guild compound. He shook his head and moved closer, only to watch as the Fae turned into a saucy little imp. Her green eyes flashed with gold, and thick black hair was braided into plaits on each side of her stunning face. Tattoos covered her arms, and her ruby red lips turned into an impish grin.

"Demon," Danu said with a throaty laugh.

"You've been standing there this entire time?" he asked, his eyes slowly sliding down the body she'd chosen for this meeting. She often swapped her images when she paid him a visit, like some sort of kinky role-play. Yeah, this one he'd tap, maybe even twice. "Nipples pierced?" he asked with curiosity and watched as she lifted her shirt to reveal perfectly pierced pink nipples.

"Of course; I know how you love it when the clamps click against the metal. Pussy is pierced too; want to see it as well?" she whispered huskily.

"You know I do," he replied dutifully. And let's be honest: The bitch was evil, but she was a damn good fuck. She played with his head, and tortured him at every opportunity, but she had her reasons. At least, he thought she did. There was one thing he knew for sure: She was as fucked up as he was. He could recognize her pain when she thought he wasn't looking.

He'd only let part of the truth slip to Synthia in the maze and she was the only being that knew even that much outside of himself and Danu. There had been a time where he had always been there for Danu, thinking somehow she would save him as she had promised when he was a child. As time wore on, it became abundantly clear that he was one of her many men. Danu toyed with her men, and she had an increasingly large appetite for Human males.

So he had moved on to others, many others until he found one who stood out. And they'd been good together, great even. Those had been some of the best moments of his very long life. The beautiful Fae female was amazing and knew how to please him. They'd become close, right up until the day she'd become rough with him in bed. But it hadn't been her, not on that day. It was Danu. She'd taken over the female, and she'd been pissed. She'd been even more pissed that he'd finally grown a pair and stopped catering to her every whim. He got a massive wake-up call when Danu had killed the girl as a warning.

That's when shit had gone downhill, and he was careful to never get close to any female again. They reached an understanding that day, one that Ristan hadn't been overly fond of, but it worked. Danu didn't want him getting attached to anyone, and her deal had been laid out for him. He could fuck and flirt to his heart's content, but anything more meaningful and the female would suffer, or worse. One of his partners died at Danu's hand, just because she suspected they were getting closer, so he tried to be even more careful. At the risk of starving, this was no easy feat.

Synthia had been the only exception so far, probably because Danu was clear where both Synthia's and Ristan's mindsets were and no fucking had ever been involved between the pair. Kissing, yes. He'd lip-locked Synthia and had enjoyed her shocked response, even knowing it would never lead to anything.

Lately, though, Danu's visits were frequent, but short and to the point.

"Too bad," she said, and watched as a mother and child walked in front of her, probably seeing only the Fae with the green eyes or nothing at all, because they would see only what Danu wanted them to see. "I'm in a hurry today."

"When aren't you?" Ristan retorted, his eyes still firmly set on the nipples. No biggie; he needed more than she could give him this time. He'd spent too much time between feedings.

"Careful, Demon," she warned. "I'm not here for me, I'm here for you. I'm not sure why you keep up this insanity of looking after this man when Synthia's more important. Her condition is precarious at best."

Ristan gave her a hardened look, his eyes rising slowly to meet hers. She could take on any image, but she'd chosen this one specifically because she knew he liked his women to be erotic both in body and nature. His body stiffened when she showed indifference to his needs, her eyes noting the bulge he was now sporting, yet paying it no heed.

Cold-blooded bitch. "I am keeping my promise to her by looking out for the old fossil. While I'm doing that, I have unlimited access to look for the relics all I want. Two birds, one stone, and all that. Seems like a good idea if you ask me, seeing that you haven't sent any visions to fuck with my head in a while. Anyway, I'm on my way back there now; I need to feed. So unless you're going to fix that itch for me, I'll be leaving now."

CHAPTER FOUR

Ristan sat below the berm of the castle, his eyes watching the suns as they set in Faery. Sunset was always his favorite time of day here, as the memories of the greatest pain he'd ever experienced seemed to fade away with the arrival of night. As if those twin orbs of light had a way of reminding him of the horrors he had survived, and the moon awarded him with solace from his sins. His eyes wandered around the beauty of his home, and he took it in with an unfamiliar eye, something he liked to do.

It was as if he was someone seeing its rare beauty for the very first time.

Faery was indeed beautiful, but it was deadly, as most beautiful things often were.

He stood and walked a short way to a grassy field just outside of the keep. They'd placed rocks in a wide sprawling circular pattern, an area he'd often used when he needed release because of the power it held. There were more ways of getting fed and releasing tension, other than fucking. He waved his arms in a pattern and released the souls he'd taken over the centuries. Their glowing, colorful auras hovered and danced around his fingers as he released them. They would make a captivating light show, which would draw the Fairies closer, and with enough of his own people around him, he'd feed.

Emotions came in many shapes and forms, but the easiest was orgasm. It released an abundance of emotions, and the Fae could refill easier through it. This was another way to feed, and one he enjoyed when tensions were high because it helped others as well.

He watched as the auras from the souls shot from his fingers and entered the space around him. To the naked eye, they would mirror Human fireworks; to Demons it would show as auras. Prisms of color erupted and filled the darkening sky as he continued to bring them forth and allow them out. He'd learned long ago to curb his soul hunger; as a Demon it was his choice of food, but it was addictive. He only took enough to curb the hunger and take the edge off.

He'd learned his lesson the hard way, and in Transition, he'd killed four out of five of his bedmates. Dead. No coming back. Immortal fucking Fae and he'd held them mesmerized and slaughtered them with his uneducated hunger. Danu had watched it, and his mother had allowed it to happen. She didn't even try to warn him or anyone else what was going to happen. She had wanted him to know who and what he was. What he was capable of. That was why he was always careful to release the soul after he'd fed from part of it, instead of taking it all, which could easily lead to addiction, not to mention the demise of his dinner. And really, who wanted to dispose of a body after feeding?

He'd only taken the edge off his inner hunger since, and he'd done the impossible, surprising even his own mother by never killing another female since his Transition. He hated senseless killing, and worse than that, he hated wasting pussy. No female should die while giving them what they needed, and he had struggled to hide his Demon side from them all.

It was a weapon, one he'd come to terms with his brothers needing, but in all other parts of his life, he hid it like a dirty little secret and hunted some pretty evil fuckers in the Human world to get what he needed. Shit, he hated it when anyone outside of Synthia called him Demon. For some reason, her saying it had calmed a part of him. As if being one was okay, and not something he should hate.

Synthia had been a surprise altogether, one he'd planned on killing, right up until he'd figured out who she was and what part she would play. Even then, he had never planned on actually liking the brazen woman who had laid claim to the scariest beast in the Horde and made him purr like a sated kitty-cat.

His mind wandered for a few moments as he thought of what would be the best music to start with, and he smiled. Coldplay's *Viva La Vida*. The lyrics and beat pulsed through him and out of him as if he himself was the conductor. He watched silently as the music whispered through the hillside and fields nearby. The Fairies started to gather and dance in the light show that surrounded him. More and more of the lesser Fae worked their way to the dancing, shimmering lights, and as he continued, they joined in dancing with him.

He moved his arms to the beat, dancing stealthily and as if his life depended on it. Fuck Danu for leaving him hard as fuck! His balls were blue, and he needed release, and yet with every pound of the beat, and with each new partner who unknowingly joined in to feed him, he felt the ache being filled.

The armies of the Horde who camped on either side of the walls joined in from their places outside the stone walls, dancing to the music which poured from him, and the prisms of souls continued to fill the sky with a blinding beauty. Silvers, blues, reds, and other colors continued to explode from his body as the Fae laughed and danced in their enchanting colors.

The tinier of the Fairies looked like fireflies as they danced to the music, their small wings humming in tune with the beat. The energy in the air was thickening and became a feast of emotions as each creature released their own angst, tension, and emotions into the air. Nymphs joined in and Ristan had to remind himself that he was already feeding as they shed their clothing and danced around him.

Ristan let it all out. The anger he felt. The tension Danu had created with her cryptic bullshit. His fear of what was coming and what would become of his world if he failed to see the future in time to save it. The stress he felt with the impending birth of his brother's children, and his inability to see their future. He allowed it all out while he could. He changed the song and enjoyed the Fairy ring, which was a continual circle that fed everyone.

It wasn't until his brother Asrian moved closer and

started to dance that Ristan really opened his eyes and looked around. He hadn't realized he'd allowed them to see his inner turmoil, and as his brother stepped forward, he placed the mask back in place on his face. It was a simple smile that he didn't feel, but still showed to everyone to maintain his place in this world.

He turned and found Synthia lounging on the grass, her hand absently rubbing her pregnant belly. His smile reached his eyes at the sight of her, and he made his way to her side. He collected the souls he'd allowed out to play as he did so. His fingers moved in the air as he fed Asrian his power to expel music from his soul for a brief time.

"You shouldn't be out here, Flower. Not with such precious cargo stowed away in your blessed womb," Ristan teased as he shook a single finger at her. She was a naughty little nymph if he'd ever met one. Which he had, and she would have tempted the saints with her sweet lips and even sweeter kiss, which he would know since he'd stolen a kiss from her long ago as he'd healed her with his own powers. The second one had also been stolen and had been sweet as sin. Pun intended.

"I had to mess with Zahruk a little, but he finally allowed me out to play with the grown-ups," she said with a wicked smile as she peered back at Zahruk, who was alert and even now looking for any hidden threat to the Princess and her unborn offspring. "So, what's up with the show?" she continued as she winced and her hand moved to another spot on her stomach.

"Fairy Ring—we will have a nice one going here by dawn. It's a way of working things out. Some Humans work out, others go mad," Ristan said, and shrugged as if it should answer her sufficiently. Ristan looked past Synthia to where Darynda silently glared and watched Zahruk. "Puzzles have a way of being solved when you least expect it," he added softly. He watched the body language between the two, the tension in their stances was hesitant, and yet there was something there. Something deeper than just sex, which would eventually come to a boil, and that was something he wanted to be around to see.

"Which puzzles are you working through?" she asked softly as her eyes went alight with interest, even though her voice held a hint of caution.

"A shit storm of information with very little time to figure it out," he replied easily. His eyes looked troubled, betraying his cheerful attitude even as he tried to contain it. Synthia had enough on her plate already; she didn't need his bullshit on it too. "Danu has been fucking me over with no new visions for the past month, and can't seem to leave me alone. The Guild is slick with traitors and your uncle is too stubborn and prideful to just walk away. Just trying to see where it all connects because it has to. Every puzzle has a starting piece," Ristan said on a deep exhale.

"You, of all people, *would* like puzzles," Synthia said with a naughty smirk on her lips. "Those first few weeks here, Ristan, I couldn't have done it without you by my side. I'm pretty sure I would have killed at least a dozen Fae before I settled in without you guiding me," she continued.

Ristan considered it and smiled at her. She was smart and blunt, which was one of the reasons he enjoyed her company. "You told me once that it's what a true friend does, and you taught me a few unexpected things as well, Flower. Just tell me what is on your mind, weighing it down, and I will help you where I can. Even if you think it's silly, sometimes it may be the most important thing," he said as he watched her for a reaction. He was surprised that he genuinely liked this female when only months ago he'd considered killing her to keep his brother on task.

"So tell me, Demon, what's bothering you at the Guild?" she asked, and he smiled. She was adept in all things Guild, as she should be since she was raised in it.

Ristan tilted his head slightly as he considered what he would actually say to her. He didn't want her to worry about anything other than the upcoming birth of the twins she carried. "I want to pull your uncle out. It's not safe in that place. Treachery is afoot and I'm watching a few of them, who I suspect of being spies. Even one of the librarians seems to be in with the Mages." He decided on just being honest and failed in masking the growl in his voice.

"A librarian; which one?" she asked as her hand continued to rub her stomach.

"She has dark red hair, and she's not very tall," Ristan disclosed, and his tone once again changed. He was warring with his needs and his inner thoughts; he hated to bring her into it. He could handle one librarian; seriously, the little thing shouldn't be weighing on his mind this much. "At least I believe she is working with the Mages, and she has access to Alden; it just doesn't sit well with me. She's a piece of this puzzle, I can feel it. Alden won't listen to me where she's concerned, though, says she's a sweet girl who wouldn't harm a fly." It wasn't exactly how the conversation had gone down between him and Alden, but he hoped Synthia might give more insight that he seemed to be missing.

"Olivia? Little mouse?" Synthia asked with a wide grin.

"If I didn't know better, I'd say she's part Demon," he growled in response.

"Olivia is sweet. She's very timid, but still sweet, from what I know of her, anyway. She's not a spy," she continued. "Well, maybe…Tell me why you think she is a spy."

Ristan considered his words and then discarded them. Instead of telling her his suspicions, or rather, speculations, he told her something that was simple and could be easily discarded by her fears. "She has red hair, and she's always listening, always," he whispered as his eyes once again dropped to her belly.

"So since she has red hair and pays attention, that makes you believe she's a spy for the Mages?"

"That's not all. I just have this gut feeling. I can't *read* her. I can't see her soul and mind." He kicked himself for it. He couldn't see her soul, and he couldn't read her at all, however; he could sense her purity, which normally hinted of virginity. He probably could touch her and read her emotions perfectly, but with the way his body tended to react around her, it was better for him to keep his distance from her. "So far, those I can't read have turned out to be Mages, as it is a powerful spell to block someone like me. Only you and the Dark Princeling have been exceptions to that rule," he said as he rolled over and propped himself on his elbows at eye level with her stomach. "You've grown a lot this week; have you talked to Eliran about it?" he asked her carefully.

She smiled widely and spoke with a straight face. "Yes; we've come to the conclusion that I've had my womb invaded by aliens which have now decided to use it to start a colony of clones."

"Ha-ha," Ristan snapped as he rolled his eyes and tried to focus on her belly, which continued to wobble with the squirming babies. "I'm serious; you're as big as a house."

"Thanks for the confidence booster," she said with a gentle shake of her head. "You think it's managed to slip my notice that I have a wide load sticker on my ass?" she asked with an irritated tone. Ristan smiled; it probably wasn't the brightest idea to call her fat, but it had worked to get her off the discussion of the Mages. "Sorry, it's kind of a sore subject with me at the moment, Demon."

Ouch, now *he* felt like an asshole. *She* was apologizing to *him!* He almost snorted, but managed to hold it in.

"Has Eliran seen the genders yet?" Ristan asked, hating that he was missing out on a lot of the pregnancy; but he was doing so in order to keep his promise to her.

"No; they seem to prefer to hide it. Every time we try, it's the same thing: Either baby will have his or her rear end in the way, or a leg is blocking us, or an entire fetus. I seriously don't care what they are, though, Demon, as long as they are healthy."

"And Ryder? How has he been these days?" he asked her, but took her sour look as answer enough. "Don't give me that look, Flower. Must I remind you that he's—"

"Fae, and love isn't something you guys do a lot? No, I get it. Really, I do. The thing is, I wasn't raised Fae and even if I had been, I'd still want love. Maybe it's a female thing, but the Blood King and Queen, they have love. Actually, even Kier admitted he loves his wife, so that's two couples that I know of that don't follow the norm. Ryder's turned me into a giant beached whale and lately, he barely sticks around to do more than feed me. He was making an effort before, and now, nothing. I get that's he's super busy, but I need him right now, too."

He smiled serenely as he was given his own words back.

"You do know he's preparing for war, right?" Ristan said as he placed his palm over her swollen stomach. His eyes lit up with wonder as one of the babes kicked him, and his heart melted. "That one must be female like her mother; she's got spunk and an attitude behind that kick."

"Well, at least we already know that I have one boy inside there," she said with that spark of sassiness she was so fond of—and, honestly, he was too.

"Just because the vision showed you handing Adam a son doesn't mean they will both be males. After all, I was wrong about who had sired them; I could be wrong about the sex of the child as well."

Visions could be altered and changed, and he felt an ill foreboding when he thought of the future of the babes she was growing in her womb.

"True, since you didn't see both of them in the vision," she continued.

"Don't go there," Ristan said softly as he nodded

to Zahruk, who had made an impatient noise indicating that he felt her playtime among the lesser Fae was over. "I haven't seen them die," he said. His eyes tightened as he watched her, and she continued to do the same, as if she thought he'd give something away. His hand continued to stroke where the babe had yet to stop kicking him, and he was unwilling to stop feeling them, as if he wouldn't get much time with them again. Something dark was coming, and it left him worried that he'd be unable to stop it.

"You haven't seen them, though, Demon; at least, not through to their adulthood. You can see Ryder's future as the King, but you've yet to see me or his children in it. I'm just worried that with the war coming, they will be born into a broken world which will be too damaged to accept them."

"That's good," Ristan responded to her with a mischievous smile. "It means you're thinking like a mother already. Now, back to what's bothering me," he said with a roguish wink. "The librarian... How well do you know her?"

It was a duck and dodge thing with Synthia. She was going dark, and quick, which forced Ristan to suck it up and change the subject back to what he'd ducked out of before by changing the subject.

"She's a mouse. Why, you thinking of fucking the information out of her?" Synthia teased. She wasn't stupid, though, and he sensed that she'd felt the switch and allowed it.

"I'm pretty sure she wouldn't know what to do with a cock if it was staring her in the eye. She's a little too prim and proper for my taste, which, as you know, I like the kinky fuckery."

"Nice mental picture, Demon; can I go toss my cookies now?" she said, wincing forcefully.

"I'm serious. She's so far from my type that I'd rather bend a Light Fae over and go to town. Better one of those insufferable pricks than that little wench. At least they'd know what to do with a cock," Ristan continued, trying to shore up his weak argument.

"Now I need ear bleach! But, on a serious note, I think you're protesting a little too much. Maybe you have a slight Demon-type crush on the poor little mouse?" she cried with a grin on her full lips. He quailed inwardly at that thought. He couldn't have a crush; he never crushed on anyone before, and he damn sure wasn't about to start now.

"She could be in league with the Mages! Who knows anymore? I can't abide betrayers, and I have had more than enough of them lately," he growled the last out firmly.

"I doubt it, but anything is possible," she finally said after she considered it for a moment.

"She's a fucking she-Demon in pretty pink heels," he grumbled.

"Oh, here now, Demon, maybe you just want her to play with your Lego parts, and tinker with your big blue balls? Just once," she said wickedly. Her eyes were alight with unshed laughter as she teased him.

Her words pulled a belly laugh from Ristan, which felt damn good considering what he'd had to deal with lately. "My balls are not blue, and I will even volunteer to show them to you for proof; can't let you go around thinking my boys are from a toy store and shit."

"Ristan," Ryder growled as he materialized behind them, and for a moment, Ristan had to remind himself that it was only Ryder, as his brother now held the same power as their father had. "You have somewhere else you need to be?"

"Not really," Ristan said absently as he stood up and began working the buttons of his pants. He loved fucking with his brothers' minds, and it was easier to hide his problems behind a wall of laughter than it was to deal with it all.

His smile grew as Synthia covered her eyes and squealed with laughter, and Ryder smiled at her reaction as well. She'd worked a miracle and she'd made him love her, even if he didn't realize it yet.

"Don't do it!" she cried between giggles.

"You show her, and I will promise to make them blue for real, brother," Ryder growled.

"She accused my boys of being blue! I only offered to let her inspect them to assure her I suffered no such disorder," Ristan said between a snort and a laugh as he watched the woman hold her belly through the laughter.

"Enough, children," Ryder said as his eyes fastened onto his woman's huge midsection with love. "You're too exposed out here, and I'd like to feed you, Pet."

Ristan stared at the space they'd stood in long after they'd sifted out and realized he'd taken too long at home. He needed to get back to Alden soon and finish his research in the archives. He knew he was close to finding the right scrolls, which could hopefully lead them to the rest of the relics.

He watched as Ciara approached him. Her dark hair bounced with each step she took. The little minx was up to something, even he could see that much. It was in the bounce of her walk, and the smile in her eyes.

"Rissy," she purred.

"What do you want, Minx?" he asked as he continued to watch her and the small fairies that filled the sky, making it glow with their frenetic dancing.

"You like her," Ciara said, and turned her eyes on him.

"Who?" He played dumb. When dealing with his sister, it was best to play stupid and let her announce what it was that she was digging for.

"Synthia," she said, and folded her arms across her chest.

"She's not like most Fae women, and she's refreshing. You'll like her once you actually try to. Stop being a spoiled brat, because Ryder is keeping her," Ristan said softly, reminding Ciara that Ryder was the King, even if it was only a subtle hint.

"I'm not spoiled. I'm simply tired of being hidden away and treated like I don't exist. Seriously, you guys act like I'm a child, and I'm not. I don't even know if I'll like her because I'm not allowed around her. It's not fair; he released the entire pavilion, and yet I only traded one prison for another."

"You've been given free rein to go wherever you want in the castle," he said, watching as she rolled her eyes. "Baby steps, Ciara. He's got a lot on his plate right now."

"Claire seems to think that Synthia will end up gone soon," she puffed and watched him.

"I wouldn't place merit on what that one says about anything. If she says the sky is falling, sister, look for it first before you run."

Ristan stood up and shook his head. He loved his little sister, but she was hot-headed and as stubborn as any of his hundred and twenty-seven half-brothers. She had been sheltered, and that was because she was the only acknowledged sister they had. He had his suspicions about a few others that were probably other unacknowledged half-sisters, such as the Brownie Malinda, who had followed them to the mansion outside of Spokane. He watched Ciara silently as she moved away from him and started dancing with one of their other brothers.

No men approached her, and for good reason. He'd watched his brothers remove those who approached her, and it hadn't been done gently. She had successfully made it through Transition, but since then, her feedings had been watched, as well as her activities. She was, after all, the only daughter born to their murderous father. Well, that they knew of.

"Don't you have somewhere else to be?" Zahruk asked as he returned silently.

"Alden is safe for the night, and I needed to feed," Ristan answered as he brought his eyes back to his brothers. "Don't you have pussy to chase? She's sending you imaginary knives, and I'm pretty sure they're being aimed at your back...or junk."

"She isn't happy with anything I do," he grumbled, which caused Ristan to smile.

"Have you tried fucking her?" was his sage advice to his older brother.

"That seems to be the issue," Zahruk grumbled unhappily.

"Really? You tapped that?" Ristan asked trying to conceal the surprise in his voice. Zahruk normally fed from women who didn't mind being shared, but Darynda didn't fall into the category. She was far from it, and came from a prominent family.

"She seduced me," he growled, and made an animalistic noise from deep inside his chest.

"Did she now? How *did* she manage that?" Ristan teased, enjoying the sight of his brother growling deeply as Ryder had when he'd met Synthia.

"She fell on my cock—how the fuck you think it happened? She caught me hungry and shit happened quickly. The next thing I know, she started talking about a relationship, like I'm that type of asshole," Zahruk explained, and Ristan struggled to try to keep the smile from his face.

"She fell on your cock, and shit just happened? Hitting the ambrosia too hard there, brother?" he asked, finally losing the battle with the wicked grin that he'd been barely holding back.

"Fucker," Zahruk said before he sifted out of the Fairy Circle.

"Right back at ya, bro!" Ristan voice was filled with laughter as he said it via the mental path he and his brothers typically spoke on.

CHAPTER FIVE

Olivia set the box of files to be archived on the mail counter, her eyes watching the hall and entryway for any sign of Justin. Her mind wandered to Cyrus and his weird obsession with her reports on the visiting Enforcer. As if the man actually wanted to be here, in this place. As far as punishments went, research and pushing papers was as bad as it got for an Enforcer unless you included death.

She had spent most of the morning pulling scrolls and other items that Alden and the Elder from New Orleans had requested for Justin to dig through. She'd written down the contents, and Cyrus had gone through the lots as she'd pulled them.

His cryptic words and calls to a higher-up left her with a bad feeling, but she was only a mere librarian, so who was she to question an Elder?

She typed in some numbers for the archives she was working on and looked up as Kendra appeared at her desk.

"Hey, girl," she said, her smile genuine; she really liked Kendra.

"Hey, did you get a chance to pull those files?" Kendra asked, her eyes scanning the library.

"I did, but I'm still not sure why you're even bothering with Demons from the 1600s," Olivia probed; she may not understand it, but she wanted to.

"Alden said he approved for me to look at them; he said I could make notes of whatever I wanted. Just no pictures and no taking them out of the library," Kendra supplied, even though it wasn't an answer to Olivia's question. She'd blatantly dodged the question. Olivia paused as she considered asking it again, and then decided to let it go since it was obvious Kendra hadn't wanted to answer it.

She was curious by nature and loved history. No, she was actually obsessed with the history of pretty much everything. She'd spent hours of her childhood; hidden in this library, scouring through books. They took her to worlds she would get lost in, and sometimes she needed it.

Her parents were a mystery to her, for the most part. Her father was unknown, but suspected to be high up in the Salem Guild. Her mother had died giving birth, and there hadn't been anyone, or any family to take her in. Without family to take her in, Salem had shipped her off to Spokane as soon as they were able to, as it was the only Guild in North America with the ability to care for an orphaned child that had magical talents.

"Here are *The History of Demonology*, *The Unclaimed Witches*, and *The Dark Witches*," Olivia said, her mind taking note of how thin the third book was. All the books had been covered in an inch of dust when Olivia had taken them from the bowels of the catacombs. "You have two hours before I close the doors for the afternoon class, but after that you're welcome to come back."

"I won't need much longer than that; I'm looking for specific events," Kendra said as she pushed her honey-blonde hair from her face and checked her notes on her phone. She was a pretty girl, the kind the boys would go after and chase for her classic beauty.

Unlike Olivia's own gaudy red hair and porcelain-pale skin. Her body was slim in a way no sandwich could fix. She would know; she'd eaten enough of them. She'd tried anything to gain some curves; she tried a lot of different techniques, some more than a few times. Her small breasts weren't even a handful, and unlike Kendra's, hers didn't make men turn their heads the way some of the male librarians were currently staring.

She scratched absently at the sprinkling of freckles on her nose. They came back in spring with the first rays of sun, faithfully. She was invisible to the men, which was probably a good thing considering how clumsy she was around them. Justin, God, he made her tongue tie in knots that no magician could magically untie.

She'd never been one to go out partying when the other girls did, and she was a hopeless romantic at heart. She spent her off hours either poring through books from the Guild or rereading her favorite romance novels. It wasn't something she was proud of, this introvert nature she had, but it was something she dealt with.

She placed Kendra's items into a bin and watched as the girl walked away, her eyes scanning the library as if she was afraid she'd be jumped. Weird. She was normally really talkative, and Olivia loved the warm vibe Kendra gave off that made her feel more like one of the girls, rather than the shy mouse she normally felt like around the others.

Olivia went back to working, her mind firmly back on Justin. He was late, as was Alden. Maybe they'd gone out to coffee? She liked coffee. Recently her daydreams included going out for coffee with a certain visiting Enforcer. Yeah, right, like that was ever going to happen. She sighed heavily and jumped as Mildred dropped a thick volume on her counter.

"These need to be returned, and Cyrus wants you to alert him the moment Alden gets in. He also said to be watchful today, and that you should just suspend the afternoon class. Those kids will riot if you do, so please don't. The rest of us would rather not take over the primary class."

Mildred was thirtyish, with drab, yellow straw-like hair. Her parents were both Elders, kind people. It was a wonder that their daughter was so serious and sour. Olivia took the heavy volume—one she had just fully archived and taken from about thirty tomes—and dropped it onto the lower part of her counter.

"I'll still teach it, and Alden hasn't been in yet. He's usually not this late," Olivia politely pointed out, her hands coming back up, and folding on the counter. "Is there anything else you needed?" she continued.

"No. Make sure you file that, and be sure to note that I took it for only a day," she said flippantly as she turned and left.

As if I don't know how to do my own job? Olivia

just barely stopped herself from rolling her eyes as she went back to cataloguing the archive she was working on. Distractedly, her mind wandered to the hours she'd spent last night looking into the description of the Demon the kid had given her, and yet the Guild held so little information on Demons that it was like looking for a ghost.

Two hours went by before the kids started coming in and the visitors started leaving. She looked to where Kendra had been and noted that Sadie was talking to the girl now. She turned and watched as the last of the kids entered.

She smiled. She loved this part of her job the most. Teaching History to eager little minds, well, mostly eager. Some hated being here, and those ones normally could be brought around easily enough with the right lesson.

"Miss Olivia," Matilda said as she slipped her tiny fingers into Olivia's hand. "No monsters today, okay?" she begged with her small lip trembling.

"Monsters are why we are here, Matilda. They're why we need to learn about them, so we can hunt them down and protect others from them."

"'Tilda is afraid of them," Clarita said, her brown eyes challenging. "I'm not afraid of them; I want to kill them, and protect people!"

The kids started sounding off, and Olivia felt her heart twist with the reality of it all. They would go out into the real world, and some of them would make Enforcer, unlike her. Some of them would die protecting the Human race from very real monsters.

"Let's sit on the carpet today," she said, her eyes

searching the faces and taking a mental head count. Having an eidetic memory came in handy at times like this. "Bryan, Kandice, and Burt, front row please. Today I'll be getting your full attention, or Alden and James will be making you run additional laps tomorrow morning. Do you understand?" she chided.

She wanted kids, but she wanted the kind that didn't happen. The kind of kids who listened, loved to learn, and behaved. She'd once confided that to Alden, and he'd laughed. He'd responded with, "A child is only silent when they are in trouble, and they only behave if bribed to do so."

"Okay, ladies and gentlemen," she said as she took her seat at the head of the class, on the small chair which could barely fit a child. Not that she was much bigger than the oldest kid here. "Today we learn about the Fae, and some of the breeds. We'll start by asking each other some very important questions."

She waited until they all looked in her direction before she continued.

"Who can give me the names of the High Fae castes? And why are they the most dangerous?"

"That's easy," Daniel called out. He had a light complexion, with freckles that covered both his cheeks and his nose. He was a smart ass most days, being the oldest of the group.

"Well," Olivia said after a moment, "enlighten us."

"Blood, Light, Dark, and the Horde. The Horde is the ugliest and vilest of the monsters and I'm going to kill them all when I get bigger and become an Enforcer. You won't see much of the Horde here because they're ugly buggers. Dark is smart, and deadly, but unlike the others, they like our world and stay in it. They don't hide, like the Blood Fae do. Those ones don't come here. They're probably afraid of us and our Enforcers. The Light is the most beautiful, and you know it's them because they draw you in with their pretty eyes and looks. Then they eat you," he said matter-of-factly.

"Good description, but those aren't facts. The Blood don't come here because it's believed they prefer to stay hidden in the shadows and remain in Faery. Little is known about them, other than that. The Horde is the ugliest of the Fae, but they don't appear so when they use glamour. They're monsters, ones without rule because their King has been missing for a long time, which makes them the most dangerous. The Light Fae, while alluring and attractive, are truly stuck-up and self-absorbed." Olivia made a face that made the kids giggle. "Or so I am told. And the last is the Dark Fae, the most well-known group of the Fae. They don't hide in the shadows, you're right about that Daniel, but you forgot to mention that they, too, are amazingly beautiful. Each of the four castes feeds on the Human race," she said, and then paused, hating the next part. "Can anyone tell me why that is bad?"

Ristan watched her from the shadows, her delicate features crinkling when she didn't like something. She enjoyed teaching; that much he was sure of. Her eyes had gazed on the children with love, and he found himself wondering what it would be like for someone to look at him like that.

He grinned to himself at the Guild teaching she was passing on to the children. The Humans hadn't gotten word yet that the Horde King wasn't missing anymore, and would have flipped if they'd known that he'd been masquerading as the Dark Fae Heir for years with the support of the Dark King, no less. Nor did they know that the real Dark Fae Prince had been hidden in this very Guild the entire time. Yep, that wasn't going to go over well when they realized the extent of the trick that the Fae had pulled on them.

He listened as the children answered each question she asked, and then as she corrected them. He liked the soft lilt of her voice, as if she had a hint of the South in her, not that he was actually from the South himself. Just the small twang, which she'd probably picked up from a book or a TV show.

He'd told Synthia that the little redhead was a Demon, but the truth of it was, she was more angel than anything else. She didn't fit the mold of a traitor, and yet, did anyone? She'd be too scared of doing it. She was too small, and very meek, as Synthia had described, but Ristan was sure she had a fire in her, just itching to get out.

Most freaks were the ones no one expected, the quiet ones. He grinned. His eyes slid further down to her plump breasts. Most men would say too small, he'd say just fuckin' perfect. Impeccable size for clamps, in his opinion. And her red lips...fuckin' hell, he'd like to see them wrapped around his cock, as those beautiful dark blue eyes watched his pleasure as it spread across his face.

Those small hips were perfect because it wouldn't take much to rock them, and he would. He'd take her hard, relentlessly, for hours. Those elegant fingers, small, and yet big enough to get the job done…

"Justin," Alden said, his voice making Ristan jump from where his filthy ass mind had gone.

The problem with actually fucking Olivia? She wouldn't know what to do if a cock came with crayon-written directions, and he wasn't into teaching as much as he was into doing.

He turned to the old man and glared. "Let's get those archives," he growled as he led the way to the study carrel. His mind firmly dismissed thoughts of what he 'wanted' to do and couldn't fuckin' do. Because when it came to that little librarian, it wasn't rocket science. He wasn't hitting it, period.

CHAPTER SIX

The halls of the Guild were almost empty as Ristan moved through them, his eyes scanning for unseen threats as he followed behind the librarian. She seemed sweet, and yet he never took anyone or anything at face value. Shit was never what it seemed, and the moment you let your guard down, you died. Now that she was finished with her duties for the day, it seemed that a little invisibility glamour and a bit of nosing around might be in order.

He slipped silently by her and into her apartment, catching the subtle scent of jasmine as he passed her. She could be innocent, but she could also be guilty of being in league with the Mages. They'd all seemed innocent at first, right up until they'd started stealthily attacking the Fae.

The Mages blamed the Fae for not being welcomed into the High Fae Castes, especially not on equal footing, as they were Changelings and not fully Fae. They'd never even bothered to come to the Horde, but then again, they hadn't wanted to be a part of the Horde. They wanted to be accepted, but every Caste had those they easily accepted, and those they didn't. Acceptance didn't mean equality, though; this was something Ristan knew all too well.

The Mages were half -human, and to the Fae, that used to be a death sentence. They were mortally flawed, as they aged, and the Fae were vain in their immortality and inability to die from natural causes. Who could blame them? They were frozen in time, at the age of their Transition, or close to it. Who wanted to watch as someone withered and slowly died as they aged? Granted, a Changeling's lifespan was a lot longer than a Human, but aging was still inevitable.

Of course, the Horde would have taken them in, had they asked. They'd been open to any Fae or creature that could in some way add to their numbers. Instead, the Mages had let their anger fester over time and had become monsters in their own right. The Mages had been systematically trying to destroy the Fae, and Faery itself, in retaliation. The Fae had traced the Mages back to the Guild's doorstep, where they'd been hiding in plain sight. The hard part was separating Witches and Warlocks from the Mages, and figuring out who was actually there to protect the Humans, and which ones were using the cover of the Guild to destroy the Fae.

Ristan swiftly slid into the entryway as he searched the room for any damning evidence. It was a small apartment with a kitchen and separate bathroom, living, and sleeping rooms all only a few steps away from each other. He caught sight of pictures—or, more to the point, frames. Olivia had walls of frames, with the original sample pictures they came with still displayed in them.

He moved his eyes to the slim female as she moved inside the room. She removed her shawl and slipped out of her flat sandals. She stretched and moved to a docking station on the counter, popped her phone into it and touched an app for an oldies station. Ristan smiled, approving of her taste in music as the Beatles' *I Saw Her Standing There* came on and her head bobbed to the beat. She softly muttered a spell and the music spread to the other rooms of the small apartment.

"Kit?" she called, her eyes moving around the room. "Kit cat, if you don't come out, mommy can't feed you," she called out, and then started dancing her way to the bag of cat food. She shook the bag, and moved around the small room, searching for the feline.

"Bad kitty," she said, her eyes passing over Ristan, and then slid further through the room. "I swear, if you got out, and you get me into trouble…" She let the threat hang in the air unspoken.

Ristan looked down as something curled around his ankle and meowed. *Found the pussy.* He smiled; yeah, he was a pussy fucking magnet. He carefully pushed the cat with a gentle foot and smiled as Olivia's face lit up as she caught sight of the cat.

"Damn, Kit, you gave me a scare. You know they'll boot you out if they discover I took you in. The Guild doesn't allow animals in the apartments," she chided lovingly, and Ristan narrowed his eyes on her.

He shook off the thoughts that popped in his head. She loved animals; who said the Mages wouldn't love them as well? Who says evil people didn't have pets? He moved further into the apartment, listening as she started singing along to the radio while watering her plants and chattering to them. For such a quiet little thing, she had a lot bottled up in there that she seemed to only feel comfortable saying to the cat and plants. She had a small snack in her kitchen, cleaned up, and then she moved into the same room as he was currently heading into.

He watched her from the empty corner of her small, but perky, bedroom. More of the frames with images of the model families filled them, even in here. Only one frame hadn't been bought and placed directly on the wall.

A picture of a woman with a pregnant swollen belly and coppery hair was on her nightstand. The woman's eyes were a vivid aqua blue, and if he guessed right, it was Olivia's mother. The background setting showed a little farmhouse with a white picket fence that surrounded it. By the vivid coloring of the tree leaves, he guessed it was taken somewhere in New England.

His eyes slid back to the woman at hand, and he paused. She was undressing. Fucking hell, he should look away. Right? He looked to the door and found the cat watching him carefully. Yeah, he knew he should leave, but he couldn't muster the willpower to actually go.

Not like he could if he actually wanted to. Sifting inside the Guild was something he had never tried. It was well-known that there were wards in place to prevent Fae from sifting in or out and he had never wanted to give them a hint of his being inside of the walls of the Guild. Too much rode on him being here.

Instead, he moved closer to the wall in the corner of

the bedroom and slid down it. She had porcelain skin, almost alabaster in color, with a few beautifully placed freckles. He held his breath as she lifted the shirt and revealed a simple white lacy bra that was sheer enough that he could make out pink nipples that begged to be nipped and pinched.

What the fuck was wrong with him? He preferred exotic women, ones who enjoyed kinky fuckery, things like nipple clamps and other toys that could make a woman scream as she discovered new passions. He swallowed as she stepped out of her skirt, and yes, his eyes slid to the thin slice of fabric that barely contained the wispy red curls of her sex.

Fuck me, she's perfect, Ristan said in his head, his eyes taking in her slim thighs and firm backside. She rummaged through the closet and tossed a few things on the bed before she bent over the dresser as she searched for something.

He waited as she left the room, and it wasn't until he heard the bathwater that he actually groaned. He caught it and ran a frustrated hand over his face. Hadn't he considered that she'd come home and bathe? No, because he hadn't thought that far ahead.

The cat moved further into the room and jumped on the dresser. Its green eyes centered on Ristan as it lay down and watched him from its lofty perch. The little bastard was looking at him accusingly. He frowned, but c'mon, it wasn't like he'd followed its mistress into the bathroom, which was exactly what he'd wanted to do.

He stood up and went to the door, his eyes scanning the rooms before settling on one that looked like an office. He entered it, uncaring that he was being stealthily trailed by the curious feline. He was almost to the office when he heard a soft moan, and his head snapped up, turning to the noise escaping from the bathroom.

He wasn't going in there. No way, no how, right? He continued into the small office that doubled as a small library, took in the neatness, and frowned. This wasn't neatness; no, this was OCD. Olivia was either a germaphobe, or she had a serious case of OCD.

He took in the minute details of the room, like how the one blanket on the recliner was folded perfectly, as in a perfect square. It had one corner that stuck out, and if he could guess what that meant, he was sure she could simply pull that corner, and the entire blanket would unfold perfectly.

Books were stacked in the single shelf in alphabetical order, and he smiled as wild romance titles stuck out, each one alphabetically placed. He moved to the shelf and ran his finger over the top, bringing it back up to his eyes without a single speck of dust. He shook his head and moved around the office, opening drawers and files, but finding nothing but documents about the Salem Guild.

Salem?

He turned as another moan sounded from the bathroom, followed by a frustrated groan. He smiled; so the little minx was having issues reaching self-climax? He heard the water shut off, and finished nosing through her things.

He opened one of the Salem files and studied several documents regarding a Witch named Carleen. He read a part of one, which detailed how Carleen had signed the birth certificate naming Olivia before the labor pains had grown too fierce. In the end, she left the father's name blank, and the child was left with her own last name. Carleen had died during the birthing, and they'd delivered the child by caesarean.

His eyes scanned the pictures of the violent birth and took mental pictures of the instruments used in the surgical procedure. Caesarian births were unheard of in Faery and he couldn't remember seeing anything in Synthia's baby books about it. His heart thudded as he considered what kind of life Olivia would have had if the Guild hadn't been there for her.

He'd often been against the Guild, but in this one instance, he was thankful that it existed. Children deserved to be loved; they were innocent. He'd often sat in the grave fields in Faery, and looked at the nameless graves of the children who hadn't made it.

The sickness was overtaking his home world, and it tore him apart to think of how the Mages had targeted the young and innocent of his species. *They* hadn't been the ones to reject the Mages, and in their bitterness, they'd struck at the heart of his people. They'd poisoned the lands, and in doing so, they'd poisoned the babes. If the land didn't accept the babes, they perished.

He pushed the files back into the drawers perfectly and moved from the office back into the bedroom as Olivia exited the bathroom in a towel. Her hair was loose and mesmerizing in its fiery beauty. It was a beautiful contrast in color against her silken white flesh; perfection. She sang out a spell in time with the music that turned it off as he slid back into place in the corner and ran his hands over his eyes.

He should have waited, but if she shut the door,

he'd be stuck on the other side. She moved around the room, and he listened. Listened to the sound of her as she removed the towel, and it hit the ground with a soft thud.

His heart began to thump harder in his chest, which surprised him, and he dropped his hands from his eyes. He caught sight of her as she lowered a silky baby blue nightgown over her head. His eyes followed it as it caressed her flesh, slowly slipping to the generous white orbs of her perfect ass. He swallowed slowly, his eyes remaining on her firm backside.

He'd tap it, and he'd pull that fiery red hair as he fucked her. Fuuuuck... He shook his head and brought his knees up to rest his elbows on them. His cock was locked and loaded in hard-as-fuck mode. He lowered his eyes to it, and considered gripping it to see if it would relieve the massive pressure he was experiencing, but he wasn't some kid; he was a Demon, one who got a lot of pussy. Pussy basically fell on his cock all the time and he took full advantage of that shit.

Yet here he was, with a raging hard-on for some green-as-fuck virgin. He knew she was; she smelled too pure to be otherwise. He watched as she pulled a thin sheet back and climbed in bed. She looked around the room and got back up slowly.

"Kit?" she called out and the cat came rushing into the room and once again moved to its perch on the dresser. "Good girl," she whispered just before she closed the door, sealing all three of them inside her room.

Didn't see that shit coming! Ristan almost banged his head against the wall, but gently placed it there instead as the lights were turned off and a bedside lamp was clicked on. He watched her as she lifted a book and began reading it.

She grunted. "Ninny," she whispered as she picked up a sexy-as-fuck pair of glasses and put them on. "Better," she uttered as she began reading silently.

It was going to be a long night.

He whispered a camouflage spell around himself, just in case he drifted off to sleep, only to wake up to his cover name being whispered. He jumped, his eyes instantly alert to any problem, but there wasn't a problem. Olivia was asleep; the sheet she'd used for cover against the cold had slipped from her body, revealing her naked ass.

She said his name again as her hand absently lowered to those lovely red curls. He smiled, knowing he should leave, but unwilling to. She was dreaming about him; well, sort of. She was dreaming of an Enforcer who didn't exist.

Her lips parted on a moan as her fingers delved between her slick folds. She was wet, and his nostrils flared with the knowledge of it. His eyes glued to what her hand was doing, and he could see that in her innocence, she was doing it all wrong.

She wasn't touching that little love button, the one that could invoke sweet screams from her lungs. Her fingers slowly trailed up the slit, and then, as he watched with his cock fully saluting her fumbled attempt, she slipped a slim finger inside.

He moved his eyes away from her hand and lifted them to her face. Her eyes were barely open more than a slit, but were on him. He could feel his magic that supported the glamour as well as the camouflage spell, which meant she wasn't actually looking at him, but he'd be a fucking fairy if she wasn't thinking about him, and it made his cock throb.

He turned his head and looked at the cat, who sat watching her as well. The cat mewled, and looked at Ristan accusingly. As if the little fucker hadn't been watching the sweet pussy get fucked as well? Fucking animals, all of them, including him. She whimpered and both of their heads swung back to her, and Ristan had to fight the urge to show her what she was doing wrong.

She worked it, abusing it as she struggled to pull an orgasm from her sweet flesh. Moisture pooled, glimmered and showed his greedy eyes proof that sweet pussy was soaking wet with a need to be fucked. Fuuuuck, this shit only happened to him.

He pushed his back into the wall and inhaled the fragrance of her jasmine bath oils mixed with the musky smell of her swollen flesh. She added another finger, and Ristan fisted his hands as he imagined his own fingers invading her tight sheath.

She'd come then, because he'd be sucking that fucking button of her flesh until she exploded her juices on his face. He moved stealthily to the bed and got a much nicer view against his own better judgment.

Her nipples were hard, pushing against her thin nightgown. Her legs were spread, and she was moving her fingers clumsily. Inefficiently. The pace she'd set was slow, and wouldn't be allowing her to come anytime tonight.

He smiled and considered helping her, but he would

be damned if he burnt his cover just to get some sweet-as-fuck pussy off. His mouth watered for a taste as even more juices gathered on her fingers while she continued to delve them inside her tight flesh.

He forced himself to go back to the corner and wait it out. His cock throbbed painfully against the rough jeans he wore. He held it and wondered what she'd think if she was faced with his ten-inch cock—which he only knew was ten inches because a pixie thought it would be funny to measure it. Considering her innocence, she'd probably run. Even some of the more experienced females he'd taken had to stop and consider it for a few moments before getting back with the program.

Of course, he'd been very selective of the pussy he accepted; most had to enjoy what Humans referred to as kink, and be willing to give him total control. They also had to be okay with him giving all pleasure and taking what he wanted.

He had a feeling that she wouldn't do that, ever. Based on what he witnessed tonight, she really wouldn't know what to do with a cock, even if he gave her step-by-step instructions and walked her through it intimately, which surprised him. With all of the romance books she had, she should know at least the basics, as the things were pretty much a step above a how-to guide! He needed to find a female, and fuck her until he sated this hunger for a simple, but beautiful, librarian. Maybe he could get Danu to glamour herself into a sexy librarian, so he could fuck his need for this one out of his system.

CHAPTER SEVEN

The Demon awoke to a gentle humming sound, his eyes scanning the room until they landed on the female, who seemed to be up and already dressing for work. He was cramped from his tall frame having slept in the corner of her bedroom.

He stood and stretched his arms, easily touching the ceiling. He turned and found the damned cat still watching him. *Who the hell named their cat Kit,* he wondered? She had personality, that was for sure, even if she *was* a mouse. She was sitting on her bed as she rolled on thigh highs, which was a sight that was too damn sexy for this fucking early in the morning.

He'd just about murder the cat for a cup of coffee. He could thank Synthia for resurrecting his obsession with the shitty brown substance, which tasted of heaven. He'd given Syn hell over it, then Darynda had worked her magic and brewed him a cup blended with chicory that had almost made his cock stand up in a one-eyed salute.

He tore his eyes from Olivia as she hooked the little black disc into the stockings she wore, and he smiled as she slid on shoes that had little sexy heels. It was a fucking fantasy of a lifetime, turning a little mouse into a fucking nymphomaniac.

Following her into the bathroom, his eyes scanned her small make-up kit. No muss, no fuss kinda girl. She dabbed some gloss onto her already rose-colored lips and then used a touch of mascara before she left the room and called to her pussy.

He gave a crooked smile as he remembered her clumsy attempt to get her own pussy off. At least it showed she had general knowledge of where a cock went, and what it was supposed to do. Damn, if his dick didn't twitch at the memory.

He watched her as she bent over to place a handful of cat food in the bowl, and then quickly washed her hands. She scanned the room and then moved past him; his nose danced with her rich, flowery scent. He loved jasmine flowers and their enticing scent.

He followed her as she walked towards the front door, stopping to pull her phone off the docking station. She powered it on, thumbed on the speed dial, and asked to be connected to Elder Cyrus.

His heart beat erratically as he considered what she'd say. He didn't get a chance to overhear any conversation, as she was told he was already out of his office.

"Can you let him know that I called for him, Janet? I'll be at my desk in about twenty minutes. He can call me there," she said into the receiver before she used a soft cloth to wipe it clean, and slid it into her pocket.

She stood in her front room, and he went completely still as she sniffed the air. Her eyes looked around as if she knew she wasn't alone.

"God, girl, get a grip. He's so far out of your league," she whispered to herself.

He slipped out the door as she opened it and headed for a vacant apartment to hopefully dunk himself under some chilly water in an attempt to shed the protruding boner which was, even now, growing harder for her.

What the fuck was his problem? He didn't like sweet and innocent; he liked girls that he could bring his inner freak out to play with. This girl? She was the sweet, white picket fence, and two-point-five kids, with a cat named Kit kind of girl. That wasn't him. Now if he could just convince himself that he didn't really want her, or maybe come up with a mantra to repeat in his mind, he would actually believe it.

He paused with his hand on the doorknob and decided to just head home. It was time to check on Synthia anyway, what with her time nearing, and he'd bought her a little present that he'd been itching to give her.

He walked outside, still cloaked in invisibility, and waited until he was a good distance from the Guild before he sifted to the mansion located just out of Spokane, which had been previously used as their home base when in the Human world. It had been completely rebuilt after the Mages had destroyed it not too long ago. It was now being used as a staging point for operations that the Horde was running to shut the Mages down while tracking the remaining relics.

He quickly made his way to the portal that would

take him into Faery, straight into the Horde kingdom. He could make a portal of his own, but he was already feeling a bit drained from using glamour and the camouflage spell as long as he had. As he entered the portal, he was stopped in his tracks by Darcy, or, rather, Danu currently wearing a "Darcy" glamour. He could see her ever-changing eyes through Darcy's sweet, brown ones.

"Danu," he said as she pushed him into an empty room. She twirled Darcy's blonde hair, and then lowered her hands to squeeze the plump breasts of the body she'd taken over.

"Demon," she said, as she began to remove her shirt, revealing rose-tipped nipples that were already hard and begging to be tasted. "I need release," she ordered.

"I needed it yesterday," he countered as he crossed his branded arms over his massive chest, which strained against the charcoal V-neck shirt he now wore. "It's all about what *you* need, and it's getting worse. Something going on that I should know about?" he demanded suspiciously, and watched as something passed over her face before she could stop it.

His heart clenched, and he got a twisting in his gut that made him feel sick. "If it pertains to the Horde…" He let his words trail off as she slid to her knees and started undoing his belt buckle.

He braced his arms on the wall and watched as she freed his cock. Yeah, that shit was loaded and hard as a fucking rock after watching his little librarian. *My fucking librarian?* He groaned as she used her tongue to stroke the sensitive fleshy underside of his cock, using long motions until he thought he'd spew his load prematurely.

Danu loved to make him lose control, and she'd throw it back in his face after she'd succeeded. It only made him more determined to outlast her. He lowered his hand and grabbed her hair as he pulled her head back and he enjoyed the surprised hiss that left her parted lips as he pulled hard. He used his other hand to grip her chin, forcing her mouth to open as he pushed his fat tip past her rosy lips.

"Take it all," he demanded as he rocked his hips, giving her time to accept his rock hard member without hurting her. "That's my girl," he moaned as he slipped further into her throat. He wasn't going to last long, and at this point, he didn't care.

He rocked his hips faster, enjoying the strangled sounds she made as she choked on his cock. Her eyes watered as he watched her, his own mouth opening to dish out encouragements as she accepted even more down her tight, lovely throat.

He exploded before either of them knew what was happening, and when he pulled out of her mouth, she stared at him in wonder, then looked around in confusion.

"Ristan," she whispered as he watched her wipe a small dribble of come from her perfect lips. "How did I get here?" she finished.

He wanted to strangle her; not Darcy, but fucking Danu. It wasn't glamour this time; it was a total hijacking. She'd done this shit too many times now. Many times she had taken over his bedmates during fucking, only to leave as soon as she got hers, which made a few of the women think him a lazy fuck. As if; he was a beast in the sheets and damn sure gave his partners a ride they'd never forget. Other times, she'd take control of them in the beginning, only to leave him to explain how he'd end up with his cock balls deep with a partner who hadn't known he was fucking her.

"Pull up your skirt and bend over, Darcy. I'll make it worth your while," he promised with a lopsided grin, and watched as she hurriedly did as he bid her. Yeah, he had an image to uphold, one that many females sought him out to experience. He'd be damned if he didn't live up to it now.

Ristan walked through the halls, his hand holding Bob, a battery operated baby that he'd gotten for Synthia. He was halfway down the corridor when Zahruk asked him to come to the armory through their mental link. He sighed as he started to glamour the doll away, only to catch Darynda as she moved in the same direction he was headed.

"Hey," he said as he moved towards her with purpose. "Can you give this to Synthia? I've been trying to remember to give it to her for days. His name is Bob," he said with a smile as Darynda looked the doll over and raised her eyes back to him.

"I can," she whispered, and her eyes rested on him. "Am I beautiful?" she blurted with an uncertain look in her sparkling bluish green eyes. "You've never tried to be with me."

"You're very beautiful," Ristan replied, uncertain

where she was going with that statement. "Why do you ask?"

"Out of everyone here, you and your brothers have never tried to take me into the common rooms," she replied.

He caught the look of hurt in her eyes, and he flinched.

"The common rooms, where we fuck women who want to be shared; those common rooms?" he asked, and decided this was a slippery slope, one he wasn't going to slide down anytime soon.

"Zahruk was there last night, and when I asked him… Never mind, I shouldn't be discussing this with you," she said, and started to move away with the doll, but he stopped her with a gentle hand on her wrist.

"The women who enter those rooms become women we all share. Some of us share them a few times a day, if not more. Darynda, never enter one of the common rooms alone. If my brother hasn't invited you, be glad for it," Ristan replied with a soft shake of his head. "It's a sign that he isn't ready to share you. He's different with you; take it as a good thing."

He moved past Darynda and watched Ryder approach him slowly. He must have been on his way to summon Synthia, but paused as he caught sight of his brother. "Ryder," Ristan said as he moved to him.

"Send Synthia to me; I'll be in the throne room," Ryder ordered and moved down the hallway, leaving Ristan to watch his broad frame as he continued on, as if he didn't have time to walk the five steps to her bedroom door.

"Well, fucking hello to you too, brother," Ristan

murmured as he sent a silent message to Zahruk that something was up with Ryder. He shook his head, and wondered how Synthia would react to the nipple clamps and dream medallions he'd given to Ryder the day before.

His gift to them had been vibrating nipple clamps and dream sex. Seemed like something everyone should experience at least once in their lifetime, right? He smiled and shook his head; it was the least he could do for them. Synthia had been upset about the sex between them, mainly because she'd wanted Ryder to handle her like she wasn't made of glass. This would stop the issue, and he had planned to enjoy Ryder's reaction, which would have to wait now if Ryder was in a bad mood, since it was hard enough to get the guy to speak openly even when he was in a good mood.

He left the hallway and sifted to the armory, where Zahruk was creating new weapons with the God Bolts that a Changeling had used on Synthia before Ryder ended his pathetic existence. Ristan was fairly certain he still had a touch of recurring heartburn from that particular soul.

"Hey, what's up?" Ristan asked, taking in Zahruk's dark blonde head before he lifted his piercing blue eyes to meet Ristan's.

"Fucking women, that's what happening," Zahruk grunted. "Ryder is giving Synthia and her little Human-ish opinions too much freedom. It's becoming a bitch to keep her protected and safe in her delicate state."

"You and I both know that he is testing her. She has to show them the stone balls she's carrying around, or we will end up fighting our own people to protect her. She can't show them weakness, and neither can our brother. We both know that is why he's hiding his feelings about her because we know how our father was. Those he's allowed inside our doors would use it to take advantage, and use her against the newly-crowned Horde King."

"You know I don't give a fuck about politics, and I'd protect her. We all would," Zahruk said as he held out his hand and Ristan absently handed him the mallet that had been beside him on the bench. "What's going on with the old man? Has there been any news or progress on the relics yet?" Zahruk asked as he started hammering the bolt flat, not even watching his progress.

That was why he was the weapons expert, and the deadliest of the brothers—excluding Ryder, who was the Horde King and could become a creature with wings that had razor sharp tips which could easily kill immortal beings. Zahruk spent much of his downtime in this armory, improving weapons to protect them from the Mages, as well as other enemies.

"I need you to order those archives we talked about from the Guild, and check into the activity in New Orleans. I'm starting to think there's more going on than we suspect. Something is off, and there's been more movement and chatter in Spokane. Also, I killed a Skinner the other day that made his dislike of Ryder known just before I took its life."

"A Skinner in Spokane, really? Shit is getting hairy. Rats bailing off a sinking fucking ship," Zahruk said as he resumed pounding on the God Bolt with the mallet.

"That about sums it up. I need to go, brother. Got a doll to watch," Ristan agreed with a smirk and sifted out in time to watch Synthia receive her present. He entered the room and stood at the door, watching her silently at first, but his mirth over her reaction gave away his presence.

"A baby doll—this is a joke, right?" Synthia asked, confusion stamped on her beautiful face as Darynda handed her the newborn-sized doll, which started shrieking with an ear-piercing cry the moment she held it. "How the hell do you shut it off?" she shouted over the wailing thing, which she held up by its leg.

"Try cuddling with it, Flower," he challenged. Synthia turned a horrified look up at him. He smiled and shook his head as he watched her, horror replaced by a soft frown.

"You ass," she growled as she tried comforting Bob with an awkward cuddle.

"Here, like this," he said as he sifted to the bed and took hold of the doll. "Gentleness is universal. Even Fae babes love a cuddle to feel secure; smart little things also like breasts."

She lifted a brow at Ristan as he swaddled the doll with a blanket, which he'd glamoured. He held the doll in his arms and rocked it gently, smiling as it stopped crying and started mewling.

"I'm probably going to be the worst mother ever known to Fae and mankind alike," she whined softly.

"No, you just need to practice making Bob here, happy," Ristan said as he eyed her growing belly. "Every mother fears that she will be a bad one. It's what makes them a parent."

"And you think handing me a doll who hates me will help? I've never had a mother, not one that I remember anyway, except for my foster mother, but those memories are mostly faded now. I've never even held an infant," she chided.

"Flower, those babes will have an entire Caste of Fae watching over and protecting them. You won't be raising them alone. A wise woman once told me that it takes a village to raise a child. You'll be a fierce mother, and no other children will ever be as loved as yours will be."

Ristan was about to comment further when Adam entered the room. Ristan felt the Dark Prince's power as it pulsed with a life of its own inside the confines of the room. He knew the princeling would fill his new role perfectly, now that he, along with Synthia, had been brought back to Faery where they belonged.

"There's my girl," Adam said as he leaned his tall body against the door with a quick nod of hello to Ristan. "How're you feeling?" he asked as his tri-colored eyes swung back to Synthia and her blooming condition.

"I'm doing pretty well, considering I'm the size of a small house. Well, minus the strange cravings and the persistent crying at random times," she answered Adam, and smiled as he shook his head.

"Synthia, you're pregnant. Crying is allowed."

"I feel like my entire body has been taken over by aliens," she admitted.

"Flower, it's time to join Ryder in the throne room. Your presence has been requested," Ristan interrupted as he remembered Ryder's orders from earlier.

Ristan glamoured her clean and did a quick change of clothes that would be more appropriate for the throne room as she and Adam bantered between each other. He felt a pull from the mental path he'd given Alden. It sounded urgent, and it was always better to be safe than sorry with these situations. He pushed off the wall and let his eyes trail over Synthia's swollen abdomen.

"Flower, have Adam escort you to the hall. I need to go help Alden, he's in trouble," Ristan said as he sifted out of the room without waiting for an answer. He mulled over Alden's urgent tone; with the approaching war, he worried that he may be too late to save him if something had occurred, and Synthia couldn't handle stress or the repercussions in her delicate condition. Too much rode on her and those babes growing in her belly.

CHAPTER EIGHT

Olivia waited just outside of the study carrel that Alden and Justin had been using, her small hands gripping the heavy files she was holding so tightly that her knuckles were whitening as Cyrus's angry words replayed in her head. He was getting pushier with his strange requests and demands that she watch over everything Alden and Justin did and report their actions directly to him.

Justin was being punished, and she hated knowing that on top of that, Cyrus was watching his every move, as if he was the enemy. It bothered Olivia, because somehow, she felt like she'd become Cyrus's spy.

She could just barely hear a heated argument coming from inside the study carrel where Justin and Alden were having a disagreement, but she couldn't make out the words. She paced, the heavy files getting harder to hold on to as she convinced herself that she was doing the right thing.

Cyrus and Alden had both been a huge part of her

life, and it was impossible to think that either of them was actually being deceitful. There were a lot of rumors going around about Alden that worried her, and at the same time she found them so hard to believe. Justin seemed honest; well, at least honest in her opinion. It wasn't like she had much experience with men; if truth be told, she was pretty sure the opposite sex was all territorial and jealous of each other.

She stopped pacing and considered it for a moment. Justin had come to town soon after the majority of Enforcers had left for Seattle; not to mention he was too perfect. The guy had a body that even Adonis would be envious of. The only thing that would make him hotter was having darker hair that was long enough to run your fingers through it.

Her phone rang, and she paused with her knuckles close to the door, which she'd been about to knock on. She shifted the files to the crook of her other arm and fumbled to answer it, and had to stifle a groan as Cyrus's gruff voice barked at her.

"Olivia, progress report?" he ordered.

"Nothing to report, they've been in the study since Justin got back to the Guild. I am just going in now. I'll call you back," she said as she ended the call and pulled an almost non-existent speck of lint from her shirt as she pocketed the phone. It was her OCD, but she had gotten it under control, for the most part, anyway. Who needed medication when you had self-control?

Justin came out as her hand would have met the door. Instead, it hit his solid chest. In her shock, she dropped the files and they both bent down to get them at the same time. Her head smashed against his, and she yipped in shock.

"I'm such a klutz! I'm so sorry," she whispered as she refused to meet his eyes, her face a perfect shade of red to match her hair.

"It's okay," Justin said, his hand cupping her chin. His eyes searched hers, and then lowered to where her shirt was askew, and he swallowed past the urge to allow his hand to slip between the cleft to test the heaviness of her luscious breasts. "Here," he said finally, as he gave an internal shake of his head and handed her back the files.

"I was just bringing these to you," she whispered, and shook her head. "Now I'll need to organize them before I can."

"I can help; I was just coming out to find you," Justin said, his lips tugging the corners into a smile as his bluish-gray eyes flashed a seductiveness he hadn't intended.

She swallowed and pushed her hair out of her eyes as she stood back up. "I shouldn't bother you," she said, but then Cyrus walked by, his eyes taking inventory of what was occurring.

"Problem, Olivia?" he asked as he gave Justin a hard look.

"No, I just dropped the files," she admitted. "Clumsy."

"Have Justin help you put them to order," Cyrus said with a sardonic smile. "He seems to be enjoying the view, girl."

Olivia blushed even worse than before. She fumbled for words, but Justin didn't seem to suffer from the same problem.

"I'd already suggested we do just that," he said genially as his smile returned, and he again offered Olivia a hand with the files.

She followed behind him, only glancing back once as Cyrus smiled calculatedly. He nodded to her as he turned and left them alone. Where had Alden gone? She looked around the room, taking mental pictures of everything she could see.

Papers and files were piled in neat stacks on the conference table that had been moved against the wall, and the sofa was pushed to the middle of the room. A small coffee table was in front of it, and she sat the folders and the strewn papers she'd saved into a pile.

"Hot or cold?" Justin asked, his eyes sending her mind to the gutter as her body responded, and she had to force her reaction to him away.

"Excuse me?" she asked, her eyes absently lowering to his lips. She chewed her bottom lip as she replayed her dreams of him. It should make her feel dirty to dream of what she wanted him to do to her, but instead it only made her moist in that untouched region.

"Coffee; I know you love the stuff and I have a coffee maker here," he said conspiratorially. "You take it hot or cold?" he asked as his eyes roamed to her mouth with a dark look in them.

"Cold, very cold," she whispered as she readjusted her skirt. She'd worn stockings for the past few days, instead of the woolen tights she'd normally worn to fend off the chill in the catacombs. The silk felt amazing, and his eyes lowered even further until his smile turned lopsided, as if he knew exactly what ailed her. "Please."

He moved to the back of the room to the tiny galley

kitchen and she heard him opening cabinets and moving things around, and then the sweet, enticing scent of chicory filled the air. She smiled, making a mental note to see if the bakery had any beignets or if they could make the heavenly squared pastries. He'd probably enjoy a taste of home, and she knew people from New Orleans loved chicory coffee, which her mouth was watering for a taste of.

"You need cream, *mon cher?*" he called. His soft accent made it sound like '*mon sha,*' and it made her smile impishly.

"Cream, please," she replied as she stood up and moved towards the desk. She could still hear him filling the coffee maker and clinking cups around, so she took the time to peek at what was open on the computer, and which file they were going through.

She scrolled through the open file and felt her heart speed up as the information Cyrus was looking for popped up. She quickly memorized what it said before she spun on her heels and moved away from the desk.

Justin was watching her as he leaned against the small wall separating the tiny kitchen. "Need something, *peekon?*" he asked, watching her with hooded eyes.

"Did you just call me a nut?" she asked softly, her eyes lowering down his long frame, and slowly coming back up to his beautiful mouth.

"*Peekon* means thorn," he said softly, his slight twang catching as he smiled at her. "*Ma fifille*, snooping through Alden's things?"

"He forgot to check one of these files back in, and I wanted to take it back with me before Cyrus caught him," she replied, surprised at how even her own voice sounded. She slid closer to him and smiled softly, her eyes watching him.

Her heart hammered wildly, and it was hard to tell if it was because she'd just been caught red-handed snooping, or if it was her close proximity to the man who had her trying to get her first orgasm out and done with.

"Is that so?" he asked as he took a step closer, and Olivia matched it with a step back towards the desk, which bumped her ass. He placed his hands palm down on either side of her small waist.

She swallowed and licked her lips. "I just needed…"

He leaned over, his face brushing past hers as he reached further on the desk and ruffled through papers. She could smell his earthy male tones, and her core chose that moment to release fluids, which she was sure soaked through her white skirt. Her breath hitched in her throat as her nipples hardened at the image of his massive body over hers.

Ristan heard the quick inhale, caught the tattletale smell of her musky scent as it flowed from her succulent flesh. What the fuck was he thinking? He was leaning over her, and pressing his hand close to her ass just to cop a fucking feel. He pulled back as his nostrils flared with the heady scent of her sweet pussy mixing with jasmine.

His cock twitched, alerting him to its readiness to bend her sweet ass over the desk and fuck it. He pulled back, his eyes watching her as he handed her the file. "Here you go, *mon mimi*," he whispered as he pulled back, forcing his body to stop its traitorous needs for this little woman.

"What did that mean?" she whispered shyly as she moved away from the desk, keeping her sweetly rounded ass from his curious gaze.

"My pussycat," he said softly with a small grin as he moved to the couch and took a seat. He relaxed a bit and placed his arms on the back and arm of it. "We should get started," he mumbled, pointing to the archives she had brought as he tried to take his attention from her and divert it back to what they were supposed to be doing.

"Of course," she said as she moved to the other end of the couch, keeping distance between herself and him.

A soft beeping noise sounded a few moments later, and he moved into the small kitchen and poured the coffee over ice and cream for the both of them. He returned, handing her the mug of iced coffee, and almost came in his pants as she moaned over the chicory-flavored substance as it met her taste buds.

He ground his teeth together and readjusted his legs to hide his hard-as-fuck cock that seemed to have a strange attraction to the little minx. "Like it?" he asked after a few moments of his mind replaying her clumsy pet-the-pony show the other night. He'd show her exactly what a real stallion could do… And so much more.

Or, he could at least tell himself that, since he'd told Alden otherwise. Despite Alden's encouragement of him having a little fun with Olivia, he doubted that he could have just a bit of fun without this sweet girl developing an attachment to him that would end badly, and he respected the old man too much to fuck him over. That was the major issue with those who were as sweet as this one. They wanted a fucking relationship instead of a *bend-me-over-and-fuck-me-hard* kind of arrangement.

"It's simply sinful! Oh wow, it's like an explosion in my mouth; my taste buds are in heaven!" she said with a look of wonder, and Ristan stared at her.

He opened his mouth to reply and closed it several times before he gave up and just nodded. He was in hell; it was official. He was in the one place in the entire world where he couldn't bend this little firecracker over that wood desk and pound into her until she exploded on his cock. He may have had Alden's okay to sample from the pastries, but he knew his self-control would go out the door with this one. He had a fucking job to do.

That was it. That was why he was obsessing about her: Because he couldn't have her. Not unless she made a move first, and that wasn't bound to happen. Not with how inexperienced she was, and how tongue-tied she became when she tried to go there.

She was cute, in an *I'm-going-to-fall-all-over-you-and-actually-knock-you-down* kind of way. He smiled as she slurped down the contents of her mug, stood up, and smiled. His eyes lowered to the sweet curve of her thighs which were now both visible through her white skirt.

"Better get that file checked back in," he said as he picked up the file he had in front of him and lifted it to her, knowing she'd have to come closer to retrieve it.

Her eyes rounded as she moved, feeling how wet she'd become. He enjoyed it, his mouth twitching to smile as her throat bobbed with her discomfort. He pulled it back and smiled. "Be careful, *peekon*, not everyone is as trusting as I am."

He wasn't trusting, but he did believe that Alden hadn't returned the file and that she was honestly trying to keep him from being in trouble. He smiled as he watched her leave, and then listened as the mental path in his mind that he shared with his brothers lit up like an angry switchboard. He stood and prepared himself to go back to Faery and see what was going on.

CHAPTER NINE

Ristan paced outside the doors to the medical ward, his mind racing from the accusations of his brother to Synthia's disappearance, and then to Danu's shit.

He had arrived at his brother's summons, only to be accused of treason. No sooner had he proven his innocence had they discovered that a Skinwalker, with the aid of Claire, had stolen Synthia from the solarium in the women's pavilion. Ristan had been sucked into the first vision he'd had in over a month, and it showed him the location of where Synthia was being held by her psycho brother Faolán and an overwhelming number of Mages as they were about to cut the babes out in a weird-ass ritualistic ceremony.

Before he could follow his brothers to get Synthia back, Danu popped in and informed him that Synthia would die. The ill-boding vision she'd taken him on had shown utter devastation in both worlds if Danu or he did anything to try to save her. It couldn't be prevented, and he hated it.

Hated knowing that soon, Synthia would be dead and there wasn't a fucking thing he could do about it.

He couldn't even warn his brother, because if he did, he could set into motion a clusterfuck that wouldn't work in the end. She was going to die, and he was going to have to step away from it and wait for his part to play out.

He waited, willing himself to stay out of the ward for now, listening as Ryder screamed for Eliran, and yet he still held back from entering the birthing room. There was no point. It wasn't time yet, from what he'd been shown. He listened, his mind racing with the hurt his brother was feeling. They all felt the Horde King's pain because they were all linked.

What Ryder felt in emotion, they did, too, as his Elite Guard. He choked on bile, knowing his part was coming. He would hate himself for it, but in the end, those babes would be his and this world's salvation.

"Fuck that; you save them! All of them!" Ryder demanded, his voice shaking the walls of the small room they were in.

"Get them out," Synthia begged, her voice just barely audible through the doors.

Ristan entered the room, his eyes taking in the carnage as blood dripped on the floor. He felt the link between Synthia and Ryder break, and knew she was dead and there hadn't been a single fucking thing he could do to stop or prevent it.

"Save her!" Ryder shouted at Eliran.

"Save the babies, Eliran; it's what Synthia wanted," Ristan pleaded with Eliran, knowing the healer was frozen with fear and indecision. "You have to save her children."

"Call for Danu!" Ryder snapped, and Ristan's eyes moved to him with sorrow.

"Save them now!" Ristan ordered of Eliran, and when the healer still didn't move, just as Danu's vision predicted, he shoved him out of the way. Eliran shook his head in alarm as he looked from Ryder to the Demon as if weighing which of them would kill him first.

Ristan moved, knowing what he had to do as he picked up a scalpel, and knowing that it could potentially be the last thing he ever did. Ristan's voice broke and his heart shattered as he whispered a goodbye to one of the only women who'd held his heart without hurting him. "I'm so sorry, Flower. I wish you could have held on for us." He pushed down on the scalpel and watched as blood trailed behind it as he opened her swollen belly to deliver the babes.

Ristan knew his brothers would help contain the beast, at least for now. He could hear the threats and taunts of the Horde King, but lives were hanging in the balance. Precious tiny beings that needed to be born, and he wondered if saving them would be enough to prevent what Danu had shown him.

Ristan could feel the seething fury of the beast that was the Horde King across the mental link he shared with his brother. Ristan tried to tune out Zahruk's voice as he tried to calm the monster that was rattling inside his brother. The monster that was, even now, about to break free and end Ristan, and he no longer cared if he died.

"I'll fucking kill you, Demon!" Ryder snapped,

his anger palpable as Ristan continued to slice Synthia open. She was no longer in pain, and Ristan held back his grief, his mind focused on saving the babes, her dying wish.

Ristan finished with the cut and put the scalpel down, and moved back to pull out one of the babes. He handed it off to his brother, Eliran. The babe was blue and lifeless, but Ristan wasn't done yet. Another babe needed to be saved. Their mother couldn't have died so senselessly, only for her children to follow her in death.

His shoulders slumped as the first babe let out a lusty wail, and his hands slipped around the other infant. He handed it to Eliran as well, and when he turned back to Synthia, his heart stopped. Everything stopped as he saw the one precious thing that hadn't been in Danu's vision.

Ristan reached in and pulled out a third babe, and his eyes moved to Synthia's empty eyes. She fucking did it. The female child was limp and lifeless. Ristan shook his head and turned to look at Ryder, who wore a look of utter devastation.

"She did it, fucking hell, she did it," Ristan mumbled, as he stumbled back from Synthia's body and handed the silent, blue, lifeless child to Eliran. "She gave you a daughter."

"Save her, please, save my daughter," Ryder begged. Ristan knew that his brother had never begged for anything in his entire life.

Ristan stepped back as Eliran and his medical staff moved into action, working to save the children. Three babes; Synthia had done the impossible and birth to the first set of triplets in Fae history. His eyes moved to her face, and he stifled the grief that tried to escape. She was dead, and he was wrong. She wasn't their salvation and he'd ruined her life by thinking it so. She'd be alive if he'd never been cursed with visions.

Danu had warned him that she was going to die and that he couldn't stop it. No one could. What the fuck was the point of it? He'd argued with Danu, and she'd forbidden him from giving warning or preventing this.

She'd shown him a world where nothing existed. Nothing. Faery and her world had both collapsed, and he knew Synthia well enough to know that she would kill him if he allowed it to happen. He moved closer to her body and his hands shimmered with a silver glow of power as he closed the bloody incision, then glamoured a sheet over her body to give her some dignity in death.

Adam sifted in, and Ristan watched as he processed what had happened. He had to have felt their bond break, because he spun in a wide circle and then he was gone again. Ristan was surprised as Adam sifted back, Adrian and Alden in tow. They both gave in to the chaos and Ristan watched in silence as everyone waited to see how many of the babies would survive their difficult birthing.

He watched as a helper moved to his brother, handing off the firstborn son. Tears slipped from his brother's eyes and it gutted him. His stomach twisted, his heart clenched, and he felt useless as he stood among his brethren, having never felt so alone in his entire existence.

Fucking Danu; she could go to hell.

Ryder broke apart. Ristan barely managed to hold his own grief at bay. He watched the most powerful creature he knew of as he crumbled. Ryder's pain flowed through his guard, and Ristan wasn't immune. He shook his head, unable to stop the pain. He watched as his niece was handed to her father.

"Your brothers hid you and protected you," Ryder whispered to his daughter as he kissed the top of her platinum curls. She was a tiny replica of her mother. A perfect innocence, her beauty untouched or tainted by evil.

"What now?" Ristan asked as he moved closer to Synthia's body.

"Don't touch her," Ryder warned as he thrust his daughter into Ristan arms and moved to the lifeless body.

She's fucking gone. It slammed into them all as Ryder felt the loss. Ristan sensed what was going through Ryder's mind, and knew he was going ask Ristan to find Danu.

"Ryder, she cannot be brought back. Danu has shown me what would happen if she intervened, and there was no world; no Humans, no Fae left. She's gone, but your children are here, and they need you, brother, we all do."

"What do you mean, *no world*?" Ryder snapped, his eyes narrowed on Ristan cautiously.

"Nothing. Nothing would be left of either world if you break the balance. This was supposed to happen, and you can't break the balance by changing it. Synthia would never forgive you if you did, and you know it."

"She's *my* fucking world," he replied in a gutted cry.

"Then tell her goodbye, brother, and let her go in peace," Ristan whispered, and pushed some of his remaining strength into his brother. He gave him the strength he'd need to tell the love of his life goodbye.

Ristan carried the babe, her small mouth already trying to suckle. Ristan pushed power into her tiny body, using his own power to make the tiny female stronger. She'd need his help; she'd need them all without her mother.

"Get out," Ryder snapped even though most of them had felt his need to be alone.

The moment the door closed, Zahruk spun on Ristan.

"What the fuck? You've not had visions in forever, and now you get one, and it's about a fucking apocalypse?" he demanded.

"Danu showed me what would happen if we tried to save Synthia. It was game fucking over for everyone. You can't fuck with the balance, and not expect it to shatter. We all know that, brother. He'll rebound; he's resilient. He may become cold, but in time he'll understand that the lives of the many outweigh his happiness, even though I wished to hell it didn't. Try knowing what's coming, and knowing that if you touch it, or stop it, you'd end everything and everyone. Try owning that for a fucking day, Zahruk."

Ristan cradled the little angel in his arms, his eyes taking in the golden ones so much like her father's. He'd been wrong before; the little princess was a mix of her parents, and she watched silently as grown men looked down at her in wonder.

"You're loved, and you are wanted, little princess," Ristan cooed to the infant as her golden eyes watched him with a look that tugged at his heart. "Your mother was the bravest woman I've ever known, and she loved you," he said, as his voice broke and his head shook at the unfairness of the entire situation.

He was still holding her when Ryder's call for vengeance went out through their bond, and he felt the pull to kill. Ryder was death, and he'd be seeking blood for blood. Ristan closed his eyes and allowed the child in his arms to bring him some semblance of peace, because soon they'd be going to war.

They didn't even have a nursery for the children because no one had thought to create one yet. They'd thought they had more time. They'd been wrong.

It wasn't until Ristan helped Ryder create a nursery in Synthia's quarters that he handed off the little girl to be tucked into the bedding of the crib he'd glamoured for her. Aodhan brought in the two cribs that he had barely finished the detail work on, and the boys were settled into their blankets. Zahruk left to locate some wet nurses for the babes, which was going to be a challenge as there weren't a good deal of lactating mothers in Faery.

Ristan and Adam realized at this point just how unprepared they were for the babes. The two left to gather supplies once guards had been stationed outside the room.

Glamoring items would be easier if they knew what the hell they were doing. They had made it as far as the portal and had been about to leave when he had felt Ryder's unease, and he and Adam both sifted into the nursery, to find Synthia alive and on her knees before Ryder.

Fucking cunt! That dirty fucking bitch Danu had known she'd bring Synthia back, and she'd made him gut her? Ristan felt anger and hatred, raw and heavier than he had in a very long time. Danu had allowed him to believe he was losing Synthia and that he'd had no choice but to play a part in it that had torn his heart out. He backed out of the room and waited outside the doors for Adam.

How could Danu be so cold? One simple clue, and Ristan wouldn't have felt as if he'd been the one to sever Synthia's life. Unless that had been Danu's sick game; to see if he'd do as she bid him to. It was possible, but if it was the case... Ristan would sever his ties to the Goddess, and let the chips fall where they may. He wanted to do everything in his power to help Faery, Ryder, and his brothers, but she was cruelly making him suffer in every way she could with his bond to her. She could kill him easily, but that would be something he'd deal with when it happened.

"She's alive, that's Synthia!" Adam exclaimed, and Ristan nodded in acknowledgment.

Yes, she was alive. She would find out pretty fast that he was the one who had cut her open on that table. Danu had taken another person from him, and he wondered if it had to do with her sick, twisted jealousy.

"Let's go shopping," Ristan said softly, his eyes holding Adam's green ones. "She'll need a lot of things for triplets."

CHAPTER TEN

Ristan sat with Alden in the study carrel; scrolls, books, and files lay unnoticed on the table and desk. A half-drunk bottle of eighteen-year-old Glenmorangie was on the table between them. His telling of the birth was sitting heavily on them both. He'd explained what had happened and what was expected traditionally as the days passed for Synthia. The presentation of the babes and the Fae traditions were of great interest to the old man.

Alden was always a sponge for anything Ristan dished out, detail-wise, about Faery. It had been a few days since he'd been to the Guild since life in Faery had taken on an ominous turn and created different demands from them all. He explained what had happened to the Tree of Life, and what the tree meant for his world, as well as the impact this would have on the babies if a cure wasn't found in time, and Alden had offered suggestions.

"He lets her do a lot of things that your own father

wouldn't have, doesn't he?" Alden asked as they poured more liquor into crystal glasses. Ristan thought for a moment as to what he could tell Alden at this time. Finding out that Synthia was really the daughter of the Goddess might be a bit much for Alden so he stayed as close to the truth as possible.

"I wouldn't say that. The circumstances are different in their dynamic than it was for my father, but he does test her a lot. He's seeing if she can stand up to the Unseelie while seeing how they accept her. He's smart, because if she didn't have balls, they'd make her a target. He knows that, so he's showing them that she's a force to be reckoned with."

"She is that," he said as he moved away and started straightening the room for the night. "She was my biggest challenge, and my fiercest warrior, so I don't doubt that Ryder is approving of her now. She'll never be an easy target, though. The girl has a sense of when she's in danger. She's a lot like my sister was, even though they don't share a shred of DNA," he said quietly. A knock on the door drew their attention.

"Are you retiring?" Olivia asked from the doorway, her eyes on Alden.

"I am," he said as he recorked the bottle of Glenmorangie, stowed it in one of the cabinets and picked up a handful of files.

"Mind if I speak to Justin on a few things I found?" she asked, and Ristan watched her.

What the hell was she playing at? He watched Alden as he nodded and said his goodnights before Olivia closed the door and moved deeper into the room. She looked at anything but him for a few moments, and then she turned and smiled at him.

"You need something, *cher*?" he asked

"Play with me, Demon," she whispered, and smiled coyly as she lifted up her skirt, showing off her red curls.

His eyes lowered, and he shook his head. "She's an innocent," he mumbled, his throat closing with the need to bury himself deep inside the tight pink delicate flesh.

"She is. The poor girl's never even had an orgasm. Why don't we use her, and I'll let her keep the memory of you giving her one?" Danu offered as she moved, using Olivia's body, and grabbed Ristan's hand, bringing it up to stroke the sweet flesh between her legs. Danu unbuttoned Olivia's blouse and let it slide off her shoulders. Her lacy bra followed it a moment later.

"Don't do this to her," he whispered as he lifted his eyes and fought against the unfurling need that tightened in his belly. His fingers skimmed her heated sex, and he shook his head. "Haven't you done enough?"

"I told you, Demon; some things not even I can interfere with," Danu said as she sat on the small table and started spreading the girl's flesh.

"You couldn't have told me she'd live? Or that I hadn't fucking gutted her? Then you pretend everything is fine, that ripping me apart and making me think I'd taken her life was just another lesson you had to teach me. What about her being your daughter, Danu? That is why you allowed us to be friends, isn't it? Because you knew I'd protect her? Guess what? I'm sick and tired of your idea of lessons," he gritted out angrily.

"Oh, my poor, poor, Demon; you want her, don't you?" Danu asked sarcastically, ignoring his questions as she slid a single finger inside of Olivia and moaned as her own actions made Olivia's body respond. His eyes were glued to what she was doing as his cock stiffened in response to the sweet sound of flesh entering flesh.

"Danu," he warned, but she pulled out the finger and moved closer to him until she was straddling his lap. The finger that had been inside Olivia was pushed into his mouth, and he groaned unwillingly.

She tasted like ambrosia. Her lush tits were exposed to his eyes and he leaned back, his mind wondering what would happen if Danu left her body now. Would she be willing to finish what they'd be doing?

He sucked on her finger, as Danu's immense power pushed through the thin sliver he'd been holding on to. Danu answered his mental musing. "She'd be in shock when I left her. Her sweet cunt would be ripped open. Yes, she really is a virgin and your giant cock would tear her apart, Demon. She's so sweet and so innocent of what a man needs. She has a crush on you, thinks the angels hung stars just for you in the skies. Do you want me to ride your cock?" she pouted softly, her motions skilled and nothing like it would be with Olivia.

"You'd be cold enough to take her first time from her?" Ristan demanded as she continued to grind the borrowed body over his massive cock, which was throbbing and more than willing to plunder the innocent flesh. He, however, wasn't.

"Yes," Danu said with a mischievous look in the sweet, sapphire eyes of the victim she was controlling. "I'd take her a few times, and I don't even have a dick. Come on, fuck her tight little body. Make her come. Teach her why women need the men I created, who I made damned sure were well-endowed," she cooed saucily. Her hands came up and pinched the pert nipples that had his mouth watering with the need to suckle them.

"Go home, Danu," he said as he remained unmoving.

"If you don't fuck me," she said as she lifted her hips, showing Olivia's exposed opening. "I'll find another to take her. She's innocent, and I know how you secretly want to eat little innocent girls up."

"I don't fuck virgins. I like a woman who knows what the fuck I want, and doesn't need directions written out to get the job done. Get out of her, and let me show you exactly what I mean," he rasped as he bucked his erection into Olivia's soft body.

"I want her to get fucked, so either you can do it, or I'll find someone who will take her. Those are my demands, Demon," Danu ordered as she scooted off his lap and bent over, showing Olivia's ass for his viewing pleasure.

"Danu," he pleaded, his eyes feasting on the sweet flesh that had moisture pooling and leaking down her creamy porcelain thighs.

"Show me she means nothing to you. Clean her pussy off, and I'll end it. That is, if you can stop without making her come first. I know you, Demon. I've been the one you used to prevent soul feasting and your weird-ass guilt of what you were born to be. Clean her pussy and I'll leave her virginity intact."

Ristan swallowed and fought down the raging hard-on that pressed roughly against the jeans he'd worn. "Fine, but don't leave this body until I'm out of this room. I want the memory of this gone from her mind. Understand? Don't blow my fucking cover, because it will only hurt Synthia."

"Fine," she said as she moved to the desk and jumped up, planting her ass on it, uncaring that Olivia would have bruises from it tomorrow.

"Fine," Ristan spat, furious for being forced to do something he thought was wrong. It wasn't right, and he knew it. Olivia wasn't willing, and, as with the others she took, he could feel what they did as they enjoyed his touch. Olivia was there, trapped in her own body, scared shitless of how her body felt and its reaction to his touch.

As if she could sense it was being abused, and she didn't like it. Of course, that changed as his mouth touched her thigh. She moaned, and her soul glowed from within. He used his tongue to rub small circles on the inside of her thighs. His own moan left his lips as he tasted her juices.

Fucking hell, he'd never tasted anything like her. His hand moved up her legs to spread her thighs, to allow more access to clean her sweet mess. His nose touched her clit, and he felt her tremble from within. Now she was willing, but he'd never take her first time from her.

He wasn't that much of a bastard.

His self-control threatened to break as his tongue moved to the slit of her heat and pushed inside. He felt pre-come leaking from his cock. His hips moved absently as he imagined he was plunging into her sweetness. He pulled her apart even further and moved his mouth over her slick wetness, and the moment he was done, he stood up and glared down at Danu.

"Her flesh is clean, and we're done," he whispered hoarsely, before breaking his own rule and sifting out of the Guild.

He'd been seconds away from taking her, and he hated Danu for it. Years, fucking years he'd controlled his hunger, and in one day, she walks in, sweet as fuck, wearing Olivia, and undoes his willpower, his self-control. Gone.

He entered Vlad's club and moved to the back rooms without even saying a word. He'd find someone who could take away the ache, and he'd be damn sure Danu didn't say one fucking thing about it.

Today, she'd gone too far. She'd been getting worse, and he'd had enough. He wasn't her bitch, and he was damn sure done taking orders from her or helping her. She must have sensed it, which had to be why she'd stolen Olivia's body tonight.

She'd done it three times in the last week, bringing him to the brink and leaving him looking guilty as fuck. Keeley had come alive against him, and she'd fought and screamed like a Banshee, and stopped just short of accusing him of rape. He hadn't even realized it was Danu until it was too late. The next female had raked his face with her nails and left before either of them had gotten off.

He was done, and with each woman Danu took over, he lost a little more control. Tonight, with Olivia, it had shattered.

"Faith, strip, now," he ordered as he pushed one of Vlad's regulars into a room and stripped out of his clothes with a single thought. She gasped, and he smiled coldly. She liked it rough, and it was a good fucking thing, because he was in a rage that needed to be fucked away.

CHAPTER ELEVEN

Olivia moved in bed, her body aching with need. She moaned as something replayed through her mind, and the image of it undid her. She'd dreamt about him again, and he'd done magical things to her pussy with his tongue, his mouth—and had he really sucked her juices from her fingers?

Looking down at her body, she groaned as she found her panties in her hand, and her pussy aching. What the hell? The last thing she remembered was returning a file, and then nothing. She sat up and looked at her white skirt, damp from her body's fluids.

Had she finally had an orgasm, and *missed it*? Why was her body on fire, her nipples sore? They felt as if they'd been pinched hard. She brought her hand up and tested one, finding her bra gone, and nowhere to be seen from where she lay on the bed.

She looked around her small room and gasped as her fingers found her pussy soaking wet, with a memory of Justin licking her aroused sex rushing back. Dream, or a memory? She heard her own rushed intake of breath as she allowed her fingers to slip inside the swollen desire of her sex.

Why was she soaking wet? When she tried to get herself off, she never got this wet. Not even dreaming about Justin, which, if she was honest, was a hot dream. But this one? This one was different. It was as if someone else had been in control, and she'd been a passenger.

She closed her eyes, and laid her head on the feather softness of her pillow, and let the distorted dream come back. Her mind was hazy, but she saw herself displayed for Justin, and watched as he became distorted, and turned into beautiful creature—no, a monster.

His blonde hair turned black and grew longer. Her fingers itched to test the silky lengths of it. Silver and black patterned eyes watched her, swirling slowly as she dipped fingers into her own flesh, and she felt it. The heat of his eyes as she slowly seduced him. His skin turned red for a moment and then back to a pale ivory, and she gasped, her body needing his touch.

She recalled moving to him, straddling his massive body. Her most sensitive flesh rubbed over his enormous cock through his jeans. Fuck, he was huge. She felt the subtle sensation of a pending orgasm. Something about this dream was all too familiar.

She watched through a trance as her own hands bared her breasts. No indication of why, or when she would have done this, but she *felt* it. She couldn't make out the words being said, or what the meaning of it was, but as she moved back to the desk and spread her pussy, he followed.

Her heart beat wildly as his hands splayed her flesh,

his mouth slowly moved to her needy core. She hissed as his tongue darted out, and he followed the trail of her arousal until it reached her pussy.

She cried out as his mouth moved to devour her flesh, darting inside until she thought she would surely explode. He did it for several moments, his tongue consuming her. This creature between her thighs was magical and purely sexual.

She felt the gentle push of her body, the tightening in the area he tasted with his mouth. The knots in her belly eased with each hungry stroke of his tongue. He parted her flesh for better access, then right when she thought she'd surely shatter apart, he stopped.

She sat up and looked around, wondering where the hell that thought or dream, had come from, and shook it off. The Guild was protected from monsters, and she wasn't an idiot; whatever had just been in her vision, or her body, had been a monster. A monster that looked much like the description the kid gave her of that Demon in the alley.

Settling for a cold shower and a lot of soap, she tried to dispel the wanton image and the tension in her body. Yet every time she closed her eyes, she saw the monster again, doing shit with his mouth that made every one of her girly parts throb with need.

She jotted it all down on paper. From the being's dark silver brands that ran up his forearms, his pale skin that turned red, to his silver eyes that had black patterns swirling in them. Everything she could mentally pull from her mind was placed on a note and shoved into her nightstand.

Eventually, she left her small apartment, and

those damned images kept replaying in her mind. She considered calling in sick, and then thought about what she'd say. *I'm having dreams of a monster doing really bad things, really well to my lady parts, so I need the day off?* As if.

She moved through the long, winding hallway until she almost ran into Cyrus. He was backed by a handful of heavily-armed Enforcers, which made her heart rate spike.

"I was just coming to find you," he snapped. "Last night, the wards went off, and we got video of something interesting in the library. Over at the study carrel Alden and Justin have been using," Cyrus said, his eyes narrowing on her. "You were there. So tell me, what the fuck was inside that office with you?"

"Wait...what?" she whispered. Her eyes misted with tears as the words and images replayed through her mind.

"You were inside that room last night," he accused, his tone condemning. "We have video of Justin going in, you arriving, and Alden leaving. It later shows you leaving, but there is nothing on the video of Justin exiting the carrel."

"No, I wasn't. I swear!" she cried, her mouth growing dry with the knowledge of what could happen. She was being accused of being a traitor! "I did have a dream," she offered. "Like I was there, but that I wasn't in control," she admitted.

"Do you understand how that sounds? Can you prove you weren't in there last night? Because I can prove you were," Cyrus said with a knowing smile that sent chills racing up Olivia's spine.

"No," she whispered. "What are we going to do now?" she asked hesitantly, knowing she was more than likely about to be sent to Seattle to be interrogated by people who specialized in torture.

"You can help us. Show us that you're not a traitor. We need to question Justin and since Alden was his sponsor, he too will need to be questioned. You can help us take them in. The choice is yours, but you have to decide now," he whispered softly as he brought his hand up to touch her face. "Choose wisely, for it would be such a waste of one so young if you didn't make the right choice."

"I'll do whatever you need," she said softly, her mind on the kids of the Guild. They'd been through enough, and she was constantly worrying about what would happen if she wasn't around to help them through the trying years until a class was chosen for them to specialize in. Plus, if there really was a monster in the Guild, her kids were in trouble.

Cyrus smiled victoriously, and one of the Enforcers handed Cyrus a bottle of wine that he offered to Olivia. "Tonight you'll go to Alden and Justin, and you'll get them both to drink this. If you don't, and we have to confront them, it could be a fight to the death for our Enforcers. This will knock them out, but since Justin probably isn't Human, you'll need to use more than just a little. I trust you can entice him into drinking it?"

There was accusation in Cyrus's eyes, and she fumbled for the right words. "What if they're innocent?" she whispered through tears.

"Oh, my sweet Oliva, what if they're monsters?" he countered. "Monsters you've been giving unlimited information to. Did you know Alden's niece went over to the Fae? Justin stays with Alden like a bodyguard when he is here, have you noticed that? I believe they have been using you this entire time to pass information to the Fae, which makes you an accessory to the crime. Do you know what the Guild does to traitors? They tie them up and slice their skin apart, and open veins until they are helpless but to beg for mercy. You and I both know that the Guild has never shown mercy to traitors."

Her hands trembled as she accepted the wine. "What will you do with them?" she asked through the tightening of her throat.

"That's not your worry; you should be worrying about how to get Justin to drink the wine," he said with an angry gaze as his eyes slid down her body.

Olivia winced and nodded.

"This is your time to shine, Olivia; to think like an Enforcer would. Our women know how to tempt the Fae, and how to seduce them. Use it, and whatever else you need to use, in order to capture the vile monster that's been using you to get information from us. If you fail, you'll be handed over to the Seattle Guild, and no one will be there help you. Help us capture Alden and Justin, and I promise to stand up for you."

"Do I go to work now?" she asked cautiously.

"Yes, but I'd change into something more desirable than that drab outfit. Use your body; it is a foolproof plan when trapping Fae. They can't get enough of Human pussy, so maybe get yours a little wet beforehand. They can smell need, and it will only add to his desire to have you at his mercy. When you have his attention, use the drink and if it fails, use this," he said as he handed her a little strip of vellum. "Get it on any part of his body and it will do the job. Don't fail us, Olivia."

Olivia watched as the Enforcers turned on their heels and followed Cyrus back down the hallway. She hadn't met any of them before today and was sure Seattle had sent their best soldiers to capture the threat inside the Spokane Guild.

She returned to her small apartment and finally allowed the sob to escape her lips. Tears streamed down her face, and she swiped angrily at them. This wasn't fair, and Alden couldn't be a traitor, he just couldn't be!

The images of the monster came rushing back, and she hiccupped as the image of him between her legs bombarded her. She'd been there, and he'd really done it. He must have fed from her and tried to take the memory. She knew Fae were capable of taking memories and images from the minds of their 'dinner's.' The dream must have been her memories resurfacing. She'd been an unwilling victim in a role she hadn't known about.

She straightened her spine, resolve setting in, cementing her knowledge of what needed to be done. If there was a monster inside the Guild, it was her duty to protect the children against him, even if she had to be bait.

Moving into her bedroom, she changed her clothes, pulling on black lace stockings and attaching them to a provocative garter belt. She removed her simple cotton bra, replacing it with one that pushed her small breasts up and showed perfect cleavage. She slid on a short dress that was black and just long enough that anyone *really* looking would see a glimpse of the lace of her stockings.

She stared at her reflection, then glared at it. "You're going to do this because the kids are in danger. They have no one, and you owe them this. A monster was between your legs, Olivia; how do you plan to pay him back?"

She didn't expect the image of the nymph in the mirror to respond, but she did look hot. The edges of the stockings showed perfectly, and the fact that she'd forgone wearing panties wouldn't go unnoticed if he was an immortal Fae.

He'd smell her sex coming a mile away.

She released the tight bun she'd worn earlier, allowing her hair to cascade down her back. "Suck it up. You can do this. You're a woman, and he's male… He's a monster, but he's male. He wants you. Goddess save us all, Hecate, please help me," she sent up a silent prayer to the Goddess of the Witches and left her apartment.

And may the Goddess have mercy on Justin and Alden, because the Guild wouldn't.

CHAPTER TWELVE

Activity took over the Guild and increased Enforcer shifts started up as Ristan watched. A flurry of activity was never a good sign, and considering he'd sifted out the night before, it could be that, or it could be that something bigger was going on.

His eyes scanned the men and the activity in the library beyond them. He could see Olivia, her red hair standing out, even in the dimly lit cubicle she often used when the library started to close down. He headed back up the second level of the Guild where the offices of the Elders were. He rapped on the door and swiftly entered Alden's office. Once he had the door firmly closed, he didn't waste a moment on pleasantries.

"It's time to get you out of here," Ristan announced as he tried to keep his mind off what Danu had done. His feeding at Vlad's club had gone on for hours with multiple partners, and yet it had done little to curb his hunger. Nothing seemed to stop his need for the little redhead, which bothered him.

"The kids? Do you have a plan for them?" Alden countered as Ristan continued to stare out the window.

"They'll be fine, but if we're discovered, you know the laws of the Guild better than I, old man," Ristan replied. "They're up to something."

"There was a breach; you know anything about it?" Alden asked, his eyes finally lifting from the files he was thumbing through.

"Maybe, but this is something else. When did they bring in more Enforcers?" he questioned.

"This is exactly what happens when they think the Guild has been breached. It is protocol," Alden said as he returned to examining the file.

"It's time to start planning your exit strategy. The kids will survive, but I for one don't want to be here when shit hits the fan, and we both know it's about to. The Mages are getting bolder, and they managed to infiltrate the Horde stronghold, which means the chances of them being here are very high."

"I won't leave those kids at the mercy of monsters, and neither will you. I know you; we've spent enough time together that I know you would protect them if the need arose."

"Be that as it may, it's too dangerous for us. We're outnumbered, and I watched them painting wards in blood that would prevent me from sifting you out. That alone is enough to tell me that I need to get you out immediately. I made a promise, old man, and I'd like to keep it."

Alden watched Ristan thoughtfully as he considered his words. They both started at a soft knock on the door.

"Enter," Alden called and Olivia's sweet face peered

around the door.

"Hey," she said shyly, Ristan felt his cock bounce to life as his balls grew tight with need. Her juices had created an obsession, and he wanted nothing more than to finish what he'd started. Only this time, he wanted her to be fully aware of what he was, and who she was fucking. But that would never happen. He could convince himself of anything, and he would make sure nothing more ever happened with her.

"I finished an entire archive today," she said as she held up a bottle of wine. "Help me celebrate?" she asked hopefully, her eyes sliding from Alden to Ristan, moving away from him quickly.

"I'd love to, but…"

"No," Ristan said, stopping Alden from continuing. "We would love to," he amended and watched her as she moved into the room in a sexy getup. He was curious to see if she realized what had happened with her body the night before.

"I'll grab glasses," Alden said as he moved into the little room attached to the office.

"You've been finishing a lot of those dusty archives, so what makes this one so special?" Ristan asked, his eyes watching her for any sign that it was once again Danu inside Olivia's body, or anything that might be off. Olivia's request was odd, as he'd never heard of her celebrating after she'd finished any of the archives she'd been working on.

"I finished all of the records that came to us from Rhode Island. It might not seem like much to you, but it's pretty huge to me," she whispered as she moved deeper into the room. When Alden reappeared with glasses, she smiled.

She handed Alden the bottle and smiled again as she sat beside Ristan. He could see the lace top of her stockings, with the delicate hooks that kept them in place. Her dress was shorter than she normally wore; his cock jerked in full awareness of the skin she was brazenly showing.

She was up to something, and he wanted to know exactly what it was. Ristan looked over Olivia's head to Alden, who nodded subtly in acknowledgment of her closeness to him. Her legs grazed his innocently, and even as the older man gave his approval, Ristan wasn't sure he trusted what she was up to.

Olivia watched Ristan. Her shyness wasn't feigned, but her mind kept replaying what had happened in the study carrel, and with her memories, came a rush of juices that made her feel like a traitor. Alden silently poured the drinks, and Olivia sent a silent thanks to Cyrus who had sent back another Enforcer with a blocker that would prevent her from falling asleep as they were about to.

They each held up the wine, and Alden made a toast that made her chest hurt with what was about to happen. She drank deeply of the red wine, swishing the rich berry flavor around in her mouth before swallowing it.

Alden poured them all a second glass, and his phone rang. Olivia waited until he moved into the other room, and then she turned on the charm, or she hoped she had, since this creature, whatever he was, had already fed from her.

She watched his nostrils flare, and as she snuck a peek at Alden returning to his chair, she noticed Alden's eyes at half-mast, his head drooping slightly. Her head swung back around to Justin, who glanced curiously at Alden. Olivia panicked and moved quickly, gently pushing Justin back down in his chair. He slowly sat back, his eyes narrowing on her.

"Olivia," he whispered softly. "This is a bad idea."

"I want you," she blurted, her eyes lowering with her shyness, as she lifted her skirt so she could straddle his lap. Her heart raced; her breathing hitched in her throat as she rubbed her wetness over his bulging cock. "I've dreamt of you," she admitted as she leaned over and brushed her lips across his softly, innocently.

Her hands rummaged through his hair as he groaned against her mouth. She was seriously in trouble if the patch didn't work. His hands moved to her hips, and his eyes lifted to hers as he opened his mouth to kiss her, and she allowed it.

She could almost pretend he was Human. Her sex dripped with moisture, and his dick was pulsing hard enough that she could feel it. Bump, bump, bump. She moaned softly as his tongue parted her lips in a seeking kiss.

Electricity shot through her, unlike anything she could have imagined. His tongue captured hers, and she moaned softly against his mouth. Her hand wrapped around his neck as she placed the patch on his skin, and then she cried out as he jerked to his feet, dropping her on her ass.

"What the fuck..." he whispered as he swayed momentarily. Her eyes widened in horror as his skin turned porcelain, and his gray-blue eyes changed to silver and began to swirl in a pattern. His hair was black, and a lot longer than it had been, and he was fucking huge!

He fell on top of her, causing her to scream as his fingers dug into her skin as he struggled against the mixture of the drugs and the vellum spell. "Fucking Witch! I'll hunt you down, and I'll take what I want from you," he whispered as his words began to slur thickly.

"I'm so sorry," she cried, but as she lay beneath him, the doors of the small office burst open and Enforcers rushed in, Cyrus trailing close behind them. "I did it," she whispered as the Demon's weight pressed against her. She could see Alden now, as she lay on the floor, his eyes watching her with a wounded look of betrayal.

"You did it, sweet girl," Cyrus said, and he smiled coldly. "Detain all three of them, and take Alden below with the creature. The raid has already begun. The entire Guild is being eliminated."

Olivia's heart stopped. "What?" she whispered brokenly.

"This wasn't just about one traitor, sweet girl; it's about an entire Guild of them. Why do you think we started moving Enforcers from here to Seattle? Alden has tainted everything he's touched," he said, and nodded to the Enforcers who awaited his command. "Take her with them, but don't kill her; she might still be of use to us," Cyrus said as a giant of a man stepped in beside Cyrus and looked at Olivia with inhumanly clear blue eyes.

"Secure the Demon; he'll awaken shortly. He's already fighting the drugs," the man said. Or, the being said; he wasn't a man, and he made Olivia's eyes hurt as she stared at him. He was a little bigger than the Demon, and his long hair was so blond, it almost looked silver.

"Bilé, we want the weapons. You promised us more weapons that could restrain and debilitate the Fae," Cyrus said as he dismissed Olivia from his mind, and smiled with an ugly, twisted look on his face as the being pulled out golden rods and handed them off to Cyrus.

"If you think of using them on me, be warned that they will not work as you think they will. We have an understanding, and if you cross me, you die," Bilé said. His image swiveled, and then he looked as Human as the men around him. He swung his head back to the unconscious creature on the floor. "Besides, you have quite a weapon right there. You have no idea what you captured with your pretty little bait. If you bring that one enough pain, he will draw the biggest prize you could imagine here whether he wants to or not. They are connected." Bilé chuckled and the sound scared the hell out of her.

Olivia felt hot, angry tears as she was yanked out of the room by Enforcers, then the entire building shook as an explosion sounded. Doors swung on their hinges and dust from the brick and mortar trickled around them. The earth at Olivia's feet shook, making her eyes water from the dust as her ears rung from the explosion.

"Let me go," Olivia pleaded, but the men ignored her. One held her arm painfully while the other took in her outfit.

"You look like fun, sweetheart," he sneered, his mottled hazel eyes sliding down her body with unmasked hunger that made her step back, only to be yanked closer as the man squeezing her arm held her there.

"There are children in the building! Babies!" she pleaded as tears slipped from her eyes to run, unchecked, down her cheeks. "Please; you're Enforcers. You're supposed to protect us!"

"Wrong," one grinned. "We're not here as friendly Enforcers, and let's just be honest, sweetheart, we're not really even Enforcers. So why don't you just shut up and enjoy the show?"

Oliva watched in horror as Alden was dragged out, blood dripping from his face; something had been done to him while he'd been unconscious from her deed. She'd done this. She'd trusted Cyrus, and now they were harming those she'd vowed to protect.

A man ran out of one of the many offices, only to be shot by one of the men who stood with her. The false Enforcers dragged her down to the library level where she saw Darrin, another librarian stop and hold his hands up in surrender; he too was killed. She sobbed as more people rushed in to see what was happening, only to be killed. Gunfire and screams sounded from the upper floors of the Guild, and Olivia cried as she slid to the floor, covering her ears.

"Stop, oh God, please just stop! They don't deserve this. They'll surrender, just stop killing them," she pleaded, to no avail.

It wasn't until she caught sight of the kids huddled behind a row of bookshelves that her heart stopped. She held her finger up to her lips and placed her hands over her eyes. She mouthed the word hide, and the moment the men moved to chase down some of the other librarians, she kicked off her heels and bolted to the kids. Some were from the secondary class, the rest were kids from her primary class, and they were huddled around one of the younger apprentice librarians, Lexie, whose leg was bleeding profusely.

"Follow me," she begged softly, helping Lexie as she applied additional pressure to the single gunshot on Lexie's leg. "I need you guys to be as quiet as you were when we trained for the drills. Can you do that?" she whispered, and helped Lexie up from the floor.

"They're going to find us," Ashlyn whispered as her bottom lip quivered. "They shot Miss Lexie; they're going to shoot us, too."

"Not if we can reach the catacombs; we can hide in there," she whispered. The kids followed as she assisted Lexie, who was somehow managing to hold in her cry of pain as she began to move deeper into the shelves of the extensive libraries. "Now, when we hit the reception area, I need you guys to move quickly. There are monsters here, so we need to be silent, but really fast."

"Miss Olivia, will they kill my mommy?" Sarah asked, her baby cheeks stained with tears.

"I think the Guild is fighting back, honey, but right now I need you to be brave. I need you to do as I ask, and I need you to do it quickly," Olivia said as she counted heads of the primary class and came up short. "Where is Michael?"

"He hid by the bathrooms," Lexie said as she tore a small bit of fabric from her skirt and proceeded to tie off the wound. "I couldn't get to him."

"Okay, I'll go back for him as soon as you guys are safe in the catacombs. Can you walk?" she asked, noting the blood already pooling and soaking through the fabric.

"I think I can, but, Olivia, it's bleeding really badly," she admitted as she met Olivia's terrified eyes.

Olivia knew based on the amount of blood flowing down her leg that Lexie's femoral artery had been hit and felt bile rush to her throat, but she refused to let it come up. She swallowed past the sob and shook her head. That was death; Lexie was bleeding out, and Olivia didn't have a single strip of vellum or a wand on her to do a healing spell to at least attempt to stop the blood flow. "You can make it," she promised.

Lexie nodded, and as more rapid gunfire erupted, she moved with the kids deeper into the catacombs. Once they were secure in one of the passages that led to the tunnels, she sat with Lexie. Her wound was pouring blood from the strenuous effort it had taken to get them into the tunnels.

"Tell my mom I was brave today, Olivia. Tell her I did well," Lexie whispered as she held onto Olivia's small hand.

"You can tell her when they come to save us," Olivia replied as she moved a few stray strands of hair from Lexie's face. Olivia's heart hammered wildly as she watched the blood, knowing it wouldn't take long.

She'd been right. It took moments for Lexie to pass away, and the kids knew as Olivia released a muffled sigh that Lexie was dead. Olivia took Lexie's hands and crossed them on her chest, and posed her as if she was only sleeping.

"Okay guys," she whispered brokenly. "We're going to play a game. In the next room is a silence ward;

it's used to keep the harp inside of it from being heard. You'll still need to be very quiet, but I'm going to leave Kenny in charge, and we're going to see who can be the quietest while I look for Michael. Can you guys do that for me?" she asked with pleading eyes as the kids moved to the small dark room where the cursed harp was.

"I'm the boss, like an Enforcer?" Kenny asked, his child eyes growing large as tea saucers.

"Just like that," Olivia whispered.

"Okay, everyone inside," she said as her eyes slid back to where Lexie was slumped over in death. Her heart continued to pound, and once the kids were hidden inside the room, she left to find Michael.

He was five, and he'd be scared to death about now. She hugged the walls as she made her way to the boys' bathroom. When she caught sight of him, she released a relieved sigh, but as he stood and ran toward her, gunshots rang out, and his small frame jerked and fell to the floor. She covered her scream with her hands, as her head shook in denial and the sight of the shattered life.

They were intentionally killing the kids! Her heart felt as if it would explode from her chest, but she didn't move. She waited for a few moments until it sounded like the gunfire was heading away from the library, then moved to Michael and felt for a pulse. A sob tore from her throat as anger took hold. This was insane. This wasn't how it was supposed to go down! She stood, moving away from the tiny body since it was too late to save him.

Olivia pushed open the doors of the alchemy room and stepped over bodies as she moved to the premade vellum, ripping off enough—or at least she hoped it was enough—to save whoever she could in the Guild. She'd started this, and she had to stop it.

Where were the real Enforcers? Because those men currently executing children were not the one's she'd served with. They were murderers. She grabbed a few items that she'd read about from mission logs and made her way to the door.

She hugged the wall again, whispering any prayer she could remember in the midst of the crisis. As she rounded the corner and came face to face with one of the men who'd been in the room with Cyrus, she used the enchanted dagger, whispering the spell she had memorized so long ago. She watched as the dagger sailed through the air, planting in the heart of the male, who looked as shocked as she did that it had actually worked.

She backtracked to the area where she'd left the children, using the vellum to take down anyone who stood between her and those innocent kids. She could hear screams and gunshots all around her, but stopped as a single tortured scream ripped through the area.

Justin. If she could get to Alden, he would be able to tell her why he'd allowed Justin inside. He wasn't the enemy since he hadn't killed children, which he'd damn well had ample time to do. Maybe together with an Elder, and whatever the hell Justin was, they could stop the senseless deaths.

She counted the strips of vellum and winced. She hadn't taken enough, and the room that held it was now across the library. She exhaled and inhaled slowly, her heart thudding painfully in her chest as she decided her next step.

"Oh, fuck it," she whispered, and headed towards where they had taken Alden and Justin. If Cyrus was the enemy, then Alden hadn't been. She'd fucked up. She had to fix what she'd done as best as she could. She had thought she'd been in the right, when she'd been so wrong. She'd been so quick to buy Cyrus's lies. This wasn't who she was, and she had to make it right.

CHAPTER THIRTEEN

He awoke to fiery pain as something was shot through him. His organs twisted as he cried out, his eyes searching for the attacker, only to find Cyrus watching him as he stabbed another bolt into his chest. He looked down and watched as another Enforcer held a knife to his stomach, pushing it through and tearing a bellow of pain from Ristan.

Blood erupted from his lips, and Cyrus smiled with wonder.

He knew this wasn't the first time they'd awoken him with torture, and he'd watched as they'd tortured Alden. He'd held back at first, taking the pain, but as time moved on, he began to scream as they tortured him in front of Alden.

Questions had been asked, about Ryder, about Synthia. He'd ignored them, feeling as they sliced strips of his flesh and broke his bones. He'd held out, screaming against the pain as they'd forced Alden to watch his torture, hoping it would bring him around to say the words they wanted to know. They made promises to let the old man go if Ristan did as they wanted him to. He knew they were lying, though. They wanted him to bring the Horde King here, and they would try to kill them all. This he knew for sure.

They'd been cutting him open, and he shook his head at Alden when the man had given a strangled cry, or maybe that scream had come from his own lips. His only thought had been for the librarian, and what he would do to her when he got out of this. Because he would, because he knew his brothers would eventually figure out that he was overdue and come for him.

"The bolts seem to be holding him; he's unable to fight us," Cyrus announced, his eyes sliding up to Ristan's with malice in them. "You really thought you'd come to my home and play?"

"Alden," Ristan asked, his body on fire with the need to reject the bolts.

"He's being questioned right over there, but I doubt he'll be with us much longer. As for you, you'll be with us until your brother comes for you. If you won't call him, then he will feel your pain and it will bring him right to us."

"He'll never come for me," Ristan snarled, his eyes filled with hatred as his skin turned from white to red. He allowed his fangs to stretch and elongate as he smiled coldly. "How'd you figure it out?" he asked, trying to buy time as he struggled against the restraints, aware of the God Bolts holding him powerless. The bolts; those idiots didn't know that the bolts interrupted his link with Ryder, and he wanted to laugh at them.

"Bilé told us after Olivia helped trap you. The Fae

could never resist an innocent cunt, now could they? She was like fucking catnip, and you just couldn't stop yourself from trying to fuck her, could you?"

Olivia. That bitch would pay dearly. He'd bought her innocent act, and when he left here, and he would, she'd pay for what she'd done. Danu had fucked him royally with her need to mess with his cock and his head. She was as much at fault as the little redheaded bitch, who he'd get to fuck now.

He smiled and laughed even as blood dripped from his lips. He'd get that little librarian. She'd beg him for death. He shouted her name.

"Olivia, you're fucking mine!" His voice was harsh, and he smiled at Cyrus, who watched him in wonder as more daggers cut him open, as Ristan continued to stare at him with murder in his eyes. "Your bolts can't hold me for long. You'll die screaming like a little bitch, and I'll eat your fucking heart while you watch me do it."

"He can't kill you," another male said as his eyes searched Ristan's face. "But I can and will, Demon. Your kind shouldn't be alive, not after what my murderous bitch of a wife did to our children, what she did to my gift. My lover," he snorted as if he'd found something funny. "I am Bilé, Danu's husband. Yes, I am a God. One who plans to kill off your race," he taunted as he reached up and pulled out one of the bolts in Ristan's shoulder, and placed it over his heart. "You should rest; they won't be here tonight. Danu needs to be present, and my spies tell me she is overly fond of you. Care to tell me why?"

Ristan glared at him, wondering why Danu wouldn't have warned them that her estranged husband was behind the Mages. When he continued to refuse to speak, the bolt pushed closer to his heart. It wouldn't kill him, but it was going to hurt like a motherfucker.

"You smell of her," Bilé growled and Ristan could see the fury building in the God's eyes.

He refused to scream as the bolt pushed into his skin deeper. Skin gave under it, tearing with white searing pain until darkness swallowed him. The blackness embraced him and engulfed his mind as his body continued to be torn apart.

His mind wandered to its dark place, the one he tried so very hard to never visit; the memories of his father torturing his own mother raced to the fore. He tried to fight his father, to save his already beaten mother from more of the monster's angry fists. He swung wildly, his small fist doing nothing to the creature that had sired him.

They were in the pavilion, where the others cowered and tried to escape his father's notice, but they could never escape. His father turned his lethal eyes to the child, and swung one fist, knocking him into the pool. His mother screamed his name as she held onto the man, to protect Ristan from his rage. It wouldn't save him, though, nothing did.

Alazander waded into the deep pool that he'd knocked the boy into and proceeded to hold Ristan under the water. It flooded into his lungs, and they burned as if hellfire was being poured down his throat. He was brought up several times, only to be shoved back under. Eventually, calm came, and with it the most beautiful creature he had ever seen.

Danu smiled at him, her eyes filled with tears as she

promised him retribution for what was being done to him. She told him that the monster that was his father would pay for his deeds with his very life, and even though now wasn't the time, he would *pay. The only thing it would cost him was his vow of servitude to the Goddess, and in exchange, he and his mother would be free of Alazander's hold on them. He agreed without hesitation.*

He woke several times after that. Each time an organ was removed, only to regrow and with it, he would come back to lucidity. His mind tried to focus on what he would do to Olivia, and with it, he took comfort.

He awoke to the sound of screaming and realized it was his own. Pain erupted as something was driven into his hands, and then his guts were pulled on. He bucked, only to realize that nothing would move. He had no control, and panic took hold of his mind.

Ristan stared at the empty, lifeless eyes of the woman he'd accepted for his Transition. He'd done this to her, ever the disappointment to his father. He hadn't been able to control the Demon, and in losing control of it, he'd fed gluttonously from her. His brothers and a few of his father's guards pulled him from her body as comprehension of what he'd done to her sunk in.

He'd been barely sixteen summers when his Transitioning had occurred, which was early by Fae standards. Now he'd once again drawn his father's ire and disgust. This time, he'd earned it for being what he was meant to be. He had wings, giant leathery black wings that flapped uselessly behind him, as he had no control over them. A tail whipped around his thighs frantically as he tried to gain control of his mind and extremities.

"Transition has exposed you for the abomination that you are," his father growled at him hatefully. "I will not allow you to remain an abomination of the Demon Legion's blood that flows through your worthless veins. You are my blood, and you are Fae. Do you understand me?" he snarled angrily. Alazander hissed as he held Ristan to the cold floor, his claws glowed, and with one slice down Ristan's back, between the wings and flesh; he severed flesh, bone and sinew as Ristan screamed in agony. Screamed and begged his father for mercy until those screams turned to promises of vengeance.

A vision of Danu came to him, soothing him and warning that it was not time yet for his father's death. Her hands soothed the pain of his ravaged back, giving him release from the torment briefly. "Soon his time will come, I promise you, sweet child. Soon he will be given his last breath."

He'd never asked or begged for mercy after that day, and he'd waited over seven hundred years for his vengeance to come. For Ryder to deliver it.

He remained still, his mind closing in on him. More memories of his past came rushing back, and with them came emotional shit that refused to shut off. He wouldn't scream, not anymore. He'd managed to stop the pain back then, and he'd do it again.

More organs were removed.

Unconsciousness devoured him again.

Unable to get into the part of the library where Alden and Justin were being tortured, Olivia went to find where the other children may have hidden. She made her way through the carnage that had been left inside the Guild. The scent of death was overpowering, yet she pushed on.

She slid her lithe frame into one of the many secret passageways that were hidden in the Guild, which crisscrossed throughout the Guild's expansive areas. Each place she searched was much like the last. Bodies littered the floors; pools of blood created a halo around each of them.

Occasionally, she'd hear gunfire as she made her way through the otherwise silent Guild. They were searching for those who had been smart enough to stay hidden, as well as the remaining children who hadn't been in the group that she'd hidden in the music room when this chaos had first begun.

Most of the older children had left around the same time as the Enforcers, to shadow them on missions while they were in attendance at the Seattle Guild. As the hours moved on, hopelessness started sinking in.

It wasn't until she hit the gym that she caught the slight sound of a whimper. Near the blown out wall, she found bodies of some of the other librarians and knew that they'd put up a good fight. Other bodies she didn't recognize lay among the mortar and bricks. Her eyes took in the hole, and she could taste freedom.

She turned to the area where she'd heard the whimper and swallowed as she made her decision. She moved towards the locker rooms and silently entered one, and then the other, finding a group of the middle-class students dirty and wounded, but alive.

"Can you guys walk?" she asked, her eyes assessing the damage the children had sustained. It took her longer than it should have, but she managed to get the kids, along with a small amount of water, to the music room where the younger kids waited.

She left them in the room as she moved through the hallway, feeling the pinch of guilt that made her hug her stomach and want to fall to the floor crying at the horrors she'd seen since the Guild had been breached. She calculated each face, and did the math, noting that at least those who were still living were safe and she'd done it. She'd saved them from ending up like most of their parents now were: Dead.

She edged closer to the dining hall. The kids needed food and other supplies to remain hidden until help arrived. They had to be starving, and she needed to at least find them protein bars, something that could sustain them until the real Enforcers arrived to stop the murdering bastards.

Olivia rounded the corner to the kitchen, and the cold steel of a gun barrel touched her temple. She turned, fully expecting to meet her death, but instead, was hit harshly with the butt of the gun. Her last coherent thought was that she'd seriously fucked up once again.

$*_\sim*_\sim*$

Daggers tore his flesh open, and he felt them touching him inside; unconsciousness was the only time he escaped it, but his immortality brought him back to consciousness each time, and back to the agony.

Death wouldn't come easily to that little redheaded harpy; he'd show her exactly what it was to be owned by a monster. Real monsters didn't stop because someone was afraid or because of pain; they were, after all, fucking monsters. She may not be wielding the tools that tortured him, but she was the conduit for them to get to him.

Unconsciousness took hold again, and he smiled as he sank back into beautiful oblivion.

When he awoke again, he used the mental path he'd shared with Alden, only to find it gone. He'd known it was time to go, and now Alden—and the kids, from the smell of it—were dead. Innocent blood had a pure scent to it. He latched onto it as souls of the dead moved around the Guild.

Death was everywhere, and he smiled, fully aware that while he was awake, he was drawing those souls to himself. Consuming them, gaining strength from them, growing stronger. Only to have it wasted as they tortured him again. Eventually, the souls left the confines of the Guild, aware that some monster was after them.

"He averages about two hours of unconsciousness, and then comes back from it," someone said.

"Keep going," a male's voice said as he peered over Ristan's face. "He no longer makes noises; why is that, do you think?"

"He's growing immune to it, but then he's also feasting on the souls of the dead," Bilé said as he ran a sharp fingernail down Ristan's cheek. "Mmm, do you smell that?" he asked.

"What?" The male asked, his eyes still watching the

Demon.

"The Fae have arrived, and I think I smell my wife, or someone bearing her essence," he smiled.

Olivia sat on the floor of the reception room to the library, trying with all of her might to stop another bout of tears. What happened in the Guild over the past couple of days would haunt her for the rest of her life; what the two fake Enforcers showed her a little while ago was seared into her mind and there was no amount of bleach that would ever get those images out of her mind. She had barely come to, and the two males had dragged her over to one of the library rooms nearby to watch as that being and several other men tortured Justin.

The sadistic bastards only had her in there for a few minutes to show her how Fae should be dealt with and she thanked Hecate for her empty stomach or she would have thrown up right then and there. Her head hung with guilt at what had happened to her beloved Guild. She felt at a loss and knew that eventually, she'd be senselessly murdered too. A hiccup slipped past her lips, followed closely by a sob.

"Stop crying. Stupid girl, what are you crying for? Huh?" one of her captors snarled angrily.

"You killed innocent people. You didn't have to kill them. They wouldn't have told anybody!" she cried.

"Shut her up, the Elder is gone. The Fae are in the building," the other male said as his teeth ground together and his eyes slid over Olivia with regret.

"You feel that? It almost feels as if we're being watched," one of the men said, his hand going for his gun while the other's gaze continued to slither longingly over Olivia's body.

"If we were being watched, Bilé would tell us," he said.

Olivia looked around the once-beautiful library and swallowed a sob. Her friends lay lifeless, along with Michael's slight frame, discarded in piles like trash. This had been her home, and they had been her family.

Ristan opened his eyes as he heard Synthia's voice. His eyes searched the room with terror, at the thought of her bringing Ryder into this fucking trap. He let out a strangled bellow of pain as another bolt was driven into his guts.

"Don't," Synthia's voice was deadly, barely audible.

"What are you going to do about it?" one of the men—he was pretty sure it was a Mage—sneered.

"I'm going to rip your guts out, and I'll do it while you're still using them. Then, after I'm done, I'll show you your insides, and give you a fucking anatomy lesson." Her tone was serious and straight to the point.

"We have a God on our side!" The man shouted with defiance.

"So what's your plan, wife? Kill me for what I've done to your children?" Bilé asked.

Ristan swung his head to the side, watching as Danu moved silently closer to her husband. Bitch better have a fucking plan to get them all out of here, considering it was just another fucking mess she'd created.

"I've no intention of killing you, husband."

Say what? Ristan was going to rip his fucking guts out through his throat!

"Ahh, then this newly-hatched Goddess must be the one who's planning to end my life."

Synthia? No fucking way. She hadn't even gotten her Goddess legs yet; she was exactly as he'd said, a hatchling. Ristan tried to move, but blackness assaulted him as he tried to fight it.

"She's not a part of this, Bilé," Danu warned. "She's mine, of my womb."

"You mated with those vile fucks!?"

Ristan watched as Bilé swung murderous eyes towards him, and he glared back. Bilé's anger shook the room, sending dust cascading from the ceiling. That's it, idiot. Bring the entire fucking place down on us. Ristan rested his head back on the slab and considered killing Danu and Olivia. Hell, maybe he'd fuck them both right before he snuffed out their deceitful fucking lives. He wondered if the Goddess's death would affect Faery. He was going to enjoy finding out.

"I lay down with no Fae; I only placed my egg where a seed could plant it," Danu sneered angrily. "After all this time, you're jealous of my children."

"I'm not jealous. You are mine! You've always been and will always be mine."

He blacked out momentarily, with Syn practically guarding his bloody corpse. When he awoke again, he glared, his strength beginning to return as someone shouted, "Showtime." He liked movies, so his mind tried to focus.

He forced his eyes to remain open, watching as Synthia took out Mages, his brethren backing her as she mowed through them.

"Missed it, did ya, Pet?" Ryder asked as he cleaned the blood from his sword. Dristan, Savlian, and Aodhan started to remove bolts from Ristan's body and free him from the shackles that secured him to the slab. One of them glamoured a loose fitting pair of dark silky pants over his lower extremities. He was thankful, as it shielded his broken and torn flesh from the Mages' endless torture.

"Always," she answered smoothly.

"The girl," Ristan snarled. His eyes were almost feral as he turned them to Synthia and his brothers. "I want her with us."

"What girl?" Synthia asked as something lit in her eyes. He felt his heart thump harder as Sinjinn walked into the room with the girl in tow, already knowing his brother's wishes from their shared mental path. "Olivia," she whispered, and he narrowed his eyes on Synthia while she struggled with her emotions.

It didn't matter. He was getting his pound of flesh from the redhead. "She doesn't talk to anyone, she doesn't get fed by anyone, nothing. Not unless I myself do it," Ristan whispered, but the amount of anger that flowed through his words carried the threat.

"Understood," Synthia whispered as a single tear slid from her eyes.

"I don't care if you're her best fucking friend, Syn, cross me on this and you'll wish you never had," Ristan growled.

"I understand you, Demon," she growled back, her eyes daring him to continue.

He was being carried out; it was fucking ridiculous, but he had no strength. His only saving grace was that he had the little bitch, and she was all his. Maybe she was innocent, or maybe she was as traitorous as he'd assumed her to be in the first place.

It didn't matter; she was his now, and he'd get revenge.

CHAPTER FOURTEEN

Olivia was sifted to the surface by the big Fae who killed the fake Enforcers that had been holding her. The wards were gone if the Fae could sift, and that disturbed her greatly. She dazedly viewed the destruction; everything she had seen over the past couple of days started to sink in and threatened to bring her to her knees with overwhelming grief. This wasn't just an attack; it had been exactly as Cyrus had said it was. This had been an elimination of an entire Guild and all of its members. No one had been spared; even the innocent had been slaughtered.

She watched as bodies were brought out, innocent lives shattered by her own actions. She hadn't held the gun, but she wondered if this attack would have had a very different outcome if she hadn't taken out the most powerful Elder and the monster he'd been keeping company with.

She swallowed a broken sob as Michael's body was brought up and carefully placed on the ground. Synthia watched it as well; her eyes rose to meet and hold Olivia's. Olivia broke the stare and watched the ground, unable to stomach her own guilt.

Justin was being helped to stand, and as she watched him, he lifted his eyes and smiled coldly, unaffected by the open wounds she could see. He watched her, as she tried to process what had happened. Her mind was on where Alden might be, and the kids still hidden in the catacombs.

Safe. The kids were safe. She'd done her job, and she'd protected the next generation of Guild members. It was the only thing that kept her going at this point. She knew Justin would end her, but then she'd meet the same fate if she stayed in this world—if those who supported Cyrus got hold of her.

Maybe he'd be quick about it. Maybe, just maybe he'd do it now.

She didn't want to die, but she didn't want to live with this guilt. There was no win in this situation; only death and destruction. All of these deaths would rock the world, and be felt everywhere. Too many innocents lost, including her previously naïve view of life.

Justin hadn't been the one responsible for this mess, but she'd heard his tortured screams until he'd gone silent, with only the occasional scream tearing through the silent Guild.

It wasn't rocket science. People died, but this? This was a fucking slaughter, one she'd unknowingly started. The why of it was killing her; she couldn't understand why Cyrus would work with that evil God and bring those men here to destroy the Guild. She watched Adam and Synthia, wondering how they felt about this; did they care? This had been their home as well, and while they were labeled traitors, they were here helping to take away the bodies of the dead, to prevent them falling into the wrong hands. But who were the monsters now? She looked at the crowd of Humans screaming at the Fae who held them away from the Guild. Were some of the fake Enforcers, even now, hiding in the crowd among the Humans?

Her eyes swept over the Fae working together to bring out the bodies of the unlucky members of the Guild. They wore black, form-fitting body armor. It made them easy to spot, even in the chaos around them. Synthia and the Dark Prince wore black, and Adam and a few others wore a shadowy gray-colored armor. She wondered at the difference, and what it signified for the Fae. Nothing she had ever seen in her reports had mentioned their armor, or what it stood for, if anything.

She felt hands on her shoulder and numbly straightened up and stepped back, knowing she couldn't fight this. She watched as Synthia said something to the Dark Prince, and then the Fae that had been guarding the dead bowed to the prince, blurred out of sight, and the dead began disappearing with them. Half a block away, she noticed a portal had been opened in the middle of the street. Her mind went numb with horror to see such a thing opened so close to the Guild, and right in front of this many Humans. The Fae who brought her out of the Guild passed her to another Fae with dark brown hair who took hold of her arm roughly. Fire flared from the palms of the first guard's hands, but before she could warn them of the children hiding in the catacombs, he set blaze to the entire Guild, quicker than anything she could have expected.

She screamed hysterically, unsure of how to explain the children and unable to make the right words come out. She cussed and cursed them all to the bowels of hell, as her heart broke, and her one purpose for believing she'd done one right thing burned in the blue flames of the Fae.

Eventually, her screams turned to silence as she lost her voice for the most part. She spoke when spoken to, and swore when the need arose, but eventually she ended up in a cell, gagged and bound as she awaited her sentence. Death by Fae? FIZ sounded great about now, to become some mindless zombie with no knowledge of what she'd done? Sign her up.

Ristan was startled awake from disturbing dreams to a darkened medical ward. He relaxed against the medical bed, his eyes scanning for signs of life, and noted a bandaged Alden on the other side of the ward, asleep. He closed his eyes, taking a small measure of comfort that the old man hadn't died on him, after all.

"Demon," Danu said, and Ristan stiffened.

"Go away, just go away, Danu," he growled, pulling on what little strength he had.

"No," she whispered. "I need you now more than ever, Ristan," she whispered, her eyes filling with tears as she shook her head at the damage that been done to her lover. "He was insane with jealousy, and this is on me."

"You're damn right this is on you. You fucking just can't stop. You fucked up, and somehow I get the jagged side of it every fucking time. I'm done. Leave me the hell alone, Danu. Find someone else to fuck with," he snapped, his pain mixing with the knowledge that this was her fault. Alden wasn't immortal, and he'd made a fucking promise that she had screwed with by stealing the body of a Witch, either in jealousy or a sick and twisted fantasy, which had created a shitstorm as a result.

She ignored him and instead held his hand against his will. He didn't have the strength to fight her hold, and as he watched her, he felt a pure, intense flood of power rushing through him as she gave him a seriously kick-ass power rush.

"I'll never be done with you, never," she warned, heat filling her eyes.

"I'm finished," he said as he lifted his head so that his eyes could hold hers with his resolve. "We've done this dance for long enough, and it's one-sided. I cared for you. It is possible I even loved you; past tense. You never even told me you were still bound to him, and I had to figure it out as I was being taken apart by your husband. I'm done being your plaything. Find someone else to fucking torture," he snarled, and sifted, his body trembling from the power she'd fed him.

Ristan had spent most of the day attempting to gain control of his form as it continued to shift from Demon to Fae form. He was able to get the location of where the Witch who had been responsible for his past few days of misery was being held by interrupting Synthia and Ryder's playtime.

Before Synthia could say more, he pivoted, leaving her in the doorway as he headed to the dungeon for a bit of payback with the little Witch. He heard the faint squall of an infant that stopped him in his tracks, and with barely another thought, he sifted into the nursery.

He saw a figure leaning over the crib as the babe cried weakly, and his body changed, turning red for battle as a monstrous growl erupted from his throat in warning. A female spun around, her eyes large and rounded with horror by the sight of him.

"Get out," he demanded, his eyes tracking her like prey that he'd easily devour. He watched as she sputtered and ran from the nursery, only to fall, and he smiled coldly. He moved to her, his eyes feasting on the soul he could see inside of her, and for the first time in a very long time, he soul-fed from a Fae. He pulled hungrily until he felt her slipping away, belatedly realizing the female was Meriel, one of Synthia's handmaidens, who would never have meant harm to the child. He forced himself to stop and moved away from where she lay on the floor, her eyes vacant on the ceiling. He could sense her pulse and soul; she would be fine in a few hours.

He moved to the tiny infant and stared down into the crib. Golden eyes looked up at him as if she knew him even in this form. He reached down, cradling her head gently as he picked her up and moved to the rocking chair.

She was weak and failing. He placed a kiss on her

forehead, giving her a jolt of power to strengthen her little body. "You are strong enough to survive this," he whispered as he continued to stare down into her beautiful liquid amber eyes.

His brothers burst into the room. Asrian and Sevrin watched him as if they feared he'd consume the precious baby's soul. Next came Ryder and Synthia, and he could hear their inner thoughts, their worries that he'd hurt the sweet babe he cradled lovingly in his arms.

She was a center, and the peace he felt when he touched her was overwhelming. He'd allowed his Demon side to show not because he felt threatened, but because it was easier to show the raw, brutal emotions that he felt. He'd been used as bait for his own brother, the one person who he'd follow blindly into battle. The person who'd protected and saved him as a stupid child. He'd never been as helpless in his life as he'd been in that Guild.

He ignored them as he allowed a soft hum of music to play in his mind, Owl City's *Vanilla Twilight*, which made the tiny babe in his arms smile. Ryder moved forward as if he'd take the mewling infant from him, but Synthia placed a hand on his shoulder, her eyes warning him to stay put.

Asrian moved to the vacant-eyed nanny who'd tried to abandon her post and was still passed out from his feeding of her soul. He watched absently as Asrian exited the nursery with the maid in his arms.

"Names are important, Synthia," Ristan growled, his hand tracing gently over the thick blonde curls on the top of the tiny babe's head. It was so soft and so precious. She'd never know pain as he had; he'd be her protector to ensure that no harm ever befell her in her lifetime.

"She's been named, Ristan; Kahleena," she said softly. "This one is Zander, and this one is Cade," she continued as she picked one up. "Do you like the names?" she asked softly, as if she was facing a monster, which almost made him laugh. He felt like a fucking monster.

"Kahleena is a beautiful name for a beautiful girl," he whispered, and raised his eyes to meet Synthia's. "She's my favorite thing in the world."

Ryder growled, and he listened as Ryder and Synthia had an argument through their mental path.

"She likes you, too," Synthia finally announced, as more internal arguing ensued about Ristan's mental stability and fears that he might harm the innocent babe in his arms. Anger and hurt surged through him at the idea that they would even think for a moment that he could harm her.

"Fuck you all," Ristan growled, as he stood and walked to the crib with his treasured niece cradled in the crook of his arm.

He watched from the corner of his eye as Synthia placed one of the boys back into his crib, and then placed a gentle, but firm hand on Ristan's shoulder.

"When you're ready, we are here. Please, make sure she's fed before she goes back to sleep," she said surprising him as she took Ryder's hand and left the room. Ristan felt his heart clench, as a tiny sucking noise started from Kahleena. He loved the name, for it was as beautiful as the tiny babe.

"I'll feed you," he said, wondering why they hadn't

fought him. He looked like a monster, and yet golden eyes stared up at him with no fear marked in their purity. As if he was her savior. He pushed even more power into the tiny female, watching as her skin glowed with golden brands, which would someday mark her skin visibly.

"You may look like your mother, Kahleena, but you've got Horde blood running through you. Your brands say you will be powerful, and with power, comes danger. That danger will never touch you, for I will always protect you. But for now, sleep, and gain strength while I tend to one of those dangers. One that needs to be taught not to fuck with our kind," he whispered as he placed a gentle kiss on her forehead and laid the already sleeping infant back into her bed. He had a date with a redhead, one who'd wish she'd never been born after he was through with her.

Olivia had given up trying to wipe her tears when he showed up. She watched him as he slowly moved to the other side of her cell. As promised, she had been gagged and her hands were securely bound. His demeanor was cold, calculated; but even she could see his pain when he moved. He shouldn't have been up and around yet because she'd listened to his tortured screams that had ripped through the catacombs for endless hours. She had seen what they did to him.

His strange eyes watched her as he carefully sat on the other bed across from her. His hands slid together, his long fingers lacing through one another. He didn't say anything, but she could see that he'd been bandaged up, and looked a little less wounded, but then again, he was Fae.

She sat silently, her heart pounding erratically as she waited for him to tell her he would end her pathetic existence. Dying a virgin would suck, but hey, she'd take the punches she deserved. She could no longer handle the hatred that shone in his eyes, and lowered hers to the ground.

"I want you to beg me for mercy," he growled, and his voice was as rough as hers would have sounded if she was able to speak.

She just stared at him, his eyes lowering to her mouth, and with a flick of his wrist, which made him wince in pain, he removed her gag.

She brought her bound hands up to rub her mouth, and lips. "Begging you for mercy won't help me," she whispered roughly.

"Nothing can help you. Not Synthia, not Adam, and sure as fuck not Alden. Not that they'd fucking want to anyway," he growled. "You belong to me now. No one even knows you're here, and those that do, won't cross me—or the King."

King? The Dark Fae King? She had seen the Dark Prince at the Guild and hoped that was who he spoke of now.

"I didn't have a choice," she whispered as she once again moved her eyes away from him.

"Doesn't matter, nothing does. If I don't care, you can bet your pretty little ass that no one else here will," he said as he watched her, his eyes burning accusingly into her skin. "What did they offer you for us? What great reward did they offer you for using your sweet little body to bag a Demon and an Elder?"

"My life," she whispered and lifted her eyes to his. "I gave our enemy records and helped them to get Guild secrets. I'm a traitor, one who would have been executed, so even if the Guild knew where I was, they'd only come here to cheer you on," she murmured as she looked at the bars.

She could get a spell out, but not one that would work to remove those bars before he choked the life out of her. She turned her eyes back to him and watched as he stood up. As he moved closer, her breathing grew labored, and her heart accelerated. Just as it had when she'd thought him an Enforcer.

"Told you that I'd have you," Ristan said, his silver and black patterned eyes watching her closely. The swirls seemed to speed up for a moment. He was still wounded, but the giant who had guard duty now stood closer by her cell, watching her for any sign of attack.

"I didn't have a choice," she whispered. "You are my enemy," she said, as she coughed over the dryness in her mouth.

"No," he laughed coldly. "I wasn't an enemy then, but I sure as fuck am now."

He grabbed her, his fingers biting her flesh as he slipped some sort of torque around her neck and chanted what sounded like a spell, but the language wasn't like anything she'd ever heard before. His hands captured her hair, yanking her head back as he lowered his mouth to hers. He didn't kiss her. He just made damn sure she knew she was at his mercy.

"Do your worst," she whispered. "I deserve it," she finished as tears slipped past her eyes and slowly slid down her cheeks.

"Tears won't save you from me; no one in here can save you, either. Remember that. There is no place you can hide from me that I won't find you. Not this world, or yours, and not even hell, little librarian," he said, but he sifted out before she could say anything, as she was once again left with the hulking warrior who just shook his head at her.

"Never seen him like that; if I was you, I'd beg for mercy."

CHAPTER FIFTEEN

The medallion on the torque Olivia now wore told Ristan the moment she'd fallen asleep, since it was linked to his own. He smiled coldly as he closed his eyes and prepared to join her in sleep. The medallion didn't just prevent her from casting spells; it would allow him to walk in her dreams, and do things there that wouldn't harm her physically here. It would be a way to see her guilt while managing to get a sliver of revenge.

He entered her dream, watching as she walked through the razed remains of the Guild, her eyes searching through the bodies. Tears streaked down her cheeks as she relived the nightmare. She was searching for something; he could feel her guilt, thick and putrid as it pushed from her pores in waves.

He shook his head as emotions poured from her. The most damning, of course, was the guilt. She stopped in front of one of the many rooms in the catacombs. A sob broke from her lips as she turned away from the room, unwilling to look inside it.

Her eyes searched the shadows, and then she moved closer to where he stood. Her head shook as she took him in. He was still battered from the torture; her dream was set during it or close to it. He could have laughed, but he knew this was her dream and not a reality. It was her mind's way of processing what had occurred during the overthrowing of the Guild.

The entire dream changed to her cheery little bedroom at the Guild. She was slipping out of her clothing while he watched her silently until she looked up at him. She smiled shyly, and he forced a smile to his own mouth.

He watched her as she moved towards where he stood. Her hands lifted to touch his chest, which was now bared in her mind, free from the still healing wounds. Her lips gently touched his abs, kissing his skin, which pulled a groan of both pain and pleasure from his lips.

Her hands trailed small circles on his skin, encouraged by his noises as she explored his body. He felt his shaft throbbing in the jeans he wore, wanting her to hurry the hell up and wish them gone. Only, she was innocent, that much he did know. Shit, she couldn't even get herself off right.

She hadn't faked that, and she'd been frustrated the next day from the inability to release the pent-up need. Not that he'd allow her to sate her needs on him; at least not he was fully healed—and then she'd be in trouble because he wasn't going to be nice about tormenting her.

He'd never intentionally harmed a woman before,

ever. He still had no plans to torture her physically, but he damn sure planned on making her beg him for mercy. By the time he finished with her, she'd know exactly what to do with a cock, and exactly how to please him.

She turned away from him, dismissing the dream mentally, and then they were back in the catacombs. She stared at the door, tears falling from her eyes. What the fuck was inside the room? What had her sobbing while she stared at it, afraid to see inside? She turned away, lifting her hands, palms up. Blood coated them, leaking from both as if they had been sliced open.

He was jolted from the dream realm as she woke from the dream.

"What the hell did you do, little Witch?" he whispered out loud.

She'd done something that even she feared and couldn't mentally deal with. Her dream had been vivid, and yet she'd seemed terrified of it. It was hard to fake something in a dream because it was the subconscious of her mind that controlled it. Whatever she'd done, he wanted to know what it was, and why she'd done it.

He sat up, his body stiff as he shook off the pain that radiated from every part of him. He glamoured on a *Theory of a Deadman* T-shirt, loose-fitting jeans, and, with his black leather boots unlaced, sifted to her cell.

The prisoner had fallen back to sleep, oblivious to the monster pacing, impatiently waiting for those pretty blue eyes to open. His hunger was back, and growing

149

by the second. This stupid little bitch was his now, and she'd feed him. She'd feed him well.

Pain lanced through his organs, and he smiled coldly as the stupid little Witch awoke, as if she sensed the danger she was in.

"Get up," he snarled, his eyes raking over her hungrily as his Demon paced inside of him with a need to devour her.

He watched as she sat up, warily, her wide eyes taking in the anger he pulsed with. His brands were glowing from his hunger, but he didn't care. She scooted back warily as he stepped closer. His eyes filled with malice as he smiled coldly.

"Question time, cunt," he sneered.

"I'm not telling you anything," she whispered. "I already answered Synthia's questions," her lips trembled as each word drifted from her tongue. "You can't make me," she challenged.

"Can't I?" he said as he sifted to the bed and grabbed her throat. "I can make you do anything I want you to—need an example?"

He allowed his magic to shimmer and slither over her, and knew the moment she began to fight it. Her nipples hardened, and her sex flooded with heat. "That's it, you weak little girl, tell me who owns you," he snarled, and his angry eyes glowed as the Fae inside of him took over. He could easily glamour their clothes off, to show her how it felt to be ripped apart and violated as the Mages had done to him, but he wasn't that far gone.

"Ristan," Sinjinn barked as he grabbed Ristan's shoulder. "Stop," he whispered with a startled look on his face as he took in the terror on Olivia's delicate one.

He'd been distracted and hadn't heard his brother sift into the cell with them.

"Get the fuck out of here, Sinjinn."

"This isn't you, man," Sinjinn said softly.

"What the fuck would you know about me? You didn't go through what I did, and you sure as fuck weren't around for the worst of it," Ristan spewed, his eyes filled with pain and something worse. Loathing.

"You don't want her like that, brother. You want her to pay, and we're all for that, but this? It's too much like old times, man. We're not those things anymore, brother," Sinjinn said softly, his eyes taking in Ristan's Demon form as he vacillated between that and his Fae form and remembered their father terrifying women.

"Those fuckers took my organs out and gutted me while she stood there watching it! What happened to me was because of her, because she tricked me," he raged.

"Be that as it may, she's still mostly Human. So if you plan to kill her, do it. But I didn't think that was your intention," Sinjinn said, his tone neutral and calming. "You want revenge and that? That's going to take time to extract. She's not protected by spells as Synthia was. If you get too rough, she'll die."

"Get the hell out of here!" Ristan growled angrily, his silver eyes swirling with black patterns as his anger turned hard and deadly.

Sinjinn sifted out, and Ristan turned back to his little traitor. "I want to know who you worked for, and if you answer the way you did before, I'll make you wish death was an option."

"Cyrus!" she cried, "I worked for Cyrus. He was who I reported to."

"Strip," Ristan growled angrily as he moved from the bed; his immense body was anything but graceful with the pain the slight movement caused his body.

"In front of you?" Olivia stammered. But she moved, doing as she'd been told as Ristan took a seat on the cot that lined the other side of the small cell.

His body reacted as she removed the dirty, ripped stockings that reeked of soot and blood..

It wasn't until she removed the dress, revealing that she wore only a lacy black bra beneath it, that he groaned as his hunger surfaced with a vengeance. Her breasts were exposed, and it took every ounce of energy to force himself not to pinch the pink tips that hardened right before his eyes

Naked, she stood before him, her modesty demanding she try to cover herself from his devouring gaze.

"Who does Cyrus work for?" he asked, diverting his energy to his interrogation. He allowed his magic to flow over her body; his hands shook with the effort.

"I-I don't know what you mean," she answered as she intertwined her fingers and held her hands in front of her red curls.

"Yes, you do. Hold your hands up," he demanded, his swirling eyes feasting on her silken flesh that was damp from his magical mind fuck. She obeyed, raising her hands over her head, if not a little slowly, and kept her eyes lowered demurely to the ground.

He waved his hand, swiftly cleaning away the blood and grime of the past few days, placing a new silver collar with the same medallion attached to it, around her neck, along with a sheer dress of ivory silk that fit loosely. It had spaghetti straps, and would be easy to remove where she was going. Not that he couldn't just remove it with a single thought, but sometimes he preferred the sound of fabric shredding.

"Cyrus worked for the Guild, you know that," she whispered, her eyes roving over her new outfit with fear. "He knew what you were because something set off the wards, but you, you were digging into files and I think he knew all along that you weren't an Enforcer."

"Cyrus is working with the Mages," Ristan hissed. "He works with them so well that they were in sync as they gutted me. But then again, I saw you in the room, too, watching. Tell me, Olivia, did you help them as they tore out my entrails?"

"I wasn't a part of that, but yes, I was dragged into this mess because I helped you!" Olivia growled back, and yeah, his cock jumped at the fire he saw in her eyes. "You and Alden made me guilty of treason because I gave the enemy files that were for Guild eyes only!"

"So that made it all right for you to turn on Alden? To pave the way for him to be beaten and tortured as he was? The only thing I care about right now, little Witch, is feeding and getting stronger so I can take my pound of flesh from your hide. You allowed someone who cared and raised you to be fucking tortured, so now, it's my turn to repay it," he said vehemently as his hungry eyes slid over her flesh, which was visible through the sheer material.

He stood up and watched as she flinched, her body trembling as he neared her. He didn't wait for her permission. Instead, he gripped her wrist painfully, pulling her body against his. The connection of their bodies, even with clothes on created a maelstrom of sensation that seemed to start and end at his cock.

He sifted them and listened as her horrified scream was muffled by the shift of time and space until they entered his quarters. Most of the Elite Guard had them all close to Ryder's chambers, but Ristan had chosen an unused section for his own.

The walls were a light shade of gray that had a deep burgundy border around it, which fit nicely with the pictures he'd created. He pushed her towards the bedroom, even as he glamoured a small cot next to his bed and a chain that would link to the collar around her neck.

His own bed was larger than most because his height needed the extra room for his extracurricular activities. He heard her gasp when she noticed the chains that hung from the seven-foot tall bedpost. It was padded and a creamy ivory color that stood out in contrast with the walls, and was always a jaw-dropper. He used it to tie women up and do some very interesting things with them.

At the foot of the bed was a white leather settee which, to the naked eye, would look like a couch, but once he opened the sides on each end, it would reveal items which he was very familiar with and would make the most skilled lovers blush.

He looked her over for any signs of sickness from sifting, as those who tended to have more Human blood in them often ended up violently sick after being sifted. He had been too preoccupied when she'd first gotten here to check for the signs. However, he was glad to see she hadn't any signs of ill effects from being sifted out of the Guild and into his world. Physically she looked well, but mentally seemed to be an entirely different matter.

"I'm not sleeping with you!" Olivia cried angrily as she tried to jerk her arm away from him. Before she could continue to protest, he sifted them to the wall, pushing her hard enough to drive his point home, and yet gentle enough that he didn't hurt her.

"You'll do whatever the fuck I tell you to," he snapped, his hand lifting up and clasping her jaw as his mouth hovered over hers. "If I say suck my cock, you will suck it. If I tell you to ride my cock, what is it that you will do, little Witch?" he murmured.

"I will not ride anything!" she gasped, but he'd already pressed his mouth against hers, and even though he'd meant to make the kiss punishing, the connection took that objective away. His lips searched hers, and when she parted them, his tongue pushed through as his mouth captured the moan that escaped hers.

His other hand moved from her chest, heading south to where her nipples had hardened. He pinched one, enjoying the noise she made that was muffled by his mouth and its sensual devouring of her sweeter one.

Once he'd released her puckered flesh, he pinched it again, twisting it gently as the sensitivity gave way to pleasure. His nose feasted on the delicious scent of her soaked pussy. He groaned as pain from his stomach sharpened, reminding him who he was with, and what he was doing. He pushed off of the wall and smiled coldly.

"On your knees," he ordered.

CHAPTER SIXTEEN

Abruptly, Olivia was shoved to her knees and before she could guess his intent, she heard the sound of metal as it clicked together. He'd connected a chain to the collar she wore around her neck. Her eyes widened in horror as she realized he was locking it with a magical seal.

"I'm not a dog!" she cried, her eyes filling with tears at her small fists balled at her sides.

"You're right. You're a fucking slave; mine, to be precise. So buckle up, baby, it's about to get fucking bumpy for you." He tugged at the medallion now attached to her collar. "Now lie down, and get some sleep. Tomorrow is going to be hell for you, little one."

Ristan shed his clothing with a single thought and watched as her eyes dropped from his, down to what was staring her right in the face. It was hard, ten inches, and needed to get off. He smiled and watched as her tongue darted out to lick her lips. Fucking hell, she was beautiful, and her scent? It had his soldier begging to be allowed to drive into those silky red curls.

He turned from her and moved to the bed, pulling back the charcoal colored comforter, his massive body dropping hard as he plopped down on the silky white sheets. He barely contained the groan from the rush of pain that erupted from his carelessness. He closed his eyes, knowing that she was going to have no choice but to lie down, and sleep.

Her chain only gave her so much room, and it wasn't enough that she could reach him while he rested; it wasn't even long enough to make it to the door or to the elegant windows that made up one of the walls of his quarters. He'd made sure of it.

"I have to use the bathroom," she said, and he popped open one eye and stared at her.

"Seriously?" he groaned impatiently. He considered being an asshole since his metabolism utilized everything efficiently so he didn't have those needs, but she would. He rose from the bed and made his way to her slowly. His soldier jumped up and down as Ristan reached for the chain and released it from the wall.

He moved across the room and opened a door, because yes, he had a toilet. He had a lot of women who visited him here, and some had personal needs as she did. He pushed the door the rest of the way open to reveal the lavish tub that could fit up to ten people easily, nine if one was a nymph who couldn't hold still. The shower was black marble, a replica of one back at the mansion back in Spokane.

Twin stone sinks that had water bubbling like a fountain were built into the vanity. He'd gotten them because the sounds were soothing. Danu hadn't seen any reason for such a lavish waste of space, but after living among the Humans, he'd come to like these comforts.

"I can use it alone?" she whispered, and yeah, he heard her clear as a bell.

He turned his back on her, and that was as much privacy as she'd get. He listened as the clinking of the chain moved, his hand releasing the links as she walked to where the toilet was. It had a small stall, one that would give her a tiny sense of privacy, but then, that wasn't his problem. He tuned her out, even as he heard the splashing of water as she cleaned herself. It wasn't until the chain was yanked, and something sailed at his head that he fully turned.

Olivia stood by the tub, launching missiles in the form of shampoo, conditioner, and other bath products at his head. He smiled. Game on. He sifted, gripped her shoulders and pulled her off the floor until she was eye level with him. "You shouldn't have done that," he warned as pain from his healing injuries burned. He sifted again, and they landed on the bed, this time, with him on top, and his little soldier pressed hard against her belly in full salute.

Not that his cock was little, but the little guy had seen wars and had been through some kinky-as-fuck women, ones who'd made his soldier sore for days afterwards with their kinky fuckery games. He'd seen a lot of shit over the centuries, and he'd even done some shit that had left love marks on his partners for weeks afterwards. Yeah, he was a soldier. He was a fucking veteran when it came to pillaging pussies. So why was it that this blushing little virgin had him hard as a rock? It probably had to do with the fact that she'd never been fucked—uncharted territory, and all that.

He ground himself against her clitoris, enjoying her loud gasp as his guy met her girl and hit that spot perfectly. His hands easily captured hers, which rose for an assault, and he smiled coldly as he looked down at her. Fuck, she looked good all pissed off, her breasts heaving from her struggling. She wiggled against him, her small hips moving to dislodge him from where he was perched on her soft, silken body.

"That's it, Liv, fight me. Fucking hell," he growled as he moved in sync with her struggles. He laughed as she immediately ceased struggling, but that heady scent of hers lingered. He lowered his forehead to hers and pressed it there. "If you assault me again, I'll do the same to you. Only my kind of assault will be one you won't forget, ever. Do you understand what I am saying?" he growled low, his breath fanning her lips as he lifted his head to look down at her.

Her eyes were flooding with tears, and her lower lip quivered. He pulled back further and replayed what he'd said to himself. He refused to cave in and soothe her. She had done this to him; she'd handed him to those evil fucks who'd torn him apart as if he was some animal that they'd shot and decided to gut and play with before eating it.

Worse, this little bitch had brought his King to the enemy, and that was something he couldn't forgive. She'd taken him down, and by doing so, she could have taken their King. They couldn't kill Ryder, but if they filled him with enough iron, they certainly could have taken him down, and it would have been game over for the Horde.

159

"I will fight you. I won't be your prisoner forever. I will get away from you, and when I do…" She let the threat trail off.

"You'll what? Throw fucking books at me? Shampoo? Conditioner? Trust me, Red, you'll never escape me. Ever. I'm not someone who plays around, not when I've been betrayed. The last person who betrayed me? They ended up gutted, and to this day I skin them myself for their flesh. Look around this room, see those pictures?"

Olivia looked, her eyes skimming the paintings of majestic landscapes that were the only thing to adorn his walls. They were beautiful, masterpieces even.

"Those are a reminder never to trust anyone, except blood, again. I have his flesh painted after it's been tanned, and then I hang it up where I can see it, to remind me. By some chance, if you do get away, know that I'll always find you. Besides, Humans can't access the portals," he warned. He wanted her terrified; and this? This would scare the shit out of full grown men, let alone his little librarian.

Yeah, so those pictures weren't so pretty anymore. She cringed and stared up at him. She could feel him pressed against her; he was massive in the size department, and his kiss had jumpstarted an array of emotions that had yet to leave her. Her body had responded to him in a way that terrified her.

"Can I move?" she asked when all the colossal ogre did was stare at her. His mouth lowered to hers; his eyes began to swirl and she moved her head, trying to stop it, even though she wanted to feel his hot kiss again.

"You need a lesson in being owned," he growled.

His hand came up and clasped both of hers together, and held them between their bodies while his other pinched her chin lightly as he sealed his molten lips over hers to steal a kiss.

This time, it was gentle, and those emotions jumped to life with a vengeance. Her body betrayed her, and she grew soft with her need, even though she knew she'd stop him before he went any further. His knee easily parted her legs, but it was all he did.

He sifted them, his body cradling hers as he took her with him. One minute he'd been kissing her, and the next, he held her against the wall until she gained her balance.

"Go to bed before I stop fighting the urge to feed from you and fuck you, until the only words you know are 'yes please,' and 'more,'" he growled as he released his hold and reached for the chain that was connected to her collar. He quickly refastened it to the wall and smiled coldly as the sound of the lock clicked. Then he dismissed her completely, as if he hadn't just aroused her to a painful level of need.

CHAPTER
SEVENTEEN

Listening to her uneven breathing, Ristan knew she wasn't asleep. She'd been tossing and turning on the cot and it was taking every ounce of his willpower to remain where he was, on his side, facing away from her. His cock pulsed, and his heart beat erratically.

He should just take her and screw his moral compass, but he'd never taken a woman by force, and he wasn't about to start now. He had a slow, skillfully detailed plan for her. He was going to make her beg for his cock, and she'd take it. Oh, she'd do more than just take it.

"I can't sleep like this," she whispered.

"Is that so?" he offered, exhaling a deep breath.

"This bed isn't very soft; I think the one in the cell offered more padding," she mused softly.

He listened as the chain rattled, and her soft groan of displeasure sounded through the otherwise silent room. He sat up after a few moments of uncomfortable silence, his eyes moving to her position in the dimly lit room. He stood, and moved to the chain, unlocking it with his touch, and he pulled her along, tugging when she hesitated.

"I'm not sleeping…" She stopped as she took in his naked body; what wasn't hidden by bandages showed angry red marks from his torture crisscrossing his impressive frame. *Fucking glow stones*, he thought as he yanked the chain hard enough to bring her within inches of his throbbing cock.

A single push on her slim shoulders and she'd be on her knees, right where he wanted her. He waved his hand, disposing of the simple outfit, his eyes raking over her erect nipples and the silky red curls between her legs.

Fuck. This was a bad idea, but he needed sleep to heal. He ignored her feeble protest and connected the chain to the headboard, then pulled on the chain until she was forced to fall or climb onto the bed.

"Touch me while I sleep, and you won't like what happens. Understand, little girl?" he grumbled as he ignored her answer and lay back down. He felt the bed move as she tried to get comfortable, and eventually, they slept.

Olivia was on fire. She mewled and moaned as fingers, very skilled fingers at that, worked her pussy over. She was lost in a dream and, considering most of them had included him, it wasn't a big surprise that this one had him in it as well.

She was pushed flat against the mattress, and she willingly spread her legs apart as rough palms directed her. One finger slid into her wet entrance, and then another, filling her to a painful level. She rocked her hips, accepting more, needing more.

Damp heat blew over her soft nub, and then his mouth was there, that tongue of his pushed hard against her love button, and lips captured her clit, sucking it into his heated mouth. His fingers were buried to his knuckles, and she had to have more of him, now.

He didn't deliver; instead one hand came up to cup her breast, and he pinched her nipples painfully. She cried out at the sensual pleasure that rocketed through her. Her own juices allowed him further entrance; his groan was erotic as it vibrated over her sensitive flesh.

His fingers pushed further inside of her and found a silent beat that brought a sensation into the pit of her belly, one she had found before, but had never successfully released. She pushed herself onto to those fingers, needing to reach it. His thumb and forefinger that pinched and teased her nipple moved to the other, and then he stopped.

"Please," she murmured hungrily, her own voice sounding unfamiliar to her ears. Fuck it; this was a dream, and she wanted him here. She wanted to know what that sensation was; to know what it was like to fall over that precipice before her life was ended.

"Please what?" he growled, and as she forced her eyes to open, she saw the lid of the settee at the end of the bed open and a few of the items inside flew across the bed to his waiting hand. What were those things?

"Oh, gosh," she whispered as she noted a small pair

of clamps, and other things she'd only seen in catalogs or described in a few of the books she'd read.

"Close your eyes, and spread your legs apart," he ordered, and his tone brooked no argument.

She mentally reminded herself that she was dreaming, and when she woke up, this wouldn't be real. She closed her eyes and felt silk as it wrapped around her head, creating a blindfold. She moaned as his fingers trailed between her thighs, until his hands captured hers and held them above her head.

"I had planned to wait, but waking up to the smell of that sweet pussy screwed that up," he growled softly, as more silk was wrapped around each wrist. She felt a tug as he tightened and then released it. She never thought she'd be into kink outside of a good book, but then she'd never even taken a man to her bed before. He excited her; no matter how much she tried to deny it, he did.

Large hands plumped her breast; his lips and teeth sucked and lightly bit her nipple. There was a sting and a burn as something metal bit into it and didn't let go. He licked it and repeated the same treatment with the other one. Clamps? This dream was getting weirder by the second. A wet, hot tongue slid down to her clit where it was sucked, licked, and nipped as a third metal bite clamped and held on. She couldn't hold it any longer; a moan escaped and she rocked her hips as the pressure from the little clamps sent a wild thrill through her.

Her pussy flooded with moisture as his fingers fondled her curls. "Gods, you're made for being fucked, aren't you, my little Witch?" he groaned and she felt his fingers as he pressed them against her heat and slid them through the mess he'd created. "I wonder if this sweet haven can stretch far enough to take me?" he questioned, and then two fingers entered her body, stretching and filling her enough that she gasped at the violation, which amplified the pleasure. He pushed his fingers into her until only his flat palm was pressed against her heat.

"I need it," she begged, unsure of what exactly she needed at this point. She rocked her hips, needing more. Her nipples felt almost numb beneath the pressure of the clamps, and her clit was swelling from being pinched. His mouth lowered to where she needed it, but the moment his tongue flicked against her clit, she cried out in shock as pain mingled with pleasure, pleasure overtook the pain, and that storm inside of her gained strength.

Ristan couldn't get enough of the taste of her. Her sweet pussy juices covered his face, coating his lips as he continued to lick her clit, where the blood flow had been restricted. He wanted to make her body betray her own wishes. Even now, she moaned for more, oblivious to the fact that this wasn't a dream.

He'd pulled himself out of her dream and awoken to her sweet body pressed against his, his cock poised at the ready as her sleek folds slid up and down it. Yeah, she was ripe as fuck with the need to be taken. Even in her sleep she'd found his soldier, and tempted him past his breaking point. He held back, remembering that she was a virgin, and she needed to be explored and ready before he fed inch after inch of his massive cock into that sweet little pussy, or he could seriously hurt her.

His eyes slid up her porcelain skin to where her nipples reddened and swelled from the clamps. This particular set could vibrate, which could make her come before she'd begged for it, so he kept the vibration off for now. Her thighs were spread wide, and while he liked the idea of her being unaware of what was happening to her pretty pussy, he wanted to see her eyes when she exploded with her first orgasm.

He flicked his fingers, and the blindfold disintegrated. The fibers caught the gentle breeze of the wind from the open windows and created a glowing cascade of white crystals. She blinked to adjust her eyes, and then he brought his fingers back to her opening. His other hand created sensations as his fingers made small circular patterns on her inner thighs.

"Do you want me to fuck you, Olivia?" he whispered hoarsely, his own voice filled with his need to throw caution to the wind and take her.

"I need to come," she replied thickly, her sultry tone sliding over his skin like a gentle caress. "Make me come, please," she pleaded, as her hips lifted wantonly.

He moved between her legs and slid his cock over her velvet folds. His stomach coiled with the need to fuck, to lay claim to what no other man or being had claimed before.

She was dripping, the beautiful sight of her juices as they flooded her core sent him over the edge and he held his cock at her pussy. His free hand reached up and removed the single piece of lacy silk that bound her hands, and then he removed the clamp that pinched her very swollen nub. He watched her as she made an O with her beautiful lips, and her eyes followed suit. He pushed the head of his cock just inside her sheath and groaned as the tightness gripped him. His muscles strained and bunched in his neck as he forced himself to remain still, his cock just barely inside of her, needing to be buried in her sultry depths.

He pulled it out, and gently slid it along the seam of her wetness, stroking her until she was moving with him, seemingly unaware that this was no dream. Her wetness would allow him entrance, and he was impatient to enter her fully. It wasn't right since she thought him her dream lover, and yet he couldn't force himself to stop. He slid his cock back to the tip of her entrance.

"Beg me to fuck you," he grunted; blood pulsed in his manhood as her tight pussy gripped the head of it painfully.

"Never," she whispered, and pushed her tight body against him, surprising him as she sealed her fate and took him deep. She cried out as pain tore through her, and he growled at her own thoughtlessness. Her pussy was wet, but it had needed to be ready for his wide thickness and long length. "Oh God," she cried out, but instead of moving away from what was surely causing her pain, she spread her legs wider, working her hips to accommodate his cock.

"Fucking hell," he groaned and held still, allowing her to use his cock to find her own pace.

She was fucking *him!* This sweet virgin was rocking her tight-as-fuck sheath around him and using his cock like her own pleasure toy. He rocked his hips and watched as her hands moved to her now very sensitive clamped nipples. Her fingers gently stroked the red tips, and a new flood of liquid filled her sweet pussy. Yeah, fuck it, she was in trouble.

He grabbed her hands, pushing them down hard as his mouth found those sensitive peaks, one and then the other as he nipped at them, enjoying the shocked gasp that exploded from her lips. She was discovering the truth, and he'd be damned if she called it off this far in. He pushed further inside her until he was buried to the hilt, and she screamed as pain tore through her, but it only lasted a few moments as he started to fuck her body.

His teeth grazed her nipple, and then he removed the clamps; one and then the other, until they were free, and then he sucked on them greedily. Her moan was bliss to his ears as the blood rushed back to those twin peaks, and he rocked his massive cock in the tightness of her sweet body.

He pulled back as her body began trembling with her impending release. He watched as she continued to use him, her sweet ass rocking as she fucked his cock. He'd planned on torturing her, but this? This was backfiring at best.

His balls tightened as she continued to slide on and off of his shaft, and then she screamed. Her eyes went wide, her pert nipples hardened before his eyes, and she exploded in screams as her body shook from the force of her first orgasm. Unable to resist, he fed on the rush of energy that pulsed from her. The taste of Fae and Human as he expected, and something else he couldn't identify. It was powerful. Something he'd never before tasted and immediately wanted more of. His eyes opened slowly and he watched her for a moment, smiling darkly as he pulled her legs up by her ankles, with no warning of his intent.

Her body was ready, and his balls ached too much to wait any longer. He spread her apart, placing one slender ankle over his shoulder and the other on his thigh as he pushed himself into her, hard and fast as he fucked her sleek, tight heat. "My turn," he warned and continued pounding her until she screamed again, her hands pushing against him as he took his turn.

Her cries were of pleasure, music to his ears as the beat of his blood mingled with them, and he exploded inside of her sweet heat. He'd never come so fast or hard in his entire life. Yet he didn't stop, not even when she tried to wiggle away from him. Instead, he captured her face between his hands, kissing her long and hard, which made her rock her hips to his tempo, as if they both heard the same song even though no music played in the room.

In the morning, she'd scream and cry foul, but he didn't care. She'd been willing; he could feel every emotion she had through his fingertips and he could see it in her expressive blue eyes that she was fully aware that this was no dream. She'd been truly fucked by her captor, and she'd wanted it with every fiber of her being.

He exploded a second time, taking her with him over the beautiful blissful cliffs, and she'd screamed his name... Okay, she'd screamed his code name, which he'd need to fix, and she hadn't said it to him, but the next time he took her, she'd scream it to the fucking heavens.

Sated and unable to keep his eyes open any longer, he cleansed their bodies with glamour, cleaning the blood from her and the bed, and yanked her lithe body against his. "You're mine now, Olivia. I own you."

CHAPTER EIGHTEEN

Walking through the gardens, Ristan mulled over his harsh words with Synthia this morning. His intentions were his alone, and he understood where she was coming from, yet he deserved his revenge.

He'd left his prisoner asleep in his bed and had stopped by the nursery briefly to give Kahleena a little boost of his Demon juice, which would keep the infant alive a little longer until they could figure out how to heal the Tree. The tiny thing was growing weaker when she should be growing strong. Her golden eyes showed her father's powers, yet she was failing to thrive, and sooner or later, her brothers would follow.

Synthia had arrived in the nursery and he'd blasted her about going against his wishes by taking Adam down to pay Olivia a visit in her cell the day before. Sinjinn had given him a mental heads-up at the time, but he'd stayed away from the cell at Ryder's command and assurance that he would personally ensure that nothing was done and that Olivia would remain his prisoner.

He'd listened as Synthia had given him advice on Olivia. He was thankful that she hadn't begged him to release her, and instead explained to him what she thought could be to blame. He'd understood Synthia's standpoint when she'd explained about growing up in the Guild, and how it was law to always trust the Elders, and follow any orders given by them. He'd smiled and inwardly chuckled at how different being raised in the Horde was. With his father, he'd managed to find loopholes and ways around doing what he knew was wrong. Unless one was very clever, death was the usual punishment for not following orders under Alazander's regime. He'd lived, though, and avoided situations that he knew were wrong, but Olivia had played the willing seductress in his fall inside the Guild.

That was the crux of it. He got what Synthia reminded him of this morning. Hell, he'd spent weeks in the Guild watching how they followed orders without asking a simple question. So the question was, was Olivia a Mage, or just blindly following orders? And what could make her turn on Alden in favor of Cyrus? Both were Elders. Every time he'd observed Olivia interacting with Alden, it seemed as if she'd cared for the old man. He'd watched both Elders for months, and Cyrus was cold and detached from the others at the Spokane Guild, while Alden had treated them like family. So was she just a great actress, or skilled in treachery and part of the Mages plan?

There were too many unanswered questions, and she was obviously not used to pleasure, which would make getting those answers an easy feat. The problem was, he wasn't used to being the asshole, and he'd hid his own pain behind his snark. But now, it was near impossible to manage with the old wounds ripped to the surface. He needed answers from her, and he needed to know why she'd done it. People had died, and while he carried no love for those who had perished at the Guild, he'd been betrayed, and worse, he'd been drugged by a tiny little female because his dick had wanted her to slip and fall on it. That pissed him off the most. One simple fucking mistake and he could have ruined everything they'd worked so hard for, and all because he'd wanted her to be the sweet little innocent thing that everyone had assumed she was.

His eyes roamed over the numerous herbs and flowers until they landed on his younger sister, Ciara. He stifled a groan as he moved in her direction, knowing that if he left now, she'd only follow him.

"Minx," he said, as he neared her.

"Hey, how are you feeling? We're all a bit worried about you," she admitted as she took his hand and kissed his palm in greeting.

"I'm doing better," he said, his mind replaying his early morning spent with Olivia. In fact, he felt a lot better since he fed from her. "How are the babes?" he asked, moving his mind to the safer subject.

"They need us to get a move on healing the Tree," she whispered as she surprised Ristan with a tight hug, which caused him to wince. Obviously, he hadn't been completely healed by fucking.

"No luck on finding a cure, then?" he asked as he pulled away, hoping she'd take the hint.

She moved to the small stone bench and sat with her hands in her lap. "They don't think I can help," she mumbled. "They act like I'm weak, and I'm not. I can fight; I've been trained by Zahruk and Sinjinn. I can help," she said, her eyes lifting to meet his with a look of sheer determination in them.

"That doesn't change the fact that you were born female, Minx, or that it's our job to protect you," he teased lightly.

"Synthia can fight, and no one says she's a female," she growled. "I'm not her, and I get it. Her lineage is superior, but mine isn't lacking either. I'm the princess of the Horde, and I can help them."

"Ciara, you're rash and young. You don't think before you act, and I know you think you're ready to take on the world, but you're not. You need to make better decisions and stop being foolish. Stop trying so hard," he said as he smiled at her, his eyes watching as a look of defiance lit in her eyes.

The air was thick with the heady scent of flowers in full bloom. His nose caught the subtle scent of jasmine, which reminded him of the sweet beauty sleeping in his bed. Lush greenery covered the stone walls that protected the gardens, and vines had sealed the cracks which had formed when Ryder had killed their father. The gardens were near the great hall where his father had impaled Dristan with his razor sharp wingtip. The kid had been close to death. Ryder had lost it, and the battle had been brutal and had shaken the foundations of the castle. In the end, he'd ended the monster that had endlessly tormented them all.

His eyes moved to the gated entrance, and to the double dragons that symbolized the Horde, and smiled. So much about this world never made sense before the change of monarchy, and now, with the impending doom of Faery, it did.

His eyes drifted back to his sister and he shook his head. "So much depends on that Tree, and right now isn't the time for a rebellion, Ciara. Now is the time to be united and fight for those babes; they need us. All of us. If you still feel this way after that is accomplished, I will stand by you when you speak to Ryder. If you approach him before that, you'll be on your own in your fight for independence."

Ristan's eyes moved to the Goddess standing at the far side of the garden. The gold lining her body was blinding, and it wasn't Danu this time. Fucking hell. He shook his head, but the Goddess paid him no heed; her eyes were on Ciara.

"Fucking hell," he whispered reverently as his eyes moved to his sister's.

Ciara twisted in her seat and scanned the garden, but her eyes came back in confusion. "What is it?" she whispered, as she absently rubbed her arms as a chill wind blew through the garden as Destiny watched her with a wicked smile on her beautiful lips.

"It's nothing we can't handle," Ristan said, his tone promising the Goddess that they were ready for anything.

Pacing beside the bed, Olivia's body ached from

where she'd been pleasured by the monster. She wasn't sure he was a monster anymore, but she needed to remind herself that he was. This wasn't one of her romance novels that would end with a happily ever after. It was a horror story.

Girl meets gorgeous guy, guy turns out to be a monster, kidnaps girl and tortures her. She dies. End of story.

She'd allowed him to take her virginity, and yet she'd done it to prevent it from being a threat that he could use to torture her with. Did she regret it? She wasn't sure yet, but she'd liked it. A lot. Of that, she wasn't able to lie about. It had hurt, but only at first, and the things he'd made her feel… Those things already made her body grow moist for more.

She was such an idiot!

She had the sheet wrapped around her, wearing it like a dress, because he'd left her in bed with nothing to wear. The chain attaching her collar to the bed was longer than the night before and allowed her to reach the bathroom without his assistance, but it wasn't long enough to get to the door or window to check for an exit or escape route.

Her breasts were still sensitive from the clamps he'd used, and every time she turned in her pacing, she was reminded of what they'd done together. Considering his impressive size, she thought the pain would have been a lot worse. The dull ache was just another reminder of what she'd done. She'd allowed it, and fuck if she didn't *like* it! She was such an idiot—or maybe she should blame her romance novels for her unrealistic expectations.

It was always the same story. Girl gets taken, girl falls in love with her captor, and he ends up loving her. It was absolute rubbish! She wasn't living some novel; he sure as hell wasn't going to fall in love with her, and there was no damned rainbow! But damn, the sex? Better than anything those books had explained. And yeah, her vagina might ache today, but the traitorous bitch was doing a happy dance to finally have seen some action.

Her body was clean, and yet she still felt his touch as if he'd burned her with it. A ripple of a tremor shot through her starting at her toes as she closed her eyes and pictured herself with him. She'd been eager, and not a single protest she'd given had sounded as if carried truth.

Memories of everything they'd done kept replaying through her mind. Since she'd woken up, she thought of little else but what he'd done with her body. *To* her body. The guy had some mad skills she'd all but purred and sang Dixie for him while he fucked her. There were other things, though, like those angry red marks from his torture intertwining with his dark silvery brands of his lineage. Along with a mark that looked like a symbol of the Fae goddess on his left pectoral. The surprising wink of silver from barbells that pierced his nipples. His abs looked as if he'd stolen them from a cover model from some male physique magazine. Then, last but not least, his cock. Nothing she'd ever read, or seen could have prepared her for that thing. It was probably considered a concealed weapon in the States. She giggled and shook her head. Here she was, held captive and mentally describing her tormentor's penis. Brilliant!

Her body had responded to his touch, and it had finally allowed itself the pleasure she'd always tried to self-achieve, but unlike when she'd tried, he had succeeded in making her body sing.

She felt his presence before the first soft footfall sounded from behind her. She stalled her pacing, and her eyes closed as she felt the blush spread across her body. She hadn't considered seeing him this soon and now knew why the morning after a one night stand was so awkward.

What was she supposed to say? Was she supposed to say anything? She was so out of her safe little world that she wanted to use the sheet as a shield and hide in its silky embrace. She felt him at her back, his immense physical presence almost palpable as she waited for him to speak.

She forgot to breathe, to move, forgot she was his prisoner until she felt the tug on the chain and was turned around by it. Her eyes lit with fire as she spun on him but sputtered out when she found him holding a tray of food. Her stomach decided to choose that moment to let out an audible growl of hunger.

"You can eat, but only if you do so naked," he said with a wicked smirk on his lips.

"I am naked," she pointed out, her hands gripping the sheet to her bosom like a lifeline.

Ristan's eyes slid down the sheet to her bare feet and back up. "Lose the sheet, and I'll let you eat. We can talk while you do so."

With shaking hands, she un-tucked the material and let it float to the ground, where it pooled at her feet. "I won't tell you any Guild secrets, or anything that could hurt my Guild."

"It's a little late for that, isn't it? Considering your Guild is nothing but a pile of ashes," he murmured as his eyes slid down her naked body.

Her nipples were red, not the delicate shade of pink they normally were. That was his doing, along with the clamps he'd used. Her hair was mussed, and the humidity in Faery had created a frizz that had it out of control. He may have bathed her with his magic, but her body still held proof that he'd taken her.

His hand came up slowly, cupping her breast before his thumb grazed her sensitive nipple. She whimpered as it caught her off guard, and sent another quiver through her body, which he saw. "Please stop," she whispered, her eyes lifting from his hand to meet his swirling silver and black stare. "I'm starving," she admitted, and she was. She was thirsty as well, and the red wine he'd brought—or she assumed that was what was on the tray—looked good enough to swallow in one drink.

"Tit for tat," he said as he waved his hand and the chain at her neck dropped to the floor with a loud rattle. "I give you a piece of food, you give me answers."

"And if I say no?" she asked as he pinched her nipple painfully, which seemed to make her lady parts drench themselves with anticipation. She blushed yet again, and tried to remove her eyes from his, but failed. The heat in them floored her, and as she watched, his nostrils flared as his lips tipped up in the corners. Could he smell her pussy growing wet with need?

No freaking way.

"You can do the math; you're a smart girl, Olivia. You know enough about the Fae and what we can do.

I could even have one of my brothers come here and question you. There wouldn't be much left of your mind but scrambled eggs if I did, so I would highly recommend you cooperate. Now, come and sit with me," he said, already heading to the small sofa in the room. She followed close behind him, completely aware of the fact that she was stark ass naked, and wetness was spreading down her thighs where they touched together.

She moved to sit on the sofa, but he took the entire seat, his eyes meeting hers briefly before they looked down at the floor at his feet. She considered arguing, but she was starving to the point where it felt as if her insides were consuming themselves.

At his feet, seated on her knees with her hands palm down on her thighs, she looked up. He swallowed hard and shook his head as he placed the tray down on what she was sure was nothing…until a small table appeared.

Magic; that had to be it. Demons must have magic that was similar to the High Fae. That had to be why her body was responding to him like some hussy with a cock fetish. "What do you want to know?" she whispered as she forced her mind away from where it was going.

"Cyrus," Ristan said, his eyes lingering on hers before he picked up a generous slice of bread, wrapped it around a piece of cheese, and popped it into his mouth. One of his hands wandered along her back, distracting her.

Olivia licked her dry lips and stifled a moan as the scent of meat, cheese, and freshly made bread tickled her nose. "What about him?"

"How long have you been working for him?" he asked, his fingers moving to the next piece of meat as his other hand continued to explore her body absently.

"Since I was twelve and started training to take my place in the library," she admitted.

She was handed a small sliver of cheese, and the moment it was placed in her hand, she devoured it with vigor. It tasted like heaven, and she closed her eyes and moaned as she chewed it. When she opened her eyes, she found him staring at her with a look that made her pussy clench tightly in awareness.

"Do you know him outside of the Guild?" he asked, and watched as her face pinched with confusion.

"Why would I know him outside of the Guild? He's an Elder, and for a while now, they have remained closed up inside one Guild or another. Before that, they didn't go out much to begin with. My entire life is inside the Guild—or it *was*," she said, and her stomach did a somersault with just how pathetic it sounded.

"And Alden, I know he has always been more involved with the Enforcers and their training, but he was responsible for you as well, right?" he asked, his fingers slowly trailing over her naked shoulder.

"He's always been active in the education and activities of training us. So yes, that is true," she said softly as a feeling of guilt fluttered through her stomach. "Cyrus was the one in charge of the librarians and the catacombs, so I left Alden's care when my field was chosen."

"So then why would you turn Alden in, when he is, after all, in charge of the Enforcers? Were you upset that you were given a desk while others got to hunt down and kill Fae?"

"Hardly; I love my job. I love working with the

children," she swallowed hard, her eyes misting with tears as she shut her emotions down quickly to avoid him knowing she'd just hit something that hurt her.

Ristan felt it, that flush of guilt mixed with pain from her own actions, but it made not a lick of sense. "So then tell me why you turned against Alden," he said softly.

"Why?" she growled as fire lit in her sapphire depths. "Why?" she asked, her body sizzling with anger.

"That is the question. I can repeat it for you if you need me to," he said smoothly, his eyes dancing with laughter. "Why did you betray Alden?" he asked, his eyes lowering from her angry lips to her lovely tits, which his large hand had engulfed. Her hand rose as she placed it on his much larger one, then actually growled at him.

"Because of you!" she snapped angrily as her other hand fisted at her side. "I didn't want to do it, but I had to because of what you did." Her eyes danced with her anger, and he'd be damned if his cock didn't take notice. "I thought it merely a fantasy of you, but it wasn't. Nor was it a dream. I saw you between my legs, doing things to me," she whispered the last, and then almost groaned as her nipples hardened at the memory.

"You saw me sucking your pussy clean," he corrected. "You almost came for me; do you remember that?" he asked, needing to know exactly what she remembered when Danu had used her body.

"I remember watching you, but it was like I was a witness, not a participant. I saw you change. I thought it was a just a dream until I got to the library and Cyrus was there waiting for me. He told me about the wards going off, and that something from within the Guild had done it. He said most likely it was the Fae. That maybe one had been inside and had sifted out. He had a video of you, Alden and I entering the carrel, but only Alden and I left. You never did. That was when I knew it hadn't been a dream. Cyrus accused me of helping you and said he'd have me tried for treason because I was giving you Guild secrets—and I *had* been! I may not have known it, but you know the Guild doesn't give two animal crackers about that. You ruined me, and yes, I did what I had to do to save my own ass."

He nodded and handed a generous piece of meat and bread.

"Did you like it, what you felt?" he asked, his eyes following her mouth with each bite she took.

"I don't know," she whispered.

"Yes, you do," he said with a smirk, his eyes lighting up with knowledge. "I felt your need to come for me while my mouth sucked on your sweet pussy. You were soaking wet, and that was all you," he growled, his eyes swirling with their inhuman beauty.

He handed her the wine, which she gulped down eagerly, uncaring when it dripped down her lips and onto her chest. She was parched and wasn't going to allow him to stop her. She finished it and wiped her mouth with the back of her hand, ignoring the cold droplets that slid down her breasts and stomach.

"Why didn't you try to warn Alden?" he asked, going back to stroking her flesh, noting that she didn't move away from his touch, but actually moved into it.

"And if he was what Cyrus said? What then? I'm not an Enforcer, and I was out of my scope."

"Scope?"

"I was out of my league, over my head. Had I known what was coming, would I have done differently? Yes, of course. I was told that you'd both be questioned."

"Well, now, we both know what the Guild considers questioning to be. You could have warned us, and we could have helped prevent what happened at the Guild," he said and felt as her guilt once again reared up.

"Would it have mattered?" she asked, her eyes and emotions closing off as if she held the switch to it, which made him examine her closely. Synthia could do the same, but then she'd been trained to withstand torture in the hands of her enemies.

"There were archives I needed and hadn't obtained yet, but I have the next best thing. You," he said offhandedly, his eyes locked onto a droplet of wine as it slid down her body.

"No," she said, her teeth worrying her bottom lip. "Those are things I won't talk to you about," she admitted.

"I can make you," he said as he sat up and moved closer.

"You could try; doesn't mean I will tell you anything," she said defiantly.

"Fucking hell, Olivia, I was hoping you'd put up a fight."

Olivia felt her body grow cold as he stood and moved to the wall. Placing his palm on a panel, which slid open, he pulled out something that looked like a giant X that was created of rosewood. It would be beautiful if it wasn't a device made for torture.

CHAPTER NINETEEN

Watching as her eyes grew large and round, Ristan knew the moment she figured out what this device was used for. She stood and he smiled. She had nowhere to run and they both knew it. He ignored her as he opened the leather restraints on the top of the X and then at the bottom. His brother had made the lovely Saint Andrews Cross with a few modifications to the traditional one. This one had sturdy stabilizer bars in the back that connected to a central axle so it not only inverted, but it could also swivel into a table position, and lock down at just the right height for even more intriguing games.

With a simple flick of his hand, the settee at the foot of his bed opened and several items floated out, each one easily caught and placed with care on the small table he materialized from his mind. He gave her a wicked smile to assure her that he had not forgotten about her and caught her eyes as he displayed the first item that was all black and looked like a whip handle with soft, fluffy tails sprouting off of one end.

"You're new to this, so I'm going to start with something easy. It's very soft for the first moment or so until you finally feel the bite and sting of it, which can burn quite nicely. It leaves a beautiful red love bite as well," he grinned wickedly as he showed off the leather tails hidden inside the soft ones. She gulped air, even as her pussy flooded and dampened further. "Now this one… I love this one too, by the way. It's little, but damn, does it do its job nicely," he said as he held it up, showing her something that looked a little larger than a bullet and was just as shiny. "Don't let its size fool you, it's very powerful. It can bring on an orgasm in less than thirty seconds. I'm looking forward to hiding this in that sweet little rose in your bottom."

Ristan turned his back and smiled as he heard the bathroom door slam closed. She was going to fight him, but by the time he was done, she'd be begging him for more. Most women loved the chase, and he was willing to bet she was no exception.

He needed it anyway. After last night, fucking her tight body had made him want to do it again, and she'd been a willing participant that was regretting it today. He could see it in her posture. The way her body blushed with the memory of what they'd done.

Today was about getting answers, and he planned to enjoy it. Her body was ready, the residual pain from losing her virginity gone. Or it would be once he healed it a bit more. Simple healing for aches and pains was easy enough magic for him. He'd made sure that he healed her aches before he'd sought his duties and it had taken him a lot of willpower to walk away after he'd stroked her sweet flesh to heal it.

"Olivia, it's ready for you, my dear," he said and smiled as he heard something slam against the door. "I like the chase," he called softly, knowing she'd hear him.

He glamoured away his shirt and boots, leaving only his jeans, and sifted into the bathroom, not expecting the bottle of shampoo to peg him in the head the moment he did. He growled and sifted again before the conditioner could hit him as well.

He reappeared behind her and hugged her naked body to his, feeling the jolt of the connection. He'd never felt such a strong physical reaction with his sexual partners, but touching her was like touching heaven. Close to it, anyway, and the sweet scent of her sex mixed with jasmine flowers drove him damn near insane.

Quickly sifting before she could respond, he pushed her against the device, knowing she'd get more pleasure than pain from it. He easily overpowered her struggles and ignored the dirty names she screamed at him while he wrapped her wrists into the soft leather cuffs. He was glad he'd asked Aodhan to use the softest leather he could find. In this situation, it would keep her skin safe from chafing with her struggles, because he knew exactly how to make her struggle, without allowing her to come until he wanted her to.

Perhaps he'd allow her to come quickly, only because she needed to get at least one out of her system so he could get the answers he needed.

He leaned over to secure her legs and caught her foot as it lifted to kick him. He gripped it painfully for a moment before loosening his hold to decrease the pain, which wasn't his intent. She might be new to sex, but her body was ripe for fucking. Her petals were sleek with the proof of her needs, and her nipples were already hard and probably aching for the sweet bite of his clamps.

Once he'd secured both of her feet, he adjusted the device until she was flat on her back, her sweet pussy opened for his viewing pleasure. He locked it into position, and she cursed and wiggled her ass as she tested the bonds. His fingers trailed softly over her inner thighs as he moved to stand between her legs.

"You look good helpless," he whispered as he continued to test her mood. She was pissed, and yet there it was: Desire. Willingness. She may be fighting it, but she wanted it more. Her heart raced, and her blood pumped, but her emotions? Those emotions wanted him to ditch the toys and just make her body sing. He raised his eyes to hers and smiled with confidence.

Right up until she started rattling off random words.

"Hubcap! Chicken dinner, taco, rabbit," she paused, her eyes wild with her search for something only she seemed aware of. "Red, red, damn you! What's the word?" she demanded, and he laughed, his eyes widening in surprise as she continued to rattle off random words.

"Are you searching for a safe word?" he asked incredulously. At her frantic nod, he laughed. "Someone has been reading some naughty books, haven't we? I must have missed that collection. I did, however, find quite a few that I scanned through while you slept," he mused, his eyes filling with laughter. "My favorite part…let's see, oh yeah. *His bulbous manhood pushed inside my sleek manhole,*" he quoted, but his words were filled with laughter.

"You were in my apartment?" she shrieked, outrage coloring her words. It only rose as he shrugged his shoulders and pinned her with a knowing grin.

"So tell me, was my cock bulbous enough for you?" he teased.

"You suck!" she growled as her cheeks tinged red from her embarrassment.

"Pussy, And I also have something you can suck on," he whispered as his fingers trailed small circles up her inner thighs. "Before we begin, little Witch, I need to set something straight. I am not a Dom, but I am one hundred percent dominant in the bedroom. All Fae males are because feeding depends on it. It's how we survive here. There are no labels, no catch phrases, not in this place. You can scream out random shit, but I'll just take it as I fucked you silly. Do not assume I am Human, because I assure you that I have no Human values. No standards that I go by will ever match yours. I am not Human. I'm not safe, and no one ever said I was sane," he said smoothly as his fingers trailed over her breasts and teased and pinched her nipple as he spoke.

"I know that where you come from, Humans have safe words because even the most experienced Dominant can potentially miss a partner becoming distressed. I'll let you in on a secret," he said, as he held up his fingers which gave off a silvery gray glow as he lowered them to trace over her nipple, drawing a warm pulling sensation around the peak. "I can feel your every emotion; everything you feel, I can sense. You can't lie to me. I will know when you are close to orgasm, or if your body becomes stressed. If I think you can handle more, I'll push. If not, I'll briefly stop and let you adjust. The choice is not yours. This is not a power exchange. You owe me a debt and I'll be the one to say when it's been paid. Do you understand?" he asked. His fingers continued to glow, his rumbling voice sending shivers to her toes, and a coil that was unfurling deep in her belly.

He moved back between her legs and could see the proof of her desire, no matter how much she fought it. His eyes feasted on her wet curls; and the pink flesh that had dampened from her struggles. If he was right, she'd more than liked the chase. It had turned her on, probably as much as it had turned him on. He walked his fingers along her thighs to her opening and enjoyed the hiss of air that escaped her lungs as he caressed her heat with his thumb.

Her eyes closed and her head tilted to the side, which made him pause, until those beautiful sapphire eyes opened, glazed with need. Game on. He pulled a different set of clamps out of his pocket first, his love of them growing with how red her beautiful nipples were today. Proof that he'd pleasured them, and fuck if it didn't make his cock stand up and salute him.

Playing with her nipples until they were at attention, he clipped the new clamps to them quickly. This pair had little rubber tips on them and little weights dangling at the end of each delicate chain. Her body arched as he tightened each clamp snugly. He slid his finger inside her folds and had to slow his own breathing as she clenched his finger tightly. "Out of all the women I've tormented, I think I'll like you the best, my sweet Witch."

"Go to hell," she whispered, but her hips bucked with wanton desire as the wine she'd drank earlier seemed to heighten her senses. "I will never tell you anything that can hurt the Guild, ever," she whispered defiantly. He enjoyed her steely resolve and the challenge.

He pulled out his finger and reached for a silver toy that was much larger than the one he showed her earlier. He enjoyed her wide-eyed stare as he pressed the cold metal against her opening. He rubbed it over her pussy, watching as her sweet juices coated it.

"Tell me about the Mages that were in the Spokane Guild," he whispered huskily as he watched her move against the device. She gave him a quizzical look like he was crazy.

"What the hell are you talking about? There weren't any Mages in the Guild. Only Witches and Warlocks," she growled as he increased the vibration and continued to use the device against her opening.

"I saw them; they were in the room using my balls for ping-pong and my intestines as the net. You saw them, too, and I want to know more about what happened."

"The Enforcers, the fakes ones," she gritted out, trying to ignore the toy as he moved it over her folds and worked her pussy against her. "They were with Cyrus the day this entire mess started. One of them admitted they weren't with the Guild," she moaned, her eyes pleading with him for mercy as her body continued to squirm against the persistent toy he wielded.

Fuck, for a newly deflowered virgin, she was wild. He watched as she glided against it and smiled as he pushed the huge tip inside, just barely. "Ooh," she moaned, and he watched as she struggled to grow accustomed to the device's size.

She'd taken him, and he was larger than the metal toy.

"Do you know why this is used for torture?" he asked as he pushed in another few inches as her juices lubricated the metal. His own cock jumped against the confines of his jeans.

"No," she mumbled, her body holding still to accept what he was feeding it. Once the device was fully inside of her, he stepped back and surveyed his handiwork.

"It has little sensors," he said holding one up far enough that she could see it. "They sense your muscles clenching and cause the device to vibrate. It becomes a cycle, which makes it vibrate, and that will make you clench more," he smiled heatedly with a thick tone that said he was enjoying her discomfort a little too much. "When I hook the toy from this," he said, pulling a wire down from the ceiling as she watched with hooded eyes, "to this…" He snapped his fingers, and she listened as something lifted from the floor. "It will fuck you. Your muscles will grow tense, and eventually you'll explode and come for me; I won't even have to do anything but watch you," he growled and hooked it together as she moved her wet heat on the machine that was buried in her sweet pussy, exactly where he wanted to be.

"I ache," she whispered, and he stood back as he connected the device, his eyes sliding over his masterpiece.

Her nipples were being pulled from the light weights, but she could easily take more. Her silk folds were stretched to accommodate the metal cock which had yet to begin to move inside of her. He'd gone easy on her placing the device inside.

Normally he was rough, uncaring of the pain because his partners expected it. Olivia was different, and he found himself taking steps to prevent pain to her body and mind. He reached for the device and clicked the machine on.

"Oh, God!" she screamed as he watched her wiggle against it. Her pussy was taking it beautifully. Stretching as it moved in and out of her core. He smiled as he leaned over and sucked her clitoris hard, his tongue flicking it as he used his teeth to gently hold it in place for his tongue's attention.

"God has little to do with this," he said as he released her and stood up. He moved to her mouth, watching as her eyes rolled with the heavy strokes of the toy fucking her. He glamoured off his jeans and gripped his heavy cock with his hand. Her instinct proved spot on as her tongue moved over her lips and they parted expectantly.

Fucking hell; whose torture was this? He stepped back and watched as disappointment crossed her face. "Tell me what I want to know," he whispered past the dryness of his mouth. His eyes slipped from her face to where the toy moved in her pussy.

Fuck, she was moving with it; he wanted to remove it and take its place. He watched as the wire sensors turned from red to green, and as she moved her sweet pussy even with the restraints holding her in place. If he hadn't been the one to shatter her hymen himself, he would swear she was used to sexual torment.

"Tell me more about the Mages, Olivia," he said, forcing his mind back to what was important.

"I...uh...shit!" she screamed as a violent orgasm

ripped through her body, his cock wept that it hadn't given her that release. Her eyes rolled back in her head, her body glistened with sweat as tiny goose flesh formed all over her skin. The noises she made as her body was fucked... Shit, those noises were almost enough to make him spill his load.

He shook his head, uncaring about the answers as he pulled the metal toy out and replaced it with his own throbbing cock. He slipped inside her wetness at the same time he released her ankles from the cuffs, pushing her legs up until her ankles settled on his shoulders, and with one solid thrust, he was buried inside of her heaven.

"Justin, no more," she cried. "No more," she begged as her body coiled and another orgasm threatened to let loose.

"My name is Ristan, Olivia, say it with me while I show you who owns this pussy," he growled and smiled as she screamed it to the heavens as she exploded around his cock.

The only sounds in the room were her screams as he drove himself into her with hard, calculated thrusts meant to hit her sweet spot, which kept her riding the wave of the orgasm after orgasm.

He fed, his hunger too much for him to contain as he pounded her flesh, growing closer with each thrust until he released his need inside of her, and yeah, he didn't stop. He fucked her until she was mumbling incoherent words, and both of their hair was slick with sweat.

He hadn't stopped fucking her until they both couldn't move; only then did he release her and take her to the bed with him, where he pulled her body next to his. Her breathing was even because she'd fallen asleep seconds after his fifth release, and at that point, she'd earned sleep.

There was something about her taste that was sweeter than he'd ever tasted before as he'd fed from her, and he felt that power which came with feeding as it pulsed through him. Something else was bothering him, though, something else that he couldn't place in his sleep-driven mind.

He ignored it as he allowed his lids to slide closed as he held her still-damp body in his arms. He could easily wash the smell of sex from them, but it was intoxicating, and he wanted her to wake up and feel just how good it felt to wake up covered with sex in the morning.

CHAPTER TWENTY

He watched Olivia sleep; her nightmare had come back after he'd left her boneless and sore. He ran his fingers over her body, his healing magic sinking into the deep tissues that would ache when she awoke. He stopped just short of completely healing her because he wanted her to remember the time she'd spent being fucked by him. She'd surprised him with her willingness to participate in her own torture, and fuck if he didn't already want to do it again. The little Witch was far sturdier than he'd expected, thank the gods for that. Witches, of course, were a lot stronger and more durable than their Human counterparts. The fucking he gave her last night probably would have killed a Human.

Soon he would need a soul to feed from, and last night had pushed him to the limits as her soul had shined from within, bright and tempting as fuck. It was still white, but it carried a tinge of red around the outer edges, but that could mean too many things for him to guess at. Feeding from her emotions was addictive enough, which made him afraid of feeding from her soul for that reason. One taste and he'd be as close to nirvana as he could ever get. Those raw emotions he'd felt during her time on the cross were conflicting. He doubted she was a Mage, but that didn't mean she was off the hook. She'd been standing beside them, and it was hard to buy that she was completely innocent and free of duplicity in what happened at the Guild.

The next logical question was how much did she know about them, or had she been as innocent as she claimed? She'd answered only some of his questions, but with the Mages growing bolder and time running short, he needed answers. Meanwhile, the desire to get his mother out of this place and to a safe location where he could protect her was getting stronger.

Olivia, on the other hand, he wanted to leave tied to the cross, so he could play with her at his leisure. She was now his favorite chew toy and fuck if he didn't want to chew on her some more. He moved away from the bed and busied himself around the room, glamouring the toys and cross clean after last night's session, while keeping quiet so he wouldn't wake her.

She'd be sore after that session, and she deserved the sleep for her body to fully recover. He could feel the tension from inside the castle, but worse, he froze as he smelled the distinct fragrance of Ambrosia. Danu had been inside his quarters.

He paused. His eyes narrowed as they searched the room for anything out of place. He swallowed a growl as his eyes found cold steel, buried to the hilt beside Olivia's head. He moved to the bed, pulled the serrated blade out of the feather pillow, and threw it across the room.

That bitch; after everything she'd done and said, now she was leaving the same warning she'd given with the other females when he'd taken them one too many times for her liking? Fuck her. He sifted to the pavilion and moved with purpose until he found his mother in her room.

"Get packed, now," he ordered brusquely. He didn't wait for her to start and glamoured luggage for her.

"Ristan," she said softly. "Why are you packing my things?"

"We're leaving," he growled.

"I'm leaving?" Alannah asked as she gently placed a calming hand on her son's shoulder. "I will not leave this place with you fighting beside the Horde King," she said with a stubborn set to her jawline. "You're my son, Ristan."

"That's why I'm going with you, and before you even think it, know this. I will fight beside Ryder, he is my king. I also need you to be safe, and I have a place I am taking you to outside of Seattle, which will allow me to help Ryder, and protect you," he said as he finished packing her clothes with a single thought of his mind.

"So you're sending me away?" she asked as she pushed her silky black hair from her face. "I am not a weakling who needs to be protected. I know exactly what is coming, and why they are coming. Danu assured me…" She stopped.

Ristan spun around on his mother, his lips drawn in a tight line as he narrowed his eyes on her. "Danu assured you of what, Mother?" he said barely above a whisper.

"You think she came to you because you were in pain? No, I asked her to help you because I could not. She has told me you were special ever since you were a child. She assured me that nothing could break you after what your father had done. She told me the Guild would fall, but that you'd pull through."

Ristan felt his inner Demon rear its head and growl. "That bitch knew what would happen to me?"

"Do not speak ill of the Gods, for they hear us all," Alannah warned.

"Mother, she is the reason I was tortured. She alerted them to my presence with her thoughtless antics!" he shouted with a white hot rage that shot through him.

It suddenly made sense. She wasn't necessarily thoughtless; she was calculated, but what else had he expected? She'd used him as fucking bait for her psychopathic ex-husband. She hadn't been standing across the street from the Guild because of his presence there; she'd been monitoring her crazy-ass ex.

She'd meant for him to sift out and set off the wards, which was why she'd persisted in pissing him off when she knew how he felt about her using an innocent woman for her games. She'd planned it. She planned it all, everything from his torture to her capturing her ex-husband.

He shook his head and looked at his mother. She looked timid and sweet, but she was a very proud princess of the Soul-Seeking Demons. Her people were feared as much for their cunning as they were for their barbarism. As it always was with Faery, beauty was often deadly and he'd always known she wanted revenge. Revenge for being enslaved by the Fae, and tortured by the old Horde King, but this went beyond that. She wasn't satisfied with the vengeance Ryder had given them all; she wanted more.

"You knew that I'd be tortured," he whispered through the hurt of betrayal. His own mother had known his fate at the hands of the Mages and one pissed-off God. "Ryder is not the same creature our father was, and yet you continue to plot against him?"

"Not him," she said. "He wasn't the one meant to rule this kingdom; you were," she said with pride in her swirling silver and black eyes. "I have helped Danu so that you would be crowned king."

"Well, mother, either you misunderstood her or she lied. Danu's own daughter sits beside Ryder on the throne, and even if he was gone, I'd never take that throne. Now finish packing; you're leaving Faery. It is past time you and I leave before you end up getting us both accused of treason."

Ristan waited for his mother to argue, and when she didn't, he sifted out, leaving her alone while he went to his brother. He found Ryder alone in the office he used for taking care of the day-to-day planning of the kingdom.

"Ryder," he said as he stepped further into the room, his eyes on the floor as he considered how to tell his king of his mother's deceit. No matter; it was better for Ryder to hear it from him rather than discover it on his own.

Ryder looked up and closed the pen he'd been using to write with, lifting his golden eyes to meet Ristan's. When Ristan refused to meet his gaze, the tension in the air grew thicker.

"I've let you down," Ristan said with a deep sigh as he scrubbed his hands over his face and finally met his brother's eyes. "My mother seems to think I should be the king of the Horde, and even though I do not share her…"

"Ristan, I'm well aware of what your mother thinks should be. I know she hates my station, but not me. I knew she was plotting to set you on my throne, but I also know you do not want it. I'm always ten steps ahead of my enemies and those who seek to place their own children in my position. Your mother is not the first to plot against me, and she won't be the last."

Ristan's heart plummeted with Ryder's words. "You knew she plotted against the throne, and yet you still have not taken her into custody as a traitor?" he asked, his hope slipping as he held Ryder's piercing eyes.

"Why would I take her into custody?" Ryder asked, his wide shoulders stretching with tension as he leaned back in his massive chair.

"She spoke out loud of her treachery to have me placed on the throne. *Your* throne, Ryder. That is enough to have her arrested and tortured to death."

"She's a Demon, a very proud one who was tortured for centuries at the hands of our father, just as my mother was. She is no different than Zahruk's mother, who thought he should be crowned king, or Sinjinn's. I knew she was aware of everything going on and, like most, they expected their children to be awarded the throne for what they endured. None of them were aware of the customs of the beast. That knowledge is something that was reserved for the closest of my Guard. You're my brother, Ristan, and my friend," Ryder said as he clasped his hands behind his head and relaxed. "What you do with your mother and Olivia is your choice. I know of your loyalty to me, and if you need a break from this world, I understand. However, I need you right now, as do my children. I ask you not as your king, Ristan, but as your brother, to help me save them."

"I'm taking my mother and Olivia away from here, but you have my word, brother, that I will be here when you need me. I need this, to get away and get my head back on right. Olivia is either under a very powerful spell that helps her to be a skilled liar, or she was clueless to what she helped do. I've been in her dreams," he disclosed, his eyes closing as he told his brother what he'd discovered.

"And?" Ryder asked.

"There's a door inside the Guild, one I'd like to take her to and confront her with, but other than that, her dreams show me nothing of her guilt. I have been sifting through her emotions and fed from them."

"You are starting to doubt she knew the extent of her treachery to the Guild?" he asked, picking up easily on Ristan's doubt.

Of course, his brother's beast could sense every emotion, which made him one of the best predators around. "I know she is guilty, but not how deep that guilt goes, nor how that information benefits us. I thank you for not interfering in it and allowing me to control her punishment. I know it isn't easy on Synthia, but this is my fight."

"You have the right to do what you wish with her, but I'd rather Synthia be left out of it. She's been through enough and losing the Guild has left a heavy weight on her heart. She's been tearing the library apart looking for answers on the Tree of Life, and I don't have the balls to tell her that our sadistic father wouldn't have given a shit about that Tree."

"And how do you keep her mind from what will happen if the Tree dies?" Ristan asked with his own heart heavy with the knowledge that it could die, and with it, his nephews and niece.

"I romance her and do whatever it takes to keep her mind from it. Time is against us, though, and each day the children grow weaker, especially Kahleena. I'm trying to figure out my next move to keep her mind from it, but I'm not sure where I go now."

"I'm not sure anything will help you there, but I also need to make one thing clear, Ryder. If you and Synthia return to confront the Guild for what happened there, I will not be joining you; right now I'd just as soon kill them all, and I know that would only hurt Synthia more. Nor will I allow Olivia to go, because she's mine now. Whatever I decide to do with her is my choice. I'll not hand her over to the Guild, and I plan to move both her and my mother before the end of today. She'll know my will and my unwillingness to sit on your throne because you're my king. But more than that, Ryder, you're my brother."

CHAPTER
TWENTY-ONE

After hours of soaking in the huge, opulent tub, Olivia's toes were looking like raisins, but she didn't care. Her body was sore from the Demon's love games and already craved more. The mere thought of his cock sent her pulse racing and her newly awakened sex drive over the edge.

She was such a masochist, and felt like one of the Viking captives in the romance novel that she'd been reading right before her dark part in the fall of the Guild. She felt like a traitor, and maybe that was why he was so easily seducing her.

He was so different from the man she knew inside the Guild, yet the same. Gone was the soft Cajun drawl; his normal baritone voice now had traces of a Scottish accent. He was taller and bigger than his disguised self and she liked the longer, silkier, inky-black hair. The silver and black swirling eyes were unsettling, yet she easily got lost in them. He was beautiful, and he was everything the Guild had taught her about the Fae. She didn't doubt that those looks could draw her to her own demise, because one look and she was a goner.

She toed the bubbles floating on the top of her bathwater and wondered how they still remained after the hour or so that she'd been in here. Maybe Ristan— she had to remind herself that was really his name now—had used magic to make the base powder of the bath salts. She wasn't sure if she should be pleased or disturbed that it was her favorite fragrance.

The rich scent of jasmine wafted through the room, and she eventually closed her eyes and gave in to the need to sleep.

She was alerted to the fact that she wasn't alone when water splashed her face and she was yanked from the tub. "What the hell?" she demanded as strong arms pulled her up as she coughed up water.

"Are you daft, or do you think to escape me in death?" he growled angrily, his hands working in an up and down motion on her back with the occasional tap as more water dripped from her mouth. Her lungs were on fire, and she was off-balance and disoriented.

"Did you try to drown me?" she accused through sputtering water and trying to get enough air in her lungs.

"Me? You were beneath the water when I arrived," he said as he turned her in his arms and looked down at her.

She felt as if she'd been asleep for only seconds, but it was almost as if she was missing time. She looked back at the tub, now missing the heavenly scented bubbles that had just been there. Her mind tried to remember what had happened but came back with only the thought that maybe she'd actually fallen asleep in the tub, and had slipped beneath the water.

"I didn't try to drown myself, I fell asleep," she admitted.

"Idiot," Ristan said, but his eyes showed a subtle sign of relief as he released her naked form and stepped back, but in an instant there was a darkness in his eyes as he looked at something over her shoulder.

Danu watched Ristan as he glared a warning in her direction. Olivia hadn't been asleep; she'd almost been drowned by a jealous Goddess. Ristan watched as Danu snapped her fingers, and Olivia's form crumpled to the ground.

"Bitch," Ristan snapped as he moved to see if Olivia had sustained damage, but she gave a gentle snore and his heart beat with relief.

"I know you spoke to your mother, and I know you don't understand the why or how of this, Ristan, but eventually you will," Danu said as she moved to where Olivia lay on the floor and knelt beside her to examine her sweet face.

"You knew what was coming. You forced me to break my promise, to fail my mission, and you knew I'd be tortured," he accused; his eyes were angry and his skin itched to turn red in warning.

"Yes, but not to that extent, Ristan," she admitted. "I hadn't thought he'd become obsessed with you if there were hints of a connection between us, nor had I thought him still in love with me. We've lived a thousand lifetimes together, and we've been at war for just as many," she whispered as her hand trailed to Olivia's swollen breast. "How many times have you fucked this one?"

"Go to hell, Danu," he said, warning permeating his tone.

"I'm already in hell, Demon," she said unaffected by his tone. Her finger slid over Olivia's nipple and Ristan felt a tight possessiveness roar to life.

"Get the fuck away from her; you've done enough already," he said, his eyes locked onto the sharp fingernail that slid over the rose colored nipple. "Get out of here, Danu. Go back to your husband," he growled, and he was as surprised as Danu by the force of his words, and the truth in them.

"Did you get attached to her?" she asked as she stood up, and her eyes turned blood red, as her hair turned black. He'd only seen her take the form of the Mórrígan once before when she'd killed the female he'd once grown close to.

"To some little Witch, one that betrayed, and helped torture me, Danu? Not at all, but I'll be damned if you get to touch her when I have my own revenge planned for her," he said smoothly, as he somehow managed to hold Danu's gaze, which he'd normally never done.

"You're mine, and you know the rules, Ristan," she said, the warning blatant in her eyes. "I can't love you, and I don't share my things. You are one of those things I prefer to keep for myself."

"You rarely even use me anymore, so why keep me? I'm not a fucking pet," Ristan warned, and felt something snap inside of him. "What you have done to me… For centuries, you have used me, and for what? To what end? How can I fight for Faery when all I want to do right now is kill you? Fuck you, Danu; we're nothing going forward. You don't get to use me as bait and then come crawling back when you need a good fucking. Find another cabana boy to fetch your towel when you need it. Kill me if you need to for saying it, but me and you? We're nothing. Get the fuck out of here."

Ristan waited until she was gone before he reached down and scooped up the sleeping form from the floor. She'd be out for a while, and knowing Danu, she'd give Olivia some vivid dreams while she slept.

Ristan didn't have time for dream walking, even though he wondered at what nightmare Danu had given to Olivia. He assessed the room and decided she was the only thing he needed from his quarters. He opened a portal, then wrapped Olivia in a soft dark blue blanket he glamoured, and sifted to Vlad's mansion, which was in the mountains just outside Spokane, nestled in the Colville Forest, and placed Olivia on one of the large couches near the crackling fire of the great room.

"Have you ever considered actually knocking?" Vlad asked as he entered the large room. He paused when he saw the blanket-wrapped form that took up a small spot on the massive couch.

"Yeah, easier just to pop in and get your attention," Ristan said with a small smile. "I need a safe place to hide her, one where people won't ask questions."

He didn't need to go into greater detail because Vlad was already aware of who Olivia was. Ristan sat beside Olivia and glamoured clothing on her since he'd spaced doing it as he'd left Faery. He smiled as the Hello Kitty pajama fuzz became exposed through the blanket.

"Ryder needs you right now more than ever," Vlad said softly, his silver eyes so light that it almost made them appear white in color. They were normally a gunmetal color, but it all depended on how much he'd fed and how recently.

"He knows I've left, and that he need only call on me," Ristan said as he huffed out an aggravated sigh. "I pissed off Synthia's mother today, and I needed to get out of there before I did something I'd later regret."

"Shit," Vlad said as he sat on one of the larger, leather chairs. "I don't know if I'm impressed or worried, shit, maybe both?" he said as he rubbed his chin before shaking his dark head.

"Don't be impressed, unless I live past this week," Ristan said, and Vlad smiled, showing off two elongated fangs.

"Lucian has a few places you might take her; no questions would be asked. I have to warn ya, though, they got some heavy kinky shit going on over at his clubs. I know you would thrive at any one of them, not sure about her," Vlad said wickedly. "My club isn't the safest place right now. Shadowlands and pretty much all Fae clubs are only open to the High Fae because of the shit going on in this world. The High Fae can hold their own, but I don't want needless blood spilled in the clubs, not unless I'm drinking it. The Guilds are calling for Otherworld blood, so I have been very selective of those I have been allowing into Nightshade lately, but it's not safe for you to go there. Not yet, anyway. Not with that one in tow."

"Lucian will want a favor in return," Ristan mused,

and weighed the option of taking her to his home outside of Seattle with his mother or taking her to a sex club that catered to the rich and famous of the supernatural world. One thing was sure. There wouldn't be any chance of the Guild or Mages finding her in that place since it was hidden by magic and Lucian seemed to be off of the Guild's radar. As it was, very little was known about him and his men, other than the rumors that circulated every few centuries.

"You want me to summon him?" Vlad asked with a wicked grin on his lips.

"Summon the King of Hell's right-hand man? No, I don't, but I need you to," he said as Olivia began to stir.

CHAPTER TWENTY-TWO

He hated feeling out of his comfort zone. Danu was notorious for making him feel uncomfortable and trying to make him lose control. The Demon in him wanted to throw things and kill shit, but the Fae in him just wanted to fuck. He decided that neither of those choices would help his current situation. He secured Olivia in his quarters at Ryder's Spokane Mansion, the safest place he could think of as a fix until Lucian could reach him, and returned to Faery.

The corridor outside the nursery was empty, except for Savlian who looked to be asleep in one of the chairs that were positioned on each side of the door, but Ristan knew his brother better than most.

"What gives?" he asked, nodding to the chair, and the wicked blade which looked like something only Zahruk could have made.

"I'm guarding the babes, but fuck me if I don't want to wander in and get all daddy day care on them. Meriel kicked me out a little while ago for diaper changes because she said they needed the contact…Still don't know why she'd want to do something as crazy as actually change a fucking diaper," Savlian said with a cross look on his face.

"They need to be held and touched; their body heat is helped by it."

"And you know that why?" Savlian asked his eyes wide in mock horror.

"I stole Synthia's book," Ristan said sheepishly as he rubbed the back of his neck. "What to expect when something or other, but someone had to be ready in case something happened."

"True that, but damn, you read it?" Savlian said as he leaned his dark head against the wall behind him. "At least someone considered what could happen if their momma didn't pull through. I think the rest of us were just assuming since you had that vision, that she'd be safe from harm or anything like that, brother."

"I always consider every outcome, and try to be ten steps ahead, just as our King is."

"No one is in there right now," Savlian said as he eyed the open doorway. "Go on in, I'm sure the little angel is awaiting her uncle's return. She seems better after you've held her," he said, his eyes keen with the knowledge that he was aware of Ristan's feeding the little minx a bit of his power at every visit.

"She won't make it if I don't," he said softly, his heart clenching in a vice as he considered the outcome.

"Hey, what you do in there, we trust you. Got it? You're family, always will be. Ryder told us that you finally learned of your mother's plotting; mine did the same shit."

"I'm sure that would have gone down beautifully with Sevrin, seeing you're both so close in age. Most people confuse you two for twins anyway," Ristan said as he considered how much shit those two did together, and the competition between them. They were good natured in most of it, but each one tried to outdo the other continuously since they'd been children.

"Hey, you know what I'm getting at. Don't let it bother you or get to you. You are wanted and welcome here among your family, brother."

Ristan smiled and nodded, his eyes meeting Savlian's with a nod of thanks before he entered the nursery. He scanned the soothing pastel hues that covered the walls. The sounds of soft gurgles and breathing eased his soul as he moved to the tiny female.

Her soul was fading, but those golden eyes stared up at him with a fighting smile. She'd be a handful when she became a woman, and he knew she would. She'd grow into adulthood, because he refused to consider any other option.

"Sweet girl," he cooed softly as he carefully slipped his hands beneath her and lifted her to snuggle against his chest. "You are your mother's child, all fire shining from within."

Ristan had helped Synthia out more than once, and hell, he'd even almost died for her. Well, what the Mages had done wouldn't have killed him, there were only a few ways to kill something like him, but it had hurt like hell.

He sat in the rocking chair with the babe, his magic creating a glow around her as he poured a little into her small body. She cooed and gurgled, her eyes aglow with a smile that created twin dimples in her cheeks. "Shit, some lad is going to get himself killed for you one day, sweet Kahleena. Go easy on the lads, for your father will think you're his world."

He pulled back on his magic as he heard the door to the nursery open. His eyes rose to meet Adam's as he stepped into the nursery.

"What are you doing here, Adam?" Ristan asked cautiously.

"How is she this morning?" he asked ignoring Ristan's question as his eyes lowered to the babe. "Her color looks better today than it did yesterday."

"She's a fighter like her mother and father."

"There's been no progress with the Tree of Life from our side," Adam said softly as he sat beside Ristan in the rocking chair, his hand briefly lifting to touch the curls on Kahleena's head. He hesitated and his fingers moved away as if he was afraid to touch the fragile child.

"We will figure it out, we have to," Ristan offered, trying to reassure Adam. He waited for him to retort.

"Demon, shit like that you get very far in life?" he asked jokingly.

"I've not hurt her, Adam," he disclosed abruptly, speaking of Olivia as his eyes moved to the Dark Prince. "That should give you some comfort, which we all know you and Synthia can use right now." He'd been able to sense the tension from the first moment the prince had made eye contact and knew what was bothering him. "You should also know I have no plans of giving her up, either."

"I'll always be a part of the Guild, so yeah, I was wondering if she was okay and all. Life is fucked up enough right now. Trying to fit back in and not fuck shit up as I go. Returning hasn't been easy, it's been a crash course from hell and sometimes I wish I could go back to what life was like before I knew who and what I really am. I grew up there, so I know Olivia was probably just doing what she thought was right, like we all used to do. I know she fucked over Alden in the process, and none of us would have done that intentionally. So what you do with her is your business, fuck her, beat, and eat her, that's on you in the end. Just remember that we all would have followed an Elder's orders, and from what I saw, she seemed pretty remorseful about her part in it."

"Maybe, maybe she's a good actress," he mused.

"Are you starting to doubt her guilt, or what her motivations were for helping Cyrus?" he asked with narrowed eyes that reminded Ristan of Synthia. One eyebrow lifted higher than the other, and those soul-grabbing green eyes smiled. It must have been one of the side-effects of being bound to her for so many years as her familiar.

"I don't know," Ristan replied as he cradled the now-sleeping babe in his arms. "Maybe you can help me out. There's a room in the catacombs, it has a door with a single music symbol on it."

"Yes, I know of a room marked like that. There are more symbols on the other side of it, and an ancient harp in that particular room," Adam answered as he stood and moved to pick up Zander, who had just woken up and had a solemn look on his face.

"Do you know why it would haunt her? I have been using dream medallions with her, and every time she sleeps, she goes to that door, and the grief she feels is overwhelming. It's almost like there's something hidden in that room which she's feels guilt over."

"Not something," Ryder said from the doorway as he leaned against it. "That's the room we found a large group of children hiding in after you had been taken out. Synthia heard the sound of their heartbeats and we were able to get them out. Someone went through a lot of trouble to keep them hidden; they were dehydrated, and some were hurt. We figure whoever hid them there is either among the dead, or left to get help and couldn't get back to them. The children haven't been questioned yet since most needed time to heal and rehydrate, and some are pretty frightened of the Fae. From what Synthia tells me of their training at this age, this is their worst nightmare…falling into enemy hands."

"How many kids, and what age?" Ristan asked as his throat tightened with his brother's words.

"I heard there was a lot," Adam added. "Some were very young, just beginning their training at the Guild's school," he supplied. He placed Zander back into his crib and turned around to face the other men.

Ristan stood swiftly and walked to the crib, but Ryder held out his hands for his wee darling. Quickly changing direction, Ristan placed her in her father's hands. His mind was moving faster than it could process as different pieces of the puzzle slid into place inside his mind.

"Something wrong, brother?" Ryder asked tensely, his golden eyes keen with interest as Ristan ran through what he suspected had happened.

"Yeah, I'm an asshole," he growled as he shook his head. "I think I made a miscalculation and I need to fix it. I'll be back if you need me."

Ristan sifted out of the nursery, leaving the men to stare at each other over the heads of the sleeping children.

The room was sumptuous and displayed furnishings and wall hangings she'd only read about in books. The bed was huge, but then again, she suspected that any bed Ristan chose for himself would need to be, to accommodate his height. This room was decorated in black and silver, which reminded her of his beautiful eyes.

She rubbed her temples and wondered if she'd been drugged or if he'd done some sort of spell that had made her black out. The last thing she remembered was being in the bath, then his heated words as he'd pulled her from the sudsy water, and then nothing. She couldn't remember anything after that. She had a massive headache, and the rattle of a chain told her that said she'd once again been securely tethered to a wall.

She tested the chain and then rose to take care of personal needs. She took her time in the bathroom and noticed that the chain had extra length now. Maybe she was gaining his trust? She chanted a charm to make the water dance with her magic; nope, it still didn't work. Perhaps he was testing her? She doubted it, more like he wasn't going to be back very soon, so she had time to stew.

Stew? She smirked; her body was filled with small aches from what he'd done, but there wasn't any real pain left behind from his play, only residual pleasure that made her itch for more. His touch wasn't even painful per se, and if she was honest with herself, she'd liked her time with him.

But even that couldn't stop the guilt of what she'd done at the Guild from percolating in her mind. She stared at her pale reflection in the giant mirror and realized the bathroom was almost an exact replica of the one she'd bathed in before she'd blacked out.

Her face was pale, which made her eyes appear larger, brighter. She didn't look unhealthy, because, for all his fluff and stuff, the guy wasn't exactly starving her to death. Come to think of it, he'd woken something inside her that had been absent before. She'd felt alive on that cross, and no matter how much she wanted to deny it, she couldn't.

A door opened in the other room, and she remained still, unable to confront him because of where her mind had just had gone off to. She turned on the tap and splashed cold water on her face, her eyes lowering to the collar of her jammies, and the lack of red flesh that should have been there from the collar chafing.

She felt him watching her before she turned and found him staring at her, his eyes swirling in an intricate pattern as he slowly looked down her body at the fluffy Hello Kitty pajamas with a soft smirk.

"Hello," he said, and nodded in her direction. "Hungry?"

"That depends, are you going to feed me, or can I feed myself?" she asked, taking in his leather pants hanging low on his hips and Doc Marten boots. He wore a T-shirt that said 'Try Me' on it, and yeah, her body responded as if he had placed some magical spell on her girly bits and pieces that gave him ownership of them.

"You can feed yourself this time," he said softly and turned to leave her standing alone in the bathroom.

In the bedroom, she found a table, small, but big enough to hold quite a spread of food on it. It had various breads, cheeses, fruit, and pastry dishes that made her mouth water with their heady aromas. She wasted no time; she wasn't about to give him a chance to change his mind.

She popped a chunk of bread, followed by a slice of fruit, in her mouth, not caring that she was totally stuffing her face and making an ass out of herself. She would rather have him watch her stuff food in her own mouth than having him doing it for her.

"Slow down, little librarian, I have no intention of doing anything to you, or taking food away," he chuckled as he sat on the bed and with a small gesture, his clothing changed to a simple pair of black silken pants, and nothing else.

She coughed, almost choking on the food that had gone dry in her mouth. He awarded her with a knowing grin, and didn't offer aid, but did nod towards a goblet of wine he'd left on the small table next to the food.

She drank deeply, her eyes holding his over the rim of the metal cup. She pulled the cup away from her lips. The wine lightly coated them as she placed it back on the table. Her eyes were wary, but it that didn't seem to bother him at all.

She was on full alert, his intent still not clear as he watched her eat as if it was her last meal. She slowly set down the bread she'd just picked up, and really looked at him as a thought crossed her mind.

"You're going to kill me, aren't you?" she whispered, as tears welled in her eyes and one slowly slid down her cheek. She straightened her spine and squared her shoulders as dread and uncertainty warred inside of her.

"Tell me about the children behind the door of the music room."

CHAPTER
TWENTY-THREE

Olivia felt a mask slide firmly into place, sealing her emotions behind it. That subtle reminder was enough to bring it all back and her chest hurt with the memories of it all. Her eyes only saw the fighting, the chaos, and the complete destruction of the Guild, her home. Her spine snapped straight and she looked at him with fire in her eyes.

"There are no children in the Guild," she whispered, unable to make it come out as anything else.

Ristan blew out a deep sigh. "That's interesting. My brother was just filling me in about a group of children that were recently relocated to Faery. A lot of children; and those kids had been hidden by someone who thought of others. Someone who wasn't evil, or only thinking of themselves," he finished.

He was lying, he had to be, and she wasn't buying it. She'd seen the inferno that had blazed through the already-devastated Guild. This was just a new strategy, it had to be.

"Go to hell," she cried, her emotions overwhelming her as images of the small faces swam behind her eyes. Her legs threatened to give out, but before they could, he was there, pulling her against him.

"I'm an asshole, but I need to know if it was you," he urged softly, his hands slowly rubbing her back as he walked them both back to the bed.

"I don't believe you," she sobbed, her chest heaved as tears ran freely down her face.

He kissed them away and pushed her hair from her face as he sat on the bed and drew her across his lap. His touch was soothing, and it only made her cry more. Where most men would have run away without a clue of what to do for comforting a hysterical woman, he continued stroking her hair and placing soft kisses on her face.

"Stop it," she cried harder, "I don't deserve this from you! I thought I was doing the right thing, but I messed up. I hid as many of the children as I could, but your people killed them when they burned down the Guild," she expelled a shuddering breath. "I know the children are dead," she whispered.

"No, they're alive. Every child you hid in that room is alive. I wouldn't lie about something like that."

"It's not possible!"

"Yes, it is. The catacombs are still there. My brothers didn't destroy them; they only sealed them to protect them from falling into the wrong hands. According to my brother, Synthia caught the faint sound of heartbeats, and they got the kids out before they sealed the entrance and razed the upper levels."

"I need to see them," she whispered.

"You can't," he replied softly, his eyes turning to steel. "Not yet. Your saving those children doesn't excuse what you did to Alden and me, nor am I fully convinced you are totally innocent. Maybe not by deed, Olivia, but by naiveté you have helped Cyrus to help the Mages, and I need to know what he was after."

"I won't help you hurt the Guild," she warned softly.

"And I don't want to hurt the Guild, either. I need for you to at least trust me on that point." At her skeptical look, he sighed, knowing that he would have to confide in her if he wanted to gain her trust. "I am half Fae, my mother was once a proud Demon Princess and I am the third son of Alazander, the previous Horde King. I am brother to the current one," Ristan said carefully, watching as the color drained from her face. "We are at war, and whether the Guild wants it or not, they are siding with Mages who have slipped into the Guild's ranks and are corrupting it from within. I am not asking you to hurt the Guild; if anything, I am asking you to help the Guild. The true Guild. The members who still believe in what it was originally created to do. Already the Mages are inciting the Humans and the other Guilds for the blood of all Fae in retaliation for the fall of the Spokane Guild."

"But...but the Fae didn't do it," she whispered. "Wait, back up. You're one of the Horde Princes? So I was in the Horde Kingdom?" she squeaked.

"Yes," he said, as her face seemed to become paler.

"So I got a son of the Horde King tortured by monsters, and now I'm your prisoner," she whispered, and her face looked a little green. "Wait, why would a son of the Horde King be in the Guild, unless you were, in fact, spying?" she questioned.

"Keeping a promise to a Witch that nothing bad would happen to her uncle while she helped my brother, the newly-crowned Horde King, try and save both worlds," he explained.

"You were there protecting Alden from the Mages, or the Guild? Was it because he was guilty of betraying the Guild?" She fired off questions until Ristan held up his hands and sat back.

"You need to listen to me. I was there because Synthia had responsibilities in Faery. I told her I'd keep her uncle safe and that nothing would happen to him because of their relationship. Not to mention, he was helping us. We knew the Mages posed a very real threat to Alden and we wanted to be able to get him out if it ever went sour. They've been inside the Guild for a very long time, Olivia. We knew they were working their way into all aspects of the Guild, but until recently, we didn't know how far they had burrowed into the inner workings of the Guilds. The Spokane Guild is not the only one having issues. The New Orleans Guild is running with backup Enforcers because theirs are disappearing and the Fae are, of course, being blamed. A few of the Elders have vanished or been killed. That's why that particular Guild was chosen to be the Guild 'Justin' came from. Believe it or not, the Horde agrees that the Fae should remain in Faery. We can't protect your people from ours in your world, so it's much easier for them and our people if ours just stayed in Faery. Unfortunately, our people have a natural curiosity and an affinity for Humans that makes it next to impossible to keep them in Faery. So, believe it or not, there are rules in place as we attempt to control the worst of them. Either way, the men responsible for the slaughter inside the Guild, those were Mages for the most part and one crazy fucked up God hell-bent on revenge. Was I digging through Guild shit? Fuck yeah, I was. We need the relics of the Fae because they belong to us. They can't even be used properly in your world. We need them to prevent our world from dying, and yours from becoming overwhelmed with the number of beings that will be flooding into it when that happens. That is why I was there. I wasn't there to fuck the Guild; I was there to help it."

"You *can* lie," she whispered. "You said your name was Justin." She paused with her teeth worrying her bottom lip. Her cheeks turned pink and she hissed. "Justin Timberland? You asshole! I can't believe it didn't click before!" she chided and slapped his arm.

"So I did, but it was for a very good cause," he said as he smirked playfully and continued. "I promise you that those kids are fine. Synthia's children, on the other hand…They need us to find those relics and save both worlds."

"Synthia has children?" Olivia asked with a perfect O on her lips that he personally wanted to test with his cock.

"Three; she gave us the first set of triplets in Fae history." He watched as she added the time since Synthia had left the Guild, and came up short. It was no mystery that time moved differently in the worlds, but most couldn't grasp the differences. "Time, of course, moves differently between our worlds. Sometimes slower, while other times faster. Right now the rule of thumb is about a quarter day in Faery to each day in your world. Fae pregnancies are also shorter than Human ones. Her heart still belongs to the Guild, and she has enough to worry about because of the Mages, and her babes being sick," he said softly as he fought the urge to taste her lips.

He watched her eyes narrow, and her teeth worry her bottom lip as she considered his words. If she kept biting that lip, it would end up raw, but fuck if it wasn't hot.

It was a new ballgame and new rules. He knew she could help him, more than that, he wanted her. He knew he could force her into playing his naughty games, but he wanted her to be willing. He didn't have to pretend he didn't want her and build excuses as to why he shouldn't want her.

"So what do you want from me?" Olivia asked with a guarded look as her hands fisted at her sides anxiously.

"Alden told me you have an eidetic or a photographic memory, and I need you to help me find items that once belonged to the Fae. You already helped me find one. You didn't know about it at the time and I can promise you that they will only be used to protect your world from mine. Because if we can't fix this one, both will die; I know, I've seen that future, little Witch, and it wasn't pretty."

"You can't see the future? No one can," she argued.

"No one should be able to, and trust me, it's not fun. I was given sight by Danu, to be able to set our people on the right path to protect our world. Tell me something: If this world dies, where would the monsters as you call us, go?" he asked, his eyes drifting from her eyes to that sexy lip she was nibbling on.

"My world," she whispered after a few silent moments had passed.

"Correct," he said and reached over to detach the chain from the collar. His fingers slid along the collar, changing it from the heavy collar to a delicate golden torque from which the small medallion hung. He watched her eyes widen, and her hand came up to rest on his chest, which sent heat to his belly, unfurling a need that he was doing his best to ignore. "Come with me," he said without waiting for her reply.

He opened a portal and sifted them to Faery, to a gigantic tree. The trunk was swathed in a thick layer of ice and the entire tree looked weak beneath the deep freeze that surrounded it. The portal closed up behind them with a wave of his hand. "This is the Tree of Life; it feeds Faery power, and helps to keep the newly born Fae alive as the world welcomes them. For some time now, it's been unable to accept most of the infants."

"Babies are dying?" she asked, and her lips formed a frown, her eyes deep with unease.

"An entire world is dying because of a grudge. It is dying over a misunderstanding of our ways that festered and got out of control. It has created evil beings that don't try to fight us directly; they prey on the innocent of our kind first," he said and turned to look at the tiny glowing lights. They weren't just lights, they were tiny beings that worked to thaw the tree, but nothing they did was working. "They are trying to kill us in your world, and they are trying to kill us here as well. We aren't speaking of policing and protecting, as the Guild was created to do. We are talking about evil trying to eradicate not just the High Fae, but all of what you would refer to as those from the Otherworld; Vampires, Shifters, Demons, Fauns, all of us."

He knew the moment Olivia figured out what was lighting the tree in the darkness. Her breathing grew shallow; her eyes grew round and then lit up. It was still one of the most beautiful places in Faery, even if it was frozen.

He glamoured a heavy parka on her, as well as other clothing that was more suited for the cold, on both of them before he took her hand and moved them closer to the endless activity of the Fairies. Her pants were leather, which looked a little out of place on her, but he enjoyed the way it hugged her ass, along with the boots that were more fashionable than most winter wear usually was. She giggled softly as the coat curved her tiny frame, and for the first time in what felt like forever, Ristan grinned.

"Those are fairies," she whispered and held out her hand as one flew in close to look at her. It landed innocently in her upturned palm and sat there cross-legged as they studied each other. Ristan grimaced when he realized it was Karenna, a fairy he had the pleasure of knowing intimately. Her breed of Fairy could go from the size of a firefly to a much more compatible size if she chose to. They were also infamous for their love of biting and nipping.

"They are," he said as he gave Karenna a warning with his eyes. She took flight, leaving a trail of glittering dust in her wake which caused Olivia to sputter, then sneeze. Karenna let out an impish giggle as she continued her way back to the others, who kept working.

"This is what the Mages did," he said, pulling his mind back to why he'd brought her here. "This tree feeds magic into Faery, and without it, the world grows weaker with each passing day. More infants will die before we can save it, but I was given visions that were supported by the prophets, that the relics are a large piece of the puzzle to not just stop Faery from dying, but reversing the damage done to this world as well."

"And you think I can help you? Even if I wanted to, those relics would be heavily guarded, probably by Enforcers who have no idea what's really going on. I've done enough damage to the Guild, and even if those children are alive as you say they are, that doesn't excuse what I did," she said softly, her eyes never meeting his as she watched the fairies work on the tree.

Ristan grabbed her hand, knowing he might be pushing her limits on sifting, which bothered him to a certain degree; however the need to show her his world overrode his concern. But those eyes? The way they lit up with the beauty of the Tree, and the tiny Fae? She was in awe, and he had so much more to show her.

He took her to his favorite place in either world. He wondered why he had done something so impulsive, since he'd never brought anyone with him when he came here. Yet it had been the first place that had popped into his mind.

The sky was lit up with deep green and aquamarine colors which mixed with the Fae version of the Northern Lights. A large pool of the bluest water he'd ever found on Earth or Faery covered the ground in a circular pattern, which was fed by a cascading waterfall that enhanced the beauty and serenity of this particular place. Vivid emerald trees stood in the far distance, with the sweet fragrance of newly bloomed flowers scenting the night air.

There was no freezing chill here, so with a flick of his fingers, he removed the heavy coat and decided to replace her outfit with a soft, powder blue baby doll dress, which made her eyes seem darker. He could see her nipples had hardened with the quick change of outfits, and he hoped it was from her wanting to be covered by him, rather than the dress.

She took in the beautiful setting carefully before he saw a small smile tug at the corners of her mouth. There was no way she was immune to the beauty of the land, because even though he'd been here a thousand times, he wasn't.

"Where is this?" she asked as she adjusted the dress for modesty.

"I don't think it's ever been named," Ristan replied, his eyes sweeping over a lush green bush that was covered in pale blue flowers that glowed just enough to illuminate the darkness. He waved his hand and the sky turned to sunset.

"How did you do that? No Fae can control the weather or the world around them," she whispered her eyes on his with wonder.

"I can create illusions, very realistic ones at that. But this isn't me; this place is different," he said, and wondered if he should control more of it for her benefit, but then again, all he'd done was think of it turning to sunset and it had. He'd never understood it, nor did he care to.

He stepped closer to her and smiled. "This is my

place. I have never seen it on any maps," he whispered. "It's full of wondrous things, deadly ones too, but it holds so much to explore and marvel at. I'd die protecting my world," he mused out loud, his body so close to hers that he could smell her unique scent, which seemed to drive him bug fuck crazy.

He reached for her and pulled her against his body. Their clothes disintegrated with a mere thought, and he smiled as she hissed from the sensation it created. He picked her up and the moment her lips touched his out of her own will, he growled.

Fuck it; he wanted her and even if he shouldn't be doing this, he couldn't help it. He glamoured a bed and carried her to it, her hands pulling at his hair as she deepened the kiss. He moaned, her hungry mouth containing and devouring the sound.

His knees hit the bed and he crawled across the mattress without setting her down. He used her weight as he shifted his body beneath hers so she could straddle him, before he finally broke the kiss. Their breathing was labored and heavy; her nipples were hard, and begged to be bitten and teased. His head rested on the pillows as he brought both hands up to where she sat straddled on him. His cock pulsed between her legs, yet he hadn't forced himself inside of her. His hands cupped the heavy weight of her breasts before his thumbs trailed softly over her taut nipples.

She moaned and arched into his touch, her pussy already wet from just their shared contact and kiss. He leaned up, claiming one nipple with his mouth before he flicked his tongue over it. He smiled against it as she groaned loudly and rocked her hips against his throbbing cock. She pushed him down and he smiled up at her, right up until she leaned over to lick his nipple ring and pulled on it with her teeth.

He swore that piece of jewelry shared a nerve with his cock, because it sent fire swirling through his belly, which made his cock hard enough that he could have come right then. He moaned as she carefully explored him, her shyness only adding to how fucking hot this was.

She snuck her tongue out and licked his nipple before her hand found the other and tested it, matching her actions to his response. Once his stomach tightened, and the hiss escaped his lips, she smiled. It wasn't a huge smile, but an innocent one that said she was enjoying being in control, and he knew the feeling.

She lifted her head, taking in the surrounding area, and for the first time noticed that she was on a bed, outside, exposed.

"Nobody knows about this place," he assured her, and her sapphire eyes looked down at him. He rocked his hips, reminding her of what they'd been doing before she'd discovered she was about to rock his cock in full view of nature.

She lowered her mouth and kissed him on the lips, and then deepened it as she pushed her tongue past his. He didn't assist her; instead, he waited for her to take control again. He was in no hurry, and that was a good thing, considering how slow her seduction was.

She pulled back, and Ristan caught movement out of the corner of his eye. A hooded figure stood in the distance, watching them. Ristan glamoured clothing on himself and pushed Olivia aside. He stood and moved quickly toward the hooded figure, but before he could get close to it, the creature vanished.

"What the fuck?" he growled, and spared a glance back to make sure Olivia was safe.

CHAPTER
TWENTY-FOUR

Olivia continued to search through the giant room; this one was definitely masculine and, like the last room she had been imprisoned in, it bore marks showing that it belonged to Ristan. Nothing indicated that it was a guest room of any kind. The room was done in varying hues of charcoal gray, with light blue drapes that framed the single window of the room, which ran from the floor to the ceiling, as well as each end of the wall. She'd already checked the window and found it securely locked. She took note of the deep emerald greenery mixed with snow and pine trees that told her she was either back in the Pacific Northwest, or somewhere in Faery that must have similar scenery.

She'd been pushed into the room without explanation or any clothing, other than a skimpy pair of panties, and left alone for what felt like hours. He'd treated her clumsy seduction as if she'd put ants in his pants and her feelings were a bit hurt as she replayed the scene over and over in her mind. She had no damn business getting busy with him in the first place. Maybe it was best he'd stopped her before she became more attached to him.

She began her search of the room tentatively, enjoying the freedom of not being chained to the wall, even though being locked inside a beautiful room wasn't much better. He at least remembered she was partly Human and had left a table laden with a delicious variety of foods that she'd unfortunately been too unsettled to eat.

Olivia knew she needed to find a way to get away from him; even if he was telling the truth about the children, she wasn't safe. At least, her heart and girly parts weren't, if she stayed around him for much longer—and that was on her and her traitorous bits and pieces.

All of the evidence of what he'd disclosed earlier pointed to him telling her the truth. Then again, all the evidence said Cyrus had been telling the truth as well, and look where that had gotten her. Ristan had brought her back here and left her so quickly that she'd assumed something was wrong, and without him being here to explain himself, her imagination took flight.

Her search of the room had yielded an eclectic assortment of books on the wide shelves, some of which had diagrams that she wasn't sure were really physically possible, and a *Never Mind the Bollocks* Sex Pistols shirt under the bed that still carried his earthy scent. The black pine dresser in the room was void of any clothing or any other personal items, so she drew the shirt over her head to provide some sort of modesty. She continued the search for information— or a way out—for some time, continually knocking on flooring and the walls to check for hollow spots that might lead to a hidden passageway. The Guild was riddled with them, why not here? She could get lucky, find an escape route, and be gone before he even noticed she was missing.

After several hours of exhausting every possibility she could think of to escape, she eyed the bed warily and crawled into it, as she considered her wanton and uncharacteristic behavior with him earlier and the blatant rejection he'd given her. After all of the cautionary tales she'd read as she'd compiled archive after archive about the Fae, she would have thought that she wouldn't have been drawn to a creature like him, not as much as she was anyway. She should be able to resist his charm and raw, sexual appeal. He hadn't even pumped up his Fae powers; this was something she was aware of on a visceral level after that one awful experience in the dungeon. He could have easily taken away any choice from her at any time he wanted. He may have manipulated their encounters, but, for the most part, he allowed her to make the choice, which went against what the Guild taught.

She'd done this to herself; the desire to have him had been overpowering, and she knew she could easily use the excuse of 'traumatic situation', but it was really on her at the end of the day. He hadn't even messed with her mind, as she knew he could have.

The Guild taught them about how the Fae could manipulate their minds, and take away free will, or make your body respond even if you didn't want it to. They were powerful beings of sex, which she knew. So why was she responding to him in ways that were so unnerving and so unlike her?

She'd never had vivid sexual dreams before she'd met 'Justin.' Since the first moment she'd seen him, everything about him had drawn her in. She'd stopped thinking with her brain and had started allowing her hormones to lead her around. He wasn't her happily ever after; shit, he wasn't even Human. He was half-Demon, half-Fae, and all wrong for her. He would end this thing between them the moment she gave him the information he needed, and she would do good to remember that. She pulled the covers up to her chin and closed her eyes, exhausted at all of the different directions her mind was roaming to.

Ristan paced Ryder's office as he considered just what the fuck had happened earlier. It hadn't felt like Danu, but that didn't make him feel any better. At least if it had been her, he'd have known who it was. She would always eventually reveal herself to him. It was part of the mind games she liked to play with him. Whoever it was hadn't done that. Instead, they'd disappeared after watching him with Olivia, and it bothered him. Partly because he had no fucking clue who it had been.

It wasn't Fae, of that he was sure, but what the hell was it? Why had it been there? It was his special place that he'd gone to ever since he'd discovered it by accident when he first learned that he could open portals, and now it was violated as far as he was concerned. He wasn't sure if it was the violation of his favorite place that pissed him off or was it the timing of the intrusion as she'd been sexy as fuck with her innocent seduction.

Fuck, she'd been sexy! A bit clumsy with inexperience, and still, he'd been about to explode from just the anticipation of her sensual assault. Normally that shit didn't send him off the deep end, but she did.

"You keep wearing a hole in my floor like that, and you'll need to fix it," Ryder pointed out as he entered the large study he used as an office.

"You know that place I found the first time I opened a portal?" he asked. Ryder was the only one who he'd ever told about it, in case he had a need for Ristan and couldn't reach him. The telepathic link to his brothers while he was inside that realm was like getting cell phone reception in the middle of the mountains.

"Yes, the one just off of Flora?" Ryder asked as he took his seat and sighed heavily as a frown wrinkled his forehead. "What about it?"

"You know how I told you that I didn't believe anyone else goes there, that every time I go; it's only been me in that place for as far as my senses will reach?"

"Yes," Ryder replied, his eyes finally resting on Ristan's.

"I took her there," he said.

"Who?" Ryder asked, his eyes narrowing slightly, the gold starting to sparkle with mirth. "Olivia?" he questioned.

"Who else? I don't exactly have an entire ward of hostages," Ristan growled. "Anyway," he continued. "Turns out, I wasn't alone with her," he said in a deep, irritated tone.

"Someone else was there?" Ryder countered. "Who was there? Another Fae, perhaps?"

"I don't know!" Ristan snapped.

"Ristan," Ryder warned, as he shook his head.

"Sorry, I didn't catch the face. I only know it was a male. It wore a cloak like what we use for the Elite Guard, yet it had a somewhat different design. The way it moved, though, it was strange. I've never seen anything like it. It was watching us, and I could feel it pulsing with so much power when I approached it, Ryder. It was almost similar to Danu's—or yours, when you let that shit leak—and I only felt curiosity coming from the creature, not malice or danger. I didn't need to even touch it to feel it."

"And you're sure the creature wasn't Fae?"

"I'm sure," Ristan replied as he finally took his seat. "It means I'm wrong about that place, and if there is a breach there, I wonder if that might be one of the places the Mages are gaining access through."

"We've always known that Faery had a few natural portals; Lucian and others of his kind have used them on occasion. Angels have also passed through them into our world, but only those who are fallen. Like Elijah."

"You think it could be one of his people?" Ristan asked as he considered it.

"No," Ryder squashed it quickly, "but I do think our newly discovered half-brother should be watched. He's half-Angel, albeit a fallen one; he's been asking quite a few questions about you and the girl that you brought in with you from the Guild."

"Why the fuck would he be asking about her?" Ristan demanded. It was one thing for him to ask about

Ristan; he was half-Demon in the company of High Fae, which would be an oddity in itself to any outsiders, but Olivia?

"I have our brothers watching him. It could just be curiosity to see how we respond to traitors," Ryder said. "He was present the night we brought you both back, and he would have seen her then. Back to the hooded figure: You think it could be a Mage?"

"No," Ristan said softly as he pulled his mind from why Elijah would want to know about his woman. *His woman?* What the fuck? Why had that even popped into his head? He didn't have one woman, he had many and often. He stood up abruptly and turned to the door, his mind in an uproar at his sudden anger at himself.

He was growing attached to the little Witch, and that wasn't an option. Shit, he'd let her control their play while some sick, twisted fuck watched it! Wait, he'd watched a lot of fucking in his days, so maybe…Nope, he was sick and twisted too.

"Ristan," Ryder called as he opened the door to leave.

"It wasn't Mages; there was no hostility, only curiosity—and something else I can't pinpoint."

"Good," Ryder said as he stood to his full height and stretched. "Zahruk said the party plans are in full gear, and that you managed to stop by and get things set up for them. Are you planning on attending as well? Synthia would miss you and worry if you aren't there, and as you know, she has enough to worry about."

"Wouldn't miss it for the world," he said softly. "Besides, it's a family thing."

"That it is," Ryder replied with a boyish smirk on

his face, which made Ristan breathe easier.

"I'll be there with bells on if it makes Synthia smile," he said in reply. He, of course, would need to figure out what to do with his little captive; the idea of that much time away from her was worrying, but it wouldn't be right for him to be a no-show after helping put the plan to lift Synthia's spirits in motion. He'd also used a very old, very powerful spell to hide his and Olivia's signature trails leading to his home. It wouldn't work to completely hide her from Danu, but it would make it harder to find. He just hoped Danu was too busy with her own concerns, like a wayward, estranged husband, to take too much interest his captive—for the time being.

The Witch in question was fast asleep when Ristan returned. Her hair was mussed and framed her face, which told him she'd tossed and turned as she finally passed out. He'd brought her to his place in the mountains, rather than back to his quarters at Ryder's mansion outside of Spokane, because if she did manage to escape, she couldn't get very far. From this room, she'd only assume she was back in the Pacific Northwest, when, in fact she was deep inside Olympic National Park.

He'd created this safe haven long ago, and no one knew of this place except for a select few of his brothers, because it was his. He loved being able to watch the wildlife that was thick in this part of Washington, which often reminded him how similar the Human and the Fae worlds could be at times.

With a simple flick of his hand, he turned on The Eagles' *Hotel California*, ensuring it was playing low enough that it wouldn't wake the sleeping beauty currently wrapped in a Sex Pistols T-shirt that he must have missed, and who looked too good in it at the moment.

He took a seat on the small sofa, noting that everything in the room was messed with since she'd probably spent most of the afternoon looking for an exit. He leaned his head back and closed his eyes, expelling a deep breath that he hadn't realized he'd been holding.

He didn't think he'd fallen asleep, and he was pretty sure he wasn't in a vision. His sight cleared to reveal Olivia still asleep in the room behind him and before him was a nightmarish place that he never wanted to see again. An imposing being, or man, that was about Ristan's same height, with shoulder length black hair that was only a bit shorter than his own, was sitting on a throne, one that was composed of living souls. His eyes were alight with laughter, as he watched Ristan process the place he'd brought him to.

"What the fuck, Lucian?" Ristan finally asked after he'd seen enough.

Humans who must have sold their souls to him were chained together and moaning as pain overtook them. Some were bleeding from what looked like welts, but Ristan knew enough about Lucian to know he didn't get off on the pain of others. Lucifer did.

"Why the fuck did you bring me here, of all places?"

he asked as Lucian just watched him closely.

"Vlad said you needed me. Was he wrong?" Lucian asked.

"I thought I did, but I have it under control," Ristan lied as he continued to watch the souls behind Lucian. Perhaps asking Vlad to bring Lucian into his problems with Danu wasn't the best idea.

"You're a curious one; you resist feeding from souls the way your brethren do, but why? You're born to devour them, as I am not. I partake in it freely, and you restrain yourself. Does the Demon within scare you?"

"I'm half-Fae; I prefer to fuck for food," Ristan said calmly, unwilling to show any weakness to Lucian. He knew more than he should about Ristan, but he didn't know everything. No one did. That was the way he preferred it to stay.

"You shouldn't hold back what you truly are," he said as his eyes appraised Olivia. "Her soul on the black market would command a very high price," he mused, ignoring Ristan's growl as it sounded. "I could resolve your Goddess issues by taking her off your hands. Problem solved and you wouldn't even owe me," he offered as though he was doing Ristan some kind of favor.

"That's not an option," Ristan snapped. "She's mine."

"You could always join me, and leave your brothers, who smother the potential you have. If you did, she'd be forced to leave you alone, or pay a very steep price," he countered.

"Never," Ristan snorted at his suggestion. "I would never leave Ryder's side."

"That's a pity," he said as he turned his midnight eyes

on Ristan and smiled coldly. "Especially with the Guild calling for blood—any blood, really," he continued. "Fanatical fucks. They wouldn't know a snake if they had one crawling up their asses."

"But you would," Ristan said with narrowed eyes. "You've got something going on; what's your plan?" he asked.

"I have my own Demons, in a manner of speaking, to fight," Lucian said with no emotion on his face. "Women are fickle creatures. Are they not?"

Ristan shook his head at Lucian's sudden switch of topics. "That's a given," he replied easily as his eyes raked over Olivia's sleeping form. "I didn't think you would come here just to talk about women," he added.

"No, I expect you didn't, but that's why I am here. You think I'm not aware of what you need? I believe you are looking for a safe location to contain your mother, and another for your little sexual hunger games with this one, no?" he said with a bored look.

"Yes," Ristan replied, "I could use some help getting my mother to a safe place, where she can't cause trouble. This one I just need for a bit."

"Perhaps when you've finished with this one, you'll find my offer more agreeable," Lucian proposed, and smirked as Ristan's face flushed with anger. "I need a certain box found; my informant tells me it's currently buried under the rubble in the catacombs of what used to be the Spokane Guild. The Guild itself is warded against my kind of Demon, as you know. Not yours, though, which is curious, no? I need that box, and I need it to be sealed when it's delivered to me," he continued.

"Is that so?" he asked. "What's inside the box?"

"Pandora," Lucian said with a wicked glint in his

eyes.

"You expect me to hand you a box with that answer?" Ristan asked.

"I do," Lucian stated. "I expect no questions asked, so please don't bother asking," he remarked as he looked up and smiled coldly at Ristan.

"One question, Lucian, give me that much."

"One, but you need not ask it. I will not use it to harm any Human. It's a gift for a woman, a very fickle one."

"You said it was Pandora's Box, so either she isn't going to like it, or she's as evil as you are."

"Evil? Who says I'm evil, *Demon*? My kind starts out as Humans before we end up as Demons. I didn't choose to become what I am; someone else sent me to hell. Like I said: Women are fickle creatures at best. No, this one deserves everything she gets," he said as an afterthought. He looked as if he was miles away as he said it, and Ristan felt uneasy and a little sorry for whoever had made this man their enemy.

"I'm sure she will get what is coming to her if you're driving the karma bus," he mused.

"She will, but not before I enjoy her company a bit. I also need the archives I was promised by Vlad," he announced as he stood up, dismissing Olivia. He turned and looked at Ristan, his eyes were a dark enough blue to be mistaken for black. "Back to your feeding habits. I can make arrangements at any of my clubs."

"Thanks, but no thanks. I have them under control."

"Sure you do," Lucian said with a tight-lipped smile. "You sure you won't let me take this one off your hands, remove temptation and all," Lucian said, and Ristan narrowed his eyes sharply, and his curiosity was aroused as to why he continued to offer for Olivia.

"She's mine. End of discussion," he warned, and watched as Lucian lifted a dark eyebrow and then shrugged.

"She's trouble, that one," he said giving Ristan his full attention. "I will see what I can arrange for you. In exchange, there is something else I'm looking for. She is a librarian of the Guild, yes?" he waited long enough for Ristan to nod before he continued. "I have it on good information that the Guild has some archives that pertain to a Coven in Salem; one of three powerful covens that existed around the late 1600s. One of the Covens became the Salem Guild. The second one was destroyed in an unfortunate fashion. Then there was a third that disappeared without a trace. Until recently, no one had any idea they might still exist. I need every scrap of information about the third Coven that the Guild has. You do understand that this is time sensitive and I need to have many pieces in place by Samhain. I require this information in my hands well before Beltane."

"Why the hell would you care about a missing group of Witches?" Ristan asked as he watched Lucian's jaw twitch with being questioned and defied at every turn. The guy was leaking raw, electrical current from his pores. He could probably light up the entire state of Washington with his power if he chose to. Ryder had it too, but where Ryder's was from his beast, Lucian's was a mystery that might be better left alone. The guy wasn't what he seemed, that much Ristan could tell.

They knew little to nothing about this man. The most disturbing rumor was that that he'd been sent to hell and had fought off enough of hell's Demons to become the right-hand man of Lucifer himself. There were plenty of other rumors about him, but Ristan knew to never trust rumors. He and his brothers had created and fueled a veritable propaganda machine about Ryder to get him into the Human world and take Adam's place as the Dark Fae Prince, so he was well aware of how to manipulate rumors.

"I'll be taking her back to the catacombs soon enough," Ristan said after a moment of silence had passed, his eyes taking in the impeccable suit Lucian wore. "We'll bring what you're looking for to the Metaline Falls club once she's found it."

Ristan didn't want Lucian entering his dreams, or taking him to visit this place again, period. Lucian nodded and cocked a smile that looked more evil than anything. "See that you do it soon, I have a Witch of my own to torture."

"I have a prior engagement that requires my presence tonight, but after that I should be able to go digging through the Guild's catacombs."

Lucian smirked and closed his eyes for a brief moment. "Your sister in law is going to need my help soon," he announced when he opened his eyes again. "Find everything I am requesting in time and I'll help her, if not, well, who knows, right?" he asked and disappeared before Ristan could answer him. The only thing that remained in the room was his cocky laughter and a cloud of smoke.

Ristan stared at the smoke that remained in the room, and he shook his head. Lucian was a mystery he didn't care to figure out, but he knew the guy was bad news. Not to say his curiosity wasn't piqued at Lucian's parting comment.

CHAPTER TWENTY-FIVE

Olivia awoke to silence. The room was still the exactly the same as it was before she fell asleep, although there was a hint of smoke that seemed a little out of place. Had someone lit a candle or was something on fire? Had she slept through Ristan returning and then leaving again?

She sat up in bed and had just swung her legs over the side when he entered the room, in only a towel. It was slung low on his sexy-as-sin hips, so his firm abs were visible, and her eyes seemed to get stuck on the trail of dark hair that started below his navel, and disappeared under the towel.

Her eyes moved of their own will, up to those perfectly pierced nipples and again, sexy as all get-out. She'd never thought she'd like a male having them pierced, but she'd surprised herself as her tongue had teased those metal rings. The way he'd moaned as she'd licked and pulled against them…shit.

He walked to the large dresser and pulled open the

top drawer, his hair sending tendrils of droplets down his well-defined back as she latched onto one and followed its progress, right up until he dropped his towel. She sucked in air as the droplet traced a loving pattern down his firm backside, but where it continued to, she had no freaking clue. Her eyes had made it as far as his ass and seemed to have gotten stuck there.

"I'll be gone for a while," he said as he turned around, giving her a full frontal view. "I have a party to attend."

"And I'm just supposed to wait around for you?" she asked tartly, realizing she really wasn't in a position to negotiate, but being stuck in a bedroom with nothing to do sounded kind of stupid. She'd needed to be busy, and the last few days she'd been stuck in either a cell or a luxurious set of rooms.

"You don't have a choice in the matter," he said as he slipped on crisp, dark blue jeans. They hung low on his hips, and her fingers itched to pull them back off of him. She somehow managed to pull her eyes from him and looked to the wall, as if it held all the answers she needed. He had to be teasing her; messing with her head. That dresser had been empty when she had searched it earlier.

"When can I see the children?" she whispered, her heart heavy with the question.

"Soon," he said offhandedly. "I promised to be there tonight, and I'm going to be late."

"Good for you," she bit out before she could think better of it. He turned as he buttoned the long, dark shirt he'd chosen and as he walked across the room to the door, he smiled.

"Sassy has always been a major fucking turn-on for me, so keep lipping off and I'm sure I have something to keep those pretty lips busy," he said with a lopsided grin. "I also have a surprise for you, but only if you promise to be good."

"I don't," she growled, taking in his appearance. He was probably going to meet with some female because she sucked at sex. Her seduction had been lame, and she was the first to admit it, but leaving her locked in a room while he went to some other woman? Screw that!

"Don't what?" Ristan asked with a wicked twinkle in his beautiful eyes.

"I am not going to be good while you are out at some stupid party!" she snapped angrily.

"It's not really a party," he stated, turning to look at her with the door halfway open.

She bolted, catching him off guard gaining her the element of surprise. He landed with a thud on thick carpet while she ran past him, through a small hallway, and down a large staircase. She didn't turn to see if he gave chase, and ran until she reached the large double doors that had to lead outside.

She threw them open and gasped. Mountains! The *top* of a freaking mountain range? Was he serious?! She took off into the woods, uncaring that she was only dressed in panties and his T-shirt, or that her feet were bare. The air was crisp, bitingly cold, and the ground was frosted with patches of snow.

She barely heard or sensed the disturbance in the air behind her and swung around, wholly planning to attack him, but was instead tackled to the ground. His body pressed punishingly against hers, and before she could scream at him, his mouth crushed against hers in a kiss that curled her toes. She moaned against it, against him. Her body responded, and that fire he normally created inside of her ignited, and she lost the will to fight against it.

They were on the ground. He was already tugging at his jeans with one hand as he used his other hand to rip the silk panties from her body. The T-shirt seemed to disintegrate. Within seconds, he was inside of her, the only sound was the mingled breathing, and moans from her lips as he fucked her on the top of his mountain, uncaring of anything but the need to be consumed by each other.

They exploded in sync, and she screamed her release, which echoed through the mountain range, telling her exactly how helpless she was here. He'd brought her home, but he'd made damn sure she couldn't escape. Dazedly, she wondered if she was somewhere in the Olympic Mountains, or if she was smack-dab in the middle of the Cascades. She was more of an indoor girl, so she only had a general idea based on what she had read in magazines.

"Fucking hell," he growled as he rocked his hips a few more times, ignoring the biting wind that rustled the yellow and orange leaves as well as his beautifully dark hair. "When I get back, this will continue, Olivia."

She moaned and closed her eyes. She swallowed the sensation of his cock buried to the hilt in her pussy to take her away from the hopelessness she felt. "Do you ever plan to let me go?" she asked, ashamed at her own wanton behavior with someone she should be fighting off.

"If you keep fucking me like this, probably not," he answered quietly before he trailed soft, unexpected soft kisses over her face. "You fit me perfectly," he confessed as she felt him growing hard inside of her again. He repositioned their bodies, picking her up gently, and smiled at her wide-eyed surprise as his cock stretched her.

He was on his knees now, his body easily supporting hers as he slipped his arms between her thighs and spread them far enough that he had full control of her. He started lifting, and then pushed her pussy down onto his engorged cock.

She exploded unexpectedly, without warning, and felt him as he began to feed from her orgasm. Her bones felt like they'd been liquefied and his arms were the only thing that held her in place as her head rolled and landed on his shoulder. The man was sensational, and better than any damn hero had ever been described in her romance books. He continued to feed, the glow from his silver gaze visible through her hair, which had covered her face.

"Come for me again," he growled, the noise louder as the echo filled the empty mountain range.

"I can't," she pleaded, but only received a rumble of masculine laughter as he proved her wrong. This one began as a dull ache that travelled through her body until she began helping him hit the perfect spot that created an explosion that made a dull buzzing noise in her head. She felt him lifting, maneuvering them upwards and moving them both; he refused to release her.

Every step sent him deeper and deeper into her body, with the occasional exit as they hit a wall, which he used to his advantage; he pounded her flesh eagerly. She hadn't even noticed entering the house until he had found that damn wall. When he finally set her down, it was only to push her head down and order her to hold on to her ankles as he gripped her hips from behind her, holding her firmly, keeping her steady. She'd thought him a tight fit inside of her before, but him taking her from behind while she was bent over? He touched places he'd never explored before. He was buried to her womb; it felt raw and erotic as he pounded her like this. Her hands gripped her ankles, as he'd commanded, and with each thrust, she cried out with the impending orgasm.

He stretched and pushed boundaries she'd never imagined pushing until she exploded again, this time collapsing in exhaustion. After some time had passed, she opened her tired eyes to find him redressing, and she had been tucked back into bed. He was devastating in his fresh clothing, or maybe it was sex-induced coma she was about to indulge in that made her think so.

"Now, for that surprise," he said as he moved to the door and closed it behind him, only to open it again a moment later, holding her cat.

"It can't be," she whispered breathlessly as she tried to sit up, only to wince as her lady bits complained at the movement. "How?"

"I told my brothers that she was probably hiding close to the Guild," he admitted. "It was only a matter of figuring out where a lost cat might be hiding. You can have your cat, but there are rules," he stated as he set the cat down to run to her owner. "When we fuck, she's not allowed in the same room."

Olivia lifted her eyes to his as her cat jumped into her waiting arms. A tear slid down her face as she kissed the little scrounge who glared back at him. He smiled at it; he'd marked his territory…a few times…and that cat could smell it on her. Yup, he'd fucked her enough that he'd be sated and not feel hunger or the need to feed at the party. A party he really didn't want to attend, as he hated the idea of leaving her here, alone.

He moved to the door and whispered a warding spell that would seal her in the room again, and looked back to find her cradling the cat as if she was the most delicate babe in the world. His stomach coiled, and he had the strangest urge to walk back and kiss her, but he forced himself out the door.

He needed to stop that shit; this unhealthy attachment to the little poppet was growing with each touch they shared. It wasn't something he allowed to happen because…

"Demon," Danu said softly, her eyes leveling him with an angry stare. "She dies," she finished as coldly as the air around the mansion.

"No, she doesn't. She's my prisoner, and nothing more," he warned, but it sounded hollow even to his own ears. "I need her alive and so do you. She is the key to finding the relics, the ones that can save you and our world. If you so much as touch her, I'll take my fucking time looking for the relics; maybe wait until the last minute, even. It's time you let it go, Danu. You had your fun with me. Let me go."

"You love me," she said, but her eyes sparkled with unease. "Don't you?"

He paused; his eyes jerked to the mansion he'd just

left and back to Danu. He felt that strange coil in his belly and knew this time it had little to do with sex. "Once," he admitted. "Once I thought you my moon. If asked who was more beautiful than the stars I love so much, I'd have said you. You don't love anything, Goddess. You hunger for control, to be worshipped, and it's not the same as love. Could you love someone? No, because you're incapable of that kind of love. So no, Danu, I don't love you."

"You will find them quickly, because if you do not, she'll die a slow painful death, Ristan!" she screamed, her eyes blazing with a mixture of pain and her own fucked-up version of betrayal.

Ristan shook his head and rubbed his temples. "I'll play my part, Danu, but you will back off, and leave me and whoever I am with, alone. That's not up for discussion. Take it or leave it," he stated, and watched as she jerked her chin up and then down as she did a nod, then expelled an angry growl.

She vanished before he could say anything more, and he rubbed his temples again as one hell of a headache started to set in. She'd been conniving and calculating in her schemes, uncaring of the collateral damage, and he'd been too naïve at the time as she began promising him the world. Nothing more than a small boy who'd thought himself blessed in the presence of a beautiful woman.

But the games began, and over time he'd started seeing through it, only to find her to be one jealous ass bitch that was lethal. Sure, he'd given her what she needed, and he'd taken what he needed as well. It wasn't enough, though. Eventually it became almost tedious to serve her needs, knowing she'd take anyone he got close to.

He dismissed the Goddess from his mind and opened a portal into the Horde Kingdom, and sifted to the pavilion which had once housed the Horde King's concubines. It was used now as more of a refuge for those who had wanted to stay within the safety it offered.

It had been the perfect place for the celebration, and earlier he'd created an illusion of the mansion Ryder had built outside of Spokane when he'd been assumed to be the Dark Prince. It was an exact replica, although the new one had been redone with more features to withstand Mages. No longer was it just a charming mansion that had been built to impress the Humans, but an impenetrable place for his brothers to resume their duties to protect their people and search for the relics.

He tilted his head as he listened on the mental path he shared with his brothers as they announced that the princess and princes were in route to the celebration. He smiled as the earthy scent of mistletoe and the rich aroma of hot chocolate teased his nose.

She'd love this. Knowing the Blood Princess—or, actually, the new Goddess of Faery—as he did, he knew she'd be able to forget what was coming, if even for a little bit. He flicked his fingers gently and raised his eyes to watch as the snow began to fall on the floor of the pavilion. What was the Winter Solstice—or—Christmas without snow?

CHAPTER TWENTY-SIX

As he reflected back on the events that unfolded over the past day and a half in Faery, he had to admit that the party hadn't been the strangest he had ever been to, but the vision he'd been unwillingly sucked into had definitely been a first for him. He didn't know what to think about the future he'd seen with Synthia, or the fact that it wasn't in the distant future, but something that would come to pass right away. There had been clues in the vision, small things that he'd seen that added up to what they were supposed to do. Synthia had seemed excited, and he'd listened to her explain what she'd interpreted from it, but he knew it was never that simple. It turned out that he had at least been right about that.

The vision supplied hope that there was a way to unfreeze the tree, and they would need his help working through the logistics on getting all of the people of Faery to that tree, and quickly. He'd been busy since then trying to fulfil his role, and throughout that time, he'd been unable to stay away from the little redhead, sifting back periodically throughout the long day to leave her a few of his favorite T-shirts, food and to make sure she was safe and that Danu hadn't paid Olivia a visit while he'd been busy.

His little run-in with the Goddess while he'd been in Faery had been less than pleasant on his end. Having Synthia call them out on their discord was a new low for him. As if he would allow his feelings for that she-bitch to interfere with the task. Not when so much rode on it, including the lives of his brother's children. No, only the Goddess herself would manipulate events and interfere with that kind of play if it suited her.

It was a relief that clues in the vision had been right about what needed to be done to set events in motion and the Tree had been unfrozen. For now, his niece and nephews were safe; however, until the remaining relics were found, this was just a temporary state and he wondered what else the Mages would think of to throw at them that would destroy the Fae—or Faery itself.

He paced another length of the living room before he stopped as he heard the soft music playing from upstairs. So his little poppet was awake and she'd found the Ipod and docking station he'd left for her. He smiled, but it was small as his mind grappled with what would need to happen next to save his family and Faery from the evil minds of the Mages. He was going to need the librarian's help, and he was going to have to woo her to their side somehow.

Before he left Faery, he had formulated a plan with Vlad and Adam that he hoped would convince her to help, and now there was nothing to do but wait for their arrival. He slumped down on the couch to wait as The Fray's *Run* played from above.

She had decent taste in music, considering how sheltered she'd been inside the Guild. His fingers tapped to the beat as he waited for his cousin, and when the knock sounded at the door, he smiled.

He stood and moved to the door, then opened it, knowing who would be there, but getting a little more than he'd expected.

"Are you going to invite me in?" Vlad asked as he smiled from the other side of the threshold.

"No," Ristan said and moved away from the door as Vlad moved into the room. "Does that shit not get old?"

"The Dracula theme doesn't," Vlad said as he jerked his head and some of his minions moved into the room with file boxes. "There are too many archives to bring out at once, and Adrian luckily had an idea of where some of the older ones were located. Might be easier to just take the librarian back there and see what she can pull out."

"How'd you even begin to narrow it down?" Ristan asked as he sat back down on the couch and waved his hand to glamour a large table for the boxes.

"Call it an educated guess," Vlad mused as he sat in one of the large leather wingback chairs. Ristan watched as both Adrian and Adam walked in, carrying a variety of different sized boxes and placed them on the table. Adrian nodded a firm hello, and Adam sat on the couch, his eyes on the boxes as if he wasn't sure about handing them over.

The living room they were unloading the boxes into was masculine and had a large hanging chandelier that had been crafted from antlers, along with high ceilings for a charming country look. Not that he'd selected it, but it served his purpose just fine. He had only used this place a few times over the years and the country living magazine look kind of worked for him.

He'd decided on more of a natural setting, and thought he'd managed the look well enough. One of the walls was finished to look like a rock face, which made it look rugged, and the bubbling fountain that was created where the kitchen would have been, had he a need for one, was soothing. He had chosen a warm crème color for the remaining walls. Deep brown leather sofas and large leather wingback chairs finished the room and made it feel more welcoming.

"I spoke to Lucian," Vlad said, pulling him back to the task at hand.

"And?"

Vlad crooked his finger and a female walked into the house carrying yet another box, but this one was looked ancient and had weird symbols that looked like runes carved into the wooden sides.

"What kind of runes are those?" Ristan inquired, his curiosity piqued at the hand-chiseled symbols in the box. They weren't like any he'd seen before, and he couldn't read them.

"Don't ask," Vlad said as he accepted the box and thanked the girl who smiled proudly at his acknowledgment, showing off twin fangs. "We couldn't find the key for it in the vault. It's warded by something darker than I've ever seen, and I'm pretty sure those runes are deadly. I don't care why he wants it, or what it's for, just so long as it doesn't come back to bite us on the ass."

"Something has to be wrong with this. We have no idea what it is, or why he wants it, but we plan to hand it over to the guy who basically took over hell, and you think this is a good idea?" Ristan mused cautiously, knowing he'd asked himself the same question when Lucian had first requested it.

They both eyed the box and shook their heads before Vlad changed the subject. He pointed at a smaller box; one that Ristan had seen many just like it at the Guild.

"That one has the files that look like they could lead to one of the relics in a location close to here; I think some of the pages are missing, though. I'm sure you can sort it out, or not," Vlad said with a tilt of his head as something caught his eye. "Is she supposed to be leaving?"

Everyone in the room turned and watched as Olivia, who had been trying to slink down the stairs and out the back way, turned to look at the room full of people. Ristan smiled and shook his head at her attire of his old Ramones T-shirt pulled down over her skimpy panties. It hadn't taken her very long to figure out that he'd disabled the wards sealing her into the bedroom. "This is Olivia," he said as he moved to her and held out his hand for hers, the silent warning clear in his eyes. He glamoured one of his fresh black Bauhaus T-shirts on her, along with a pair of jeans and white Keds, making her look even younger. "My guest, I guess you could say."

"I don't think they call kidnapping and holding someone hostage a *guest*," she snapped with a fire in her eyes that made his cock respond.

"Well, drinks and conversation didn't work out so well for us before, so we will have to make do now won't we, Olivia?" he taunted wickedly and she blushed furiously at the reminder of what she'd done to get herself in this situation.

"It's my pleasure," Vlad interrupted with his eyes on the little Witch who had yet to accept Ristan's outstretched hand.

"And you would be?" she asked, ignoring the hand as she moved to sit on the coach, only to stop as her eyes moved over the archive boxes. "How did you get those?"

Her eyes moved from the box to Adam and then Adrian before she gasped and covered her mouth with her hand. Ristan watched her as she dropped her hand and shook her head.

"I went to your funeral," she said softly, her eyes misting with tears until she caught the glimpse of fangs in his mouth as he started to respond. "Not you too! Is anyone from the Guild actually what they used to be? This is crazy! I feel like Alice when she fell down the damn rabbit hole."

"Some, I'm sure," Adrian said as he scratched his head and gave a quick look at Adam. "Larissa was, and she really did die."

"I liked Larissa, she was smart and nice to us when she dropped off your coven's assignment files," she said as a rush of emotion ran through her. Her eyes slid to Vlad and back to Adrian with understanding dawning on who Vlad was; she was quick-witted. She also could put two and two together and come out with the correct answer.

Adam looked up and then away from them as he concentrated on the files, unwilling to speak of his dead lover. He indicated the files, quickly changing the topic. "You know these files, Olivia. We need your help and we are here to help you understand what is going on and to get you to see the truth of it all. As you can see, I am Fae. One hundred percent Dark Fae; I am also the Dark Prince," he said and held his hands up when she started to interrupt him. "Let me finish," he said softly, as if trying to remain calm, which considering he was newly transitioned, wasn't always an easy feat. "I didn't know what I was, not any more than Synthia knew what she was. It wasn't malicious on our part to hurt the Guild or betray it in any way. We can't help what we are, no more than you can. I know you feared that the children were hurt because I know how much they mean to you. They made it out alive, as Ristan has already told you. Alden made it out too; he and the children are all safe and well cared for right now."

"How do I know it's the truth? I thought he was dead," she pointed at Adrian and shook her head. "Nothing makes sense anymore, and I don't know who to trust." Her eyes moved to Ristan and then to Adrian. "Tell me about the children and how they escaped."

"We got them out, but some were badly dehydrated and in need of medical care. They were a little dirty and scared, but other than that, you saved them, and for that we thank you," Adam said softly, and Adrian agreed.

She nodded grimly and her eyes lingered on the files for only a second before landing on the wooden box.

"That is very dangerous," she whispered as she stepped back away from it, which only made Ristan more interested in the contents.

"Do you know what's inside of it?" Her eyes moved to Vlad as he spoke.

"No, but I know it was in the Guild vault and I can also tell you what the runes etched on it mean."

"You can read those?" Adrian asked as his turquoise eyes swung to Vlad and then back to Olivia with a curious glance.

"It says: *Stupid-ass-people-shouldn't-touch-evil-things-they-cannot-read!* Did you not notice the dark magic that it pulses with? Because that right there should have told you to leave it alone, and how the hell did you get into the vault?" she demanded as she inched back from the box.

"It's not pulsing anything," Adam said as he reached up and touched it, much to Olivia's dismay.

"Don't touch it!" she shouted and expelled a shuddering breath as everyone turned to look at her.

"What's it feel like, Olivia?" Ristan asked, his heart pounding from the terrified look in her eyes.

"Like evil, pure, unadulterated evil," she admitted and stepped closer to Ristan for protection without realizing it. Everyone else in the room, however, did.

No one said anything as they waited for Olivia to speak.

"You can't feel it?" she asked, her eyes widening as gooseflesh broke out upon her naked arms. "It's bad, and no one should touch it with bare hands. The Elders said it's cursed, or something to that effect. It was in the vault and heavily warded for a reason; it needs to go back if the vault is still intact. The Elders placed it there to ensure it never fell in the wrong hands," she uttered, and inhaled a shaky breath before she continued. "That box is bad news; even the runes speak of a serious curse."

"I feel nothing from the box," Ristan said with eyes narrowed on her.

She stepped a little closer until their bare arms skimmed, and he paused at her nervous energy and the overwhelming fear she was feeling. He looked at the box again and frowned at the idea of handing it over to Lucian, but they'd made a deal with him already and he wasn't the type to just let it go.

"So, getting back on subject," Adam said as his eyes moved to the boxes of archive files and pointed at them. "Those are missing pages, and I know the Guild didn't keep the old archives together. I spoke to Alden about some of the protocols, and as you can see, we started going through them only to find he was right. So, where would the other pages be?" Adam asked, and smiled softly. "Come on, Librarian; help us like you used to do in old times. Help us prevent the worlds from colliding and save Human lives, because believe it or not, we still care about what happens to them."

"Is that why you saved the boy? Because you care about Humans? Or was there another motive for what you did?" she asked, turning her eyes to Ristan and leveling him with a knowing look.

"I saved him because it's against the Horde King's rules to kill children. The boy was innocent and he would have suffered horribly at the hands of the Bás Mall. His parents would wonder about him for the rest of their lives because that creature wouldn't have left anything for them to find. No parent deserves to go through that," Ristan said softly as he moved her to the couch so he would be close enough to feel her mood.

She was edging towards surrender, yet she still didn't trust them, and with good reason. She'd been raised to fear them, to fight against them even if she was doing so from the library. He understood the fear, yet so much depended on her helping them.

"Adam," Ristan said and watched as the Dark Prince turned to look at him with inhuman eyes and brands that pulsed from the power he was still learning to harness and control. Well, shit, that wasn't a good sign. "Reel it in," he said, hoping the kid could manage it. They all turned to look at him and Olivia let out a yelp of surprise as she watched Adam struggle against his form, to hold his glamoured Human image. "Tell Olivia what will happen to Synthia's children and the entire realm of Faery if we can't find our relics in time."

"They'll die, all of them. That includes Synthia's children, most of the Fae, and when the remaining Fae abandon Faery for Tèrra, then we can include the Human race as well. As you can see from how I currently look, I am Fae and I can't lie anymore which can sometimes suck as I haven't quite gotten the hang of how to play Fae word games. So once again I ask you, Olivia, from an Enforcer to Librarian of the Guild, help us save both worlds. Those who breached the Guild were not members of it; they're who we are fighting against. As of right now we must consider the fact that none of the Guilds are safe and have most likely been infiltrated, as ours was, by an enemy of both the Guild and Fae. Help us destroy the fuckers who hurt our own," he implored. "Help us find them so we can eliminate them and make sure that they never do to someone else's home what they did to ours."

"Said like a true prince," Vlad said from where he'd watched the entire speech with a smirk. "I have to deliver something to Ryder, but after that, if you need me, Ristan, you know where to find me."

Olivia watched the vampires, including Adrian, walk out. She turned first to Adam, and shook her head before answering him.

"Take me to the catacombs. I'll help however I can, but I won't do anything to compromise any other Guild," she said as she expelled a long shaky breath before continuing. "I can't just sit around and do nothing," she said. "Not when those monsters could be already planning to hit another Guild."

"Guess we're going on a field trip," Adam said as he smiled at Olivia.

CHAPTER
TWENTY-SEVEN

The catacombs were, in fact, whole and preserved, just as he'd told her. They walked together down one of the many tunnels that led to cavernous pathways that she knew like the back of her hand. She would pause occasionally, peering at the little knots that had been carved into the stone walls.

It was the perfect chance for her to escape, and she was sure the Demon knew it as well. She'd passed by several closed doors that hid old relics behind them, all of which held a great amount of power, but none that would do Faery a lick of good.

She could lead them down one of the many paths with traps, which the Elders had set after they'd finished building this Guild, but if what Ristan and Adam said was true, she needed to help them. Adam was most definitely Fae, and she knew enough to know that he couldn't lie.

Growing up in the Guild, it had been explained often enough why the Guilds had been created and oftentimes the Elders would ask them to imagine a world without the Guild policing the Fae. Total chaos; the Humans would always be on the losing end.

She stopped again and ran her finger over the cold stone before she turned back to Ristan and caught her breath as his masculine scent teased her senses.

His mouth quirked into a knowing smile and his hand lifted to cup her cheek, uncaring that Adam stood not more than a few feet away from them. His eyes swirled with that marked Fae glow, and then he dropped his hand as if he remembered they were not alone. She cleared her throat nervously.

"I can't really make out some of the smaller glyphs. I'd need my reading glasses to be able to see them, and in the dark it would still be iffy. I actually would do a lot better if I still had my contacts," she muttered embarrassedly.

"A Witch that needs reading glasses," Adam quipped, amused by her words. "Didn't know Witches needed reading specs," he laughed.

"Yeah, well, it's just one more reason why I didn't make the cut to Enforcer," she grumbled and Adam looked like he wished he could take his words back. Ristan stopped her and gently placed a thumb over each of her now closed eyelids, pushing a small amount of power through her eyes, adjusting the shape.

"You still have to wear those glasses in bed if I request my librarian back," he whispered in her ear as his lips brushed over it before removing his thumbs from her eyes. She blinked and narrowed her gaze on the glyphs. She barely contained her little sob of glee as she found she could clearly see the tiny markings.

She gasped, her hands moving to her eyes as she rubbed them just to be sure it wasn't her imagination.

"How did you do that?" she whispered as she looked at the markings, first standing at a distance before moving up closer.

"Magic," he said and wasn't prepared when she threw herself at him and wrapped her arms around him.

"Thank you!" she squealed, and then noticed that Adam was watching them. She self-consciously backed away from him, but couldn't hide the smile that remained plastered to her face. She bit her bottom lip to hide the smile and got back to the matter that they'd been discussing. "It's not far from here, but the path is going to get a little slippery. There's water on the stones from one of the city's main water lines that has been leaking into the catacombs on and off for years." She whispered, as if she was afraid she'd be overheard.

"Lead the way, I'm enjoying the scenery," Ristan said with a seductive tone. His eyes lowered slowly, sending heat swirling in her belly as her pussy flooded with need. His eyes settled on her sex, which was covered by the jeans, and then he turned to look for Adam, who had sifted out.

"Where did he go?" she asked as her head moved to look further down the dark corridor, past where the small flashlights they carried could light the way.

"He's newly Transitioned, and you smell like you need to be fucked," he said with a voice filled with gravel. "He needs to feed often and I'm not ready to share you," he finished as he stepped closer, forcing her against the wall.

"What are you doing?" she whispered as she

looked up into his eyes. His mouth hovered above hers. Confusion mingled with desire, and that created a soaking mess in her panties, while fear and uncertainty created an ache in her chest.

It was too much. *He* was too much. This emotional overload was entirely his fault! She shouldn't be here with him, and yet she wanted his sexy lips to move the last inch and press against hers. She wanted her daydream fantasy of him fucking her in the catacombs to come true, and that was so bad.

She absently licked her lips and knew the moment he'd seen her submission because his mouth crushed against hers. They both moaned together as his hands lowered to her hips and picked her up until her legs were wrapped around him, and he ground that massive cock against her damp opening.

They were so wrapped up in each other that they hadn't realized Adam had come back until he coughed and their senses slowly came back. She was swollen with need, and wanted to growl for the ex-Enforcer to get lost so that she could live out this fantasy, but luckily she held her tongue and released her legs as she was slowly set on the ground again.

"Unless you two plan to invite me, I think we should get what we came for," he said from behind them.

Olivia felt Ristan tense, and his eyes glowed with a shimmer of silver that reminded her of what he truly was. It still amazed her that she didn't feel any unease or panic with the knowledge she was being taken by a Demon. No, at the moment, she wanted him to make Adam leave so they could pick up where they'd just left off.

He smiled against her mouth as he claimed it once more, and then whispered against her ear. "I'll make that fantasy of yours come true, pretty girl," he promised.

She gasped and looked up at him in surprise, but refused to ask him how he knew of her daydreams, but then he seemed to know an awful lot about her. Like her books, the ones that had been in her home office. He'd also been in her apartment, but how many times?

She tried to gain her balance, only to have her knees threaten to not hold her weight, which Ristan hid from Adam as he held her up and smiled down at her from his impressive height. His hands skimmed her waist until she stepped closer to his body, and turned to continue down the passageway and away from him.

She was so occupied with thoughts of her body's reaction, as well as her overwhelming emotions for him, that she forgot about the slick walkway and almost fell flat on her ass. Ristan caught her easily and instead of just helping her to stand; he easily picked her up and carried her over the slippery path. She struggled against his hold at first, but it was futile and he only tightened his arms around her.

"Stop fighting me," he warned playfully as he swatted her bottom and walked deftly on, sure-footed through the slimy, water-covered stone floor of the catacombs.

"I can walk," she fumed.

How freaking embarrassing? He was carrying her like she was an infant. The indignation of it burned her cheeks while her body burned from his touch.

"I can't give you directions like this," she continued, trying to get down before she ended up doing something stupid being this close to him. Like turning her head and smelling his unique scent that fucked with her senses even now. It was like he had some sort of aphrodisiac cologne on that had a direct link to her ovaries.

"You can," he said softly as his hands tightened around her body protectively.

"I'd rather walk," she continued.

"I'd rather be buried in your sweet flower," he mused in a hoarse voice. "I can send Adam away and I can make it happen," he warned. "My balls are starting to resemble Smurfs, so hold still or I won't be responsible for my inability to resist fucking you."

She swallowed and barely managed to hide the smile that formed on her lips at knowing he wasn't immune to her body, just as she wasn't to his. She wasn't sure she should be so excited at having left his balls blue, but she was. It was that simple. He wanted her, and she was beginning to think that either he was having the same issue as she was with being unable to stop the fire between them, or he was just having fun at her expense.

She pointed to the far wall on the left and he moved in that direction until she was able to place her hand on the wall, which would help her read the slightly raised bumps that had been left there by the builders as directions for whoever used the catacombs.

According to some of the things she'd dug through during her tenure as a librarian, this passage had once belonged to one of the original covens and had been abandoned around the turn of the nineteenth century. The Guild had decided that the intertwining catacombs of this passage made it the best place to house anything that the Covens or the Guild wanted to hide because they thought it would confuse any enemies. They'd never even considered the Guild falling from within.

They'd never considered that they could be harboring something like Synthia or Adam, or that one of their own would switch sides. War was ugly, though, and as they made their way through the passage, Ristan explained a little more about why Synthia had been at the Guild. Why Adam had joined her was a little more confusing.

Cyrus, however, was a Mage, or he had been turned to the Mages' side. How they'd done it was unknown, and it was irrelevant now. She was finally placed on her feet as the flooring became dryer, and she was finally able to think past his touch as they neared the music room, as the kids had often called it.

She stopped cold in her tracks as that night's event replayed in her mind, and her emotions warred with what she'd assumed had happened. Her first fight and actual kill had happened that night, and so had the days of torture for the man who stood beside her. His hand trailed up her arm and she allowed him in, to feel the warring emotions of guilt, betrayal, and confusion. How it felt to play her part, unwillingly. She allowed him to feel her horror at being asked to betray him and Alden. Then she remembered the coldblooded murder of the child that happened before her eyes and shut it all off. Like a switch, she closed off the emotions and turned to look at him as she tried to fight the tears that threatened to spill from her eyes.

"There's no one in that room anymore," Ristan said softly, but to show her he had been telling the truth, he pushed the door open.

She swallowed and moved forward. Her heart pounded as she replayed in her mind everything that had once been in the room. There was nothing out of place. Everything was exactly as it was before she had hidden the children there. There were no small lifeless bodies littered upon the floor, and the only blood was minuscule, from where one or two of the wounded had been.

Her mind processed the remaining items in the room, and then she turned to Ristan. She shook her head in confusion, but it was quickly replaced with hope.

"You got them out," she whispered brokenly before the heavy sob in her chest exploded and she cried openly with relief.

Ristan was at a loss for what to do, but gently pulled her to his chest and held her as she cried with relief washing through her as she absorbed the truth of what he'd already told her. Those children were alive because she'd fought for them. This tiny slip of a woman had fought against men to save children from being slaughtered, and that gave her bonus points in his score book.

"They're alive, and they have you to thank for that," he said as he kissed the top of her head and held her away from his body so he could look down at her. "Now, we're on a time crunch," he informed her. "Where are the missing pages to the files that were in the boxes?"

"Down a few more corridors and then down to the bottom floor of the catacombs," she said. "Basically, we're going to the pits of this place, where they used to do sacrifices to Hecate," she said with a shiver in her voice.

Ristan smiled as her bottom lip trembled and had to fight the urge to nip it before he ended up making a scene in front of the silently brooding Adam, who watched them still.

"And the box? Do you know where the key to it is?" he continued.

"I think the box and the key were separated, and I've no idea of where it would be. I just know that it is pure evil and Gods help us if it falls into the wrong hands," she said before she wiped at her eyes and led them out of the room and towards the darkened staircase that led to the deepest part of the catacombs.

CHAPTER
TWENTY-EIGHT

It was at least a mile or more before the path leveled out and no longer descended. Ristan whispered a spell that lit the huge wooden torches that were affixed high in the stone walls, lighting the entire wide, round room that had an altar in the middle of it. Ristan paused as he took in the handwritten warning runes, which had been carved into the stone columns that ringed the room.

"This wasn't just used for sacrifices, was it?" he asked as Adam followed his lead and took in the runes. Those were dark runes, once used to summoned beings and creatures that had no business being here.

"I don't know," she admitted. "I've been down here many times; however, each time I was allowed here, I was escorted by an Elder. They never spoke about the runes and they always said it wasn't safe to come alone. Some of us thought that it may be haunted."

"Haunted?" Adam asked, his eyes moved around the room and Ristan felt a twinge of regret. He'd lost

Larissa, and she'd come back as a ghost for one night with him. The kid had been through hell, and while he felt for him, he also knew that everything had a reason for happening.

"At least that's what librarians used to think but I don't know if it was true for sure," she replied as she moved to one side of the room and pushed on a stone that made a large creaking noise. Dust exploded from the wall, and as she pushed, another room was revealed.

"A secret passageway?" Ristan asked with a childish smirk.

"They're all over this place," she said with an impish grin. "You could literally hide down here forever if you had food and water."

"The Witches who first lived here created a den, one that no Demons from any plane could enter," Adam said, citing the teachings of the Guild. "It's said that this place is blessed by Hecate, and that altar was created from stones that came out of her own gardens. In the Witch community, the stones are sacred, but blessed stones are more so. These ones with the runes, I can't read them and neither could Synthia. We were taught about them, though, since it was part of our history when we were learning. I'm surprised with how old you are, that you never learned to decipher them." Ristan shot Adam an annoyed glance.

"You need to practice our teachings a bit more, little prince, if that is what you think. There are many different types of runes in this world as well as in Faery. I only learned what I needed to, and those are not from my world. I did, however, learn to read the runes of the Vikings, mostly because those fuckers loved to party," he said with a wicked smirk. "Dristan is fascinated by their study, and Ryder had a love of them, as well; he even used some on the fountain outside of the mansion. Even some inside," he admitted.

"How'd he know which runes he was using?" Olivia asked, her eyes narrowed as they adjusted to the dimly lit passageway.

"He's Ryder; we don't ask him how he knows anything," Ristan answered dismissively and took the lead. He had pulled a torch from the wall so that Olivia wouldn't be walking in blindly, as he and Adam could see as well in the dark as they could in the light.

He was starting to trust her, but too many things had happened, and at the end of the day, they were on opposing sides in a war. She'd saved those kids when she could have just run. If she'd run, he still would have tracked her down to the ends of the earth, but she hadn't.

Instead, she'd sacrificed her own freedom to ensure others had survived. His feelings about his torture hadn't eased, but his feelings about her part in it were.

He continued down the narrow passageway, noting that whoever the hell had built this hadn't taken into account that not everyone was the same size. Occasionally his head would almost touch the low stone ceiling and he would have to crouch down a little further. Eventually, they walked into an open room, and Ristan felt his skin crawl with the hundreds of Human skulls that littered the shelves that had been carved into the walls. And from the looks of it, they'd been placed there as a warning.

"What the fuck," he said, and heard Adam grunt behind him.

"Those would be the sacrifices," Adam said as he moved past him and smiled as he pointed to an exquisitely carved wooden casket. "Meet Jane Doe, unknown female who was left whole. The only one, though. Someone took some time preserving her and creating this beautiful box to entomb her in. It has some sort of preservation charm on it; otherwise the wood would have disintegrated long ago."

"And you guys keep saying we're fucked up?" Ristan mused as he shook his head.

"Hey, wasn't like *we* did it," Adam said and winked at Olivia. "I found her when I was fairly young," Adam explained. "Me, Synthia, and Adrian wanted to scare Larissa. Since it was close to our exams to see who would be finalized and where we would be placed inside the Guild, we wanted to celebrate. No one knew where they would be sent off to, and we could've easily been separated. I bet Larissa that she was too chicken-shit to come down here, and she surprised the crap out of me when she took me up on the dare."

They listened to Adam as he spoke, and Ristan smiled; it was the first time he'd really spoken of his fiancée since she'd been murdered.

"So Synthia, being Syn, decided that we all had to come down together," he said, lost in the memory. "No man left behind, and all that. Anyway," he laughed. "We all came down here, and somehow Adrian had stolen a few bottles of Alden's scotch, and we'd been drinking pretty heavily, and God bless Adrian's moronic ass, he started running down this hallway because it had been left open. We'd just taken a tour of this place earlier in the week, but we hadn't been shown this section.

We ended up following Adrian until we found her. The runes say she was the beloved of whoever inscribed it. However, if you look at this carving," he said as he bent down a little and carefully wiped away some dust. "She was sacrificed to save her coven from evil. Or something to that effect," he finished and turned on his haunches to look up at Ristan. "At least that's the legend that Alden told us when he busted us down here, and made us promise to never sneak down here again after that," he recalled.

"That is the legend; there's a lot more to it than that, all of it contradictory and none of it really makes sense, although many have tried to figure it out over the years. We know that animals were typically sacrificed to Hecate," Olivia said hesitantly, but at Ristan's encouraging nod she continued. "However, in the old days, they did use black magic in some rites, which could include Human sacrifices. But Hecate wouldn't have welcomed it; she prefers the outcasts and animals. There are some ancient tomes that say if a Witch sacrificed her powers to give Hecate strength, she could be reborn. With dark magic, all bets are off when it comes to the actual reason she would have been sacrificed. There are also runes marking her casket that describe several curses. It could be that she was the one who had used black magic, and they wanted her to not be rebirthed again. Or, sometimes those who are murdered are considered too damaged in mind and soul to come back, so a curse could be placed on them to prevent it," Olivia said, as she caught the hint of melancholy on Adam's face. "It's hard to say what really happened here without something to back it up. I can say for sure that she is cursed, but not why. It also has a section that someone scratched out, and it's not certain who would have done it. Maybe kids who found it or maybe someone from her own time period who tried to remove a certain set of runes," she explained.

"Murdered ones should be given the right of rebirth too," Adam growled.

"Larissa was a great girl," Olivia said gently, her hand touched Adam's shoulder lightly before she stepped back and pointed to the casket. "I am not sure if that is what happened to her. Those runes," she pointed to the small ones that wrapped around the casket. "Those say she wasn't sacrifice per se, she took her own life to protect her coven. Adam, her remains are not the only ones intact," she said softly as she moved deeper into the next room without waiting to see if they would follow her.

She waited for the torches and the men before she pushed open the heavy wooden doors and pointed. "Same runes are on those ones, and yes, they all seem to have the same preservation charm on them. All of them are Jane Does. Well, most say unknown female, except one. Her name isn't legible, though. The only thing you can read is my beloved and a single letter M. If you look at these," she pointed to nine caskets, some more elegant than others, but each crafted with love. "They all say the same thing, except the runes on this one. This one has a divided mark, as if she knew she would die and tried to escape being reborn. We do know that in the old times, if a Witch knew she would sacrifice her life, or would die soon, they would create their own caskets. Each of these runes signifies something she wanted but couldn't have in the life she lost. Say children, or a husband. Love was normally a huge one back then because being able to trust a man was harder back then, back when Witches had to hide what they were and couldn't share it with anyone not of their coven. So if you look here," she pointed at one of the runes Ristan had spied on several of the caskets, that were similar in styling to the box Lucian had requested. "She wanted to find her love again, meaning she'd found him but she either lost him, or he left her." She turned around and found both men listening to her with interest.

"So what, they just entombed them here, and forgot about them?" Ristan asked after he'd stared at the beautifully etched wooden casket for a few moments lost in thought. "They've been given final rites?"

"No idea," she said as her hand traced the symbol for beloved. "It's unclear to the truth of why any of them are here. We can only speculate and go off what is written in the runes."

"So you don't know why they are down here, or why they are all women?" Adam asked as he rubbed his temples with his fingers, as if he had a headache.

"No, but if you look at this rune, it is a particular curse. A memory one, which means in her next life, if she is reborn, her memories will come back to her about what happened in this life, or this body per se. Such as dreams, they will remind her of what happened. Since she didn't create this coffin, I think someone else wanted her to remember. Sometimes people are cursed to remember the past, mostly in dreams or simple things. So something as simple as opening a door can trigger a memory of something that happened in their past life. That is why it's considered a curse. People are not meant to relive the past because eventually it distorts reality. Each one has the symbol of that curse, just as each one has the symbol of love. If I had to guess, I'd say she wanted to remember something about her love in her past life, maybe to find him again. Or maybe he placed the runes to find her again. There's no file on any of them, and I'd know because I have searched high and low for them because they intrigue me. It also makes my brain itch about why so many say the same thing, almost to the point that maybe it leads back to one coven."

Olivia moved to the far end of the row of coffins, and then looked at Ristan. "At least that's what I think. I've done a lot of research over the years on these remains. I think these ones were originally from Scotland." She motioned to several of the coffins. "I'm not sure if you were aware of the Witch trials around Aberdeen in the sixteenth and seventeenth centuries, but that was the catalyst for some of the Scottish Covens to flee before they could be captured and killed. They came across in waves around the time of each of the trials. One group came across before the Pilgrims landed at Plymouth and were thought to be one of the lost colonies. They just went into hiding and reintegrated themselves into society with the Salem settlement. Others came after Plymouth; those ones landed in a settlement in Nova Scotia and moved their way south as well as the ones who came in through East New Jersey and travelled north. Guild records showed that each of the groups could all be traced to a huge Coven outside of Aberdeen.

"Those groups also brought many of the things that

were sacred to them. These caskets would fall into that category, even though it was very impractical to put them on a ship. When the original Guild in the Americas was formed, there was a huge fight between Covens that were pro-Guild and the others who wanted to remain hidden. They wanted to protect their children from persecution and not just from Humans or the Fae. The Guild wanted to take on the world and show them they were not evil but here to help them against the Fae. The Salem Witch Trials solidified the fears of each group and the Guild in the Americas was formed and the Covens that didn't join the Guild went into hiding. Over time, the other Covens seemed to fade out of existence. Most think they are gone, but we know they just tend to blend in with the Humans or have formed separatist Covens. The Spokane Guild wasn't founded until way after these catacombs were built, but the first founders of this Guild had felt the magic of the Leyline, and suspected that one of the other Covens had first inhabited it, which told them that at least one of the Covens must have escaped the persecution of the Salem Witch trials. We aren't sure if they were the ones who left the caskets here, but it would support the theory that the Covens line either died out or abandoned the craft. That part is still a mystery, as there are no records to go off of. Only rumors," she said softly as her eyes remained locked on the caskets.

Olivia moved to one of the newer coffins and knelt near the front of it as she dusted off the markings. "This rune here states this is a coven Witch. It doesn't state which coven, though. This rune here," she pointed at another rune. "That is a death rune. This one here, though, says she was powerful. Very powerful, and she died very young. So it is possible that she was sacrificed to give her powers to her coven to protect them."

"How does that work?" Ristan asked, amused by her enthusiasm on the topic.

"Her blood would have been drained from her body and fed to sanctified lands, similar to the way the Leylines work. The blood calls to other Witches, and can be used to increase their own powers. It would have been custom for them to celebrate one who had made such a sacrifice to the line for their Coven's sake, not bury them in a hidden tomb without as much as a name to honor them or their bloodlines. It's almost as if they wanted to keep these women hidden," she said as she rubbed her arms. "Many catacombs have dead buried in their walls, or at lower levels, but not like this. I do know that Alden tried to figure out who this one was, and he used her hair and a locator spell, mixed with dried blood from her casket. He couldn't locate any living bloodlines that he could scry for. It's simply a mystery as to why she and the rest of the nameless women are here."

"I wasn't aware that Alden tried to figure out who she was," Adam said as he ran his hand over the casket.

She shook her head. "He did it recently, but nothing came from it. I do, however, think all of these remains should be taken to consecrated ground and buried."

Olivia's faced beamed with her words, and Ristan had a hard time containing his own smile and the nerdy words that he wanted to spit out. Instead, he redirected her to the reason they were here to begin with.

"That's cool and all, but we need to speed this along

and get those files and we need to get the hell out of the creepy tomb," Ristan said as he eyed the rows of caskets. "I agree that the poor girls should be put to rest, and given their rites."

"You think they still care?" Adam asked.

"Why wouldn't they?" Ristan retorted. "They most likely gave their lives to protect their people, and that takes heart. Most people these days don't understand that. They would sooner kill a person for a dollar than do the work. They basically expect good things to happen to them, and don't get up to do it for themselves."

"Damn, tell us how you really feel," Adam said with his tri-colored green eyes smiling. "Somebody hasn't eaten today."

"I'll feed soon enough," he said in reply as his eyes travelled over the Witch who was already moving on to the next room. She scurried about as if she'd been down here a lot more than she'd let on, but he kept that information to himself as he mulled over the room full of caskets with the matching runes for the box Lucian wanted. If he hadn't spotted how the runes matched, he wouldn't have let her get that far into the history of the Guild without moving her along. One never knew when the smallest detail would be needed at a later date.

It could have been a coincidence, but he wouldn't bet his nuts on it. On another note, after that little spiel, she would know exactly where to find information on Lucian's missing coven; he needed to figure out how to get it out of her without Olivia thinking she might be betraying the Guild.

"Finally," he said as they entered a room that looked out of place, considering it looked like a library.

"So those missing pages should be in here, but I have no idea where the key is," she said and turned on them. "Here's the deal," she smiled and Ristan narrowed his eyes on her. "I'll help you, but afterwards we are done. You let me go. I am sorry that I had a part to play in what happened to you but as you know now, I was tricked, and it will already haunt me for the rest of my life."

"Olivia, if you're asking to go back to the Guild," Ristan warned, and then paused as she held up her hands.

"Not the Guild, you know they'd 'retire' me as being compromised as soon as they saw me." She said retire with air quotes to be sure Ristan had understood her meaning well enough: 'Retired' basically meant shot on sight. "I just don't want to be locked inside a bedroom and left there."

Adam coughed to hide his laughter as he started to move inside the room, around the arguing couple. Ristan watched him and wondered why he was so uneasy with her asking for her freedom. Why the hell did he feel this twisted need to tell her no?

"I'll consider it," he offered as he met her beautiful eyes, knowing he was lying. It was something he knew he wasn't going to even begin to consider, and if that made him the world's biggest asshole, so be it. "Now, the pages, get them, please."

She stared at him for a few moments before she moved into the room, pulling books and throwing them at him.

"Hey," he said, but she smiled sweetly and threw another at his head until Adam's laughter caught her attention, and she hurled one at him, too.

"You shush!" she growled as she spun on the Demon. "You! I've been a good little prisoner, but you know I was innocent. I know you can feel my emotions, remember? You told me you could, so feel them now!" she said as she threw yet another at him.

"Okay you two, need me to leave for a few moments?" Adam asked with a cheeky grin on his face. "I guess you should probably feed her, too. You're starting to sound like Synthia and Ryder."

"Out," Ristan growled without looking away from Olivia.

"Done," Adam said, and vanished.

CHAPTER
TWENTY-NINE

"Do we have a problem?" Ristan demanded once they were alone.

"Yes, I'd say we have a problem. I know I fucked up, but being dragged around to help you should buy me at least some redemption! I've been a good little prisoner—shit, I even like some of the things we do— but there's a limit to how long you can keep me. I am not some slave to fulfill every little kinky desire you come up with! I have needs too! Like I *need* to go out and do things. I *need* to have the freedom to choose where I sleep, or where I walk. And I really *need* to choose my own damn clothes!"

He smiled as she ranted, her eyes growing larger and a little brighter as her rage rose. His big body moved towards hers and she refused to back away from him. He smiled, knowing exactly what was about to happen. Pissed off, no holds-barred-fuck-session. His favorite kind, well—one of them.

He slid his hand around the back of her head,

grabbed a handful of her gorgeous, silken curls, and tightened his hold on it until he pulled hard enough to steal a moan from her lips. His other hand found her pussy as it slid down the front of her jeans.

"You know what the sexiest thing about you being pissed off is?" he asked as he applied pressure to both her heat and hair. "It's that you don't back down from me. You know I could easily kill you, but you still stand your ground. So different than I thought you'd be. I kind of like it."

She swallowed and moaned as his fingers pressed harder into her silken flesh, while the hand that tugged at her hair worked alongside the other, creating a multitude of sensations that already had that storm building again inside her belly. The sexiest thing about him was that she didn't know what he would do and once he got an idea into his head, there was no stopping him. It turned her on, and it shouldn't.

He walked her backwards until she was pressed against an old oak table. He smiled roguishly as he slid his hand out from her heat and with a pulse of power, the old files, books and dust flew off the table with a crashing noise as he used one hand to lift her up without losing his hold on her hair.

"I'm starving," he growled as her clothes were glamoured away.

Olivia gasped as his fingers came back and started working her pussy. He pushed two inside and pulled them out hard and fast. She trembled at his assault and wondered where the hell that angel on her shoulder was; the one who was supposed to make her tell him no. It was as if the little devil on her right shoulder had attacked the little shoulder angel on her left, tied him up in duct tape, and was even now cheering Ristan on to do bad things that felt entirely too good. It should have been a bad thing, right? Wrong. She loved that little shoulder devil right now.

She spread her legs, giving him better access to fuck her with, and he growled his appreciation. His fingers continued fucking her until he released his hold on her hair and her head rolled back without the added support. His mouth slid down to her already wet pussy and started devouring it even as his fingers fucked her.

"Oh, God!" she screamed, uncaring that they were in the bowels of the catacombs in a room that was covered in dust and shadows. His eyes lifted to meet hers as he sucked, stroked and nipped at her clitoris.

"God isn't making you scream right now, Olivia, I am," he growled as he briefly came up for air, then he took a moment to lick and suck his fingers clean, which was almost enough to send her reeling over the edge. His own clothes disappeared and before she could remind herself where they were, he was buried inside of her warmth and she exploded.

"Fucking hell, Liv," he growled as he watched her fall into the abyss of pleasure. Her back arched and her hands moved to pinch her own nipples. He moved faster; the sound of flesh hitting flesh and their moans were the only noises in the room. His hands gripped her hips, using and leveraging her body how he wanted as he drove deep into her until his own release rumbled through him.

She exploded again and he fed from her, his hunger devouring her orgasm with eagerness. He loved the sensation of feeding from her, the intense desire to never stop and the pureness of her soul tugged at his Demon, which he forced to remain quiet this time. Soon he would let it out to savor a small taste of her soul—just not yet. Not until he could control his need to feed from her emotions. That was the only way he could reasonably be sure his Demon wouldn't take all of her soul in its greed.

Her body quivered around his cock as he pulled back and lowered his mouth to touch hers. His eyes met hers and found her smiling as he reluctantly slipped out of her warmth. She gasped as his mouth claimed hers in a soul-deep kiss, one that should never have happened. His heart sped up, matching hers as her hands cupped his face and met his kiss head on.

"You drive me insane," he growled as he glamoured clothing back on them. This time she was dressed in a white cotton baby doll dress with a red sash around her slender hips. He replaced the Keds with a pair of white leather flats and smiled as she looked at her feet as he helped her to stand.

"You forgot something," she said and waited expectantly.

"No, I didn't," he smirked and pointed at the dusty tomes and scrolls.

"I have no panties, no bra either," she replied as she crossed her arms over her breasts self-consciously.

"I know, because that was only half of what I plan to do to you today," he answered smoothly; his voice had a deep timbre, filled with confidence.

"What would you do if I said no?" she asked, and he caught the slight tremble of her lips.

"In all of my time alive, I've never forced a woman to do something she truly did not want."

"Oh," she whispered. "But the first time…" her words trailed off.

"The first time I felt your willingness and though you may have been dreaming of it, you wanted it. I felt it, and you know the truth of it, Liv."

"My name is Olivia," she said as she narrowed her eyes on him. "Let's get the other pages of those files and get out of here," she said through a tight-lipped pout.

She had been willing and she knew it, but the knowledge that he knew it sucked. Was she really that easy to read? Or did his fingertips answer every question her body had without her needing to speak the words out loud? She nervously cleared her throat.

"You do know that I am not a Barbie Doll, and that this outfit and most of the others are very impractical, especially for places like this."

"Those outfits might be impractical, as you call it, but they certainly improve the view." He grinned roguishly. She huffed and expelled a shuddering breath as she moved towards the old tomes, only to be thrown backwards by a ward she hadn't expected.

Ristan caught her in his arms before she could hit the wall and they both stared at the apparition that was in front of the tomes. A woman stood there, her eyes white as she turned her head to look at Olivia. It was a spell, and a very powerful one, too. Olivia had heard about these types of spells; they were guardian spells used to prevent the archives from falling into the wrong hands.

She stepped closer to the woman, only to have

Ristan pull her back.

"Fuck that," he growled in warning.

"It needs my blood to let me into the files," she explained calmly.

"Just your blood?" he questioned.

"Watch and be quiet," she hissed as she pulled a small piece of wood that littered the floor and pricked her finger with it.

She held her finger out and Ristan watched as the apparition touched the blood and then held it to her nose.

"Not quite Human, nor quite Fae, a Witch you are and something hidden," the woman spoke, as they both tried to listen to her distant voice. "You are pure of heart and pure of soul, come inside and seek what you will."

She vanished, but the spell would still be in play. "Stay back," Olivia warned and moved forward through the small round stones she could now see on the floor. She should have been paying attention earlier, not lost in the after-sex glow, which had made her sloppy.

She walked lightly, her eyes on the stones as she stepped over them into the warded area and expelled a shuddering breath. She turned and smiled at Ristan, but his eyes weren't on her, they were on the shelves that were moving on their own and opening an entire library that was hidden behind the wooden shelves.

"Wow," she whispered breathlessly, and walked towards it without waiting for Ristan, who was unable to get past the wards.

"What the fuck is this? I've never been stopped by any of the wards in the Guild."

"They're not just for Fae, but a lot of other creatures, too. This area is one of the oldest sections and the early

Witches were afraid of a lot more than those that were visiting from Faery," she replied without looking at him. "This is weird. The wards here are a lot stronger than any I've ever felt before."

"What the hell does that mean?" he asked, his tone turning angry. "You need to come back," he warned.

"Afraid I might stay here and not come out?" she teased.

"No, I'm afraid that it's more than it seems. I've never been unable to walk through a ward placed by the Guild. Which may indicate that these ones weren't placed by the Guild," he mumbled.

"Then who would have placed them?" she chimed, and turned to look at him.

"Maybe it belongs to the Witches who built it, the same ones that left people in a ritualistic mausoleum to rot," he snapped, his eyes moving to each corner of the room she stood in. "Get out of there, you're not safe."

"Why? Is it because you can't touch me in here?" she taunted playfully.

"Olivia," he said impatiently, but she turned around and began to touch a large pile of books that looked ancient.

"Oh my, gosh," she whispered fervently. "Do you have any idea what these are?" she asked excitedly. "These are actual grimoires! These books were used by the first Witches back in the old country, and then brought here with families and passed down to generation after generation of Witches."

"Synthia didn't need a grimoire to cast spells," he said.

"No, but she needed vellum for a lot of her spells,

which is what the pages of these books are made from. Each spell in these has been created from spells handed down since the beginning of our history."

"Grab them and get what we came for so we can go," he urged uneasily, his eyes on the ancient-looking books.

"I can't take them," she replied as if he was missing a screw or more in his head.

"Why not?" he asked cautiously, unfamiliar with the books—he could feel they were leaking power.

"They're not mine, and I sure as hell don't want to be tied to one of them if it decided it wanted to claim me. A grimoire is more than just a spell book. It contains a piece of a soul from every Witch who has ever used it. It's sacred, so I'm not sure why they would even be locked in here unless someone didn't want them used. They could be dark magic, but I've only heard of a few people ever turning to dark magic. Most Witches that used Grimoires found a balance. They could dabble in the dark arts, but it was easy to get lost in it. Those who got lost normally started turning against their own covens for more magic, which is bad, very bad."

"Okay, get the hell out of there then," he growled again, his eyes daring her to argue.

"Fine, but that key could be in here," she teased with a brilliant smile as she walked out and the room closed behind her.

CHAPTER THIRTY

The great room of Ristan's home, where they currently sat, was littered with archives and small stacks of papers from the catacombs. Olivia's mind remained on the old library they'd discovered, and yet that tingling warning itch in the back of brain had yet to dissipate. She'd been inside that section a few times before and that had never happened, no ghost-spelled reaction from the room. No secret room opening up to reveal ancient secrets, just a boring room filled with missing pages from different archives. So why had it been different this time?

Why now? Was it because the Guild had fallen and the other wards were down? It could be. It could be just about anything, though. Some spells on different parts of the catacombs had to do with moon phases, or the planets being perfectly aligned.

Another warning that kept making her brain tingle was that Ristan had requested for her to pull anything that she knew of that pertained to the three original

Salem Covens, specifically the fate of the one that had vanished. He had, however, promised her that the information wouldn't be used to harm the Guild; it was needed as a part of a deal with someone who had promised to help Synthia when she needed it. Olivia was all for helping Synthia, but only if it didn't harm the Guild in the process. The real problem she was having was that if she was right in her suspicions, they were looking for Kendra's Coven. Not that she knew it for a fact, but it fit with what she'd found of that Coven, and Kendra was one of the only people before now who had asked for any files related to those Covens.

"What is this one?" Ristan interrupted her thoughts as he handed her another few pages that looked like they were related.

It was like a jigsaw puzzle since the missing pages hadn't been placed into the tomes correctly. Whoever had filed them should have been taught how to correctly catalogue them—or they might have been in a hurry and skipped normal protocols.

"This page goes in this one, I think," Olivia said as she reached over him and pulled out one of the archives. Her breasts, still missing a bra under her dress, skimmed his arm and she swallowed her response to touching him as her nipples hardened and her cheeks flamed. She could see the areola through the white dress. That meant he could see them, too.

His hand lifted from the papers that he'd just set down and his fingers traced the fabric of the dress, his eyes lifting to hers as he made a growling noise deep in his chest that rumbled up. It seemed to have a direct connection to her center, because her pussy dampened with readiness. She swallowed her own moan and did her best to ignore him.

"I smell you," he said confidently as he pulled her dress up as she continued to concentrate on the task before her. His fingers found her nub and began gently working it; then all hope of working washed down the drain.

She refused to lose the battle of wills they were waging. Of course, his fingers would be the victor, but she was going to pretend he didn't make her shatter every time he touched her. She leaned back and spread her thighs to allow him further access as she pretended to focus on the paper she held in front of herself. He laughed, and before she could guess his intention, he slid to his knees in front of the couch, and his hot scorching mouth started to work her pussy.

"This…this one goes with that…one," she whispered huskily as she tried to ignore what his mouth and tongue were doing. He'd cleaned her up the moment they'd returned and now she was going to be in need of a long cold shower.

He brought one finger to her slippery heat and pushed it inside of her until it was buried there, but he pulled it back out as his mouth left her wetness and started trailing kisses over her inner thighs. Eventually, he entered her with two fingers and she allowed her head to fall back against the softness of the couch.

She continued to hold the pieces of old parchment in front of her, refusing to give in. it wasn't until he added a third finger and sucked on her clitoris that she gave up. His mouth was addictive; his tongue sucking and licking the right places as his skilled fingers filled her until she had to rock her hips to take more was even more amazing.

Papers dropped to the couch as he continued to fuck her with his fingers. She moaned with abandonment as he moved them faster.

"Good girl," he growled as he pulled his mouth away to watch as he fucked her body with his fingers. His other hand freed his cock, and before she could tell him that they needed to work on matching up the files, he was buried in her pussy. "I can't get enough of you, my sweet mouse," he murmured as he picked her up easily, even from his position. He sat on the couch and shifted her on top of him, still impaled on his cock, and his own motions stilled as his eyes held hers. "Ride me," he whispered and lowered his eyes to where their bodies were joined together.

"I...I don't know what to do," she whispered, and he smiled and gave her soft murmurs of encouragement as his hands gripped her hips firmly and moved her up and down on his shaft.

"Male and female were made to fit together. Some more so than others," he said as he held her body up until only the very tip remained inside of her. He dropped her and she screamed as his cock stretched her body until it molded to fit him perfectly. "Fuck, you feel so good; I could spend eternity here, inside of you."

"I need to come," she growled, surprising them both as she lowered her mouth to his and claimed his kiss. She started to move against him and he groaned with need as she controlled the movements—fuck if he wasn't happy to just let her use him.

She was a little clumsy as she found a rhythm, but

it just turned him on more as he helped to steady her. Her movements were unhurried, and every time she slid back down or rocked her hips on his cock, he had to force himself to not take over. Her musky scent and the innocence of her moves were seductive, even to him.

It wasn't until her eyes met his that he lost it. His hands cupped her face as she pulled back from the kiss and screamed as she exploded around his cock. He wasn't done, though; he pulled her back to him, his movements slow as he continued to bring her pleasure as he cradled her body with one arm while he held her face with his other.

He kissed her deeply, enjoying the slowness of this escapade. He'd never taken it slow while fucking, and this time there was a connection in the way they moved together, her body against his and his against hers. He kissed her harder, wondering why he needed to kiss her at all. Normally he didn't lavish kisses on his partners; as a rule, kissing evoked a connection, yet he felt as if he would drown without her kiss.

His mind whirled with what he was feeling, and the new feelings that he was sure he had never felt before. Confusion took over, yet he couldn't stop taking her slowly and with a tenderness that was still new for him. He wanted to fuck her hard and fast, to dominate her, and yet he liked this slow, leisurely session more than he had ever liked fucking Danu—or any other female, for that matter.

Her hands lifted to her breasts, and instead of removing the dress with glamour, he watched as she pulled it down, revealing her perfect tits, and pinched her own nipples. Fucking hell, she was the hottest thing he'd ever seen in his life.

She came again; this time he cradled her through it and knew he was in serious trouble, because he allowed the Demon to slip out, and nibble at the sweetness that was her soul, his cock buried deep inside of her as she gyrated and cried with her continuous release that was fed by his own feeding. He joined her and was lost to the pureness and deliciousness of his sexy-as-fuck librarian.

When they were a heaping mess of limbs and both struggled to catch air, he should have pushed her away. Instead, he rained kisses over her forehead, neck, and mouth. He felt like he was starving, and she was the only one who could satisfy that hunger.

"The papers," she whispered between kisses.

"Fuck the papers," he said softly as he continued to kiss her, high on the powerful sensation of the little bit of her soul that he'd taken inside himself. She was innocent, and he was an asshole. He could sense it now, in her touch and in the pureness of the taste of her soul.

"I can't do this," she whispered as she pulled away from him and he was left sitting on the couch with a raging hard cock that begged to stay sheathed inside of her. "I can't..."

"Can't what?" he asked, coming back to his senses as the sting of her moving away from him hit home. "Can't fuck a monster like me?"

"I can't get attached to you," she whispered brokenly right before her shoulders shook as tears slid down her cheeks.

Ristan paused as he sat watching her. She adjusted the dress and ran from the room, and he didn't go after her. Instead, he sat still knowing that if he went after her, he'd end up doing what he had just fucking done. Again. He'd be tender, and allow his emotions to get in the way of what he needed to do. He wasn't going to allow himself to get attached to her, and he would just have to keep trying to find reasons not to. He damn sure wasn't going to get attached ever again. Those consequences were too high.

He glamoured himself clean and dressed, and started picking up papers. "Fucking hell," he growled in frustration as he stared at the stack of books, scrolls, and papers, then back to the door where the little Witch's sobs could be heard.

He was an asshole, but in the end, it was for the best that she didn't want to get attached to him either. He knew he couldn't keep her, and it was probably time he started thinking of what he would do with her once Lucian's requests were fulfilled and the relics were found. He wasn't sure he could hold Danu back if it wasn't in her interest to do so.

Olivia slid down the bathroom door and buried her humiliated face in her hands. She'd felt a connection to him, and it scared her. He would never want her in a way that she could hope for, and yet she had felt every kiss to the depths of her soul. Every thrust of his cock inside of her body had left a mark.

She'd never experienced anything like this and it terrified her. Fae didn't fall in love, that much was a given based on the Guild's teachings, and what if his plans included making her fall in love with him just to torment her? What if that was how he really intended to get revenge, even though he said he'd understood what happened?

When his fist pounded on the door, she jumped, and somehow made it to her feet. She wouldn't fall for this dark Demon; she needed to escape him, and if helping him got her a chance at freedom, she'd do it. She opened the door after she'd wiped the tears away and looked him right in the eye.

Ristan stared at her, the defiance in her eyes mixed with the acceptance of what had happened between them. Shit, he wasn't even sure what had happened himself, but he'd liked it. Too much. He stepped aside and watched as she moved past him to piece together the papers that had been discarded while they'd made love.

His stomach churned, and a cold sweat broke out on his skin as the words he'd just thought got stuck on an endless loop. Made *love. Made*…love. Made…*Fucking Gods!* He wiped the sweat from his face on his forearm and shook his head as denial took over his mind. He hadn't just fucking thought that, no way in hell!

He left before he could do something that he would regret, or say something ridiculous as the emotions ran through him. He sifted outside and let the chill air run through him and clear his head. He needed to get back on schedule and it was time to take the librarian to do as he'd said he would.

CHAPTER
THIRTY-ONE

In a futile effort to take her mind off the Demon, she sat on the floor and continued to work through the stacks of papers, books, and files. She hated that her heart beat wildly at the array of emotions going through her. She needed to get away from him before she ended up falling for her captor, because when it was all said and done, that's just what he was.

She stood and moved to another stack of papers, and picked them up, scrutinizing them as she scanned them. Nothing made sense; the files they'd retrieved from the catacombs, they were all wrong. Pages were still missing, and the supposed relics he was referring to weren't mentioned in the pages at all!

She mentally replayed her training and how they'd worked the archives. Her heart sped as realization dawned on her and she could have sworn that the proverbial light bulb lit up above her head.

"This isn't working," she told herself and smiled. "It's not working because you're not doing it right." She mentally saw the files in her mind and her eyes moved over the stacks. "You're an idiot!"

"You're not an idiot," Ristan said softly from where he'd entered the room quietly, just in time to watch her berate herself. "I need to apologize for earlier," he started, but she held up her hand for silence.

"Not now, I'm being brilliant," she quipped as she grabbed for the pen and started writing down letters for each file. "I thought...well, I thought the missing pages were in the room we visited in the lower levels of the catacombs, but I don't think they are. You see, I'm not the only librarian with a photographic memory, and I've been adding things up. One, what is the safest way to hide sensitive information from an enemy? Two, why hide something where people would know to look? And three, what if you could have an entire file saved in person's mind that not even they knew about?"

"I don't follow," he said.

"I have the files up here," she said tapping her head. "Think of it like this; if you want to hide information from an enemy in a way that they could never decode it or access it, yet you needed to keep it on hand; where would you put it? You wouldn't put it all in the same file, because if your enemy wanted it, they'd go straight for it. So I think the more sensitive archives were split up and then sent to different parts of the catacombs. However, I know I wasn't the only one who could easily remember the files, so what if the librarians are a type of backup memory drive?"

"Like a flash drive for a computer?" he asked as he turned it over in his head.

"Exactly," she said with enthusiasm as her eyes lit

up with the idea. "Think about it, though. We didn't use computers to back them up, as the Guild library system was initiated before computers were even an idea, and once they became commonplace, security was always an issue. In the Guild system, the librarians would process the mission logs or the archives as they came in from the other Guilds, then we would have another librarian check our work, then they would go into another section with the Elders before they were finally filed away. I think the Elders would decide which information was classified and needed to be split up and they were the ones who hid the pages that had been separated. As it was, I was lucky I knew where some of the hiding places were for the separated pages because I'd gone with a few of the Elders when they filed them. I just didn't know exactly what was going on at the time. I was still pretty young and they didn't tell me what we were doing other than filing old archives. I do remember one time that they couldn't find all of the pages to an archive that an Enforcer had requested from a mission; the Elders couldn't find them, and Alden asked me to write down the missing pages word for word, because I had it here," she said and tapped on her head again.

"Well fuck me, you're a backup hard drive for the Guild," he said with a smile that touched his eyes briefly before he shook his head. "Brilliant bastards," he mumbled. "This entire time we've been wondering how those archives never end up in enemy hands or how to get the ones on the relics back and couldn't figure it out. It's so simple and yet also so complex that no one would even consider it."

"If it's actually true; but either way, I can get the

information on these ones. I'm not sure what we should do for any archives I didn't process myself," she said with a beaming smile that lit up her eyes.

"So they gave them to you, and you have them all in here," he asked as he tapped on his temple and winced. "And now I have you."

She expelled a breath and nodded her head. "Yes," she admitted. "Now that I think about it, I thumbed through a lot of the archives as I returned them to the shelves..." she trailed off in wonder as the impact of the Guild system hit her. Sure, it was a system that had flaws, but it was probably more secure than most corporations had set up on their computer networks and subject to hackers on any given day. "Anyway, this also means that we don't need to continue searching for missing pages because I have them in my head."

"Good," he said as he closed his eyes. "I'm going to bed," he announced abruptly as he stood and moved towards the door. He waited for her to follow, but when she just stood watching him, he grinned. "Easy or the hard way, little librarian, tonight I don't care either way. Hard way will get you fucked here and now; easy way will probably postpone playtime for the morning. Decide."

"I'm coming," she said as she moved in his direction and watched as his eyes smiled at her.

"No, not yet. Trust me; you will know when you are coming, because you'll be screaming like earlier." His eyes sparkled with mischief as he grinned wickedly.

"I need sleep," she hissed, then gasped as his magic slithered around her skin, and before she could protest, she was dressed in a creamy satin nightgown that showed off more than it hid from prying eyes.

Once they entered his bedroom, he pointed at the lights, flicked his finger down to dim them, and crawled across the bed without a care in the world as his clothes seemed to melt away from his body. She, however, felt the unease of having his huge, now naked, sex God body bared before her eyes. He turned over slowly, revealing a very impressive erection. She slid onto the bed and gave him her back as she pretended to not notice it.

"Get some sleep; tomorrow we will be heading out," Ristan warned, as his hands wrapped around her waist and pulled her close against his body, cradling her tightly to himself. She didn't stop him, because based on his past actions, it would have been pointless to even try.

She replayed the day's events and felt elated at her discovery and proud to know that she hadn't just been pushing papers around as a simple librarian. That her place inside the Guild had meant something, and had been a meaningful position that not just anyone could do. Her joy faded a little as she thought about her other discovery of the day. She was feeling an emotional connection with her captor, and she found herself wanting to delve deeper into it, which was insane. She found that she enjoyed having sexual relations with him, but it should end there, right?

She'd needed the connection of his mouth against hers as much as she'd needed him to be inside her body. His touch felt like fire and it kindled her desire until it was a smoldering blaze that not even the most skilled firefighter could put out. She also liked talking to him; he was intelligent, funny and, since she had come to really know him, she didn't feel that awkward or self-conscious.

His body cradled hers, and she closed her eyes as tears welled, and her heart pounded against her chest with what was happening. She was more than falling for her captor; she had already fallen for him.

She was addicted to his company, his touch, and his kisses.

This was so freaking bad!

Ristan felt the moment she'd fallen asleep and opened his eyes. He'd felt her emotions, and knew she was just as screwed as he was. He sensed what she was feeling as she'd come to the realization that she was becoming emotionally attached to him—and damn if it didn't bring warmth to him that left him reeling with a sense of joy he'd never felt before.

This was new territory for him, and he wasn't sure he wanted to tread into this kind of new terrain. Every excuse he made up to stay away, wouldn't last more than a moment or two and his resolve kept failing. He couldn't get enough of her, and even though he knew he'd developed feelings for her, he wasn't sure staying around her for much longer was healthy for her.

Eventually, Danu would come to him. Their little tiffs wouldn't be enough to make her leave him alone for very long. Olivia's life would be in danger at that point, and he wasn't sure that he could honestly say that she was his prisoner and he was only torturing her because their relationship was evolving; he just wasn't sure where it had taken a turn into her being more than his prisoner.

He held her against his body, protected in his embrace, and considered his options. One, he could keep her as his sex slave. That held a great deal of appeal and many Fae had pets like that. But it might break her spirit, and that wasn't something he wanted to do. He loved watching the fire in her eyes and he enjoyed finding ways to provoke it. Two, he could have her help him look for the relics and help them with deciphering the archives. He could consider it payment for her part in his capture and let her go once she finished helping them. He at least owed her that much.

His stomach churned at the thought of her leaving this bed, let alone leaving his world. If he could figure out a solid remedy to his problem with the Goddess, maybe he could have the best of both worlds. He shook his head before he placed a soft kiss to the back of her neck and closed his eyes. He needed to pull away from her, because letting her go wasn't going to be an easy feat.

He shifted in the bed as he heard Ryder call for him through their shared mental link, and he groaned softly with the summons. He sat up as he gently detangled his limbs from hers and whispered a spell to strengthen the wards that surrounded the house that would hopefully make it harder for Danu to find his or Olivia's signature traces leading to this location. He knew he couldn't hide from her forever; she was a Goddess, after all. As it was, he was buying time to figure out how to fix the issue.

He moved from the bed slowly and glamoured on

his armor that designated him as one of the Elite Guard before he opened a portal and sifted into Faery.

Ryder was in the war room, spreading an ancient scroll across the table as he lifted his eyes with a subtle greeting to his brother.

"For the love of the Gods, tell me you got something on the archives?" Ryder asked as he picked up more papers and tossed them into the stack Zahruk was still adding to.

"I don't think you'll find any useful information in there," he said as he sat beside the growing stack. "Olivia had a breakthrough, but it's not certain."

"Elaborate," Ryder said as he took the chair opposite Ristan.

The men turned as Synthia entered the room, her eyes glowing as she smiled at Ristan. She moved gracefully as she slid into the chair at Ryder's side.

"What's going on?" she asked as she took in the faces of those in the room and Ryder gestured for Ristan to continue.

"Olivia has a photographic memory," he explained. "She doesn't think it's a coincidence that she and a few of the other librarians had the same ability. She thinks that it's how the Guild keeps the archives safe from enemies. The librarians are like the backup drives for the Guild."

"It's inside her head," Ryder mused. "What if she was killed? They'd lose the information. Technically, it's brilliant, but there are a lot of flaws in that plan. Too many unknowns," Ryder mused as he considered Ristan's story.

"That's the thing; they would send new mission logs

and archives through two librarians and then through an Elder before they were filed. Olivia thinks the sensitive archives were split up by the Elders and sent to separate areas of the catacombs. Just imagine how much information she could have potentially absorbed as she looked through those tomes and scrolls before she refiled the returns in the library catacombs. Speaking of which, I took her to the catacombs today and we found some strange shit. One being a mausoleum full of caskets, the other being a room that she hadn't known about which was filled with grimoires. She brought back files and a lot of loose pages that should have made the archives we have make sense, but they don't fit or pertain to the archives in any way."

"There's a lot down there. Too bad you didn't sense any relics when we went through there the first time." Synthia shook her head and placed her hand on the top of Ryder's comfortingly.

"Just wards," Ryder agreed. "I would have sensed the relics if they'd been inside the walls of the Guild."

"I don't think the Guild would have left them there, at least not at the Spokane Guild."

"No actual relics, a lot of information, though. We did get the cauldron because of the information stored there, and I did get a good lead on another relic, but until I'm certain what and where it is, I don't want to get ahead of myself."

"I'm sure you don't," Synthia agreed as she smiled. It evolved into a grin in her excitement as a thought struck her. "I know Olivia was given a file by Marie that pertained to a dagger; I know because I was the one she asked to hand it to Olivia. It was weird, and at the time

I thought the same. It was a long while back and Olivia was fresh out of training. Marie insisted that I give her the file and only her. I'm wondering if Marie was a little clairvoyant, because if it is what I think it is, we have the location to the dagger and it could lead us to the other relics."

"You gave Olivia the file, but that also means another librarian had the same information," Ristan noted.

"Maybe, but maybe not, Marie was there when I handed it to Olivia, and she remained in the room. She was also the one who helped the librarians and taught them how to navigate through the catacombs. If she knew what I was, and could sense the future in the way that you can, Ristan, maybe she only wanted me and Olivia to know of its existence."

"I guess I better go ask a Witch about a dagger," he said as he pushed away from the table and stood.

"How is she?" Synthia asked, her eyes sharp as she took in his proud stance and smirk that lit in his eyes.

"She's mine," he said with a short grin. "I have a few loose ends to tie up. After that, I'll be heading out to see what I can find. I'm going to need someone watching my back, though, because I'm sure if we figured it out, the Mages are not far behind us," he admitted. Even though he could handle most the shit those sick, twisted fucks could throw at him, he'd be moving with a woman at his heels and he wanted to be sure nothing happened to her while she helped them.

"Be careful of the devil," Ryder said with a wicked grin. "That one could be far more dangerous than he appears. You let us know when you need help; you know we will come when needed. There isn't one of us who wouldn't draw swords to aid you."

"I'm counting on that," he said as he stood and moved from the room.

CHAPTER
THIRTY-TWO

Olivia awoke to the sensation of being stared at. She stretched her arms and stifled a yawn as she sat up in bed to find Ristan watching her as she slept. She quickly wiped her mouth with the back of her hand to be sure she hadn't drooled in her sleep. He smiled as if he'd read her mind and shook his head.

"You snore," he said playfully.

"I do not," she said, watching him as a smile formed on his full mouth.

"Then explain to me why the trees have all run away and are hiding even as we speak?"

"Seriously, I snore?" she asked in a worried voice.

"You do," he teased. "Up," he coaxed as he snapped the covers away and used his magic to wash her instead of wasting time with a shower. With a quick flick of his fingers, he dressed her in a baby-blue cotton dress that made her eyes pop vibrantly. It had a full-length skirt, which he wasn't too hot about, but he wanted her to be comfortable when he broached the conversation he needed to have with her. "I need you awake, then I need you to listen to what I have to say."

He reached around to the table he'd set up with an array of food and beverages, grabbed the coffee, and ran his fingers over the rim of the blue mug until steam rose from it. She watched him with wonder in her eyes as he heated the coffee for her.

"Warm, but not scalding with a dash of fresh vanilla crème and one packet of sugar, as you prefer it. There is also fresh melon and other fruit for your breakfast," he said as he handed her the mug and watched her as she lowered her nose to inhale the warm, fragrant vanilla.

He'd watched her enough to know exactly how she took her coffee, and that she preferred fresh fruit over bacon and eggs. He also knew that she hated going to Starbucks because she thought the baristas didn't make the coffee strong enough, but she wasn't against buying it to brew at home where she could make it strong enough for her taste.

She sipped the coffee and moaned as she closed her eyes with a smile. "This tastes like heaven," she murmured between sips.

He enjoyed watching her eat, and since he didn't need Human food, he didn't join her, but he did enjoy watching as the juices from the plump melon balls tried to escape her lips as she devoured them. He loved the way she ate without a care to what or who was watching, unlike many Human girls he'd observed who pretended to be full after only a few bites. Olivia always ate as if she was being given her last meal.

Once she was finished, he handed her a tissue he glamoured and held out his hand for hers as he took her out of the bedroom so his brain could be where he needed it, and not on the giant bed and sexy vixen he wanted to bend over it.

"Just spit it out!" she said when they'd reached the living room where archives and papers were still scattered everywhere, which he knew had to be driving her OCD over the edge.

"Synthia gave you a file on a dagger shortly after you first came out of training; do you remember it?" he asked, his eyes watching for any sign of agitation as his fingers absently stroked her palm.

"Yes," she replied honestly. "That was a very long time ago."

"Marie told Synthia that she was to give it to you, but at the time it seemed strange to Synthia because you were pretty new to your duties."

"Yes, I said as much. I thought it should go to another librarian who had more experience to take care of it than I did. Marie told me I had to file it, but it was strange because normally an Elder from the library would be present, and Marie was more of an *everything* Elder. She knew the entire running of the Guild from top to bottom, and she told me she needed me to do it. I remember Synthia bringing it to me, and I remember her having a strange look on her face as she looked around at all of the older librarians," she said as she made a face and continued. "However, instead of it being handed off to another librarian to be double-checked after I'd finished processing it, Marie took it. She simply stated that she wanted to be sure I'd double-checked the file."

"Did you tell anyone about it?" he asked as he watched her.

"No, never; Marie was an Elder and I trusted her one hundred percent. She was kind, and she cared about us," she sighed heavily and turned troubled eyes to Ristan. "She loved us, and I think if she had been alive to see the Guild brought to its knees, she'd die again."

"Marie was murdered," Ristan pointed out.

"They told us that she was killed by a group of radicals," she corrected.

"They tell you what they want you to know, just as they've told you all Fae were evil. Tell me, Olivia, do we still seem evil to you?" he countered.

"I can't answer that," she whispered. "I only know what they told us. I also know she was different than the other Elders. She taught us things that mattered and about self-worth. She was also the sweetest woman I'd ever met. I just can't imagine that someone would actually want her dead, not even after all this time has passed."

"A few weeks ago, I am sure you couldn't imagine a Guild Elder conspiring to kill everyone in his own Guild, but shit happens. People keep secrets; we all do it. So back to the dagger," he replied.

"It's in Ireland," she replied absently and tenaciously circled back to their previous topic. "The Elders told us that Marie was killed by a group of radicals outside the Guild. If she was really murdered inside the Guild…"

"The parents of the students would have panicked; Enforcers would have called for the blood of an invisible enemy. Alden believes she was killed by another Elder, one who wanted to take her place."

"Cyrus took her place," she whispered breathlessly.

"That he did."

She seemed to consider his words for a moment and then nodded as if she was willing to let that line of thought go for now. "Okay, so there are a few things that don't make sense, while some of it does. The dagger was supposedly hidden in Dublin, Ireland; the archives stated it was in the catacombs of Saint Patrick's Cathedral. I remember quite a few details from the records, but I would prefer to double-check those facts against the ones in the Guild Library before anyone heads off to the cathedral."

"Ireland?" he asked with a lopsided grin. "Ireland is full of myths and legends, and it's the perfect place to hide something."

"Ireland," she confirmed and nodded her head. "Coffee me," she smirked. "Please."

"Fine, but we need to get some things together. I have to see someone before we can leave for Ireland and you'll need to come with me. Do you happen to know anything else about that box?"

"Other than the fact that it's evil?" she quipped. "I know that Marie knew about it. She thought it should be destroyed. Problem is, no one knew enough about it to know how to successfully destroy it. She spoke with us openly about things like that, as if we weren't just a bunch of kids in training, more like we were adults who would be soon in charge. I'm still not sure about where the key might be, but, Ristan, whatever is inside that box, it's beyond anything I've ever felt before. It's like raw, burning evil that radiates from it as if it's a life force itself," she whispered shakily.

"So is the man we are going to meet," he said softly as his palm touched her cheek. "I'll pack you a bag and we will leave within the hour. After I've concluded my business there, we will leave for Ireland."

"And how will we get out of the mountains?" she asked with a worried look. "More sifting?"

"For you and the box of evil, I'll drive," he said with a grin. "I'm not flying in one of those death contraptions over an ocean, though, so to Ireland, we will sift."

CHAPTER
THIRTY-THREE

He brought around a Land Rover that looked as if it had never been driven before. The interior was black leather, while the exterior was an opalescent white. He had driven in silence for over an hour when he turned off the highway, pulled to the side of a deserted stretch of road and parked before he looked at her with a knowing grin. "I know you are uneasy about travelling with the box, but the man who we are taking it to isn't stupid. He needs it, and we need him to be on our side for the upcoming war. Sometimes having the biggest, meanest evil villains on your side is the best plan. He won't unleash hell on earth, because he can't rule it if he does. From what we've heard, Lucian is always in control and wouldn't have need for something like this to unleash evil. He is searching for something. We have no idea who or what it is, only that once he finds it, he'll probably go back to where ever the hell he came from."

"What if he opens it with no real idea what is inside

of it, and something bad is unleashed?" she asked worriedly, her fear clear to see in her beautiful eyes. "What if you're wrong about his motives and he knows what is inside of it and lets it loose?"

"Then we send Ryder to kill it and him if need be," he stated simply, as if it was an easy choice. "Ryder is the Horde King, and he won't allow any harm to come to the Humans because he loves Synthia. She loves the Humans, and was raised as one of you. Trust me, Olivia. She is still an Enforcer, just one with her eyes wide open now. Yours are opening as well, and you see what was wrong inside the Guild, even if you can't openly admit it yet. Adam, Adrian, and Synthia still ask me every time I see them if you're okay. What does that tell you?"

"Loyalty, but I don't understand it. One day they were the elite, the best Enforcers of the Guild, and the next they just disappeared. How could they go that long without knowing what they were?"

"Synthia was an infant when she was brought to her adoptive parents. She was spelled, her true powers cloaked. She was branded to suppress her Fae powers and to keep her looking like one of you for as long as possible. Adam is her familiar, or was until she was reborn as a Goddess. He was accidentally pulled here when her guardians were murdered, and his parents had thought they'd lost him. Being connected to Synthia and always within close proximity to her helped kept his powers suppressed as well. As they aged, Adrian saw that Synthia had more power than he did, and he knew she was so much more than he could see, so when Ryder had Vlad offer him immortality and more power than he could have as a Warlock, he accepted the gift.

They weren't flawed, nor did they do it to fuck the Guild over; they just became what they were supposed to be."

"It's almost unbelievable," she whispered as he put the SUV in gear and pulled back onto the highway. "We were told that they had betrayed the Guild, and hundreds of mission logs were pulled and combed through. I hated questioning them, ya know? Like they had infiltrated the Guild and lied to us the entire time is how we were made to feel, but even as we combed through the mission logs, the facts all checked out and eyewitnesses to the missions were brought in, questioned and nothing changed. They enforced the laws of the Guild with utmost respect. Synthia was found to question her orders more than other Enforcers, but now I think she may have been catching on to what was happening before anyone else. She was always the noisiest about any assignment that she thought was bullshit," she mused with a small grin.

"She's perceptive and persistent," Ristan agreed. "And stubborn as a mule," he added with a laugh.

"You like her," Olivia asked as a pinch of jealousy set in.

"I think if my brother hadn't claimed her, I'd have tried for at least a taste of her. She's got a fire that most men would love to sample."

"And I don't," she said quietly as she pulled her legs up in the seat and wrapped her arms around them.

"You have an inner glow, a slow burn that ignites and flares gloriously, but you're not the same as Synthia is. She's a fighter who jumps into the fray without thinking first, and you...You're a thinker like me. You try to see things from every angle, and you do question things—for the most part."

"I didn't ask enough questions before I handed you over to Cyrus, and if I could undo it, I would," she said softly. "With all of the things I know now, I wouldn't have given you up—or Alden, for that matter. I am sorry for my part in it. I know you won't believe me, but I am sorry."

He smiled and turned to look at her, really look at her. Her hair caught the sun and from where he sat in the driver's seat, she was beyond beautiful. She was the perfect combination of fire and ice. Her sapphire eyes glowed with her own inner purity, while her red halo of hair made her skin seem a little paler than it had this morning.

"You're beyond beautiful, Olivia. I have never wanted a woman as much as I do right now. If I had more time, I'd pull over and show you what I could do with your sweet body pushed up against the hood of this SUV."

"Really," she whispered throatily, but as she spoke a bolt of lightning cracked across the sky, making her jump.

The storm hit the mountain range with a vengeance. Snow and sleet were making the road treacherous, and eventually Ristan caved to Olivia's nervousness and pulled over at one of the many mountain retreats to rent a room. Once they were inside, he glamoured her some dry, fresh clothing and then did the same to himself.

He snapped his fingers and a crackling fire lit in the elegant fireplace. He could've sifted her to Lucian's club and sent one of his brothers to retrieve the Land Rover, but he wanted this time with her. He wasn't sure why, or what would become of it, only that he enjoyed her company.

He'd just given her a steaming mug of peppermint cocoa when the violent storm ripped one of the storm shutters away from the window, which made her jump again and spill the cocoa.

"Ouch," she cried as she set the cup down and held her burnt fingers to her lips. He moved to her and took her hand into his much larger ones; a soothing coldness emanated from his hands that would ease the pain of the burn as he healed her. "That feels better," she admitted and lifted her eyes to his with a smiled. "Thank you."

He leaned to her, his mouth claiming hers with wild abandonment before he could stop himself. Her hand forgotten, he pulled her body close to his and waited for her acceptance before he deepened the kiss.

He easily picked her up and headed to the bed, but she struggled against him and he stopped himself, forcing his body to cool the ardor that she created with a single look. He stepped away from her and glamoured a new storm shutter over the window. Satisfied it was secure, he turned to look at her.

She stood almost fully naked, dressed only in a pair of lacy pale pink panties, and the thick fur slippers he'd glamoured on her feet. He swallowed and forced himself to remain still, as if she was a skittish animal that could easily be spooked.

"Take off your clothing, and lay on the bed, please," she whispered huskily. He raised an eyebrow at the abrupt request.

"Olivia…" He'd been about to give her an out, so she wouldn't feel obligated to fuck him. However, his curiosity got the better of him and he wished his clothing away as he walked to the bed, laying on it with a cocky grin. "You're not planning something bad, right?" he teased and watched as she smiled.

Her hands came up to gently pinch her pink nipples which had a direct connection to his cock. He barely managed to stifle the groan as she stepped closer to the bed, her eyes feasting on his body.

"In the books I read, I often dreamt about men made for this, but I was sure they didn't really exist," she confided. "Your body is perfect," she whispered as she brought a hand down and trailed it over his muscular, defined abs. Her fingers barely touched his skin as she traced a circular pattern in his flesh.

She straddled him as she had in the beautiful place in Faery he'd taken her to, and lowered her lips to his pierced nipple. Her teeth clicked against the piercing on the first one as she gently tested it with a soft pull. She felt his cock as it rose up and curved against her opening. She moved to the other and hid her smile as his cock jumped again when her tongue flicked against his hardened nipple.

"Damn, girl," he growled breathlessly as she reached down and started to work his long, thick cock with her hand. He bucked his hips and reminded himself mentally that she wasn't used to this, and outside of his experiences with Danu, neither was he. Other than Danu, he hadn't allowed any other female to ever have control of him.

He lifted his head as she climbed down his body and his heart did a somersault as her tongue darted out to lick her lips as she stared at his cock. He shifted to sit up and rested back on his forearms. Then, as he watched her, she leaned in closer and used her tongue to reach out and taste him.

His entire body vibrated with the simple act. Fuck, he was in so much trouble with this one. Her lips kissed him, and before he could guess her next action, she'd taken the tip between her lips and slid her mouth down until she coughed on it. He smiled at her ineptness, but fuck if it wasn't the hottest thing he'd ever seen.

Instead of giving up, she took him into her mouth again this time slower. His head rolled back and his arms buckled against the bed as he pushed his hips, feeding her more until she tightened her hold on his cock and began slowly working him over until he looked up. Her eyes were liquid fire as she allowed his cock to slip from her mouth and crawled up the mattress until her body was above his.

"You drive me crazy," he said shakily as he watched her slowly straddle his body, her hand positioning his cock where she wanted it. She was a wet mess, and she slid him inside her pussy easily.

"Ditto," she replied as she began moving her body in a rocking motion. She was the most beautiful fuck he'd ever had. He smiled as he growled and turned her over until her back was on the mattress and her thighs spread wide apart. His cock slid out of her sleek heat and before she could protest, his body shifted and he buried his face in her wetness.

"Ahh!" She moaned and screamed as he used his nose against her clitoris as his tongue pushed into her. He may not have the ability that Ryder had to grow a larger cock, but he was a Demon. His tongue swelled until it filled her and his eyes feasted on hers as wonder lit in their oceanic depths. He pushed it further until she squirmed against him to get away from it.

His tongue caressed the sweet spot as she cried out, her body growing slick with sweat as he continued to push his tongue deeper while it fucked her G-spot, right until she exploded with violent tremors and a few choice cuss words that made him smile against her soaking wet pussy. He pushed her legs further apart as his tongue went back to normal size, and he shifted his body around until his cock was back at her entrance.

He plunged into her body without allowing her to come down from the cloud she was currently occupying, and took her with a force that would leave her sore until he decided to heal it. His cock was gripped by her pussy as if it was refusing to give it back, or maybe it was hugging it. Who didn't like a good hug with a vagina?

He pushed her legs up, allowing them to close a smidge as he raised them for better depth. She cried out as he pushed deeper into her welcoming heat. He bent his face over her body and nipped at her perky nipples, rolling them between his tongue and teeth until he felt her slipping over the edge again. Only then did he allow himself to find release as he sipped a taste of her soul, her pussy feeding his Fae while her soul fed his Demon.

This time, he didn't have to pull back on his Demon; it controlled itself and only took a small sliver, seeming content with that. As if it wanted to please its host by not wasting this treat so he could have more in the long run. Ristan knew he would never get enough of the way her soul tasted, addicting and dipped in a purity that was hard to find any more in the Human race. He took her four more times, enjoying each orgasm as she screamed out his name and God's. As if God would ever approve of her screaming his name while she was being fucked by a Demon? He smiled when she mumbled incoherent words until she passed out.

Yeah, he was going to have a hard time letting this one go.

He curled his body protectively around hers and slept, blissfully unaware of the Goddess who watched them from the reopened storm window, her ire rising at what she witnessed. Ristan tucking his much larger body around the librarian's, and then kissing her forehead tenderly.

Ristan felt her presence before he caught a glimpse of her rounding the cabins. He finished loading the few things they'd brought with them into the back hatch as Olivia came out and got into the passenger seat of the Land Rover.

His eyes scanned the snow-covered woods as he moved to the driver seat and bent over to start the engine so that the heater would kick in and keep her warm. "I'll be right back," he said as he gave her a gentle smile and turned to move to where Danu had slipped into the woods behind the cabins.

He had just broken through the brush when he caught sight of her further down the trail. She was dressed in a white robe, her features obscured from his vision as he approached her. His heart sped up, but he knew he had to face her.

"Danu," he whispered, wondering how he could explain Olivia to an ancient Goddess who had a black spot where her heart should have been.

"Your time is up, and it is time for her to die," she whispered and turned to look at Ristan with blood tears running down her face.

He paused and hated the sick, twisting feeling that entered his stomach at her angry words. He felt his heart turn cold in his chest and he shook his dark head at her.

"If you kill her, Danu, you'd better kill me too," he whispered. "I am not the child who thought the world of you any longer. I did love you at one time, I am sure of it now, but you didn't love me back. You can't love anyone because I don't think you've ever been taught to love. You can't understand it because in your world it doesn't exist. That's why we, the creatures you created, are flawed. You forgot to love those you created, and in turn, it made most of us unable to comprehend what it was."

"Love is a weakness," she snapped. "I am a Goddess! I can have no weaknesses. If I loved every one of my children, it would only paint a target on their backs for other vengeful Gods and Goddesses to use against me. I created the Fae without love because I needed them to be stronger than the race before them and to not have weaknesses that could get them killed. I made you to be killers, ones who would fight until your last breath for me and in doing so, I had to give my soul! I will die if you are too distracted by a tight pussy to save Faery, so you now know your real flaw."

"I played my parts, I fulfilled every task and demand

you set before me; I helped heal the Tree of Life," he growled, hating that she thought she could stake her claim on his life after what she'd done. "I will help find the relics, but I've already told you, Goddess, we are done. What you did to me? I can eventually forgive you for that, but your constant need to control me, and the blatant disregard for the fucked up situations you leave me in? I'm over it. Touch Olivia and I will end my part in saving Faery. I help fight for Faery by choice, not because I can't survive elsewhere."

"You fight because it's your home, and your people need it to survive," she whispered as she wiped at her eyes.

"We would survive," he replied with confidence. "We would easily take over this world and make it our new home, but we want ours. That's the difference, Danu; we will survive at any cost. You, on the other hand," he said leaving it open as he shrugged his shoulders. "Leave the little Witch alone; who I fuck and who I fall in love with is not up to you. I don't know what's happening between us, but I am willing to see where it goes. That's my choice."

"I could easily flick my fingers and kill her," she said as she narrowed her eyes on him. "But I fear you will have to learn life's lesson on your own. Lesson number one, your pretty little redhead just stole your car because she can't wait to be rid of you. Lesson number two, she seduced you enough to get you to let your guard down, and it worked so well that you forgot there's a box inside the car that one certain Demon will kill to get," she said with a whisper filled with self-confidence. "Maybe he'll find her first, or maybe I will. Tick tock, baby," she said with a nasty laugh as she snapped her fingers and disappeared.

"Bitch!" he roared as he spun and sifted to the spot he'd left Olivia in, only to find her and the Land Rover gone.

CHAPTER
THIRTY-FOUR

Olivia sped onto the highway and didn't
stop until she had put over a hundred miles between
herself and the Demon. Her heart ached with every mile
she drove and she considered going back, but then she
would remind herself over and over again that he was
her captor and there would be no future with him.

Captor, meaning he'd taken her by force, played
kinky fuckery games with her, which, if she was being
honest, wasn't such a bad thing. Well, if she was being
honest, she'd enjoyed it far more than she was willing to
admit. But, freedom! No more being locked in a cell, no
more being confined to a bedroom. No more worrying
that she was teetering on the brink of losing her heart
to a Demon. She felt as if she was channeling William
Wallace and even now should be painting her face blue
as she drove each mile to freedom.

Twenty minutes later the tears came, and with them
the stark, reminder that she had absolutely nowhere
to go and no one she could safely approach without

alerting Cyrus, or the people he worked with that she still lived. Apart from Alden, everyone she'd considered her family had died at the Spokane Guild.

The one small comfort she had, if Ristan was telling her the truth—she prayed to Hecate that he was—was that the children she had hidden in the music room were alive and would be sent to their parents. She still wondered what would happen to the little ones who didn't have parents. The ones that weren't lucky enough to have an advocate to fight for them. She'd been one of those children, and she hoped that Synthia and Adam would look out for those children and do the right thing where they were concerned.

She silently wiped away the tears and turned the music on as she drove past nameless towns and country houses, through the sprawling, snow-covered countryside. She passed cows, horses and other animals as she made her way back to I-90 and onto the interstate, which ended up taking her back to Spokane and the Guild.

Huddled in the blankets she'd found in the Land Rover, she waited across the street from the ruins of the Guild until midnight had passed, and then the dawn bloomed on the horizon. It was serene, but as she fought the courage to get out of the safety of the SUV, she considered the facts.

She had nowhere else to go. Sad, since this wasn't much of anything anymore. It was a pile of rubble that sat above extensive catacombs that ran underneath most of the city.

She had no one. Not even her cat, since it was left behind at the mansion in the mountains. At least if

Ristan kicked it out, she knew Kit would survive, unless she got eaten by a bear, which would suck.

She had nothing. Not even a spare change of clothing should she slip and fall in the mud. She could just imagine the things that Demon had packed in that bag, and was willing to bet nothing in it would be suitable to wear in public. His tastes in clothes were more in the range of kinky to downright inappropriate. Although, she had looked okay in some of them, considering she never would have worn anything like those clothes if he hadn't glamoured them on her.

She was homeless. She was hungry, and the chill from outside was beginning to soak through to her bones.

She blew out the breath she hadn't realized she was holding and eyed the rubble as she exited the Land Rover, leaving the keys in the vehicle since technically she couldn't keep it. She didn't own it. A very sexy, probably very angry Demon did. She stood in the early morning haze and watched as the sun rose before she finally moved toward the Guild.

She had to go in through the back wall, climbing over piles of stones, and carefully made her way down broken, teetering stairs as she headed into one of the secret entrances to the library and catacombs. She wasn't even sure why she'd come back here. Probably because it was familiar, not to mention the Land Rover wasn't going to go anywhere else right now. The little gas light was on and she didn't have a penny to her name. If she tried to pull money from her bank, it would alert those within the Guild that she was still alive, and she preferred them to believe she had been killed by her captor or taken to Faery. Everyone knew that Humans didn't return from there.

Her foot slipped and she hit the rocky floor of the tunnel hard; her palms burned as she pushed herself off the floor and stood back up. Her arm stung and as she could feel blood as it slid down the back of her forearm where she'd banged her elbow on the stair as she fell.

"Why the hell can't I sift? That shit is so much easier," she screamed at the empty room.

She moved into the soot-covered library and stood in silence, as if she was holding a silent vigil in it. Most of the library had collapsed at the entrance to the catacombs. All that she could see from this side was charred remains and soot. She reached a breaking point and screamed as loud as she could. Birds flew from within, trying to escape the Banshee wails. She moved to one of the desks that was half burned and half undamaged and kicked it.

"Ouch!" she shouted as she jumped around trying to hold her wounded foot. "Why me!?" she asked the sky that peeped through the ruined ceiling. "Why? I wasn't bad, was I? Was I some major bitch in a past life, so you give me this one? Leave me abandoned and alone without a single person to care about me? Why me?" she whispered brokenly as she slid to the floor. "I don't even kill spiders."

She sat in the soot and dust, hugging her knees with her back against the desk.

"You don't even kill spiders?" Ristan teased as he stepped around one of the pillars in the room.

She jumped and then groaned. "I'm not going to get close enough to one to kill it, so no."

He laughed and, uncaring about his own attire, he sat on the floor beside her. "You stole my car and left me in the middle of fucking nowheresville."

"I did," she said as she rested her head on his shoulder. "I needed a moment of freedom."

"Is that why you were shouting freedom in my Land Rover for twenty minutes, or my personal favorite moment was when you were singing at the top of your lungs to *Fight Song*?" he countered as he reached for her abraded palm and healed it before he gently did the same with the other, as well as her elbow.

"I like that song," she whispered softly. "I have nothing left," she surprised herself and him by saying. "I've got nowhere to go, and no one would even notice if I disappeared." He'd been in the car with her the entire time! Mixed with the emotions that she was dealing with, and now knowing that she'd never been actually free of him, she expelled a breath and shook her head.

"That's not true," he said.

"It is; it's sad, but it's true."

"I noticed you disappeared," he clarified with a gentle grin.

Her eyes moved to him and she rolled them. "Of course you did, I stole your car, which is like a felony."

"So I should find some handcuffs and a paddle and show you what it's like to be really punished?" he asked as he lifted a brow, as if he was intrigued with the idea.

"I mean it," she said. "This was my home, and I had nothing else. No backup plan. The Guild always wanted us to cleave to the safety of the Guild, although Marie used to encourage us to think beyond the Guild, to a life outside. I thought I had more time. I thought I'd save up and move out someday, maybe plan a life and find a beefy Enforcer who had an obsession for dorky librarians who'd never been kissed."

"You're what, Olivia, twenty?" he asked as he rested his head back against the desk.

"Twenty-one," she said, as if the one year meant something to him, which it didn't.

"Most Humans don't have shit figured out by twenty-one, the exception being which foods they like, and even that much is iffy. Had the Guild not fallen, you probably would have ended up stuck here way past your forties, married to some Warlock who went after younger girls when he went through his midlife chaos."

"Crisis—and no, I'd have married a handsome one who only had eyes for me, who enjoyed cooking and pampering me. He would have wanted a big family and he'd be perfect. He'd be my mate in love and life," she stated with dreamy enthusiasm.

"Lay off the books, damn. Who the hell did you plan on marrying? A male version of Mary Poppins?" he asked with a sideways glance.

She laughed and turned to look at him. "I guess my expectations were a little high. I just wanted to have a family and love them as they would love me. It sucks being alone, ya know? I had the Guild, but they're not the same. I just never really fit in. Marie told me that when I was born, the Elders of Salem thought that my father was one of the more powerful Warlocks assigned to the Salem Guild. No one knows for sure because my mother died having me and didn't tell anyone who he was and he didn't come forward to claim me when she died. It put me at a bit of a disadvantage when I came here.

"Anyway, once I was old enough to understand what was going on around me, I could see that other than being a girl, I didn't have much in common with anyone here. Mary used to tease me about boys and how they viewed me more as a little sister and less like someone who they could date, and the men in my books were way better than the boys I was growing up with. I wanted to fit in, and I wanted to be normal. It just didn't happen for me. I couldn't even access my magic the way the other kids could. I have it, but I can't channel it the same way so I had to find ways to make it work so I could blend in and not attract too much attention. Fin, one of the other librarians, could use his to send archives back without leaving his seat, but mine was weaker. I could return them quickly enough, and, of course, doing it manually ensured that it was without mistakes. I did create a system that worked, and had a few cheats thrown in so that I was as quick as the others. I didn't party like the others did, though; that was my own fault because I was shyer than the others and I didn't feel comfortable joining in. I just wanted someone who that made me feel normal."

"You are normal, Olivia. You are as normal as someone who grew up inside a place like this could be. I get that you were sheltered within the Guild, and raised to follow orders, which makes you very naïve, but I know you have dreams, and you're a good person. Other than stealing my car, you've probably never even broken the law."

"I forgot to pay for a coffee once," she admitted, and he smiled.

"And what did you do after you discovered you hadn't paid?" he asked as he looked around the room.

"I went back and paid for the damn coffee. I was so unnoticeable, that the guy at the counter said he'd never seen me before and refused to take my money."

"Ouch," he said. "I doubt he failed to notice you; either he was trying to give a pretty girl a free cup of coffee, or it was because you were wearing one of those drab skirts that did nothing to show off those sexy-as-fuck legs. Still, if he failed to see the beauty on the outside, I know he couldn't have missed the beauty you radiate from within."

"Gosh, is this where you compliment me and then," she stopped as she held her thumb up to her neck and dragged it over her throat dramatically, "off me?"

He laughed. "I should spank you; I didn't enjoy you impulsively ditching me, but I did enjoy your driving."

"Wait, back up. You…" She paused as she replayed what he'd said earlier. "I was watching for you; how the hell?"

"I think somewhere between screaming freedom, and crying your pretty little eyes out, you missed me sifting in and I was at a loss for the weirdness of the situation. I was also pretty sure you wanted some alone time."

"I needed some time alone to think. A lot has happened, and I needed time to process it," she admitted.

"And did you?" he asked carefully.

"Sort of. I am starting to think I have a serious case of Stockholm syndrome."

"Stockholm what? What the hell is that?" he asked, giving her a curious look.

"It's a psychological condition where a hostage or a kidnap victim forms an unnatural attachment to their captor," she said with a lopsided grin as he grimaced.

"Let me guess; you think you have this because you like me and I turned out not to be the world's biggest asshole? Ever consider that maybe I'm just addictive and habit forming?"

She rolled her eyes and elbowed him. "Nope. Now I'm starting to think you just suck."

"No, but you do it pretty well," he said as he pulled her close to him and kissed her cheek. "We have somewhere to be, and we need to get cleaned up. Vlad advised me to dress accordingly; and by dress, he meant nice evening wear, black tie and all of that. I can think of a few good things that tie could be used for afterwards, though."

"Where are we going?" she asked curiously as he helped her up.

"To the Gates of Hell to meet a Demon about a box."

CHAPTER THIRTY-FIVE

Once they were back in the Land Rover, he glamoured them both into clean clothing that would be more suitable for where they were going, or at least that was what he told her. He was hot in just a basic t-shirt and jeans, but decked out in an Armani suit with a crisp white dress shirt, silver tie, and matching cufflinks? Oh, Lord help her, she couldn't keep her eyes off of him.

He'd dressed her in a little black dress that had long sleeves, a sweetheart neckline, and the back was left open in a dramatic low drape to mid-back. The short skirt had high slits up to her hips which thankfully made it more comfortable to sit in. Her shoes were black, peep-toe stiletto pumps, and he'd even created tiny crystal roses that embellished the top of them and softly sparkled at her in the dim interior lighting of the SUV. She had complained about her hair, and he'd wiggled his sexy fingers and her hair had been swept to the side and placed in a loosely braided bun on the side of her head. Soft tendrils of hair had been left free to frame her face, giving her a sensual look.

It wasn't something she would have done herself, but paired with the red lipstick and heavy kohl eyeliner, she had to admit that overall, the combination made her look hot. From what she could see of herself in the tiny mirror, she looked like someone else. Of course, she'd never worn much makeup other than her normal dab of mascara and lip gloss, but she felt more beautiful tonight than she ever had before.

She wasn't worried until they pulled up to a nightclub that seemed to materialize in the middle of nowhere. He sifted out of the car and opened her door before she could do it herself. He accepted her hand as she lowered herself from the Land Rover, kissing the inside of her palm gently before he released it. Her heart clenched at the courtly gesture and she couldn't help but smile at him.

"Club Chaos?" she questioned as loud music sounded from within. "All sinners welcome?" she whispered as the door opened and a couple walked out with matching smiles.

"It's an inside joke of the owner's," Ristan explained as he rounded to the open hatch and pulled out the bag with the box in it.

"That thing shouldn't be given to anyone," she said as she took an involuntary step backwards.

Ristan shook his head as he closed the hatch and held out his other hand for her. She accepted it begrudgingly, her eyes on the box-shaped bag. She had never been able to get close to it without feeling sick to her stomach, and that just made the curiosity of what was inside burn brighter for her.

She had never hidden her curiosity about the many sacred objects housed at the Guild, which the Elders had indulged to a certain degree. Some objects had been off-limits to touch or examine. She'd once been asked once to hold an ancient tome, which had given her the chills for an entire week afterwards.

They approached the door and she stumbled on the heels, but Ristan quickly held her up and gave her a curious look.

"I'm sorry," she said quietly. "This is a little out of my comfort zone."

"You mean you never left your bedroom or those damn books long enough to go out to a nightclub?" he teased with a carefree smile.

"I didn't have a lot of friends," she admitted.

He paused at that and turned to look at her. "It might be better that you weren't very close to those who died at the Guild," he replied solemnly.

"It doesn't make it easier that we weren't good friends. It actually makes me feel worse. I had a hand in what happened. I have to live with it; even if they weren't close to me, Ristan, they were my people."

He didn't get a chance to answer her, as the wide club doors were opened by a huge, intimidating man with an actual man-bun. It normally was a turn-off when a man had his hair up in a bun, but this guy was seriously pulling it off. He was heavily covered in tattoos up his arms and neck, and his eyes were a vibrant crystal blue.

"What the fuck do you want?" he growled, his eyes raking over Olivia and then Ristan.

"To speak to your boss," Ristan said without

showing an ounce of fear, unlike Olivia who wanted to bolt back to the safety of the car.

"Is that so?" the hulking man asked as he snickered. "You got some balls, Demon. We thought for sure you'd send it in the mail."

"Snail mail sucks and they lose half the shit they get paid to deliver. So, is he here or not?"

"He's busy," the man said, his eyes sliding back to Olivia and the low neckline of her dress. "In his office upstairs," he finished. "Go on up, if you dare."

Olivia perked up at that. *If you dare?* Was this guy serious?

Ristan placed his hand on the small of her back and pushed her past the man guarding the doors. Inside it looked like a lot of the clubs she'd seen in magazines or described in books, with gyrating bodies that pushed against each other as they danced to the beat of the music.

The room was large; black lights outlined the dance floor and colorful lights swirled and bathed the dancers, while the bar was lit up well enough for the bartender to pour drinks without mixing up the bottles. Not that it would have mattered if it hadn't been, since the bar itself was glowing with bluish green light from beneath the mounted glass that topped the bar. There was also a wall of glowing lights spanned from one end of the bar to the other.

"Wow," she shouted to be heard over the loud music.

"Darklands is better," he shouted back as he moved her easily through the crowded room. It wasn't until they reached a door that had the words 'Sinners Lounge' on it that he paused. He turned his head in her direction, smiling wickedly. "You're going to see some freaky shit when we go through these doors. There are rules, Olivia. One, you belong to me," he reminded her as he tugged lightly on the torque around her neck. "That should keep most away; however, if anyone should ask, I am your master, your lover, and no one else is to touch you. Two, don't make eye contact with the men; it's considered a challenge to most. Three, don't leave my fucking side for any reason. We get in and we get out, understand?"

"What the hell is behind that door?" she whispered breathlessly as his rules replayed through her mind.

"I'll show you," he said with a wicked grin before he pushed the doors open and pulled her gently through them.

Pulsating, sensual music and muffled moans of multiple people exploded around them the moment he pushed the door open, and the sound of it closing behind her was deafening. It was as if they had left the safety of the real world—and she immediately wanted to turn and leave.

She halted, unsure if she wanted to continue past the entrance. "What is this place?" she whispered. She jumped as the sound of a whip meeting flesh along with a woman's moans of pleasure erupted from only a few yards away.

"This would be an exclusive, invite-only sex club. One of the most notorious ones on the West Coast of America," he explained with a lopsided smile.

"I need to go," she said as she shook her head, unsure of what the hell they were doing here. She listened to the moans and the whip as it snapped against the flesh again. Oh shit, she needed to run, quickly.

"I have you; no one here will touch you, Olivia. You're mine."

"I don't belong here," she whispered vehemently.

"Every woman deserves to be set free from the confined cage society tries to lock her into. Come; see what it is before you just reject it."

He didn't give her time to argue as he grabbed her hand and pulled her around the corner and into a room where the whip was meeting flesh, and the subtle moans of pleasure grew louder. A crowd surrounded a woman as a huge hulking man wielded the whip.

She was naked and secured with rope that made it impossible for her do anything other than stand on her tiptoes as she was whipped from behind. Welts crisscrossed her back, butt and thighs yet the skin didn't look as if it was broken. Bile rose in the back of Olivia's throat, and she pushed it down reminding herself that she'd been tied up once, and she'd enjoyed it. A lot more than she ever thought she would.

Olivia forced herself to remain stoic and ignore the people who encouraged the man to continue the woman's punishment. She counted each lash, and as the crowd shouted, she watched as he dropped the whip and moved towards her, his hand gripping the woman's hair harshly as he cupped her pussy with his other hand.

Olivia couldn't imagine being placed on exhibit as this woman was, and yet she looked as if she wanted this.

"She's willing?" Olivia asked in a barely audible voice.

"She's more than willing," a woman with bright red

hair said as she turned back to answer Olivia. "She's chosen to serve him, and most of us would beg on our knees to be served by him. Look at his cock," the woman said as her eyes moved back to the naked male, who did have a hugely erect cock that he was currently rubbing between the woman's legs. The woman moaned and did her best to bend her hips for his touch.

Olivia angled her head a bit to find Ristan watching them, his hand subtly rubbing her exposed leg through the side slit in her skirt. Her body responded to him as the sound of flesh meeting flesh resonated in time with the tantric music. Her eyes moved back as the couple fucked in front of the crowd, but as quickly as he had pushed inside of her, he pulled out as yet another woman was added to the scene, this one carried by four men and placed before the man.

This one was beautiful, and had blonde hair and green eyes. She was younger than the other woman; Olivia figured this woman was at least as old as she was. Her arms were secured behind her back, and as Olivia watched, the male switched partners. He moved to the new girl, easily picking her up as the crowd gave him their approval. He hoisted her onto a raised platform, forcing her to balance on it as he gripped her hair, and, without waiting, pushed his cock into her body as she screamed.

The crowd gave murmurs of appreciation as he took her from behind, and as Olivia watched, others moved in behind him, some moving to the forgotten woman, each helping bring her down from the ropes, and before she was even fully allowed to stand, two men were buried inside her body.

She cried out as if it was a gift, and Olivia turned to look at people in the crowded room. Some were pleasuring themselves as they watched as others took what the person beside them offered. More couples and threesomes were making use of the comfortable-looking loungers that ringed the room. Olivia felt her cheeks grow heated from the scene before her, and before her heart could burst from her chest, Ristan held out his hand for her.

"We can go now," he said softly, waiting for her to gather her scattered wits before he led her from the room and down another hallway.

"That wasn't right," she whispered through a dry mouth.

"They wanted it, and if they didn't, they wouldn't be here," he said quietly, reminding himself as to how naïve she really was. "Not everything with sex is black and white; there's a lot of gray area. Some like to behave badly, so they will be punished or they like being an exhibitionist. Some women need it to get off, like those women out there. To them it's not degrading, it's freedom. It's freedom to be who they really are without being judged for it, or hiding it. Too many people in this world spend their lives thinking they are sick and try to stamp down and hide their desires, when in reality, everyone has their own kinks. Not everyone's ideal sex is monogamous, or simple. At least those here have embraced what works for them and no one gets hurt unless they ask for it." He grinned at his little play on words as she shook her head slightly.

"I don't understand it, I get that. But I would never do that, nor would I put myself on display for others to see," she said out loud, needing him to know where she stood on it. "I prefer a closed door, and if that makes me a prude, so be it."

"Most have their reasons for what they do, and some just don't give a shit what others think. Every woman in that crowd, except for you, would have jumped to be in those women's places. They didn't come here to just hang out, they came here to fuck. It's a sex club, not a mall, Olivia, and by Fae standards, that was very tame." He gave her a warm, indulgent smile. The scene out there, by Human standards, had been wild. For a sheltered girl like Olivia, it was probably the wildest thing she'd ever encountered.

"I'm not sure why the ownership is so insistent on the dress code if they're just planning on ripping each other's clothes off anyway," she mused thoughtfully, and heard a soft chuckle from Ristan at her observation.

He gripped the bag tighter as he walked her up a flight of stairs and through a hallway lined with dark windows. She occasionally turned her head to stare at her own reflection and wondered just who it was who stared back at her. She had seen a lot over the last few days, and she'd never considered herself judgmental. Never. This went way beyond anything she could have ever imagined and she wasn't sure if it was the shock of watching people be 'punished,' live and up close like that while an entire crowd had witnessed it, or how she'd felt watching it.

Ristan turned them towards a large door and knocked on it as she chewed her bottom lip nervously. She wasn't even sure why she was so nervous. The only thing she knew with certainty, was the further down the hall they'd gone, the more uneasy her nerves had gotten.

"Enter," a male's voice said. Ristan twisted the knob, and Olivia felt the uneasiness of her nerves spike to screaming levels.

CHAPTER THIRTY-SIX

The office they entered was immense.
The entire wall directly across from where they entered the room was glass. It gave the occupants of the office a bird's eye view of the nightclub below. Olivia figured it must have been made of two-way glass, or a mirror, which she must have missed as they'd entered the club earlier.

A man stood with his back to them, watching the revelers in the nightclub. He was similar in height to Ristan, and his black hair barely skimmed his broad shoulders. From where she stood, she could see the fine details in his suit and knew it was tailored and probably cost more than her yearly salary at the Guild. He didn't turn in their direction immediately, so Olivia continued to look around the office.

It had a masculine design with dark mahogany and leather furniture, obviously belonging to the man who couldn't be bothered to turn towards them. On one of the walls was a painting of a beautiful woman with caramel colored hair. She was wearing a dress from the early 17th century, and even though she didn't smile in the portrait, her eyes seemed to look straight through the viewer, and Olivia could sense the woman was more than just beautiful, she was powerful.

Olivia couldn't help but stare at the painting. Before she could stop herself, she was moving towards it with an itching in the back of her skull that gave her the notion that the subject in the painting resembled someone she knew. *Kendra?* No, this woman was more delicate than Kendra, and her eyes weren't the same color. She did look as if they shared some sort of a familial bond, and this beautiful woman was dressed in an elaborate gown that probably would have been the height of fashion sometime around 1610.

"She's beautiful, is she not?" a deep male's voice said right next to her, causing her to gasp as her eyes moved to the man beside her. She hadn't heard a single noise to alert her that he'd even moved. The man seemed to be oozing power, and had somehow masked that power when they'd first entered the room. She felt as if she was standing next to a transformer that was actively conducting power. Raw, physical power.

"She's very pretty," she agreed.

"And deadly," he added.

"She looks as if she was looking beyond the painter, to something or someone in the background. Whatever it was, it made her uncomfortable," Olivia said, sensing the woman's mood from the way she held her body; it was tense, as if she wasn't posing by choice. "Almost like she didn't want to sit for this painting," she amended.

"That's an astute observation from only looking at it

for a few moments," Lucian said.

"Her hands are the giveaway. Her knuckles are white, as if she's tense," she pointed out, not daring to actually touch the painting in case it was actually real. It looked real, yet it also looked like it was painted with oil based paint. It also looked as if the red of her lips was a beautiful shade of 'Dragon's Blood' which was a pigment made from Asian gum resin that women used long ago to color their lips. "Is this real?" she blurted.

"Very," he said softly, his eyes locked on the woman's as if he was lost in memory.

"Do you know how much this is worth?" she asked as she turned to fully look at him, and paused.

He was freaking gorgeous, but where her heart beat faster for Ristan, it sank to her stomach and the hair on her nape rose, so she took a giant step backwards. His eyes moved to hers, holding them captive as she paused. *Black?* What the hell kind of creature had black eyes? His irises were almost the color of midnight. He smiled; she almost expected him to have fangs, but instead he had perfect teeth.

"Olivia," he said as he nodded his head. "It's a pleasure to meet you."

Olivia turned to find Ristan and found she'd almost scooted right into him as she'd sought safety. He was less than an inch away and she welcomed the heat his body offered along with the protection.

"Olivia, meet Lucian," Ristan said as he pulled her body against his.

She held out her hand for Lucian to shake, only to watch as he dismissed it and moved away. Her eyes moved down the length of him and didn't mind the view as he moved to his desk.

"You have what I seek?" he asked when he was seated and looked in their direction again.

"I do," Ristan replied as he swung the bag off his shoulder and moved to where Lucian was seated. He carefully placed the bag on the desk. Ristan opened the top of the black bag and slid it down around the box as Olivia watched. Ristan pulled out several file folders that had been on the top of the box and set them on the desk before pushing them closer to Lucian. Lucian's eyes closed briefly, but whether it was in relief, or something else, she couldn't be sure.

"The Guild had it, yes?" he asked, his eyes briefly moving to Olivia and back to Ristan.

"They had it," Olivia answered, her body tensing as the box was handed to Lucian; something inside of her warned her to run. As if she could sense he wasn't what he appeared on the outside, and all of her alarm bells were going off like crazy.

"It belongs to the Guild," she said as she moved to take a seat in the chair beside Ristan.

"Is that what you think?" he asked softly, as his eyes moved with her as she lowered herself in the chair, following her with humor marked in their inky depths. "Just because they claim something doesn't make it theirs. This box was stolen decades ago."

Decades ago? He barely looked to be over thirty. His fingers gently caressed the box, which drew her eyes to it. She had a sick feeling in the pit of her stomach, and a sense of foreboding she couldn't shake.

"Do you know what is inside the box?" he asked, his eyes never straying from her face.

"No; neither did the Guild, from what I was told. I have no idea where the Elders hid the key, or if they even had it."

"It doesn't need a key," he said with his lips curling into a sardonic smile. "Hence why people who don't know what something is shouldn't fuck with it."

"How does it open then, if not with a key?" she whispered, her curiosity getting the better of her.

"The world isn't ready for it to be opened," he said assertively. He opened the file folders that Ristan had placed on the desk and briefly skimmed through the pages. He pushed away from his desk and opened the top drawer, from which he pulled out what looked to be an old set of skeleton keys. He pushed them across the desk to Ristan and sat back in his chair. "These keys belong to a cabin just outside of Chelan; it's heavily guarded by Seekers, and the runes have been placed by a powerful coven of Witches. No one can get out of it once they've entered unless the owner allows it. This is the deed," Lucian said as he opened a lower drawer and pulled out a package. "Congratulations," he said crisply. He used a dagger that had a bone handle to cut the package open, and the look of pure bliss on his features made her wonder just what type of bone it had been created from. He pulled out a piece of paper and placed it on the desk and slid it to Ristan. "Sign it and the house and ninety-two acres it sits on are yours. Of course, the Seekers will be a permeant fixture there since they died on the land. They'll protect you and anyone who is inside the house."

"Seekers?" Olivia asked, and her eyes narrowed as he turned those midnight eyes in her direction.

"Cursed souls," he explained slowly. "They've been prevented from entering heaven or hell, and are much akin to Revenants. Only where the Revenants terrorize the living, the Seekers work in the opposite to protect them."

"So, ghosts?" she questioned.

"Not quite. More like cursed souls who have no place that their immortal essence can go to. They are outside of heaven or hell—purgatory or any of the 'circles' Dante described," he explained as his eyes watched Ristan's progress and narrowed on him. Olivia turned to Ristan and watched as he carefully read every minute detail of the Deed of Trust he'd been handed. "It is also important to keep in mind that Seekers prefer to protect only those who they deem worthy of it. If they find the occupants lacking in the moral department, they can make the stay on the property quite hellish."

"Oh," she replied easily and folded her hands in her lap as she turned away from the obsidian eyes that looked through her, rather than at her.

"Is that why you're so eager to be rid of it?" Ristan asked as he lifted his head to smile at Lucian.

"Actually, they don't tend to fuck with me," he said absently as he looked over the paperwork. "It's done," Lucian said as he pushed a button on his desk and nodded at Ristan. "Our business is concluded, but you're more than welcome to enjoy the club for as long as you wish. I had a room cleaned and furnished for your preferred taste of pleasure. I thought you'd prefer not to share your woman, since you were protective of her the last time we met, and you'll not be disturbed for the duration of your stay. The doors to the club have been secured for the night and there's no leaving until morning. Safety measures against my enemies. You understand, I hope."

"We've become very selective of who we allow inside our own clubs as well," Ristan admitted, even though he didn't like the idea of Olivia being locked in a sex club with creatures that belonged in hell slinking around it.

Olivia turned a wide-eyed look at Ristan as the scene from earlier pushed into her mind. She was about to turn and ask Lucian if they could make an exception for them to leave, but he wasn't in his chair, and she hadn't heard him even move, again!

"I don't make exceptions, little girl," Lucian whispered against her ear before he pulled out her chair for her to stand. Ristan moved so quickly that she hadn't even heard him until she was pulled close to him, and the room grew tense. The air was thick enough to cut with a knife. Her eyes moved from Lucian's to Ristan, and back.

"Thanks," she said uncomfortably as she stood and turned around to look at Lucian, who almost seemed to be taunting Ristan with a smug smile on his lips.

"I have business matters to attend to, but if you need anything or the accommodations are lacking, my men will remedy it. The doors open at six AM," he told them smoothly.

He smiled and moved towards the door Olivia looked back at the desk where the box had been, and then at Lucian who had nothing in his hands. The box had vanished, and she could no longer feel it, or that foreboding sense of unease and evil. Then again, she could no longer feel the palpable power that had oozed from Lucian, either.

Lucian held the door open, indicating that their business was concluded.

"One more thing," he said as they walked towards him. "The files you brought me are missing some pages," he announced. "Vlad's favor depends on them being found."

"I have the missing pages," Olivia said, unsure why she was volunteering the information. She pointed at her head. "Here."

"Curious place to file things. I prefer them on paper; see that they are documented on parchment before you leave the club in the morning. You do understand that having something in your head is not the same having it in writing unless you are offering to lose that pretty little head of yours?"

Ristan growled, his eyes glowing with warning as surely as his brands that lit up with his ire. He stepped closer to Lucian and smiled, showing his teeth. "That pretty little head belongs to me."

"So it does," Lucian conceded. "Parchment was my first option; I will see that it is delivered to your suite."

"Thank you for this," Ristan said as he held the package of papers in his hand, and held Olivia's hand in his other. "When I leave here, we are done. You'll honor the agreement to owe Vlad his favor for the files as was promised."

"Yes, and I will also help your brothers fiancé, as promised. Unfortunately, our paths will collide again soon enough, I assure you of that. Whether it is by choice or necessity has not been revealed to me yet.

There are forces in play that neither of us have much knowledge about, and though it may be a riddle now, soon it will come to pass. I am aware of the state of Faery, and the war with the Mages, and he will ask me to help him. Your brother, that is. He's a very powerful creature," Lucian said as his eyes took on an unnatural gleam. "A very strong ally to have a favor owed to, no?"

"If you try to misuse…"

"Your brother is the mythical Horde King. He would never make that mistake, nor would I misuse his help, as it may come in handy in the future. Now, I have a matter that requires my attention. Enjoy the room, but be sure to spend time on the missing pages before you leave in the morning," he warned. "Wouldn't want that favor to be voided," he finished, dismissing them.

Ristan and Olivia were escorted by one of Lucian's men down several flights of stairs to a set of doors that opened for them automatically, as if by magic. Ristan paused and looked to the bulky guard who smiled with his eyes, rather than his mouth.

"The doors will lock once you're inside, and will reopen at six AM sharp. Lucian said you'd need parchment and ink. They have been provided for you as well as a table. Look around the room and make sure it has everything else you require before I seal you in."

Ristan eyed the man and then pulled Olivia inside with him. "We're good as long as you supplied food for my woman."

"There's a fully stocked fridge and bar. There are cameras in the room, but Lucian has instructed us to disable them, since they have live feeds to his site. He said it would be best, since you're territorial, that we not share what happens tonight."

"Good idea; I'd hate to start a war over a porn video," Ristan mumbled as he took in the Saint Andrews cross, a padded wall that held lengths of chain to secure a willing victim to, as well as boxes of adult toys that had yet to be open or used. "I think it's time we bid you goodnight," he muttered.

"As you wish, but remember, your time here ends at six AM, and not a minute past."

"Understood," Ristan said, as the nameless man stepped back and smiled wickedly at Olivia. "She belongs to me, and has fully submitted."

Ristan wasn't sure why that had come out of his mouth, but it had, and for the first time in his life his inner jealousy was rearing its ugly head. He wanted to shout that she was his to every male in this place. She was becoming more than just his prisoner, she was becoming his obsession. He couldn't get enough of her, and the idea of setting her free was abhorrent.

He listened as the door closed and a lock clicked into place from the other side. He hadn't wanted to stay here, but he'd known before he'd brought her through those doors that he might be stuck in here with her from dusk to dawn.

Ristan turned to look at Olivia, only to smile as he found her inspecting the wall of toys. Each had a small, rather elegant price tag on it, probably because Lucian charged his members for each item they used. He had to admit it; the man had a killer instinct for business.

He ran sex clubs, night clubs, and a porn site that brought in millions of dollars each year. Ristan himself had considered running a similar club once. Ristan had helped his brothers create Sidhe Darklands before Ryder had come to this world in the guise of the Dark Fae Prince. They'd needed a reputable place they could use for gathering intelligence on the Mages while maintaining the cover they'd created for Ryder. Sidhe Darklands had become more than just a club; it had become an endless buffet for them, where they could openly feed. Those who wanted something darker had only to ask.

She was stuck on the beads, her head tilted to one direction and then the other and he had to stifle a laugh. She moved to one of the dildos that was larger and made of silicone, and her hand moved to the box before she pulled it away as if it had burned her.

"Pick a couple; I'm more than willing to show you exactly what each one can do," he said as he moved closer to her. "We have twelve hours of nothing to do but fuck."

"I'm starving," she lied, her cheeks turning red as she turned around to face him. She moved past him and towards the fridge and minibar.

Inside the small fridge were a couple containers of whipped cream, strawberries, and other assorted fruits and foods that could be used in ways other than just nourishment. He shook his head and looked around the room at the cameras, and noticed one had yet to shut off.

He walked over to it and continued to watch as the red light blinked signaling it was on. He reached up and tore the camera from the wall. He tossed it in the small garbage can and turned in time to watch as Olivia licked her whipped cream-covered finger. He groaned inwardly as he moved towards her.

It was going to be a seriously long night.

CHAPTER THIRTY-SEVEN

Taking another finger full of whipped cream from the bowl, Olivia then grabbed the bowl of strawberries and moved to the giant bed, thought better of it, and continued to stand awkwardly as she held both the containers.

Ristan had taken a seat in the only chair in the room and she was not going to sit on the bed and have him watching her as she ate berries and whipped cream. She swallowed the bite in her mouth and was about to ask where she should sleep when he removed his tie, and set it aside, and then slowly, precisely, started unbuttoning the crisp white dress shirt without removing the jacket.

The black jacket was snug, but then again she preferred it that way on him, since she was more than a tad bit addicted to his body. He slowly undid the cuff links and pushed off the jacket. Her mouth went dry as he smiled at her, unbuckled the belt and slowly pulled it from the waistband next.

The shirt slid from his shoulders, revealing his wide

chest and brands. The way they pulsed and glowed drew her eyes to his magnificent chest and abs. He didn't remove his slacks; instead, he sat back in the chair, unafraid of the erection straining against the silken fabric. He rested his hands on the claw armrests of the chair and watched her as if she was the most desirable woman in the world.

In his presence, she could almost forget that she was a simple librarian, who hadn't kissed a boy before she'd met him. She had never felt sexy in her life. Not even on the eventful day she'd mistakenly betrayed him. In his arms, though, she did. The way he looked at her made her breathing heavy, labored. Her breasts felt heavier, and her pussy was a constant flow of her desire when he was near.

She smiled back at him, dipped her finger to the knuckle in the heavy whipped cream, and then as she watched him, she slid it deep inside her mouth and listened for his groan of need. It didn't come; instead he smiled with approval and crooked his finger at her.

Making sure her hips swayed in the sensual dress, she slowly made her way to where he was still seated. When she stood right in front of him, his eyes lowered to the hem of the dress, then higher to where her nipples pressed against the material, hard and ready for his attention.

He'd planned on taking her fast and hard, then using the hours between now and dawn to ravish her body endlessly. But after the experience when they'd returned from the catacombs, he wanted to take it slower and enjoy his time that he had left with her. He wanted to talk with her, to make what they did last. Instead of just fucking her, he wanted to take things slowly. It was odd, how what he wanted to happen and where events usually led him were often two very different things.

He swallowed past the uncomfortable dryness in his mouth as he considered what it could mean, but dismissed the thought before it could take him down a path he wasn't sure he was ready to follow yet.

"You're so beautiful, Olivia," he whispered, surprising them both. Normally he'd resort to something snarky, or hide behind the sarcasm that he'd used to disguise what he was really feeling. Instead, he smiled and crooked a finger at her.

The moment she was close enough, he removed the bowl of berries from her hand, slid it onto the small table, then the whipped cream, right before he claimed her mouth, which tasted of both. He groaned at how delicious she tasted with the hint of strawberries still on her full mouth.

She pulled away from the kiss and he smiled. A light flick of his fingers and music filled the room. Imagine Dragons' *Second Chances* played softly; his hands already worked to lift the skirt of the dress as his mouth once again claimed hers.

He reached down and lifted her small body until she was forced to wrap her legs around his waist. Her moan was music to his ears as he took her to the bed, uncaring that he was moving faster than he had wanted to. He pulled away from the kiss and looked down into her sapphire eyes.

"I think I have more feelings for you than I should have," he admitted. "Feelings aren't supposed to make sense, though, right? They confuse the fuck out of me and make me twisted inside," he whispered as he gently touched his forehead to hers. "Tell me it's not just me who feels this connection," he muttered.

"It's not," she whispered as a single tear slid from her eyes. She wasn't sure why she felt the emotional bond to him, but she did. He was like consuming a steak after a steady diet of vegetables and saltine crackers. Juicy and rare, she couldn't get enough of him, and she was fucking starving. "I feel this pull towards you, and I'm not sure I should do this, but I can't say no. I don't want to say no. I want you," she whispered brokenly, and moaned as his mouth pressed hard against hers.

His knees parted her legs as he slid his hand between them and pressed against her pussy through the soft material of the dress. "This is mine now; you realize I'm never letting you go, right?" he assured her, his voice held enough command that she was helpless to do anything other than moan her consent.

"Say it," he growled huskily.

"It's yours," she confirmed on a murmur and then moaned as he glamoured the rest of their clothing away and his flesh met hers.

"All mine," he agreed as he sat back on his knees and took in her naked perfection.

She didn't have huge breasts, but they were perfectly rounded and her nipples were created to entertain his favorite fantasies. The slick, wet curls that shielded her pussy drove him insane for some reason. He'd glamoured a lot of hair off in his days, which was an easy thing for him, but he couldn't bring himself to touch her perfect patch of red curls.

Danu had been right. She'd seen through him as to

what he really desired, which was vastly different than the type of female he normally had pursued. The type of female he'd convinced himself for centuries that he wanted, not just for their safety, but also for his own sanity. It was always at the forefront of his mind and the reason he'd gone after the kind of females who were used to quick sex and being alone when they woke up the next morning.

Perhaps that was why it was so hard for him to understand why this shy, naive female who'd been untouched by any other man created this maelstrom of emotions inside of him. Everything about her was perfection to him, which was saying something, considering he'd always looked at his sexual partners and found something he didn't like. Perhaps that was what made it easy for him to hit it and quit it. With Olivia, he loved everything, right down to her frown when she was lost in whatever was running through her pretty little head.

He lifted his hand in the air; from the wall lined with toys, a package flew through the air and into his hand. He used his teeth to tear the package open and carefully placed the dainty clamps on her stomach as he lowered his mouth to her perky nipple.

She groaned and lifted her hips as she rocked them against his erection. He pulled hard from one nipple before he lifted his head and stared between their bodies to where his pulsing cock was being rubbed by her sweet pussy. Fuck she was so hot; her innocence was addicting. He reached down between them and sat up a bit, using his cock to slap her soft nub, which pulled a soft groan of frustration from her lips.

"You want that buried in your sweet, tight pussy, don't you, my good girl?" he taunted, his eyes never leaving hers as they grew heated and languid from her need.

"Yes," she replied huskily as she gasped for air. This creature made her insane with need, leaving her bones as nothing but mush when he finished with her, and to know that he wasn't immune to the same feelings she'd been having was overwhelming.

He smiled and moved back to her breasts, his mouth hungrily licking and sucking against her flesh. She was in heaven, she had to be. These sensations he created, a storm unfurling in her womb to move through her every nerve ending; he did this. His hand moved to the clamps that were still on her stomach, and picked one up. She felt a slight pinch as it was clamped onto her nipple.

He sat up and nipped at her other sensitive nipple with his teeth, creating a moan in her throat that threatened to explode from her lips. Her eyes remained on his as he clamped that nipple as well.

The pressure applied from the clamps was perfect, but the moment he turned them on with a remote she hadn't noticed before, her body stiffened and that moan left her lips as her eyes closed in pleasure.

He laughed at her response to the clamps, which forced her to open her eyes about the same time she felt him sliding whipped cream over her midriff, and lower.

"What are you doing?" she whispered, half worried, half curious as to why he'd just lathered her in whipped cream and was even now grabbing a berry which he rubbed against her pussy before licking it lazily.

"Don't worry, Olivia, I love to play with my food,"

he assured her as he doodled the berry on her whipped cream-covered stomach, his innuendo easily understood as his mouth lowered and that sinfully long tongue stroked the side of her belly.

She moaned and let her head fall to the soft blankets covering the bed. His mouth continued lavishing, licking, and nipping against the cream as music played in the background. She vaguely wondered why she wasn't horrified at what she was doing; she should be ashamed by her own eagerness to fuck him, but this wasn't just fucking anymore. This was something entirely more emotional to her than that, and had been for some time. His fingers brought her back to reality as two pushed inside her tight slit, then slid back out.

"Look at me," he commanded, his tone brooking no argument. "I'm going to get more cream," he whispered. "You're going to give it to me, right?" he asked with an amused look on his face as he lowered his mouth to her pussy. "You're all strawberries and cream, even when it's not lavished upon your sweet curves," he murmured as his tongue slid out and trailed firmly over her slick folds. "I want you to keep count of how many times you come tonight, got it?"

She mumbled something incoherent and he stopped, turning off the clamps and moving his mouth away from where she needed it the most.

"Understand?"

"Yes," she whispered even as her hips rocked with need.

"I'm going to get one out of you quickly," he growled. "Then I'm going to bury my cock inside of you and fuck this sweet flesh until I come, and then, oh then, sweet girl, I'm going to make you come for hours until you beg me to stop."

"I will never beg you for mercy," she whispered, there was a fire in her eyes that he knew he'd created.

"Is that a challenge? Because I love being challenged in the bedroom," he replied as he turned the remote for the clamps to the highest setting and moved his body close to hers.

"You're teasing me," she whispered through the moans of pleasure as he rubbed the thick head of his cock over her wet pussy. He used his hand to control it, slapping her clitoris at the exact moment she needed pressure, and she knew it was from his touching her, feeling what she needed and when.

He continued until she exploded from the combination of the clamps and his cock beating firmly against her pussy. As she came, he pushed into her wet cove and rocked his hips as she continued to come around his wide cock. It took him seconds to explode as her body pulsed hungrily around his shaft. He immediately pulled out and cleansed their bodies before he lifted her leg with his hand and slapped her ass firmly with his free hand.

"I said keep count."

"You spanked me!" she whimpered, and he smiled.

"Oh my sweet little girl, you have so much to learn about my world," he warned with eagerness in his soul that he hadn't felt in a very long time. "And I will enjoy every moment of your education." He let his hand land firmly against her rounded ass cheek and then reminded her to count.

"One!" she whimpered on a hiss.

"Good girl," he said as he bent over to kiss her already kiss swollen lips. "Ninety-nine more to go and maybe I'll give you a break once we reach one hundred."

Ristan watched as her body buzzed with the powerful clamps and smiled as he sensed her next orgasm already growing. Fucking hell, this little Witch was his match in every way. Her body was his own heaven, and her pussy was the golden gates which allowed him to be somewhere a Demon like him could never go.

CHAPTER
THIRTY-EIGHT

Ristan had been true to his word, and the moment she whispered the last number, one hundred, he finally awarded her with a small interval, but only so she could purge the missing pages onto the provided parchment. Olivia managed to sort through the jumbled mental notes in her mind and transferred the pages that Lucian wanted, along with some notes she thought might be needed to decipher the missing parts.

As soon as she finished, Ristan cleaned them both up and glamoured Olivia into a fresh pair of jeans that hugged her perfectly in all the right places, leather boots, and a Black Sabbath *Fairies Wear Boots* t-shirt. With a wink, he glamoured himself into fresh jeans, boots, t-shirt, and finished his wardrobe with a long leather coat. He 'd barely thrust a cup of steaming hot coffee into her hands when the door clicked open, alerting them that it was time to go. He wasted no time sifting her back to the Guild so that they could get started on cross-referencing the information in her head with actual details from the archives in the catacombs. If Olivia was right, it wouldn't be long before they had the elusive dagger.

He'd sifted her back down to the catacombs where he now sat at one of the small wooden tables while she pulled out several files for him to scroll through. He'd flicked his finger and Fall Out Boy's *Disloyal Order of Water Buffaloes* echoed around them. Olivia grinned at the sacrilege of him blaring music in the catacombs, but hey, who was going to shush them? Her eyes fell on a bowl of jelly beans that had appeared on the table and her heart skipped a beat. He must have discovered her sweet tooth as he'd spied on her. She'd always kept a bowl of the candy on her desk with the intent that it was for others, when in reality she was addicted to jelly beans.

"Here's another reference to the church in Ireland. It's discolored, but if you look at the archive here," she said as she displayed the scroll for them to see; her arm grazed his which sparked a jolt of emotion through her. "And here," she said as she pulled out another one. "I think it's speaking of something that is not of the Guild, but was considered pretty important to the Fae, and if you look at this one," she continued as she pulled out another scroll and rolled it out in front of him. "This one speaks of the importance of keeping it hidden from the Fae at all cost. Sound like it could be what you're looking for?" she asked, her hand grazing his as she placed the other slips of ancient paper beside him.

"This is the one Marie spoke to you and Synthia about, right?" he questioned.

"It is," she said, but she paused and shook her head.

"It makes no sense, because it all points to Saint Patrick, but no one knows for sure where he was buried, not to mention he died in the mid-fifth century. You told me that the relics were stolen from Faery when the Templar Knights were still in power. Saint Patrick's Cathedral in Dublin was originally built around the time their power was starting to decline—wait a second." She scrunched her nose in puzzlement as she studied several scrolls. "It's all wrong; look at this," she said holding up a map. "This points to a stairway, but it's not on any diagrams of the cathedral. It also leads below the water table, which would make it a stairway into nothing," she growled with frustration. "It's stupid, because the water table is so high under the cathedral that the builders decided there could never be a crypt or any catacombs under the actual cathedral itself. The tombs would be ruined; they'd never chance it."

"Unless it's a lie, and they want you to think that it was impossible to have catacombs beneath the cathedral," Ristan pointed out.

"Yes, but the high water table isn't a lie. It's been pretty well-documented over the centuries."

"Look at this place, Olivia," he said as he used his arms to indicate the room they were in. "There's no map with these catacombs on it. They're hidden; the entrances are open to the Guild alone, hidden under the city of Spokane. Each entrance has been memorized by Guild librarians and passed on as tribal knowledge from generation to generation of librarians. Each entrance from the outside leading to the catacombs is concealed with magic, Guild magic. You can't get around the idea of high water table, and I'm sure they were counting on anyone else being stuck on the same stumbling point that you are. There's no proof that there isn't a secret door that leads into an underground room in that cathedral, which means until we can prove it otherwise, we need to believe that they hid the dagger in that church. There's another church less than a ten-minute walk away, Christ Church, which does have catacombs. I'm willing to bet that they both have more than the public is aware of, because Ireland has always been wrapped in secrets. From the beginning of their history, the land has been coveted. The Fomoire and Tuatha Dé Danann terrified the Gaels and they learned to hide their secrets well. The Roman, Viking, and Norman invaders that came after just solidified their predisposition to hiding their best secrets, usually wrapped in whatever religion prevailed at the time."

"So you think it's been purposely kept from the public? It's a little hard to hide from prying eyes, and over centuries, no less," she sighed, closing her eyes briefly with as she pinched the bridge of her nose. "The only way this one has remained secret is because the Guild never let the general public in. Those churches are tourist attractions."

"There is that," he agreed. "But they wouldn't have been when those churches were built and I'm not convinced that they wouldn't have used magic to protect it," he continued, his eyes slowly looking around the giant room they were in. "Take this place, for example; the exits that lead out into the city are protected by magic. No one outside of the librarians can access those doors because they've been spelled."

Olivia nodded with understanding, but it didn't

solve their problem. "If they've been spelled, we won't be able to open them, either."

"That's not entirely correct," he said impishly. "My magic undoes most spells and wards that an average Witch can cast. When Synthia first entered the Dark Towers, we knew it because her magic pushed against mine. It's also why being here was such a bitch for me; my magic conflicted with the amount of magic being used daily in the Guild. I think there are either secret rooms, catacombs or more, hidden in the churches in Ireland, because these scrolls not only point to their existence, it also documents that the first Witches Guild had origins in Ireland. We have known where the Guild originated for centuries, but these scrolls confirm what we have suspected all along; that the Guild was created for more than just fighting Fae, and considering that the Mages were hiding here, it's probable."

"You know a lot about our history, and considering it's not public knowledge, that's telling. You don't look old enough to know everything that you do. Just how old are you?" she asked with her eyes on him and a curious twist on her lips.

"Old enough to know better, young enough to do it twice and see if it gets my rocks off," he grinned and watched as her mouth curved into a beautiful smile before she giggled openly, which did things to his heart that he wasn't sure he wanted it to.

"You're not anything like the Guild told us or taught us to believe. I've read a ton of magazines and studied those Fae to an extent, but those ones are more formal. Some even seem as if they are from another time, stuffy and stuck up. So are there more like you, or are they like they appear to be on TV and magazines?" she asked with curiosity gleaming in her eyes.

"Be a bit boring if we were all the same, now wouldn't it?" he said as he leaned back in his chair, watching her intently as he tried to figure out where she was going with her questions. "Are you the same as every other librarian of the Guild?" he countered.

"I'd like to think I wasn't," she admitted. "I'm trying to understand you. I can't understand a lot of things, and nothing the Guild taught me seems to carry weight. It's quite scary knowing that I never questioned anything. I just always thought that they were on the right side. It's difficult to swallow the truth I guess." She paused, watching him as he stared at her.

"Can I ask you something?" he asked.

"If I can do the same after I've finished answering you," she said with a bright smile.

Ristan felt his heart sink, because people normally only asked him about his family, not caring about him in particular. Of course, he'd never been of the mind to care too much about what people thought. Caring was a dangerous slope.

"In your apartment at the Guild, all of the walls had picture frames, yet every one of them had the stock photos of model families that came with them upon purchase. Why?" he asked, watching as her lips tugged down until she frowned.

"I had planned to fill them," she admitted. "I was going to get married and give birth to as many babies as I could so that I could fill them all. I was lonely and wanted family," she laughed softly with the memory. "I started collecting those when I was twelve, and I just never got around to getting rid of them. My turn," she announced. "What was it like growing up as a child in the Horde?"

"Fine I guess, as long as I remained out of sight," he said with a shrug. "I heard you teaching the children about the Horde, so I know you understand that the Horde is and will always be the strongest of the Fae and it is true that all of the 'monsters' of the Otherworld tend to make up much of the Horde. The Horde appreciates and actively recruits strength and gives safe harbor to those creatures that are not welcomed by the other Fae Castes. Safe harbor does not always mean acceptance, though. Part of the Horde King's role is to keep the most dangerous of the Otherworld creatures away from the weak, so it is best that they stay with the Horde," he said and swallowed hard. "My father was brutal. We may be the strongest and the deadliest of the Fae, but the Horde itself is not evil as everyone says."

"Your father was," she whispered, her mind mentally perusing a full set of archives that had been dedicated to the carnage they knew had been done by the Horde King.

"He wasn't stable, and he knew it, I think," he admitted. He wasn't sure why he was speaking of his father with her, only that it didn't give him that sick feeling he normally got when he spoke of Alazander. "When I was just a child, he tried to kill me on several occasions."

"That's horrible," she gasped. "He was your father!"

"He has a lot of children," he said softly, his eyes unfocused on her and looked away briefly. "He took the things that his wife and concubines loved, and tore them apart. For my mother, it was what she was, one of the most fierce and proud Demon princesses of the Soul-Seeking Demon clan. He took her horns, tail, and wings shortly after she arrived here. Once I arrived, he went after me. I was her only child, so he used me to get her to be submissive and compliant with anything he wanted. He did it to them all, and a few went insane or catatonic, like Ryder's mother. He was the hardest on her, from what my mother said. He gave her three children before she went crazy. Ryder saved my ass more than I care to admit, but that's how life was." He swallowed the painful memory and continued. "My father hated me, and I'm sure it was because I took after my mother's side instead of his, which was illogical, as all Fae take after the mother and they inherit the brands of their father. He continued trying to kill me, until one day the Goddess asked me to become her servant, and I willingly accepted in exchange for the protection of myself and my mother."

"The brand, the one on your chest, is it her mark?" she asked as her eyes lowered to the spot which was concealed by his shirt.

"She accepted my vow and almost immediately I began to have visions of the future. The visions didn't protect us from my father, although it did change my value to him. Something that is not common knowledge with the Guild is the change that the Fae go through when they come into their magic. Transition. The High Fae didn't know about the Demon Haze and assumed that my father's blood would win out in this when it came my time to go through Transition. I killed four females. Violently, and I don't remember much of it," he said as he made a disgusted noise. "It was such a fucking waste. The Demon awoke; he was starving, and they died because of arrogance and ignorance that could have easily been prevented." He was startled as her soft hand wrapped around his.

"That's sad," she whispered, and he looked up to find her eyes wet, and no damnation as he'd expected her to have in them for him after hearing his tale. "What happened when they discovered that you'd accidently killed them?"

"I couldn't change back to Fae. For about two or more hours I was stuck in my full Demon form. That's when my father took them from me. Everything that made me a Demon, he took. My skin still turns red, and I have a nice set of fangs that tend to show when I fight; that wasn't something he could take away and for the most part, I have learned to control it. Unfortunately, he couldn't take the hunger that had been awoken from feeding off of souls, and he compounded the problem by forbidding me from soul-feeding in Faery. Ryder brought me here, trying to keep me alive. It became something he did for me often until I learned to open portals on my own. I've been trying to control the Demon for centuries, just skimming souls so that it doesn't kill by taking the entire soul. It's not common for Demons to be able to hold back the hunger, but somehow I manage. It's a bitch to harness it; he's always there, waiting. I don't think it's anything like what my brother has to deal with since he killed our father, so I don't complain about it. Can't change genetics, even with the Fae," he said, watching as she continued to watch him, her sapphire eyes wide with acceptance, and not a trace of revulsion.

"Has it ever fed from me?" she surprised him by asking. "I mean, I know that when the Fae feed, their eyes glow. I noticed it when you were…" She paused as if she was looking for the right words.

"When I fucked you," he said with a sardonic smile on his lips. "Say it, sweet lips. Fucking. I fucked you. I enjoy fucking you. You fucking get me," he said and they both laughed. "To answer your question, yes, I've fed from your soul. It's unlike the others I've nibbled at, and that's all I took. I don't dare take more, because as I do, it becomes harder to stop at just a nibble. I can feed from fucking, or emotions, but the Demon has to be fed as well," he concluded.

"I taste different?" she asked, her eyes wide with surprise.

"I've not tasted too many Witches; they are not easily seduced by their enemies."

"Do I taste good, at least?" she asked with a worried look.

"You taste like heaven wrapped up in a bowl full of sinful deliciousness."

"That's a strange combination," she laughed as Ristan watched her. "What happens when you take a piece of the soul?" she asked softly.

"They regenerate. Most take a bit of time to heal, but yours heals more quickly than most. It could be whatever else is mixed in your genealogy, or it could be simply because you're a Witch. As I said, I have not made it a habit to feed from Witches."

Olivia felt horrified by what he had told her, but it had created this beautiful creature who hadn't hurt her, and had actually been gentle with her since day one.

"Do you miss him?" she asked.

"Who?"

"Your father," she continued. "I have never had one, so I don't miss him since I never was given the chance to know him. You lost him though, and even though he was pretty much Satan wrapped up in Fairy dust, he was your father."

"No; in fact I helped Ryder kill him, and don't regret it even for a moment. I hated him and he hated me solely because my mother is a Demon and I took after her. Demons aren't exactly accepted by the Fae. Most Fae, anyway. My brothers don't care what I am, but my father took that hatred to extremes. Growing up, that was something I had to come to terms with pretty damn quickly. I decided that they could fuck themselves if they didn't want me around. I found ways to insinuate myself in with them, eventually. The sight from Danu was a blessing, as well as a curse. No one should have to see some of the shit I have seen in my lifetime… It was valuable though, and needed. I may have been through some shit, and trust me, it wasn't easy to go through, but I did find a way through it. Kind of like you. You didn't feel like you belonged; you were shy and you retreated. From what I saw at the Guild, it was like you didn't want to attract attention. You also didn't have anyone who recognized what you were going through. I at least had two brothers that supported me as a child. I figured out a way to force myself into any situation I wanted to be involved in and other ways around the rules I thought were unfair. Things have changed for the better since Ryder killed him, and we have been working to get the Horde back to what it once was since the day our father died. The Mages are fucking the plan up big time, though. Finding the relics that the Templars stole will go a long way towards righting a lot of wrong, Olivia," he said softly.

"Seems almost impossible to have gone through so much," she agreed. "I do believe you about the relics, and I do want to help you find them," she said with an easy smile. Her eyes slid down his body, taking in his well-defined abs that the shirt failed to hide. "You know, if you have been around for as long as I think you've been, you are seriously robbing the cradle with this one," she laughed as she pointed a thumb to herself and expelled a breath with a smile.

"Tell me, sweet girl, do I fuck like someone who needs to pop a little blue pill an hour before its go-time?" he asked cockily, his eyes smiling as he used magic to pull her body closer to his.

"No, and maybe it's your age that makes you like me, so I shouldn't argue with numbers," she whispered as she looked up at him and felt her chest tighten. "You strip me bare, and see through everything. You see me in a way that lets me know that you know everything about me, my flaws and those imperfections that most guys run away from. You see the real me and yet you still want me, and maybe I'm a fool for questioning it, but why? Because my soul tastes sweet, or is it something else?"

"The taste of your soul has little to do with it. Unlike the others, Olivia, I can see the purity of your soul and I can look beyond it all because I know what's really in here," he said as he placed his hand on her heart.

"Many people would have run out of the Guild, leaving those children to whatever fate the Gods had in store for them, but you ran *to* them. It shows on your soul. It gives it a gold tinge, which is normally reserved for those who give their lives for others, and yours glows with it. I didn't want to see it before, and often the soul can reflect what the being feels, which, for a while there, was guilt. As a librarian you know that sometimes the most beautiful covers have the dullest story hidden in their pages, while the most used or plain cover can have the most beautiful world created within its pages. Don't they teach you to never judge a book by what others think of it, and that only someone willing to take the time to read it for themselves will know what truly is inside of it? With you, there is a beautiful cover and a marvelous story inside that is still being written."

Swoon! She barely contained the tears as her heart thumped against where his hand rested. She leaned to him and placed a soft kiss against his lips.

"You should have been born a poet," she whispered as she pulled away.

"Screw that," he laughed as he placed a gentle kiss to her forehead. "I'd rather be a porn star," he said as he pulled away. Shit had just gotten a lot deeper than he was comfortable with, and he still needed to figure out how to keep her from being a target for Danu's rage.

"So we're going to Ireland together?" she asked as she watched him move away from her and return to the files.

"Yep," he said in confirmation. "I don't think it's a good idea for us to go alone, though, so I'll need some time to get a few others to join us."

"A few of the Horde?" she asked with a slight tremor of unease in her voice.

"My brothers," he confirmed, his eyes settling on her as she swallowed any argument she'd been about to voice.

CHAPTER
THIRTY-NINE

Ireland was freezing, but luckily
Ristan had glamoured her into a warm black coat with a
soft, knitted black scarf and a pair of Bear Paws that had
matching fur trim on them; now she didn't even notice
the chill in the air.

After seeing the huge gatherings and crowds on a
Sunday at the cathedral, they decided to play it safe
and wait for Monday when the visitor volume would
be much lighter. If that didn't work, they would have
to make a try on the cathedral at dark. In the meantime,
they had decided to just blend in among the tourists
and locals. Olivia was game for the adventure that
Dublin offered and couldn't wait to see the sights of the
historical city.

Everything around this city was alive. Laughter
filled the air as tourists milled through tours, or the
many sites of history. Ristan had even set up a tour at
Trinity College that she hadn't expected since it was the
weekend.

They toured the old library at Trinity College, and the glass displays that held some of the world's oldest books. She couldn't contain the smile that crossed her face or the excitement as they toured the exhibition of the ancient Book of Kells. It was the actual illuminated manuscript of the four gospels of the New Testament that was written in Latin by monks in Ireland in either the 8th or 9th century. Her fingers itched to touch the binding or any of the pages.

Next they'd gone to see Dublin castle, which was beautifully kept and even though it was completed almost eight centuries ago, it was still a magnificent sight. She was so enthralled with everything she was seeing, that she hardly even noticed the two Fae who trailed behind them as Ristan pointed out anything and everything that might interest her.

It wasn't until they were on the cobblestones of the Temple Bar District that she actually watched them as they danced to the musicians that played along the streets and corners of the district. They'd been in Ireland for less than six hours at this point, and Olivia was really enjoying the perks of sifting and the three men accompanying her who were acting like any of the Human men sightseeing or hanging out in the area.

Aodhan danced with the girls, any girls, really. He smiled and accepted the hand of any maiden in the area who offered, like a bee moving quickly from flower to flower. Sinjinn was a bit more selective, but that didn't make him any less active or charming. She watched them, laughing until Ristan pulled her to him and forced her to dance one of the traditional dances. She hadn't laughed this hard in ages, and it felt good.

Folk music filled the area, and they danced to it with total strangers. Ristan kept his hand on the small of her back protectively, which she liked.

"Admit it," Ristan shouted over the music.

"Admit what?" she asked with heated cheeks from overexerting herself dancing.

"You feel it," he laughed, his hand tightening against her back as he used it to guide her away from the crowd.

"I love it," she admitted. "I've never traveled, well, unless you include the trip from the Salem to Spokane when I was a babe. Most librarians get to do some travelling. I was never offered, though," she said without any resentment at being stuck in one location.

"I couldn't imagine it," he said.

"Imagine what?" she asked as she accepted a cup of hot apple cider from one of the many vendors. She waited for Ristan to pay the man before she turned and continued down the cobblestones.

"Being unable to travel, to see the beauty of the world," he admitted. "I love this world, even if I don't understand the way they think sometimes. I mean, this world's perception of beauty is mind-boggling at times," he said and laughed when she gently slapped him on the bicep.

"That's probably because you grew up with extreme beauty around you, People here are easily influenced by beauty and tend to judge a great deal based on looks. I guess it's a flaw in our make-up, but oftentimes it is easier to believe someone who is pleasing to the eye than someone that isn't. Example; the news anchors are always good-looking and pleasing to the eye. People here watch the news and take in what others say and are often easily tricked into thinking certain things that they really shouldn't."

"It just seems strange to me that so much emphasis is placed on beauty here, when I could give two shits about what they consider perfection. In my world, I'm marked and judged on sight because of the way I look, because my appearance identifies me as a Demon. However, Demons have a well-deserved reputation. Here, so much isn't deserved based on looks, take you, for example; red hair in my world is considered variety. Danu detests boring and predictability. Here, red hair is considered a genetic mutation. Frankly, I have never seen such a lovelier mutation." He smiled fondly and swept his hand behind her head, bunched her hair up, and let the stands slip slowly out of his fingers. "Those little freckles across your nose are also mutations. Fae don't have freckles, so I think those little mutations make you more beautiful. I guess you will have to forgive me for not understanding cruel idiots here who use the idea that those are mutations to go out of their way to hurt redheaded people; I think the term is 'ginger-bashing.'"

"People are easily influenced and go with what they know," she said softly, as she mulled over his words and how they made her heart soar. "Most of them are influenced by how they were raised. Take me for example; I grew up being told that I should hate the Fae. I was fed a steady diet of it, and so I did."

"To a certain extent, I understand what you are saying. There also comes a point where a person has to just say 'fuck it' and make decisions on their own that don't involve hurting others." He looked at her meaningfully. Since her eyes had been opened about what was really going on with the Guild, she was forming her own opinions and she had become even more beautiful to him. An ideal pairing that he never thought he would ever experience.

"Hey, you left us!" Aodhan's voice interrupted his thoughts as he walked up beside Ristan and smiled briefly at Olivia. "Let's go get a drink, I'm thirsty as hell," he said and started up the road.

"Temple Bar Pub?" Ristan asked, his hand absently finding hers and heading in the direction before anyone had finished answering him.

"Shut the front door! Really? I can't wait to see it!" she said eagerly. "I read about this place so many times; this whole area is a historical landmark," she said as they continued to walk. "It used to be St. Andrews Parish, and before that, it was an honest-to-God Viking settlement."

"Now those were some Humans who knew how to party," Sinjinn said as he grabbed a felt leprechaun top hat from a stand and held it up to his head. "Is it me?" he asked, much to the amusement of the lady at the stand.

"For eight euro, it can be you all you like it to be," she said as she held out her hand for the money.

"Four of them, please," he said.

Olivia was excited by the history of this place and couldn't get enough of it, but watching three grown men, or Fae, putting on leprechaun hats was a high point. They looked so normal, so human. It was hard to tell them apart from the tourists or even locals, except for the fact that the three tall males were inhumanly beautiful.

They entered the Temple Bar Pub after handing

the hats off to a couple of kids, and took a seat in the back, away from the college aged kids that seemed to be filling the place up. They'd just ordered a round of Guinness pints when a gorgeous brown-haired woman with an ample bust approached them, looking directly at Ristan.

"Can I get you anything?" the waitress asked, flaunting her goods at him as she leaned over to show off her generous breasts.

"We're good," he said, and turned to look back at Olivia, but Miss No Dignity wasn't finished.

"I bet you are," she laughed. "I mean can I get you *anything*, even something off-menu?" she smiled.

"I think we're good," Ristan replied, his eyes slowly moving from the waitress to Olivia.

"Maybe you should have her go look for her dignity?" Olivia snapped, and then slapped her hand over her mouth in shock. She'd thought it, but she hadn't meant to say it out loud.

"You can help me," Aodhan said matter-of-factly as he winked at Olivia.

They watched as Aodhan scooted his stool away from the table they were seated at and made a smooth exit through the crowd and out the front doors of the pub with the waitress in tow.

"That wasn't weird at all," Olivia mumbled, her nose scrunched up as the knowledge of what was about to happen outside played in her mind.

"More?" Sinjinn asked as he lifted his hand to stop one of the other waitresses. "Another round, please," he said with a charming smile to the younger waitress.

"That wasn't normal," Ristan said after a moment.

Looking around the packed room, he noticed many inhuman creatures; some had been expected. However, the woman in the far corner with the beady eyes and sharp teeth, also known as a Hag, wasn't.

"Fuckin' hell," he growled as he pushed from away from the table. "That wasn't random, it was selection of the fittest," he growled. "It's a damn Hag. Olivia, don't move until I come back for you."

Ristan didn't wait to see if she listened, but she did. She watched as he ran from the bar with Sinjinn close at his heels. The doors flew open just before they reached them, and closed the moment they were outside.

"Another drink?" he waitress asked as she offered a steaming cup of coffee with vanilla cream thickly piled on the top. Olivia's nose wrinkled as she told herself that she'd had enough coffee already today, and sleeping would be a problem if she indulged, but those little flakes of chocolate on top of the cream seemed like a crime to waste.

"Thank you," she said as she accepted it and used her finger to dip into the cream and pull out a few bits of the shaved chocolate to nibble on. Minutes went by, and people milled about as she waited for the men to come back.

She'd finished the drink a few moments before she felt the wooziness start. She must have reached her coffee limit, or perhaps it was the lack of sleep from Ristan's sexual marathons that was kicking in. She leaned back against the wall and people-watched the crowded bar while enjoying the live music until a voice whispered against her ear.

"Make a sound and I will slit your throat like butter, bitch," Cyrus growled.

"No," she whispered silently.

"Come with me, or I'll give the word to kill your Demon lover right now," he warned.

"Cyrus, please don't do this," she begged, her lip trembling from anger and the idea that once again, this monster had Ristan in his custody.

"Get up and move or you'll both die right here, right now."

Tears slipped down her cheeks as she brought her hand up to wipe at them furiously for being caught again. The torque she still wore would prevent her from casting any spells, and a few choice ones came to mind that she would have loved to try on Cyrus. With another swipe at the tears, she did the only thing she could think of and used her teeth to tear at the skin near the palm of her hand, smearing her blood on the edge of the table and stool as she stood up.

If Cyrus was lying, she wanted Ristan to know that she hadn't betrayed him again. She tried to make eye contact with several of the people around them, but, like most people at a bar, they were too busy on their phones or socializing with their friends to take notice of what was happening so close to them.

"That's it, slut, move it," he sneered hatefully.

"I am not a slut," she hissed.

"You spread those thighs for him, have you not?" he countered as he moved her towards the back exit.

"Go to hell, Cyrus. You're surely destined for it anyway. You killed innocent people, people who trusted you to keep them safe," she said venomously as she turned a cold stare in his direction, only to feel the bite of a knife as she did.

"I'll go to hell, Olivia, right after I send you there."

CHAPTER
FORTY

Ristan and Sinjinn entered the dark alley close to the pub and found Aodhan pressed up against a wall, his eyes closed as the waitress worked his cock, looking as if he enjoyed it. Both he and Sinjinn winced as they realized what she was doing to their brother.

Aodhan moaned and Ristan growled as she turned to look at them, pulling Aodhan's cock from her mouth; her serrated teeth dripped blood as she smiled. "You want a turn?" the Hag asked, her smile revealing her monstrous teeth even more.

"Nah, thanks, I like my cock with its skin on," Sinjinn said as his armor appeared in place of his clothes and he pulled out blades. "But you? You'd look right pretty without skin; don't you think so, Ristan?"

Ristan remained silent as he materialized a long dual-bladed sword in each hand. His armor shimmered into place as he slipped into a battle stance. "Get the hell away from him," he warned coldly, his words barely above a whisper, but holding enough warning to make a full grown monster stop cold—but not this bitch.

"He's mine! I earned him. I got you away from her. I did my part, and now I get my reward!" the Hag sneered, her body contorting from the shapely, pretty waitress to her true form.

Her skin melted, revealing boils and rotted flesh, her fingers extended into razor sharp talons. Her hair changed from a glossy brown to dull gray until it matted, and fell from her scalp, exposing even more sores.

"Shit, get off me," Aodhan muttered dazedly holding himself up against the wall as he tried to figure out what the hell had just been tasting his cock.

"Fuck," Ristan said, sending out a call for help on the mental link he shared with his brothers. The thing about these ugly bitches was they went everywhere in packs, so somewhere close were others just waiting to weave their dirty magic on him and Sinjinn. Hags were deadly to Humans, but to a Fae caught in their web of seduction, they'd end up wishing to the Gods for death.

"Eyes," Ristan warned, knowing his brothers could see and hear what he and Sinjinn were experiencing through the link. "This bitch has friends."

"That she does," Sinjinn agreed as he turned in a circle to check the area.

Ristan felt the air shift, and then overwhelming power that rippled around them as the Elite Guard entered through a portal close to the bloody scene. His mind was replaying the Hag's words, and fear for Olivia was plaguing him as he faced the deadly bitch that was soon to die. He knew her sisters were here somewhere close, waiting for just the time to attack.

"Ristan," Ryder's deep rumble came from beside him and his heart stopped briefly because this was the second time he'd taken the king away from Faery.

"You shouldn't be here," he grumbled, but if he was honest, he was grateful. "It's a Hag, probably one of three or more if she holds true to form." He noticed the newly familiar face of Elijah with the group and nodded at him. "Don't let one of these bitches near you, bad idea to do so; they only need a tiny prick of your skin to make you helpless," he explained as he jerked his head in Aodhan's direction as an example.

"Elijah, sift Aodhan back to Eliran the moment we move this creature's attention onto us," Ryder said crisply, and Ristan turned his attention the half-Angel, Half-Fae.

"What the fuck is he doing here anyway?" he snapped, watching his new *brother* suspiciously.

"He's here because he can fight like hell, and for reasons he has shared with me, he's requested to join the Elite Guard, and needs to prove himself worthy," Ryder growled as he turned his piercing golden eyes on Ristan. "Don't question me," he said firmly, warning Ristan that they weren't alone and he was the king. Ristan hid the look of disbelief he was sure had flashed across his face. Less than a week ago, Elijah had been leading his own little group of outcasts and challenging Ryder for leadership of the Horde. Not like he would have been successful, but this was an interesting turn of events.

"I think this is a diversion," Ristan said smoothly, not missing a beat as he changed the subject back to the matter at hand. "Something is off about this. Hags don't typically fuck with the Fae, but this one said Aodhan was her reward for luring us away," he explained.

"Why would they want to fuck with the Fae?" Synthia asked as she pushed Ryder aside from where he'd blocked her view. "I'm not helpless," she scolded him.

"You're still learning your new powers," he argued. "I need to be able to focus."

"Duly noted, Fairy," she replied with a soft smirk. "Jesus, she's ugly," she whispered with a crinkle of her nose in distaste. "She also smells of death."

"She *is* dead, or, more to the point, undead," Ristan explained as the Elite Guard worked to surround her as she moved in a hypnotic motion, trying to lure them closer to her claws.

"She's going to try and pierce their armor," Elijah said as he nodded to the Hag, who was now lunging at the closest Elite Guard.

"It's bitch-proof armor," Ristan laughed, even though he didn't think the situation was remotely funny.

"Someone should..." Elijah stalled his words as a gust of wind made his hair fly up.

Ristan snorted as he watched the king of the Horde raise his hands. Her head contorted in a blur of movement and, before he could count to three, Ryder stood there with the Hag's head in his hands as her body fell to the ground.

"Kill her?" Ristan offered.

Elijah turned to give Ristan a pointed look, as an ear-piercing shriek filled the dark alley around them. He barely had time to prepare for the attack as another Hag rushed them. He sidestepped easily away from the Hag's claws. He rushed forward, taking the head from the Hag, and right when a third would have taken Elijah's head, Ristan swung his blade at Elijah, instinctively knowing he'd duck in time.

His blade met flesh, rotten flesh, the blade slicing through it like butter, ending the battle prematurely. Elijah stood and glared at Ristan, but the moment he turned to the headless body, he shook his head, and his hand lifted to his neck with the knowledge that he'd almost lost his own.

"Get Aodhan to Eliran," Ristan ordered as his armor shimmered back to his everyday clothes, and he sifted back to the doors of the bar. His heart was in his throat as he opened the doors, pushing aside bar patrons until he found the table where he'd left Olivia. Empty.

He stopped one of the waitresses and asked about Olivia, only to be told that she'd left through the back exit with an older male fitting the description of Cyrus.

"Ryder," he said, knowing who was at his back.

"She could have left willingly," Ryder offered quietly even as Synthia glared up at him, not quite sharing his belief.

Ristan paused, his mind warring with his emotions because he didn't know for sure. He couldn't believe that after the past few days together that she'd just leave, could she? He opened his mouth to accuse her, or to damn her to the winds, but nothing came out. He shook his head, and the soft hand that touched his made him pause.

"Stop," Synthia said softly; her halo of platinum hair looked as if she'd been zapped by electricity. "Don't do that, come with me now," she whispered and lifted her hands for his willingly placed his hands over hers.

One moment they'd been in the crowded pub, and the next they were standing on a small island that was surrounded by the pounding surf of an oncoming storm. Waves crashed around them, the saltwater spraying high in the air and lightly wetting them.

"What the hell, Flower? Why did you bring me here?" he whispered the questions as he looked at their surroundings.

"Breathe, Ristan. Just breathe," she urged, feeling his turbulent emotions.

"How did you do this so soon?" he asked, his eyes watched her as if he expected her to turn into Danu. Synthia was her daughter, after all. Consciously he knew it was Synthia, but shit had been getting strange in his life, so he wasn't surprised by much these days.

"Magic," she said with a slight smile. "Let's talk it out before you jump to a conclusion which will end in you being an ass," she finished.

"She's gone, and apparently she left with Elder Cyrus. Is it a coincidence that the man she left with fits the description of a man who tortured me?" he asked softly as pain lanced through his chest.

"I'm taking us back now. No one will hear us or see us. Everyone in the pub will be frozen, so we can take a better look at the scene. We will see what the facts say, and let them speak to you, Demon. Sometimes things aren't really how they first appear, and you have doubts. Let's see where the facts lead us, shall we?"

"This is stupid; we should be looking for her," he growled.

"Don't you growl at me, Demon, I get enough of

that from your brother. Look at the pub as if it is a crime scene, and not a place where Olivia left you to go off and do random acts of evil." Her eyes searched his for a moment before she continued. "Alden has the children talking again. They finally opened up and they explained what they saw, and it was that mouse fighting to save their lives. She saved them, Ristan. She may have screwed up, but I don't think she would do it again," she said firmly. "I've allowed you time to do as you wished, but I think we need Olivia alive. So I need us to be on the same team again."

"Fine," he said, even though the pulse in his jaw hammered wildly as different scenarios ran through his mind.

They were back in the bar and other than the group of Fae males, Synthia had managed to freeze everyone in the pub. He looked around at the people who continued to look at something or other on their phones or frozen in mid-sentence or a laugh with their companions. The waitress who had given him Cyrus's description looked at something as if she was unsure what to do about it, but then a young couple a few booths to her left were spilling a drink, so she'd probably decided to ignore what had her worried, and do what her job entailed. Ristan watched as Ryder and the rest of the Fae made their way to the table.

"Blood," Synthia said as she leaned over and looked at the table. "This is where you were, right?"

"Yes," he said as his heart flipped in his chest and skipped a beat.

"Was she wounded before?"

"No, I'd have noticed it. None of us were bleeding

from any wounds," he acknowledged.

"In emergency training, if a Witch is in a difficult situation and chooses to spare the lives of those around her, they're instructed to leave a blood trail. So say if a Witch had been worried about protecting someone, the Witch would have gone willingly, but to signal that they were in danger, they'd leave a trail so their coven would know that they needed help."

He paused. "So she left me a sign?" he asked cautiously, as if he was afraid to believe it.

"She not only did that, she left you a few," Synthia said as she pointed at the frame of the rear door, which was also smeared with blood.

"Unfreeze them, and let's follow it," he urged.

"About that, I'm not so good with unfreezing people yet," she admitted sheepishly.

"What happens when you try?" he asked hesitantly.

Ryder snorted and shrugged at Ristan's curious look.

"Well I haven't blown anyone up yet, but I'm not ruling it out. One of the stones beside the Fairy pools blew up and almost took off my head last time I tried this."

"Shit," he said as he looked past her to where his brothers waited, watching them. "Was that during the freeze, or when you tried to end it?"

"When I tried to end it, of course," she answered in mock horror. "You think I would try it on actual people for the first time? No, I tried it on some sheep that were close to the pools and it freaked me out a bit when the rock blew. This is my first actual attempt on people, and to be honest, I'm a little freaked out right now," she laughed with a naughty twinkle in her eye.

"How long does it last?" he asked worriedly as he looked around the room.

"Cyrus won't kill her," she said comfortingly as she tried to evade his question. "Not until he gets what he wants from her, which, if everything Vlad and Adam have reported back with is true, he's probably looking for the relic, too."

"Speaking of which, just how long have you had Adam spying on me?" he asked as he started for the exit, his brothers followed closely behind them as he guided Synthia along with them.

"You think I wouldn't keep track of you? Ristan, you kept me sane when I thought I would go crazy with everything happening to me. When you freed me from the mansion, it bonded us. It made us friends, and there's a lot I owe my friend for. I needed to know you were okay, and while I promised to keep out of it, I also needed to know you didn't cross a line with Olivia that you couldn't come back from."

"Friends don't spy on friends, Flower," he said as he absorbed what she'd said.

"When we found you in that room, you were gone. You scared the shit out of me, Demon. Ryder filled me in on some things, and for a while, I was really worried that you might not come back to us. You saved my babies, and I needed to know if we were going to have to save you, even if it meant saving you from yourself. Okay, so where is the relic?" she said, changing the subject with a dismissive hand.

"Saint Patrick's Cathedral, we think."

"I don't think there are any catacombs below the cathedral where the Templars could hide it, so maybe one of the graves in the walls or the flooring?" she offered.

"We talked it over, Olivia and I, and we think that there might be an entrance beneath the cathedral that was hidden. I know it says that when they built it, the water table was an issue, but how many times in the history of the Guild and the Freemasons have they made shit up to keep people from looking?" he stated.

"That sounds about right, so why would Cyrus take Olivia? Would it be to get information on the Fae, or do you think he knows about the relics and wants her to take him to it?"

"I don't know," he answered, and for a brief moment, he wondered if Olivia had reached out to Cyrus. It was strange, him appearing here out of the blue like this. Was the blood trail a signal for him, or another trap to lure him?

"She hasn't had any contact with the outside," Synthia said, guessing his thoughts. "No access to a phone, and she doesn't have the ability to communicate to anyone without one. Unless she isn't a Witch, and in that case, we could have misjudged her again, but I don't think we have. Think; does anyone know you found it?"

"There were some people with Vlad; they came with the archives, but he trusted them. Adam knew, and Adrian," he announced. "I guess it could have gotten out, but I doubt it. Vlad would kill anyone he thought betrayed him and they know it."

"Then I guess we better hope everyone unfreezes pretty quick here, so we can get you to a cathedral and save the damsel," she said impishly.

A guilty pang crossed his mind that Olivia was now a damsel that might not even be able to defend herself because of the torque he'd placed on her.

"And if we're wrong?" he asked.

"If we are both wrong, then she must die. If she's fooled us this much, she's more dangerous than either of us thought and I'll put her down myself. If we're right, we'll need her help."

The room came back to life with a deafening boom as everyone resumed what they'd been doing.

"What if someone had walked in?" Ryder asked impatiently, cutting off a scathing glance from Synthia.

"I would have frozen them, too," she shrugged.

"And if you accidently blew up an entire pub filled with people?" he asked. "I could live with it, but you?"

"They didn't blow up!" she growled.

"You two need a room, or maybe a corner? Pressing matters here, no time for a timeout to fuck about it," Ristan growled impatiently.

"Next time, practice in a situation where I won't have to give them a push back to life. Stick with the sheep for a bit, Pet," Ryder said, as they continued to ignore Ristan with their personal matters.

"I'm never going to learn if you keep undoing my mistakes," she complained with her hands on her hips. She winked at Ristan and moved closer to Ryder, her king. "On to bigger problems, there's a Guild Elder who has Olivia and we need to figure out what he's doing here and what he really wants."

"Then let's be smart about it, and make a plan," Ryder said as he pulled Synthia closer to him and gave his brother a reassuring look. "Let's go Witch hunting, brother."

CHAPTER
FORTY-ONE

Olivia was forced at knifepoint into a waiting van, and something was pressed against her face. The sickly-sweet scent made bile rush to the back of her throat, and blackness seemed to swallow her whole.

When she awoke, it was because rough hands carried her into a darkened cathedral, and she was placed on a cold mosaic floor. She feigned sleep, listening to Cyrus as he gave instructions in a language she'd never heard before. The men with him left to do as he'd bid them, or at least she assumed they did, since her eyes remained closed.

"You should have listened to me when I told you he was a monster," Cyrus sneered and kicked Olivia in her abdomen, forcing her to give up the façade that she was still drugged.

She cried out as the pain assaulted her, and then he kneeled beside her and turned her face towards himself in a punishing grip.

"Stupid whore; I should have allowed them to kill you with the other worthless fucks in the Guild. Lucky for me you didn't die in the chaos," Cyrus said with his eyes drilling holes into her.

She felt nausea swirling in her stomach, and an anger churning through her that wanted justice for all of the innocent blood he'd spilled.

"You didn't have to kill them," she whispered through his hold on her chin.

"Oh, but I did. You see, new Elders will soon replace those who follow the old rules and one by one, each Guild will be replaced with a new world order. Instead of protecting the Humans from the Fae, we will eradicate the Fae, and the Humans will buy anything we tell them. Simpleminded fucks, all of them. Oh, don't look at me like that," he warned. "You know, the Guild actually thought it could make a difference and the truth is, they never have. They thought to police the Fae, but they're weak. We all have Fae in our genetics, but some of us have more magic than others. Witches and Warlocks are just watered down bloodlines. They are created from a stupid Human whore fucking one of the monsters and the spawn of that union reproduces again and again. Nothing like we have in our lines. We are stronger, faster, and more powerful than those of the Guild."

"You're making no sense," Olivia gritted out. "We have done nothing to you!"

She knew now just how bad this monster was because there wasn't just hatred in his eyes, there was madness. He smiled coldly, his mouth twisting coldly; the resulting smirk was full of hatred.

"You have no idea what I am, and neither did the Guild. They don't know just how far embedded we are into their ranks. Harold, the Elder who runs the Seattle Guild, he's just like me, Olivia. We started with the New Orleans Guild last fall; it was so fucking easy to take it from within. How do you think I knew your lover couldn't have been from there? Because I was down there for business at the beginning of November, and by December, all of the Elders of New Orleans were dead or under our control. One month is all it took to change the leadership of an entire Guild, and the others will fall in line just as easily."

Olivia quickly calculated the timing and grasped his meaning; for at least two weeks, Cyrus had known for sure that the requests from New Orleans Guild were false. No wonder he had been so meticulous in his monitoring of 'Justin's' activities towards the end.

"Why are you telling me this?" she whispered, buying time. She knew the answer. He didn't plan to let her live long enough to tell another living soul that all of the Guilds were in danger of being compromised.

"Do you have any idea just what kind of monster might already be brewing here?" he asked as he finally released his hold on her chin and moved his hand to her abdomen. "Did you even fight him? Or did you just spread these legs and welcome the beast between them?" his hand moved to her pussy and she froze.

"You don't want a Demon's leftovers, do you?" she taunted, chancing that it might send him over the edge, but she figured it was better to be dead than to let someone like him touch her.

"Bitch," he said as his mouth curled with hatred.

"Did you know the Guild breeds librarians specifically based off their parent's gene signature? All of the others in your field had been matched by the Guild, except yours. Of course, your mother held the right genes, but your father, no one knew who he was. Like mother, like daughter? Was she as much of a whore as you?" he asked.

"My mother died giving birth, but you already know that," she replied as she glared at him.

"Are you sure about that? The Guild has strict laws in place for the ones who don't follow the rules. You wouldn't be the first child to come from an emergency surgery due to the mother passing her expiration date."

"What the hell does that mean?" she asked.

"They kill their own people more often than any of you thought. In fact, young Adam was supposed to die on the mission to the Dark Tower because no one knew who his parents were and the Guild doesn't chance unknowns. Synthia was kept close after the Fae attacked her parents, or who we thought were her parents. They kept their little secret well, but then their station within the Guild allowed them to do so. You were kept close, in case anything evolved from the man who donated to your DNA. How many of your friends went missing while you were kept in that library?" he asked as he stood back up, towering over her.

"Only a few," she whispered, but they had been sent to other Guilds, right? It wasn't strange for people to be shuffled around to other active Guilds. "The Enforcers who left for Seattle?" she whispered the question.

"That was me. I sent them to their deaths. Couldn't have them mucking up my glorious win when I took down the Spokane Guild ahead of schedule. Alden was growing suspicious and the Spokane Guild took a lot longer to infiltrate because of the old bastard. Years—it took us years to break into the ranks and become what was needed to earn the trust and respect of everyone there."

Olivia was about to curse when one of the men returned. "We found it," the man announced, his eyes moving to where Olivia was on the floor. "We still need her?" he asked, his own eyes morphing from green to blue and back again. *Mages.*

"Unless you got another Witch in this place, her blood is the only thing will open the doors."

"Get up," the second man said as he reached down roughly and pulled her up to her feet. "Try anything and I'll slit your fucking throat," he warned, waving a black folding knife at her that looked like one of the Benchmade Bedlam knives that the Guild issued to Enforcers.

"Jeffery, we need her alive. The blood of a dead Witch won't open the doors to the catacombs."

She knew it!

There were catacombs beneath the cathedral!

She cried out in alarm as Cyrus pulled her to her feet by her hair. Tears burned in her eyes from the pain as she forced herself to move. Her mind was numbed against the blade Cyrus once again held against her flesh, and her feet moved automatically, as if autopilot had taken over. She was being used once again, this time, though, she'd be damned if she gave them what they wanted.

Last time she hadn't been the only one who had suffered for their actions; these sick, twisted assholes had escaped any sort of prosecution because no one knew they were responsible. She'd been taken prisoner. They hadn't suffered at all. She'd been accused of the treachery that these men had been guilty of. They had lied to her, used her, and innocent people had suffered for it.

Marie used to say that life was funny in the way that the guilty often never were accused of their crimes and oftentimes ended up being the winner of whatever game they'd played. That sometimes you have to turn the odds to your favor, play the same game as the enemy, and make yourself the winner of their game.

"The catacombs are real, then?" she asked, her mind processing what she could do to change the odds to her favor without her ending up skewered at the end of the knife Cyrus held to her back.

"They are," he said roughly as they started down a set of stairs that led to the lower level of the cathedral. "The first of our kind helped build this cathedral. They kept the catacombs a secret, even though it took a large effort on their part. Imagine building this back then, and all of the work they would have had to do to make sure it remained hidden. The catacombs are so vast that it's believed they also run through to the college," he explained, and for a brief moment, Olivia knew why she'd so easily believed him.

She'd trusted this man because he'd been with the Guild since before she had been born. People who helped raise you weren't supposed to turn on you. Life wasn't supposed to be that cruel. It wasn't supposed to turn your mentors into your enemies, and have them dragging your ass down an eerie set of steps by knifepoint; it just wasn't.

"Why did you turn on us?" she chanced the question.

"I was never with you to begin with," he answered harshly. "I was born here in this world. My mother was a whore, much like you have become. She thought she could make one of the Fae love her, but he didn't care for her in the end. She even told him about me, and he beat her until she bled out; luckily, the Guild found her as she lay dying and cut me out of her corpse. So you see you and me have similar situations. Both of our mothers were worthless whores, but where I went along the right path and joined with the Mages, you took the path of our mothers. Did you even fight him?" he repeated coldly, "or did you just spread those legs and invite the enemy in with welcoming eagerness?"

"You left me to die, and yes, I did fight. Right up until I learned that he wasn't the enemy—you are. You killed hundreds of innocent people. You didn't have to do it; we trusted you. We were on the same side!" she said, her eyes moving over the stone walls as she processed the rooms they walked through.

"I was never on their side, not even as a child. I wanted them to all suffer because they were weak!" he said cruelly. "They could have killed so many of them, but instead they only sought to punish them. The deaths in Spokane were necessary for the greater good. We needed public goodwill so the Humans will support us when we eradicate the Fae. They are monsters! They are nothing more than heartless beings that feed off of humanity. They deserve to be slaughtered and you know it! The Mages have iron mines, and soon they will move the iron into Faery to weaken her even more, and then the war will start. I will not be on the losing side, ever, so shut up and move," he growled as he pushed her hard enough to make her lose her footing and fall to the cold ground.

Once again he used her hair to pull her up, but at least they were done with the stairs. They stood in front of a wall that had been built with stones. She was so busy looking at it that she didn't see the attack until it was too late. He released her hair and reached for her hand, using the other one to slice through the palm of her hand with a combat knife. The knife was ridiculously sharp as it left a deep gash across her palm, and blood spattered on the floor. She yelped and fought his hold as he gripped her wrist painfully and pushed it against the wall, smearing her blood over the stones in the process.

"You asshole!" she sobbed as pain shot up her arm as her palm was pressed against the stone wall again. Another of the men punched her in the side of the head, causing her to see blackness, but it was short-lived as the room started to tremble, and the wall began to crumble, revealing a wooden door.

"We did it," Cyrus said, ignoring the hand he still held that was dripping blood profusely. He eventually dropped it as glowing words appeared on the door. "What does it say?" he demanded as she brought her hand up and cradled it protectively to her chest.

"Abandon all hope, ye who enter here," she lied.

"Stupid bitch, what does it say?" he muttered as he reached for her hand and pushed on her wound viciously with his thumb.

"Ahh! It says only those true of heart can open the passageway!"

"Open it now, Grant," he said to one of the men.

Olivia stepped back, or tried to. Jeffery held her captive as Grant placed his hand on the door and tried to force to open. He turned after a moment to say something, but his scream was the only thing that came out.

His body jerked in pain and he fell to the floor as his skin turned red as if he was being burned alive. The smell was horrific, and his eyes met and held hers as the whites turned blood red, and smoke escaped from his nose and mouth as he burned from the inside.

"Open it!" Cyrus snarled as he gripped Olivia, ignoring the man who was dying a horrifying death at their feet, and shoved her hard against the door.

Her heart raced painfully as she did as she was told, and the moment her fingers touched the ancient wood, it glowed and she felt calmness from within. She heard a bolt on the other side groan and slide and was able to push the door open. Cyrus shoved her haphazardly out of the way, into the room beyond the doorway.

The wood stopped glowing, but it didn't matter because the walls inside the room glowed with the writing of the Guild or whoever had created this place. It didn't look like any Guild she'd ever heard of or seen depicted. Skeletal remains littered the floor against the walls, as if the inhabitants had rested against it, and just died.

"It's true, the believers died after sealing the secrets inside!" Cyrus said, answering her unasked question. "Do you have any idea what this place is?" he asked excitedly.

"No, but I'm sure you plan to tell me," Olivia

answered as she looked back to the man who remained on the floor still screaming for mercy.

The vast room they now stood in had numerous passageways that led to places unknown; each one had golden writing that glowed above it. Cyrus had been right; one was marked with a painted Gaelic symbol for the Holy Trinity, which she figured was the tunnel that would eventually lead to the college, as Trinity College was built over the former Priory of All Hallows.

She felt at odds, as if by opening that door, something bad had happened. Something worse than letting this monster inside this secret place; her stomach coiled with unease. Her palm burned from being cut with the blade, and her body thrummed with power that wasn't hers.

Books lined shelves, along with skulls that had been painted in spelled ink. A few even glowed with the same mysterious words and ink that lined the walls. Water sounded in the distance, probably from where the builders had rerouted it away to form the catacombs.

The smell of the room was nothing compared to the man who was burning from the inside out; it stank of rot, dust, and mold. Piles of ancient scrolls lay abandoned beside those who had died inside the room, but she didn't have time to examine them.

"Which one leads to the Fae relic?" Cyrus asked coldly, his eyes filling with greed as he turned to her.

"That one," she said, pointing at the passageway that had a painted depiction of what the ancient texts had shown as the symbol for the Fae in the early days. It was a rough painting of an incredible beast that had extended wings, and looked as if it had been depicted by cavemen.

"Move," Cyrus snapped as he pulled her unwillingly with him.

CHAPTER
FORTY-TWO

Ristan entered the cathedral before anyone else. His mind was processing the scene as he moved deliberately through the cathedral towards where the scrolls indicated the entrance of the catacombs would be. Olivia was with Cyrus, and he knew the moment the man got his greedy, murderous fingers on that dagger, she was dead.

"Look," Synthia said as she pointed to a knitted black scarf that had been discarded on the mosaic flooring. "Where are the stairs?" she continued as Ristan retrieved the scarf with a frown on his beautiful face. He'd glamoured the scarf for Olivia when they arrived in Dublin.

"This way," he stated as he led the group of Fae through the cathedral to the stairs that led below it. "Watch for traps; if this was the Guild, they wouldn't have left anything unguarded without some wards," he directed.

Ristan's heart raced and his insides felt as if they

were going to explode with the fear he felt for Olivia. He'd never felt this fear for anyone, or this need to kill everything in his way to get to the little librarian who had woven herself into his soul.

"Blood," he announced as they came to the stairs. His fingers touched the small streak of blood on the handrail; he brought them to his nose and felt a sense of unease. Why wasn't she healing? Her wound should have closed, or at least stopped bleeding by now. Unless she was purposefully keeping it open to show him where she was?

They moved as a group down the stairs and through several rooms until they came to a sealed door with a charred corpse smoldering on the floor in front of it. His heart stopped until he identified it as being male, or at least it had been at one time. All that remained was a black skeletal figure who looked as if he'd been melted.

"What the hell is that?" Synthia asked, but it wasn't directed to him and he watched as she semi-knelt next to the charred remains. "I'm going to guess this stupid asshole didn't read the writing or else he didn't take it seriously," she announced. "We have a big problem, gentlemen," she continued. "The door states that only the pure of heart can open it, and I'm going to make an educated guess and say that he wasn't exactly pure of heart. If this is early Guild like you thought, it's probably blocked against pure Fae blood."

"Then break it down," Ristan growled.

"It's not that simple," Syn explained. "It says blood is needed, and from the look of it, they used Olivia's blood to open it." She pointed to blood splattered on the wall and the ground.

"That's not from a flesh wound," Ristan whispered a sick feeling in his stomach. "He cut her badly," he muttered with a tightening in his heart that was foreign to him.

"She's alive," Synthia said softly as she placed a reassuring hand on Ristan's arm. "This door wouldn't have opened for the dead, nor would be easy to steal blood from a living Witch to open it. They'd be smarter than that. He'd also want her alive just in case anything else called for her blood."

"If she was able to open this door…" His words trailed off.

"Then she was never guilty of the crimes we thought she committed," she said as she tightened her grip on his shoulder as she examined the door closer. "We need to find the nearest Witch, or someone who is pure of heart."

Before they could turn to leave, Elijah moved to the door and placed his hand on it.

"Don't do it," Synthia warned, her head shaking slightly. "We can find another way," she pleaded, but he kept his hand firmly on the wood as everyone froze.

"Fucking hell," Ryder growled as he pulled Synthia to him, away from any danger.

After a moment had passed, the door glowed and everyone let go of the breath they'd been holding as the sound of a bolt grinding on the other side of the door echoed through the room. The door opened to reveal another room and Ristan felt his stomach uncoil as a sense of hope flooded through him.

"Which passageway, Flower?" he asked as he moved into the room and looked at the skeletal remains near the door as well as the bookshelves filled with ancient tomes, scrolls, and more skeletons that lined the room, along with the entrances to quite a few passageways that seemed to spread out to different locations beneath the city.

"Probably the one with your father's picture above it," she said as she raised a finger to point at the one with a roughly painted image of the beast that her fiancée now housed inside of him. "I'm just guessing that it's not Ryder since this room smells like it hasn't had clean air in it since it was sealed and it's the old king painted there."

"How would they know? He was never overly fond of coming to this world, and only did so to perform the duty he was assigned to by Danu; even at that, he was typically circumspect so that Humans wouldn't see him, that is unless he was seeking another woman to carry his babe," Ristan said.

"The Guild knew a surprising amount of info about the Horde King, but nothing had been proven. Just rumors of his deeds and what to watch for to protect the Humans," Synthia explained as they started down the narrow tunnel.

"Where do the others go?" Ryder asked as he moved closely behind Ristan and Synthia.

"I think one goes to Trinity College, one to the other cathedral, and I'm not sure yet about the others, but they could be like ours in Spokane, and used for storing things. The Guild worked closely with the different churches in the old days. You also have the Freemasons, who were around when this place was built. It's likely that they converted whoever worshipped here to their cause. This place is heavily warded, but it's also has a lot of power in here, so I'd bet that we can expect some fairly nasty surprises. See this," she said as she paused to point out the gold veins that ran in the tunnel walls. "Those veins look to be gold, but we all know that gold wouldn't be used in a spell, but it is used with the magic of Leylines. It's a heavy metal, so it would absorb and conduct the magic."

"Which would help hold whatever spells they used to protect this place," Ryder answered as his own golden eyes glowed.

"It would also make them more powerful than a normal ward," Ristan pointed out.

He'd been about to say more when he heard Olivia scream out in pain. He moved to run, but his brother held him back.

"Let me go!" he growled in warning.

"I am not letting you go," Ryder snarled. "They probably know that we are here by now and are using her to bait you. You run to her right now and you may as well slit her throat for them. We need a better plan," he said, and Ristan swore violently in frustration.

"We could just run in and toss a few Hail Marys out, seeing that we are under a cathedral," Synthia offered sheepishly.

"Are you always a smart ass?" Ryder asked with a lifted brow at her sardonic smile.

"Nope, sometimes I'm asleep," she offered with a lazy shrug.

Ristan ran his hands through his hair in frustration as they stood in the narrow tunnel, and the sick realization dawned on him. "He'll kill her if she stops being useful, and you know that her usefulness will run out the moment he gets that dagger."

"Listen," Synthia said as she tilted her head and listened to the sound of rushing water. "Aqueducts?"

"Rushing water, and it's close," Ristan agreed.

"We knew that they weren't lying about the water table, so it's possible that they rerouted it to build the catacombs. Weirder shit has happened," Synthia agreed.

"We keep moving," Ryder said, his eyes still focused on the walls. "The wards are building in power, which means they are getting ready to do what they were created to do, and I'm willing to bet it was to repel the Fae if they ever got past the entrance. I sense it now, so we should move quickly."

"Let's go, then," Ristan said, pushing forward as he saw a light that was growing bigger towards the end of the tunnel. They neared the edge and paused.

The passage had opened to a narrow walkway that seemed to go on forever as it descended into the caverns. Gold veins in the rock glowed and shed a surprising amount of light that made navigating the walkway a little easier. It had taken them well over three hours to find a way across the rushing water that ran well below the walkway they hugged. It wasn't very big, but big enough to walk single file if they held on to the jagged rocks that were on one side of the narrow walkway. Obviously the Guild hadn't made this to protect the objects just from the Fae, since they could easily sift to the other side.

Cyrus swore violently as his foot slipped and he barely avoided falling down the deep ravine to the furious rushing water below. She smiled behind his back, wondering what her odds were of pushing both men in and heading back to the pub, and somehow managing to sneak back to her table. Fantasy, she'd actually need a time machine to manage it.

Her thoughts wandered to Ristan, and if he would even come for her. He would come for the relic because his sole intent was to prevent the death of his world, or getting everything they needed to save it. She looked longingly at the other side of the ravine and the narrow walkway they must have come down at least an hour ago; she was lost in that thought when she felt a hand gripping her shoulder and shoving her inside an alcove that she hadn't noticed until she was on her hands and knees in the dirt.

"Guess there's no traps here," Cyrus sneered as he entered the room.

Olivia fought against the pain from her hand as she raised it from the ground. Her eyes scanned the room, taking in the many relics and artifacts the small cave-like room held in it. There were golden objects and glittering piles of ornamental jewels.

Her hand throbbed with pain, her cut filled with dirt from the floor. She sat back on her knees and looked around the room for a weapon since both men seemed to have forgotten she was even there. She slowly moved away until her back found the wall. She waited as her body pulsed with pain. Her head and face smarted, and her knees had joined her list of complaints. Her torn jeans showed that both were bloody, as well as her other hand from the fall into the room and the subsequent rock surfing session.

"There's millions worth of jewels here," Jeffery said as he smiled with glee.

She held her tongue even though she wanted to call him an idiot, since most of these objects were here for a damn good reason. She could feel the power from them; mostly the bad ones, as she had been able to feel the same vibe from them as she did with the box that they'd given to Lucian.

Her eyes moved around, but no weapon presented itself, not until Cyrus reached down and held up a wicked looking dagger; its handle was encrusted with jewels, and he smiled with an ugly twist of his mouth.

"This dagger," he whispered and looked as if he was about to start licking it. "This is one of the weapons Bilé promised us. This can kill the Fae, with a single piercing of the creature's skin."

Olivia felt her blood run cold as she watched him and the realization hit as to why Cyrus knew about the relic being in this particular place and had shown up at the same time they did. He must have spotted her with the Fae when they arrived and took a chance that they were here for the same reason. "The Fae would never use something so girly," she exclaimed. She wasn't sure why she said it, only that she knew it was the relic Ristan had been after.

She heard a woman shout and peered through the entrance of the alcove. Synthia was on the walkway on the other side of the ravine, her golden halo of hair striking a contrast with the golden writing that covered the wall behind her.

"Cyrus, we've got a problem," Jeffery said as he moved to the entrance and looked across. "A few problems," he amended.

CHAPTER
FORTY-THREE

Ristan watched Synthia in the middle of the narrow walkway, her magic fighting against that of the wards and looking across the ravine into a small alcove. He could sense that Olivia was close, but other than that, he had no proof of life. Both he and Ryder had tried sifting across, only to find out that whatever wards were written on the walls were preventing them from doing so.

His frustration was growing more with the scent of blood in the air. *Olivia's blood.* He wanted to rip Cyrus's throat out while the asshole still lived. Her usefulness to Cyrus was most likely at an end, and she was hurt. She was fucking defenseless and he had no way to reach her. Guilt ate at him, but the hopelessness was the worst.

He tore his eyes from Synthia as Cyrus walked Olivia out to the edge of the walkway, and his world spun from its axis.

"He's got the relic," Sinjinn muttered. "Fucking hell," he swore.

"Come on! What are you waiting for?" the male with Cyrus leered as he turned and groped Olivia while his eyes remained on Ristan. "Oh that's right; no Fae magic is allowed inside these sacred walls, and it looks like you can't fly."

"Enough," Cyrus said with one arm firmly around Olivia's chest, pinning her against himself and pushing the blade of the jeweled dagger closer to Olivia's neck with his other hand.

"What are you waiting for? Kill her!" the man begged, his eyes lighting up with his craziness.

"All in good time," Cyrus assured him.

Olivia looked at Ristan and smiled her goodbye. Tears filled her eyes as she tried to push all of her feelings into that one last look. She wasn't going to let these crazy assholes take him again, and if she could see his frustration at being unable to get to her, so too could they.

She brought her torn palm up to Cyrus's arm across her chest. The old man was cocky and sure in the knowledge that she couldn't do anything to help herself, and the moment Jeffery took another step closer to the edge, she grabbed Cyrus's forearm with both hands, leveraging herself against him and brought her foot up and kicked Jeffery's knee with every ounce of strength she possessed. He stumbled forward and slipped off the walkway, his screams echoing until a splash stopped them. She'd be damned if she let them get away with their crimes against her people. The Guild and its members deserved to be avenged.

Cyrus screamed in rage as he turned on her, his normally pale features turning a mottled red, as he moved to attack her.

Ristan watched helplessly as Olivia looked at him. Her eyes showed him everything that neither of them had been able to say out loud. His heart dropped as the blade pressed closer to her throat, and she did the last thing any of them had expected.

He watched her as a small smile filled her soft mouth, and then before he could tell her to wait, she grabbed at Cyrus's arm around her chest and used him for leverage as she kicked at the other man's leg, causing him to lose his balance and slip off the walkway and down the ravine to his death. Cyrus screamed with hatred, and she was caught in his hold.

"No!" Ristan shouted at her, knowing she wouldn't listen.

Her hand moved to her throat and she barely avoided having her throat cut open, but her hand wasn't so lucky. She brought her head forward and slammed it back into Cyrus's, catching the Elder unaware. Blood oozed from his nose as he reflexively dropped the jeweled dagger to staunch the bleeding.

Olivia dropped, using her weight to get free and she scooped up the dagger and turned to Ristan and threw it with everything she had left in her. She smiled with triumph as she turned back around.

Ryder extended his hand and caught the dagger before it could fall into the ravine. The dagger glowed, morphed, and extended into a shining sword. Ristan shook his head in horror at what Olivia had just done. She'd just thrown away the only weapon she had against Cyrus.

Ristan's blood stopped, his heart fell to the ground.

"Stupid bitch!" Cyrus shouted as he pulled a serrated combat knife from her chest and stabbed it back in again.

"No!" Ristan's strangled shout ripped from his throat as he watched helplessly as Olivia was stabbed over and over by the same man he'd thought she'd betrayed him with. She slid to the walkway, her arms feebly trying to hold the madman away from herself. "No! Olivia!" His gut wrenching howl shook the catacombs.

"Oh my God," Synthia whispered as she turned and slammed her hands into the walls and screamed in Latin. Her arms pulsed with golden brands as she screamed a nulling spell, but the magic of the cathedral still rendered the Fae unable to sift. "Ryder, change now," she urged, but she knew he couldn't.

"I can't, Pet," Ryder growled in frustration as he moved closer to his brother.

As they watched, a hooded figure materialized on the walkway with Olivia and Cyrus. Power radiated outwards and a glowing double edged sword appeared in the being's hand. Thin, glowing whitish-silver brands traced up his muscular arms. With a swift stroke, Cyrus's head flew into the ravine, his body following a moment after. Elijah hissed and bent down on his knee as he tipped his dark head in respect to the hooded figure.

"Who the fuck is that?" Ristan asked as he tried to regain his footing.

"Gabriel, the Archangel, her father," Elijah admitted softly.

"What?" Ristan asked as he swung his head from Elijah back to the dark figure.

"I sensed her when she arrived in Faery and thought she may have been one of us. I needed to confirm it before I told anyone. The story was common knowledge within the Host—about Gabriel falling in love with a Witch from the Salem Guild—and there was talk of a child being born from that union. He fell for a while, but they called him to return to his rightful place. When he returned to the Sanctuary to negotiate, we heard that his woman died and the child's fate was unknown. He searched for her, but the Guild doesn't make it easy to find their people."

That being had been in the clearing with them, and watched him with Olivia. He needed to break the wards that kept him from sifting; this inability to get to her was driving him insane. He watched as the Archangel turned and looked right at him with glowing eyes.

He'd expected him to just leave the catacombs with Olivia, but instead Gabriel vanished and reappeared beside him with her bloody and broken body in his arms. His cloak vanished and the tall being before them radiated power. He was as tall as the Fae, his hair was a long fall of coppery red hair that brushed his shoulders, and his sapphire eyes still glowed at Ristan. Gabriel's eyes were the same deep, beautiful blue shade of sapphire as Olivia's. He looked back at her, trying to will her to just open her eyes for him.

"She's in stasis as she becomes what she was meant to be," he said as he faced Ristan with no fear.

"You can't take her," he challenged.

"I can and I am; she's my daughter," he retorted.

"She's mine," Ristan stated firmly, his body tensed for a fight.

"Your kind cannot help her with what will come next. She's an Angel, and you, a Demon. You cannot keep her; we are at cross purposes," he growled.

"Where are you taking her?" Ristan asked, knowing the Angel was right, yet everything within him wanted to snatch her from his arms and run with her. Deep in his heart, he knew he couldn't expect her to stay with him after everything he'd put her through.

"To Sanctuary, where she will be given her grace," he explained. "She needs to know what she is. She needs to decide her fate without influence." Ristan studied Gabriel as he considered the implications of his words. His hand reached across to trace Olivia's lips and his mind struggled between what he wanted to do and what was the right thing to do.

"I have to help her fill the picture frames. I wanted to get her new frames and fill them with memories of us," he pleaded softly. "I love her, Angel. I've always known she was special, but she's so much more than she knows. Tell her that for me, please."

Ristan barely finished whispering the words when the Angel vanished, leaving Ristan with a hole in his chest where his heart had been.

*~*One month later*~*

Ristan sat by the gurgling fountain in the gardens

and watched Sinjinn and Aodhan speaking quietly near the gates to the gardens. His fun-loving brother had been quiet since the incident with the Hag and no one was sure how much he remembered of that day.

Ciara sat beside Ristan with her knees pulled up to her chest, which was something that reminded him of Olivia. Everything reminded him of her. He missed her and her stupid cat that he'd brought to Faery seemed to miss her, too. The relic had been secured with the others, and his brothers tried to occupy his mind with anything they could come up with, but nothing changed.

He hated this 'poor me' bullshit, but his heart was missing. Elijah wouldn't tell him how to get to where Gabriel had taken Olivia, or even if she was willing to see him. The waiting was killing him, and he was failing at being patient. But he would wait for her. He was willing to wait centuries if she'd still have him. The dream medallion hadn't been working since she was taken from him and he had to assume her father had taken it. Hopefully it wasn't at her request.

"Enough," he heard Danu whisper as everyone in the garden with him froze. "Snap out of it already."

"You should teach your daughter how to do that trick without worrying about blowing shit up," he muttered.

"We need to talk," she said, ignoring his words.

"Go away," he laughed. It was cold and lifeless—exactly how he felt.

"It's been long enough, and yet you won't stop sulking. She's an Angel, and I'm pretty sure I don't have to explain that your kind and hers are oil and water; Gabriel covered it pretty well, I think. I can help you get through it, though."

"You can get bent, Danu. I'd rather go find the den of the Hags who had Aodhan than go back to what we were. I won't go back to that meaningless life. I did my part. I got the relic and lost the girl in the process. I made your wishes come true. Do me the courtesy of leaving me the hell alone from now on," he growled.

"Was I really that bad?" she asked, and for a moment he felt bad that he'd reacted so harshly, but it was gone quickly and replaced with anger that she just didn't get it.

"Yes, you were a cold bitch; a heartless harpy who fed from my pain. You may not feed as you created us to, but you got off on it. You could have saved me at any time, but you chose to stay the course and didn't really protect me from my father as you promised. During my Transition, you could have warned me what would happen, but you chose not to. You set me up at the Guild as fucking bait and used me for countless other incidents. So this is me, Goddess, choosing to walk away from you."

"She's doing well, but she's conflicted on where she belongs," Danu whispered as she sat beside Ciara and touched her cheek.

"Ciara is?" he asked.

"Olivia," Danu said, shocking Ristan into stiff attention. "She is being given a choice. She will make it soon, but I don't think it will sway in your favor."

They sat in silence as Ristan digested her words.

"You knew what she was, didn't you?" he accused.

"I knew from the moment that I entered her, but what's the fun in giving away the ending?" Danu replied airily. "I would have figured it out even if I hadn't taken a ride in her; Gabriel wasn't the only one watching you two in that little world you thought was your own, and eventually I hear everything."

Ristan blinked at the realization of what she was saying and ran his fingers through his hair with the knowledge that he'd never really been alone there, and made a mental note to keep his fucking clothes on the next time.

"You couldn't kill her; you knew what she would become if you did, yet you still threatened me with doing exactly that," he said with a mixture of pain and betrayal in his eyes.

"I am a Goddess, Ristan. I can kill her, but the blowback wasn't worth it. I knew it would only be a matter of time before her father eventually traced her to the Spokane Guild and found out what had occurred there, and he would have taken her sooner or later."

"Just when I thought you couldn't get any colder, you do," he growled.

"This one is about to have fun, though," Danu announced as she kissed Ciara's cheek. "Destiny has her eyes set on her, so I'm guessing it will be a grand adventure."

"Ciara has been through enough," he growled.

"Nothing worth fighting for ever comes easy. You should know that, my beautiful Demon. If it's too easy to grasp, then one should never reach for it."

They both sat in silence before Ristan spoke sadly.

"I would have fought for you if you had asked it of me, but you weren't willing to let me in, not even to help you. You bound me to you and led me on in a passive-aggressive no-win game, but why?" Ristan asked.

"You were right," she laughed ignoring his question. "I don't love as you do; even though I created my people without it, you still learned it. You learned that love is above greed or taint. It's worth fighting for. I know you love her, or loved her. You may even love her centuries from now, but unless a miracle happens, she is lost to you." She wouldn't have asked for help and they both knew it, but he also knew that in his entire time with her, she'd never really asked for anything for herself, only this world. Sure, she took pretty much anything she wanted, but in the end, she always had Faery and the safety of its people as safe as her final goals. "My sister warned about this; that it would eventually happen. I wasn't ready to give you up, and I am still not," she admitted.

"Danu, I need you to let me go. I can't do this with you anymore; it needs to be over between us. Even if I lose her, I still won't willingly go with you."

"You know, I have often wondered if I loved my husband. I now know that I do, and that even with his flaws, I love him still." She sighed, considered something for a moment, and seemed to come to a decision. "I don't want to; however I will release you from my service, Ristan. I cannot stop the visions as they have become a part of you. I hope you understand and can forgive me eventually," she whispered and ran her fingers through his mussed hair, and kissed his cheek softly. "For what it's worth, you were my favorite, and I do love you in my own way. I always have."

CHAPTER
FORTY-THREE

Olivia picked her way through the remains of the Spokane Guild with an odd sense of déjà vu. Her bones and body still ached from the change, but more so, her heart ached from leaving Sanctuary. She'd enjoyed her time there, but it lacked something. It wasn't her home. She'd felt like a visitor who was observing some foreign world. Her father had been amazing and had filled in a lot of the blanks where her mother had been concerned.

He'd genuinely loved her mother, and had been torn between his love for her and the call of his own people, which was why he had returned to negotiate a plan that might satisfy everyone when Carleen died in childbirth. He'd returned to Salem only to find Carleen dead and all traces of her child had been wiped from the Salem records. Olivia had already been sent to Spokane by then, and even though he'd tried, he hadn't been able to locate her until he followed up on the tiny scrap of hope that Elijah had sent him.

As they pieced through the past, Olivia wondered how different things would have been if the Salem Guild had kept the records of her birth, rather than forwarding them on to the Spokane Guild along with Olivia when she was a baby. It was an interesting twist of irony that Marie had given the documents to her once she was old enough to understand the difficult circumstances of her birth.

She'd spent days listening to her father's version of his time with her mother, and how he'd fallen in love with her. Her mother had had an amazing soul and had also been a librarian just like she was. Upon hearing how Olivia grew up and the sense of isolation she had felt as a child, Gabriel admitted that this was likely due to a spell that he and Carleen had cast upon her for protection before her birth. Children of angelic unions are very noticeable and she would have attracted too much attention, so they had decided to disguise her until an agreement could be made with the Host. Only a soulmate or someone who could see the soul itself would be able to see through the spell.

After only a few days, however, she started missing Ristan, and after a few weeks had passed, she made her choice with the support of her father. In the end, his story had moved her and showed her that love was worth fighting for, and that she was willing to start over with Ristan, but this time it would be on equal ground.

She had fallen, she had no idea how to find Ristan, nor did she know how to gain access to Faery. Once again she found herself picking her way through the secret entrance and back in the catacombs of the Guild. There were sounds of activity in the catacombs, and she planned to figure out exactly what was going on.

She descended the stairs slowly; her wings itched to be allowed out of her flesh, but she kept them in, hiding them from whatever was going on in the remains of the once great library complex.

She could have imagined a lot of things going on, but what she discovered was the furthest thing she could have imagined.

Alden and Synthia were pointing to the damaged ceiling and making notes on parchment as Adrian and Adam were carrying a damaged desk to a pile of charred wood in the corner of the receiving room. The kids milled about, giggling as they carried books and other items to the far side of the room. The Horde King stood next to a few of his men as they watched the entryways. He was also the first to turn and look at Olivia, and he smiled as if he'd been expecting her.

He made his way to her, but not without the men following closely behind him, which Ristan had once explained was protocol for the Horde King, who oftentimes tried to evade them.

"About fucking time," he said as he smiled at her.

"I was a little bit busy," she said sheepishly.

"Synthia is going to drive me bugfuck crazy over you, so personally, I'm glad you're back," he said as his golden eyes sized her up. "You fell," he said, it wasn't a question; somehow he knew.

"I did," she whispered and felt alone again, even with a room full of people.

"Welcome home," he said softly.

"This isn't my home anymore," she answered. "I don't really belong anywhere."

"You're never alone," he muttered. "The Fae owe you for what you did, and it won't be forgotten."

"Thank you," she whispered.

"No, little Witch, thank you," he said and turned to leave.

"Excuse me, but where is he?" she whispered the question through her dry mouth.

"He's right behind you," Ryder answered with a subtle nod of his head and a wink.

Olivia swung around and looked at Ristan, fighting the urge to throw herself in his arms. He looked as worried as she felt. He also looked as if he too was struggling against the urge to throw himself at her and wrap her up in his warmth.

"Hi, you," he said barely above a whisper, as if he was afraid he'd scare her if he spoke too loudly.

"Hi, you, too," she replied.

"Synthia and Alden are making plans to fix your home," he said sheepishly as he rubbed the back of his neck nervously. He'd never been this unsure in his entire life. He wanted to pull her into his body and sift her to his bedroom, and feed his starving body for days.

"This isn't my home anymore," she answered as she began to chew her lip nervously.

His heart leapt at her words, but then the thought of her considering Sanctuary as her home filled his mind and it sank again.

"No?" he asked as he looked around the suddenly silent room.

"No, I learned something in the last few weeks," she answered shyly.

He swallowed. "What did you learn?" his heart

plummeted as he considered what she would say.

"I learned that sometimes a home isn't a place, it's a person."

"Your father," he said as he shook his head. He felt sick to his stomach and wanted to sift away before she could agree because he wasn't sure he could handle knowing she was alive somewhere, and that he couldn't touch her.

"No, Ristan, it's you. *You're* my home. I love that you love me, and I love you. I love that you want to fill those frames with me," she said as she fought tears and lost. "I want you to be my home. I want you to be everything to me. Be my everything, Ristan, please," she pleaded.

"Fucking hell," he growled as he pulled her into his arms and smothered her with kisses. "I lost my heart when I saw what Cyrus did, but then I lost it again knowing that every day you were alive and I couldn't kiss these lips, look into these eyes. I'll love you until the end of time, and be your happy ever after, Olivia. I want to be your male Mary Poppins and I'll even say stupid words like 'sleek manhole' if you want me to."

She laughed through his kisses and the tears as the room erupted in laughter and cheers. She wanted nothing more than to be alone with him for a few days, snuggled up against his warmth in a bed.

"Question," Synthia said as she interrupted them. "Hate to interrupt, but I need an answer and soon."

Olivia turned to look at Ristan, but it wasn't him who Synthia was speaking to. "Me?"

"Yes, Olivia, you," Synthia said as she smiled at Ristan.

"Okay," Olivia answered.

"We're starting a new Guild. Alden is heading it up, but I still have a war to prepare for, so I need some more help. I need someone who is good with kids and won't be afraid of the fight we will face against the other Guilds when news breaks of what we are doing. I need someone I can trust to help me run this place—a Sanctuary for everyone, no matter what species or race they are. I need someone who can be the face of this place. It's going to be a while before we can rebuild and it's actually running, but if you're willing to help, we'd be glad to have you with us."

"You trust me enough to help you after all that I've done? After what I did to Alden?" she whispered in shock and looked at her old mentor, who smiled and nodded at her with a twinkle in his eye.

"You opened those doors to the catacombs, Olivia. What you did, you did because at the time you thought it was right. So help us save others from making the same mistakes. Help us make a home where everyone is welcome and laws are not decided by a bunch of corrupt people with too much power. Help us rebuild the True Guild."

"I'm in," she said as she hugged Synthia warmly, and then pulled away. "I'm sorry," she replied.

"For hugging me?" Synthia asked. "I think we're about to be sister-in-laws, so hugging is more than okay, it's expected. So is babysitting, though," Synthia said with a smile.

"Synthia, this shit can wait," Ristan interrupted and pulled Olivia closer to him.

"So it can," she agreed and winked at Olivia.

Ristan wasted no time opening a portal and sifting them to his quarters in Faery. He smiled against her cheek. "You smell like heaven, literally," he laughed.

"You smell like you need to fuck me," Olivia purred with a saucy grin on her lips.

"I will never let you go, Angel girl," he replied.

"Listen," she said pushing him away from her. "I'm just a girl who fell for you. Literally. Think you can handle it?" she laughed softly as she slipped off her coat and began to undress. Magic flowed easily through her now. With every day it grew more powerful and she learned new things that she could do. She had mastered the art of changing quickly; however, teasing him and seeing what he would dress her in seemed like it would be a lot more fun.

"I can accept anything that ends with you undressing," he purred.

"Good," she replied as she slipped off her bra and tossed it at him as her wings unfurled and created a breeze in the room.

"Beautiful," he murmured, taking in the thin, lacy whitish-silver brands that now decorated her arms, and the glossy black feathers of her wings.

"Like them?" she asked with a soft smile.

"No, I was referring to you," he replied softly. "I never thought I would get you back, and the moment I started to accept it, I started to die inside."

"I almost stayed there, but then I thought about never seeing you again, and I knew when my father said that you didn't want to let me go. And he told me that message…I knew any chance of me staying there was ruined."

"I'm sorry," he said and ran his fingers through his hair. "I did warn you that I was habit-forming."

She laughed softly and shook her head. "I'm not sorry, because I want to spend the rest of my life loving you—if you feel the same?"

"I love you, Olivia; I'll never let you go again. Ever," he said lovingly.

"Good. Now, I think one of us is way overdressed for the occasion, and by one of us, I mean you."

"I agree," Ristan smirked as for the first time in his life he felt an unconditional love that was just for him. He wanted to spend the rest of his life showing her how much he appreciated that unconditional love and he wasn't going to wait to do so.

See you in Faery!
~~*

About the Author

Amelia Hutchins lives in the beautiful Pacific Northwest with her beautiful family. She's an avid reader and writer of anything Paranormal. She started writing at the age of nine with the help of the huge imagination her Grandmother taught her to use. When not writing a new twisting plot, she can be found on her author page, or running Erotica Book Club where she helps new Indie Authors connect with a growing fan base.

Come by and say hello!

http://amelia-hutchins.com/

https://www.facebook.com/authorameliahutchins

https://www.facebook.com/EroticaBookClub

http://www.goodreads.com/author/show/7092218.Amelia_Hutchins

A Demon's Dark Embrace

The Elite Guards

Made in the USA
Middletown, DE
09 July 2020

12310782R00255